MW01273753

Regards to Tammy

Jean Dell

THE OTELLO OMEN

Note for Librarians: A cataloguing record for this book is available from Library and Archives
Canada at www.collectionscanada.ca/amicus/index-e.html
ISBN 1-4120-2236-3

This is a work of fiction. Characters, names, incidents and places are products of the author's
imagination, or are used fictitiously, and are not to be construed as real. Any resemblances to
actual persons, living or dead, events, locales, or organisations, is entirely coincidental.

Printed in Victoria, BC. Canada. Printed on paper with minimum 30% recycled fibre. Trafford's print shop
runs on "green energy" from solar, wind and other environmentally-friendly power sources.

Offices in Canada, USA, Ireland and UK
This book was published *on-demand* in cooperation with Trafford Publishing. On-demand
publishing is a unique process and service of making a book available for retail sale to the
public taking advantage of on-demand manufacturing and Internet marketing. On-demand
publishing includes promotions, retail sales, manufacturing, order fulfilment, accounting and
collecting royalties on behalf of the author.

Book sales for North America and international:
Trafford Publishing, 6E–2333 Government St.,
Victoria, BC v8t 4p4 CANADA
phone 250 383 6864 (toll-free 1 888 232 4444)
fax 250 383 6804; email to orders@trafford.com
Book sales in Europe:
Trafford Publishing (uk) Limited, 9 Park End Street, 2nd Floor
Oxford, UK oxi ihh UNITED KINGDOM
phone 44 (0)1865 722 113 (local rate 0845 230 9601)
facsimile 44 (0)1865 722 868; info.uk@trafford.com
Order online at:
trafford.com/04-0064

10 9 8 7 6 5

For Yvonne and Frederick
Who believed
And
For Gwendolyn
Who will

ALSO BY JEAN DELL

The Fanciulla Fate

The Tosca Taunt

THE OTELLO OMEN

Jean Dell

OVERTURE

The bullet penetrates the singer's other eye, and lodges in the trunk of the budding oak tree.

But no blood flows.

Satisfied, the shooter gazes at the revolver, raises it in both hands, aims and fires once more. This time, the bullet hits its mark: it shreds the throat, the most famous throat in the world.

But no blood flows.

The shooter exults in this successful marksmanship. Both eyes, both eyes and the throat. Once more the shooter indulges a fantasy, that nevermore would the singer sing his songs of love and death.

But no blood flows.

The shooter treads through the sodden grass to the oak tree where the poster of Carlo Paoli, now mutilated by three bullet holes, stirs gently in the spring drizzle. The shooter removes four green tacks which hold the target photo to the tree. A torn remnant of print under the likeness of Paoli's face reads, "Metropolitan Opera Gala AIDS Benefit, April 24: Singing are Antonio Amato, Mia Mitsouros, Carlo Paoli, John ..."

The shooter wraps the tattered paper around the revolver.

The skilled marksmanship is honed to perfection.

The shooter feels buoyed, exultant, ready for anything.

One

Carlo Paoli clutched the railing of his Fifth Avenue penthouse balcony, staring down at Central Park as the light faded with the afternoon. Leafless trees appeared from above like fungi, mushrooming over the snow dusted grass. Manhattan's dull roar reached him even here. Turning abruptly, he stepped back inside, rejecting the cheerless view, too reflective of his mood. He strode to his library, seeking distraction.

The phone rang. Carlo hesitated, debated letting it ring until his answering service picked it up, then forced himself to seize the receiver. "Hello. Hello! HELLO?"

At first there was only silence. Then a voice whispered, rasping, throaty, genderless. The phone connection deteriorated; Carlo could make out only a few words between bursts of static. He heard, "…too late—your promise or—suffering—all things lovely—death where—"

Carlo felt the back of his neck prickle. "Too late? Too late for

1

what? What promise?" He realized he was shouting. He lowered his voice, trying to sound calm, in control, unafraid. "I don't know what you're talking about! Who are you? Why are you doing this?"

He stopped. He heard the harsh, uneven breathing. From the beginning it had been like this; bizarre messages he could not understand, uttered in a grating androgynous voice, followed by a hoarse breathing.

The inside of Carlo's elbows felt wet. He heard a click followed by the anonymity of the dial tone. He noticed his hand trembling as he replaced the receiver. Should he call the police yet again? Each time he called, their response was the same. What could they do more this time? Could they possibly be right when they repeated that there was likely little to fear?

He felt a rivulet of perspiration run down the middle of his chest. He could not live like this; he must do something about these calls—but what? He had already changed his private number and still the calls continued.

Unused to feeling powerless, he struck the desk hard with his fist. It repaid him with an unpleasant splintering sound, as his gold fountain pen bounced off the desk onto the floor where it rolled under the silky yellow skirt of a low armchair. He seized the telephone, intending to call the police again, hesitated, and, with frustration tensing his shoulders, he slammed down the receiver.

"Likely some excited fan," Sergeant Donlevy had said weeks ago when a frightened Carlo had summoned the police after receiving the first three phone calls. Coming into the Paoli's over-furnished sitting room for the first time, the policeman had sat uncomfortably on the edge of the spindly antique chair towards which Carlo had motioned him.

"We don't get this kinda thing much with opera singers, Mr Paoli. I wonder how they got your unlisted number? Just change it—that should solve your problem."

"Signor Paoli," an irritable, shaky-voiced Carlo had interjected.

"Nothing much we can do, you know," Donlevy continued. "We'd need a helluva lot more harassment than this to start investigating, Mr Paoli. Just be a bit careful is all."

"SIGNOR Paoli," insisted Carlo, the loudness of his voice signalling his suspicion that Donlevy was less than brilliant. He felt a tight stomach pain, an unwelcome nausea. "I thought I *was* being careful by calling you in. Are you seriously telling me you can't do anything until ..."

"You've got it. Not until somebody tries something."

"So when he does try to kill me, you have a better chance of finding him, right? Especially if he succeeds."

"Kill you? Nobody's threatened anything specific, Mr— Signor—Paoli. From what you said it was all kinda vague. Why did you say 'he'? You got someone in mind?"

Carlo was further irritated by the sudden expression of suspicion on Sergeant Donlevy's broad face. "Don't you think I would have mentioned it if I suspected somebody? I'm not that stupid, for Godssake. Its just a way of talking about the ... whoever. It could be anybody; some damn jealous tenor, even some soprano. I can tell you nobody knows better than a tenor that women can commit crimes too. Goddamn prima donas."

"Well, uh—you be careful, Signor Paoli, but don't panic. You singers use bodyguards much?"

"Occasionally; I myself have an aide-bodyguard who— "

Sergeant Donlevy stood up. "You tell him to keep an eye out, but my best guess would be these calls mean damn—uh— don't mean a thing."

With that, Sergeant Donlevy had left the apartment. And no unwelcome phone calls had whispered down Carlo's phone wires for days, until this dusky, menacing afternoon.

Carlo, with unwelcome nausea rising again, stared uneasily at the phone on his Louis Quinze desk. Remarkable traces of red in that burnished mahogany. He had sung enough operas set in symbolical stage settings to make what he realized were paranoid connections—red, like hate; red, dark and opaque, like blood.

Whoever would make such frightening phone calls? And, even more germane, why? Carlo knew he was being operatic, but he was absolutely, devastatingly certain he was in grave danger. He was at the point of talking to himself. *"If I ever find out who this bastard is, I'll— I'll— "* The muttered threat hung, incomplete.

Carlo looked wildly around him, desperate for distraction. He stomped into the music room and struck middle C on his enormous white grand piano. He would rehearse, that's what he would do. He would sing *Celeste Aida*. That bloody aria should take his mind off anything. He wished he had never contracted to sing *Aida* this season. Damn voice killer, that opera.

He assayed an ascending half-tone scale. His throat was tight; he felt as though he was strangling. He impiously complained to the deity. "Christ, don't let this tension ruin my singing: the voice is in trouble; I can feel it. And all those young tenors like dogs snapping at my heels. This must be how Richard Tucker felt about me when he was aging, oh God, about the age I am now, and my career had just taken off — "

Carlo stared rapidly around the room, seeking comfort from his carefully chosen possessions. His eye lit on an ornately framed etching which he cherished despite its now unfashionable sentimentality. It depicted a magnificent stag at bay, trying to save itself from a vicious attack by three slavering hounds. Carlo all at once identified miserably with the stag.

He began to reason with himself. Needing desperately to find a convincing reason that the phone calls were not actually death threats, he began to wonder whether they came from a jealous and clever tenor, someone in competition with him, someone who would understand the harm that tension and fear could do to the operatic voice.

Shadows crept across the room. A pale curtain trembled as if moved by an unseen hand. Carlo shivered. He strode across the study to a closed, glass fronted cabinet, which held his increaseingly large collection of Enrico Caruso memorabilia. He reverently took out his most recent acquisition, a score of the opera *Aida*, in which the great turn of the century tenor had written astonishingly private comments. All thoughts of threatening phone calls filtered away as he basked in his pleasure at having beaten out his rival Caruso memorabilia collector, tenor Antonio Amato, for this score. Tony had recently outbid Carlo for Caruso's stickpin, so this was sweet revenge. Carlo decided it was time to divulge his *coup* and to show Tony this new treasure.

He dashed through the long sitting room whose brocaded

yellow silk walls glowed with a subtle, sunny sheen. Throwing open the door of the bedroom he shared with his wife Diana, (although too often these days she banished him to the guest quarters), he strode into the room. The sweet scent of her perfume met him as he approached her.

She reclined on a yellow *chaise longue*, wearing a blue satin negligee. Her eyes were closed, the corners of her wide, pretty mouth turned down. A small leather-bound book had fallen to the floor beside the chaise; Carlo craned his neck to see that she had been reading love poetry. He was faintly pleased by this; perhaps the poetry would remind her that there was more to being a good wife than she seemed lately to believe.

Carlo toyed with the notion of telling her about today's unnerving phone call. He decided against it, because, ostrich-like, she continued to side determinedly with the police, and her usual "Don't be silly, Carlo; the police say there's nothing to worry about," was not what he needed to hear. He needed comforting, and nowadays that was something she seemed unable to do for him.

"Diana, you awake? Di? I want to show Tony Amato my Caruso *Aida* score. Let's invite the Amatos to supper beginning of March; Tony told me he'll be back in town recording *Carmen* then."

Diana opened wide her lovely green eyes. Annoyed though he was with her of late, Carlo wallowed briefly in his pride at having such a renowned beauty for his wife; it gave him considerable satisfaction to think he was the envy of all who saw her with him.

At the moment, however, the corners of Diana's mouth

remained fixed in the downward position. Carlo had awakened her from a surprising, unexpected dream about another man, a dream she would not dare divulge to anyone. Besides, although she didn't know why, she always awoke angry when she was abruptly roused from a sound sleep..

She heaved a martyred sigh. "Can't you see I'm resting, Carlo? Don't you ever think about anyone's interests but your own?"

"Sorry, sorry sorry, but it *is* dinner time. You have to get up soon to dress anyway. God knows it takes you long enough. If you don't get on with it we'll be too late for our reservation at Coco Pazzo."

Diana, seeing where Carlo was looking, tugged her negligee briskly, concealing her long legs. He wasn't suddenly going to decide they had time for that. Not if she could help it.

"Don't be ridiculous, Carlo. For us they'll hold the table all night."

"I'm not being ridiculous; and as usual I bet you've forgotten what I planned for us afterwards."

With difficulty Diana stopped herself from glancing heavenwards. "Now what are you talking about?"

"The play, for Godssake, the new comedy that's getting such great reviews, with that English sonofabitch Mallory Mancroft and that fellow Pollock Braun. Force yourself, Diana; you might manage to remember. Anyway, what about the Amatos?"

"Tony and Jen to supper?" Diana sighed again. "I suppose we must, but you know I don't much like them."

"What do you mean, you don't like them? Since when? I thought you and Jen were great friends. Well, I like them. You'll just have to put up with them."

"Yes Carlo, I will. I'll add them to the long list of people I just have to put up with, for you." Diana took satisfaction in seeing Carlo suddenly redden; one point to her, in this little fencing match.

"I feel *so* sorry for you, Diana. What's the matter with Tony and Jen, for Chrissake?"

"Must you use blasphemy in my presence? You know I dislike it."

"Sorry. You going to answer my question? What's wrong with the Amatos?"

"Oh, you know as well as I do, Carlo. Stop playing the innocent—it doesn't sit well on you, you're too old for it. It's Jen. She's such a hypocrite. Everybody's heard the gossip that Tony plays around—none of you can hide that kind of thing any more and a good thing too, now the tabloid journalists are always on the prowl. But Jen still acts like he's some sort of god. It's so phoney."

Carlo surprised even himself by rushing to the defence of a rival tenor. "You're wrong, Diana. You can't believe everything you read in the tabloids, for Chrissake. Tony and Jen are good together. And I for one don't believe Tony plays around. But even if he does, maybe Jen is willing to put up with it; maybe she really loves him anyway."

"Love, warts and all?" Diana scoffed. "That's not my idea of love. People have to deserve love, at least before they get any from me."

"So I've noticed."

"Are you trying to be sarcastic?"

Jean Dell

"No, I'm succeeding."

Diana squeezed her eyes shut, forcing a lonely tear to escape and course slowly down the curve of her cheek. Carlo watched this dispassionately, mentally preening with the thought that if only they had children, what great looking kids they'd be. Then he saw a second tear descend.

"Oh for Chrissake Diana, I'm sorry, I didn't mean to ..."

"Oh yes you did. You come in here and disturb me when I'm trying to rest because I want to do you proud tonight at Coco Pazzo; you know how everybody goes there to stare at everybody else. And then you ask if we can entertain people I don't like, and then you insult me ... oh, go ahead, invite Tony and Jen, invite anybody you like; you will anyway so why bother asking me? If you were this selfish with Ilona no wonder your marriage broke up."

She turned away from him, covering her eyes with her rose-tipped hand as though life were too painful to look at.

Carlo uttered an operatic sigh that would have done justice to an anguished *Pagliacci*. He stalked out of the conjugal bedroom and into his study where he dialled Tony Amato's telephone number. Jenetta Amato's warm voice had but to say "Hello" to remind Carlo irritatingly of how lucky Tony was. Jen acquiesced happily when Carlo proposed supper and a viewing of the Caruso *Aida* score.

"I'm sorry I can't talk now, Carlo, but I was just going out the door to dinner and then to hear Tony and Mia's *Boheme*."

"I'm glad you're well enough to get out again, Jen."

"Thanks, Carlo; it's slow going, but I do see light at the end of this tunnel. Anyway, I look forward to your supper March

9

first—and Tony will be thrilled to know the Caruso score has been found. Say 'hello' to Diana for me."

That lucky Tony, Carlo mused. At thirty-seven he was just reaching the pinnacle of his profession. Carlo thought wistfully that the climb upwards was better than actually being at the summit, because once at the peak, there was only one way left to go.

Two

"I sn't Amato marvellous!" whispered the elfin young man in the second row to his rotund woman companion. "Weren't we lucky to get these seats?"

Jenetta Amato, sitting directly in front of the enthusiastic youth, smiled to herself as several heads around her swivelled to glower at the perpetrator of this sacrilegious whisper. Then all heads pivoted back towards the stage of the Metropolitan Opera.

There, barely in control of his supposedly professional anguish, tenor Antonio Amato as *Rodolfo* bent over the tattered couch on which lay Mia Mitsouros in the role of *Mimi*, his now "dead" mistress. As the audience waited for Amato's ultimate invocation, *Mimi* winked at him.

Dio, how could Mia even think of destroying his concentration like this? Her hand, clutched in his, squeezed hard as his honeyed voice soared in the sob-edged "Mimi, Mimi!" The orchestra's final chords underlined *Rodolfo's* yearning cry. Conductor James Levine slowly lowered his baton. Now the famous gold curtains of the Metropolitan Opera descended in graceful folds as though bowing to the deafening explosion of applause for tonight's performance of *La Boheme*.

On the other side of the closed curtains, Tony yanked Mia up from the couch. "*Cielo,* Mia! Why do you do these things? What are you trying to do to me?"

Mia emitted her coloratura laugh. "Do to you? See if just once I can make you lose your concentration. I love your accent when you're annoyed. And listen to that applause, Tony darling. You sing better with me than with anyone else and you know it."

Tony felt the hot blood rush to his face. He snapped, "I sing always fine, with you or without," and turned away.

For their curtain calls the cast assembled quickly on the set which depicted a shabby Paris garret. The baritone who had sung *Schaunard* led the line of singers through the break in the long silk curtains. An uproarious ovation greeted them. The electricity of tonight's love affair between audience and performers crackled through the great ruby and gold theatre.

Tony, grim-faced, acknowledged the applause. He had long ago stopped trying to smile for his audience immediately after singing a tragic role—he was too trapped in sincerely felt emotion. He was not like Mia, he thought wistfully as they bowed hand in hand. What she achieved was brilliant; she was dazzlingly convincing in her dramatic roles, all the while indulging, on stage and off, in an outrageous, irrepressible sense of humour.

By the time Tony took his third solo bow, he had climbed far enough out of his emotional depths to smile his little-boy smile, as his more adoring fans called it. Audience members threw flowers to him; with a skill born of long experience he caught some and ducked others.

Like most of his fellow tenors, Tony loved the role of *Rodolfo.* His throat knotted suddenly as he bowed; would he be able to sing *Rodolfo* again, or would the coming gamble with *Otello* ruin his voice for such a lyric role? Surely, surely it would be all right, it would work out ... wouldn't it? To conceal his fear from the audience, he momentarily bent his head as he picked up a spray of dark red roses. He waved, bouquets in both hands, as he walked off the stage to the addicting sound of applause.

Jamie MacTavish, a music critic from *The New York Times* sitting in his usual row G seat, decided that the phrase "The true successor to Caruso's golden legacy" was too hackneyed. But how else to express it? "Great singing actor. The Tom Hanks of the operatic stage." Or should it be Al Pacino? That would make a good analogue, since Amato and Pacino were both Italian. More or less. Not like the American Carlo Paoli whose claim to being Italian consisted solely in using the Italian version of his real name, which was Charles Pauling. MacTavish found this ridiculously pretentious, but then Paoli was neither his favourite person nor his favourite singer. For Paoli had succeeded with Mia Mitsouros, where MacTavish had longed—and feared—to try. The critic sighed. He wondered whether Amato was troubled about his forthcoming operatic gamble, pushing his voice into a role that some believed might be too heavy for it. MacTavish himself was not concerned. Amato had not made a career misstep yet; why should this be any different?

As for Mia Mitsouros, she was always splendid, although

MacTavish had detected a sliding out of character just before the death scene. When La Mitsouros lost her concentration, it generally meant she was developing an itch for someone. Lucky devil. Maybe this time it was Amato. That would make interesting copy, to add to the rest of the titillating items about Mitsouros. As for Amato, MacTavish could never understand how the public was expected to believe a tabloid press which reported with equal fervour on the bliss of the Amato marriage and on Tony Amato's supposedly roving eye. In any case, whoever Mia's latest itch might be for, MacTavish was wistfully sure that an affair with La Mitsouros would be anything but dull.

Swept along with the departing crowds, MacTavish glimpsed his reflection in a glass door metamorphosed into a mirror by the night beyond. He saw a slight forty-year-old with a long face to which the adjective "handsome" would never be applied. For a moment the fantasy of his childhood recurred, that of being the frog who is transformed into a prince by the kiss of the fair maiden. The fair, the too fair Mia Mitsouros—she who unknowingly had dragged his fantasy into adulthood. Mother read me too many fairy tales, he thought ruefully.

The well-dressed audience swelled from the portals into Lincoln Centre Square, that meticulously policed island of peace in the centre of the restless megalopolis.

Meanwhile, on stage inside the theatre Mia linked her arm firmly in Tony's. They walked through the stage area, so vast the *Boheme* stage setting itself seemed dwarfed by the cavern in which it was placed. They passed the backstage bank of television monitors needed by the stage manager; they passed the flats of stacked scenery and props. An elaborate Italianate altar leaned drunkenly against a flat depicting an ornate wall.

The singers strolled arm-in-arm towards their dressing rooms. Around them swirled the familiar backstage after-performance activity. The smell of sweat mixed with scents of greasepaint and removing cream. Cheerful voices relaxed in chatter, although the energy which had driven tonight's *Boheme* still charged the atmosphere. Tony often thought this was the best moment of all, if your own performance had been a success. As tonight's had been; as, Tony freely admitted, were all his roles sung with Mia.

Laughing and joking, the performers unwound, happy to chalk up one more well-received presentation. They basked in their pride for a job well done. Too soon the satisfaction would ebb, as each musician analyzed his own performance, looking for ways to reproduce the successes and eliminate the flaws.

By the water cooler in the anteroom Mia stopped suddenly, and since her arm was so tightly linked in Tony's, she brought him up short.

"What now?" he asked, exasperated.

"This," she replied, reaching behind his head and pulling him down towards her so suddenly he had little chance to stop himself. She kissed him with an ardour that would not have been inappropriate in the seduction scene from the opera *Carmen.* Tony felt himself reluctantly respond to her, his body finally succumbing to what his mind had known for some time.

But Tony forced himself out of Mia's embrace as he saw his wife coming towards them.

Mia, unfazed, said, "It's good to see you out again, Mrs.

Amato." Her eyes gleamed; her arm was still linked in Tony's. "As you can see, we're celebrating yet another triumph. He's wonderful, our Tony, isn't he?"

Mia squeezed his arm and looked up at him proprietorially. Tony disentangled himself abruptly from her. Her soft coloratura laugh rang out.

Jen's smile did not reach her eyes as she said, "We can't credit Tony with the whole triumph; you were superb, Miss Mitsouros."

Mia grinned her yes-I-was-and-don't-I-know-it smile. There was a short silence.

"Well my darlings, I'll leave you to your undoubtedly many domestic blisses. I hope you're feeling as well as you look, Mrs Amato. I ... we were all so sorry about your ... about you losing ..."

Mia, trapped unexpectedly by a grief of her own, was rescued by Jen. "We did appreciate your letter and flowers. Odd how it takes a disaster to make you realise how caring people are. I hadn't known that you had lost a child too ... it's so hard ..." Jen's voice tightened, trailed off. She looked with sympathy at Mia and said almost inaudibly, "Please, won't you call me Jen?"

Tony winced inwardly at the sharp edge of sorrow in Jen's voice. When did time begin to heal grief? Their Gianni, the last child Jen could ever have, had nearly killed her during his harsh birth three months before. And Gianni was so damaged in the cruel process that he died after a month of tenuous, difficult life.

Now Tony's assistant called to him from the dressing room, "The hordes are on us, Mr Amato. Even more people than usual waiting to see you."

Tony and Jen turned from Mia to push their way through a small group of laughing, gesticulating performers and a few privileged fans, to escape into his dressing room. Tony closed the door of the small room and sat down in front of the brightly lit mirror to remove his makeup. Putting her arms around him from behind Jen kissed the top of his head, and grimaced at the taste of the hair spray he needed to keep his unruly dark curls in place when performing without a wig.

"Tony love, I do hope they check all these fans who come backstage—sometimes I get scared, we live in such violent times ..."

"Don't be silly, Jen, who would hurt an opera singer?" He stopped, reflected, grinned. "Well, except maybe another opera singer ..."

She hugged him hard from behind his chair. "You certainly did justice to the Sacred Trust tonight, love."

"I wish you didn't call it that, Jen."

She smiled wryly at him. "What else can I call it? That's how we live, as though your voice is a sacred trust. Sometimes I ... you were great tonight. O Tony! I hope you're still singing when we're a hundred years old."

"A hundred! The vocal cords will be used up long before then, the rate I am going." He swallowed hard. "Maybe used up by May, who knows?"

"Don't even think it, Tony. Don't give the gods ideas ..."

Tony, his face smeared with removing cream, smiled at her reflection and was disturbed to see her turn away, trying to hide from him eyes filled with tears. He knew the tears had nothing to do with concern about his career, and perhaps even nothing to do with Gianni.

He sought for the right words in English. It would be so much easier for him in Italian, but Jen's Italian was not fluent enough for such subtlety. "Jen, I ... Mia ... I should have ..."

She held up a warning hand. "No, Tony love, don't say any more. You've had such a triumph tonight; let's just revel in it!"

"Jen, if you are angry, I feel better that you should tell me," said Tony, his conscience demanding either salve or penance. But apparently she would give him neither. She put her forefinger on his lips.

"Tony, no. Life's triumphs are for celebrating. They don't come along so often that anyone can afford to spoil them."

He pulled himself from the chair, unsure whether he should respond. He walked across the narrow dressing room to his shower. As the hot water washed away the perspiration with which he was drenched after the effort of making his unamplified voice fill that huge theatre, he found himself wishing he could emulate Jen's ability to share jubilation. Even tonight as she hurried backstage to reinforce his triumph with her joy, he had marred her pleasure by responding so enthusiastically to Mia's embrace.

Changing quickly into a navy blazer and grey slacks, he started for the door as his assistant called in, "The fans are lined up all the way down the hall, Mr Amato."

Now Tony hesitated. He turned to Jen who leaned against the wall watching him with sad dark blue eyes. Catching her in a breath-stopping hug, he exclaimed, "I love you, Jen. I need you. Never leave me!"

"Tenors! I must have been insane to marry one!"

"But it is a glorious insanity, yes?" Grinning, he dashed out to the Green Room to receive his public.

Tony never tired of meeting the people whose appreciation of opera (and especially of his talents therein) made his career possible. To advisers who said that he was never careful enough with his security and that he gave too much of himself to his fans, he replied, "Giving too much is not possible. Without the audience I am nothing."

Tony took up his position inside the Green Room facing the door through which his burly assistant ushered a few fans at a time. The assistant appeared casual and easygoing as he went about this task, but actually he was examining each visitor as carefully as he could, to ensure the safety of his employer and of the other people backstage.

Confronted by the actual Presence, fans seemed nervous, often becoming virtually mute, or foolishly babbling. Tony felt it incumbent on him to make them comfortable, so they would realize that he was just a human being trying to do his job like anyone else. This attitude had left him open to the criticism that he was faking humility. He was surprised and angry at that censure.

Tonight's fans blurted out the usual comments.

"You're the best tenor in the world."

"You're as good as Jussi Bjoerling."

"Thank you for seeing your fans; don't you ever get tired?"

"May I have your autograph?"

"May we take your picture? Gertrude you take a picture of Mr Amato with me I do hope it turns out oh thank you!"

The Otello Omen

A stunning dark-eyed woman stood in the doorway now: she looked familiar to Tony. His memory abruptly kicked in; he and Jen had met her at a reception after the last Carnegie Hall Benefit. She stepped towards him, smiling. Grasping his hand firmly, she catapulted herself against him, kissing him on the lips with enough warmth to disconcert her male escort and saying with her mouth against his cheek, "You remember me, Mr Amato, we met at the reception for..." Tony thought, there are dangers with these fans, but not the ones Jen talks about — nobody will take out a gun or a knife and hurt me. More likely somebody gives me laryngitis with all this kissing and then I can't sing for a couple of weeks. He smiled mechanically, and with deliberation turned to greet the couple behind the osculatory beauty. Her smile became a rictus; Tony was faintly amused as she seized her companion's arm and flounced from the Green Room.

There were still more faces to be addressed — so much warmth and appreciation directed at him. Tony thought suddenly, "*Dio*, but I am tired; I must make the effort, not many more people now, what is this woman saying? What piercing eyes she has."

"... and I know you sang *Che Gelida Manina* just for me Mr Amato. We have met before you know, once after *Fanciulla* here, and once in Washington when you sang *Butterfly*; of course you remember me?"

Tony cruised about in his memory as he shook her hand and peered into the plain, unfamiliar face with its halo of heavy auburn hair. Nothing. Better find out if he was forgetting something particularly important. "Naturally I would not forget, but please refresh my memory."

"Why Mr Amato, of course you remember, it was backstage in Washington, and I always wear this same jacket to the opera, the one you touched."

Now I understand, thought Tony. Time for a kind lie. Kind lies never hurt anyone.

"Of course ... of course now I recollect. It is a pleasure to meet you again."

Turning on her the full force of the famous little-boy smile, he gently reached past her seemingly rooted self to shake the hand of the man waiting behind her. She turned away, an expression of strange exaltation on her broad, bony face. With relief Tony realised that the last group was being ushered in. In just a few minutes he would be with Jen, going home.

Three

Hannelore Crasmann glanced back once at Antonio Amato as she left the Green Room; then she lovingly stroked the left sleeve of her precious jacket as though it were a cherished pet. She was exhilarated. This encounter had gone so well. Not like her first attendance at the Metropolitan Opera so long ago, which, she reflected, had been in equal measures triumph and disaster.

In the brightly lit area under the Metropolitan Opera building where automobiles came to collect and deliver people, Hanne felt safe. But at the edge of thought was the insistent awareness of perils she might meet before she was safely inside a taxi and on her way home.

Hanne was curious about that blonde woman standing alone outside the stage door near the navy Mercedes limousine. There was something familiar about her. The woman clutched a splendid sheaf of dark red roses, and gazed unsmiling into the harshly lit middle distance of the pickup area. Hanne decided to stay; something interesting might happen to help her recognize the blonde woman. And staying postponed the inevitability of braving the night streets.

After a long chilly wait, Hanne finally saw Antonio Amato come smiling down the passageway accompanied by the heavy-set man who had been with him outside the Green Room. Amato stopped to chat with the eagerly waiting fans. Hanne watched him ensure that no-one was left without a smile and a word. He exploded into laughter at the last fan's *bon mot*. The man with him strode away, waving goodbye, as Amato came up to the blonde woman. She moved towards the car and the chauffeur jumped out of the front seat to hold open the door for her and Mr Amato. Of course! The woman was Antonio Amato's Canadian wife Jenetta, the well-known watercolour artist. Hanne supposed that must be an enviable life; but for herself, she cherished a different fantasy.

The limousine pulled away. There was nothing left to see; only one security guard now kept Hanne company. She had delayed her departure as long as she could. She walked with reluctant steps to the wide, brightly lit street-level exit of the driveway, disinclined to leave what felt like safety. Although she had walked here many times late at night after attending an opera, she had never felt secure. She turned towards Columbus Avenue. On her right loomed the broad staircase which led up to the Square at Lincoln Centre. It was so open, so brightly lit even at this hour; why did it feel menacing? Surely nobody would be loitering there; surely she would get to Columbus Avenue without misadventure; surely she would get a cab without trouble. So far everything had gone well tonight.

The man lurched from the shadows and stretched his long arms towards Hanne. She flinched inwardly, but remembering articles advising women to adopt an assertive demeanour on city streets, she clutched her shoulder bag tightly against her side and hurried up the stairs, looking neither right nor left. Her heart thrashing painfully, she brushed quickly past him as he shambled towards her. She heard him mutter something about spare change for food, and, resolution fleeing, she broke into a run. Up, up to Columbus Avenue, "Oh, thank God, there's a cab, and he's, no, he's not stopping, do I dare look behind me, what if that man is coming after me, oh, this cab's stopping, thank God!"

Hanne yanked open the door and jumped in. Breathlessly, her throat aching from running and fear, she told the driver her address. Hardly one of New York's most prestigious, but respectable, and, at least when she was inside the vestibule door, she felt comparatively safe. Once there she rushed up the slippery, newly varnished wooden stairway to the fourth floor and, her keys ready, unlocked the door to her apartment.

Closing the door behind her, she locked it quickly—two bolts, a chain and a padlock.

"There, I'm all right now, I'm safe," she said out loud, her breathing still hard, painful.

Slowly she took off The Jacket, the one she would wear when at last she realized her long-held dream of meeting the tenor she believed to be the world's greatest, Carlo Paoli. Of course, thought Hanne indulgently, for career purposes he had chosen to emphasize the Italian side of his family, having Italianized his—to him—too American-sounding name. Carlo, her beloved Carlo, who had once brushed her Jacket with the back of his hand as he came out of the stage door of Carnegie Hall.

She felt more confident about meeting Carlo because of her rehearsal with Antonio Amato tonight. She would say more or less what she had said to Amato. Wouldn't she? What if Carlo said something to her that made it impossible for her to use those phrases? What other things could she say? She had to let him know how much she cared for him and for his singing, how much joy he had given her over the years, how long she had waited for the fulfillment of at last meeting him again, how much she worried about him if she read that he had cancelled a performance.

She ran her hand slowly over the soft cashmere of The Jacket. She had bought it last year in one of her frequent shopping expeditions to the secondhand clothing stores; it was not at all stylish but it had such a soft feel, such a delicate rose colour, and the very same day she bought it Carlo had touched it.

She hung it carefully on its hanger, a special padded one she had found in the after Christmas sales at Macy's, a Christmas present no-one had bought. Because, thought Hanne, because it was destined for me, for my Jacket, for Carlo's Jacket.

From her tiny ill-lit entrance hall she turned into the parlour— at least she liked to call it her parlour. Of course it was her dining room too, and at night her bedroom, but right now it was her parlour. She could still smell the fried tinned corned beef she had eaten for her quick supper.

There were photographs everywhere—hung on the walls, propped up on the coffee tables, even leaning on the book-laden shelves of the precariously high brick and plank bookshelf. At first glance, it looked as though Hanne must have a huge family of male relatives. On closer perusal, however, it could be seen that all the photographs were cut from magazines, from newspapers, from posters; then carefully matted and tastefully though inexpensively framed. And they were all of the same person; they were all different poses of the heavy-set, conspicuously handsome Carlo Paoli.

Hanne threaded her way past two small photo-laden tables to the shelf which held a crystal ball, an ouija board and a compact disc player. She turned the music on. The CD she wanted to hear was already in the machine—Carlo Paoli's latest recording, called simply, *I Love You—The Love Songs of Carlo*.

Was it too late to phone Carlo? Did she dare do it from home now that numbers were traceable? She had, by dint of clever research and a friend at the telephone company, discovered his private number, and it gave her such joy to phone and sometimes hear his voice say hello. Of course she hung up right away, but that thrill lasted for days. Maybe tonight it was too late, and doing it from home too risky. Besides, a singer needed his rest.

To the impassioned strains of *Be My Love*, Hanne gyrated slowly, unbuttoning her rose and grey print dress, and dropping it gently to the floor. She languidly drew her slip over her head, dancing now to the melody of *Somewhere My Love*. Down came her grey panty hose, and she unhooked her brassiere to the music of *Mona Lisa*. As she twirled, she caught sight of her image in the glass of a big framed poster of Carlo. She saw a tall middle-aged woman, heavy set but not fat, a big woman with an

Jean Dell

exaltation on her wide, plain face that made her reflection seem beautiful.

She stopped dancing, amazed at her beauty, her sudden beauty after forty-five years of being plain. Hanne had heard that love makes every woman beautiful. And how Hanne loved! She tossed her mass of auburn hair, the one real splendour she possessed, and pulled open her beige sofa bed. The sheet ripped again on the metal as the mattress unfolded, one more sheet damaged, but tonight Hanne didn't care. Soon she would meet Carlo.

She lay down on the bed and, with her hand between her thighs, she brought herself quickly to moaning, engulfing orgasm. But she didn't know she was doing it to herself, for in her exalted state she saw Carlo above her, thrusting and caressing, singing softly of *La Vie en Rose*.

Soon. Soon. Soon.

Four

In the automobile pickup area beneath the great auditorium, Jen had held the sheaf of roses and had waited impatiently for Tony. She understood too well what she teasingly called the Sacred Trust; she did not always like what it entailed.

With her peripheral vision she kept a check on a husky well-dressed man, whose hands were thrust deep into the pockets of a camel-hair coat as he waited with a group of fans for—for what exactly? What had caught Jen's attention was that he stared fixedly at her, edging gradually closer to her. She moved nearer the car, so she could jump in if the man invaded her space too closely. But he turned from her abruptly as the soprano who had sung *Musetta* flounced out the stage door. Only a tall red-haired woman, standing some distance away, continued to stare at Jen. With disgust Jen reproached herself for paranoia.

Tony and his assistant finally emerged into the harshly lit outside corridor. Fans lingered still, some hoping to speak to Tony, some wanting his autograph, some merely wanting to stare. The tall Tony looked up from signing autographs, seeking Jen and grinning at her over the crush of people around him. A young woman took advantage of Tony's momentary inattention to throw her arms around his neck and plant a red-lipsticked kiss firmly on his cheek. Jen smiled at Tony and shook her head indulgently. But her actual feelings were less tolerant.

All these women! Thank God I can trust Tony ... I hope ... oh, of course I can ...

Finally every fan was satisfied. As Tony's assistant strode away to retrieve his own parked car, the chauffeur opened the door of the hired Mercedes limousine and Jen climbed in, sliding across the seat.

Tony sat down very close beside her and encircled her shoulders tightly with his left arm. He buried his face in her short fair curls. "I love your perfume, no, I love you, Jen. Never leave me. I need you."

"I know you do, Tony. Just make sure you remember that, will you?"

"There is nothing wrong with *my* memory." He hugged her again.

"I know. But there are plenty of applicants for my place."

Tony stared at her. "Plenty applicants for mine too, Jen."

"Is that the best you can do?"

"No, it is not the best I can do ... " Gently he turned her face to him and kissed her. They grinned conspiratorially at each other.

The limousine, its grey interior smelling luxuriously of new leather, moved quietly through insomniac Manhattan. Jen gazed intently at the people of the night. Some were dossed down on benches lined against the low stone fence of Central Park. Looking like pathetic bundles of rags, these creatures of a desolate twilight world were lost for a merciful moment in the oblivion of sleep. Other twilight people shuffled along, sad ghosts of the night, thought Jen, wondering how she could create a watercolour which would do justice to that despair.

Two couples hurried home along the other side of Fifth Avenue, walking quickly arm in arm close to the ornate facades of the apartments. Close, so that if the constant intangible menace became tangible, they could appeal for help to the night doormen, who kept safe the sanctuaries of the rich so they could sleep in peace.

Tony lifted Jen's hand to his lips and kissed it. "When I have more time, I will learn the sketching. You will teach me. Look out there; I could draw for so long a time just from this."

"If you really want to sketch, you'd better try to find time now, Tony. I can't imagine the demand for you lessening for years."

"Unless I blow the voice away singing this *Otello*."

Jen stopped him by putting her finger on his lips. A police car screeched past them, sirens howling.

Tony was pensive. "Maybe I could draw on the planes— is the only time free. Time is the—how you say? *Nemico*."

Jen giggled. Even when she was sad, her sense of humour was never far from the surface. "Tony, you *are* funny when you've been singing Italian and your English disappears."

"Okay, okay, what have I said now?"

"Time, it's the enemy. *Nemico* is Italian."

Impulsively Jen hugged him, saying wistfully, "Oh Tony, I

wish I loved you less..." She put her head on his shoulder. For her their bond was a tangible presence, holding her so closely that when they were half a world apart she would waken suddenly in the night and know, rightly, when something was going very well or very badly with him. The intensity of that bond frightened her. For there were too many women strewing too many temptations in Tony's path for Jen ever to feel completely secure in her marriage.

The limousine glided to a stop in front of their white stone apartment building, and the chauffeur opened the door to let them alight. The opera-loving night doorman hurried from behind his small counter inside the rose marble foyer, to open the door and to ask eagerly, "So, Mr Amato, did it go well?"

"As usual, Joseph."

"You know what he means by as usual, don't you Joseph? He means the usual major triumph." Jen's pride was palpable.

But Joseph quickly interrupted with, "Have you heard the news tonight? I'm warning everybody as they come in—you just can't be too careful," the doorman continued.

"What's happened? We haven't emerged from opera to real yet."

"Old Mrs Harrison Algernon—you know, in the penthouse—her chauffeur was helping her out of the car in front of the building, and when he turned to shut the car door this fellow came running and grabbed her purse and knocked her down. Got away with it too. The chauffeur tried to tackle him but didn't make it, and he fell too. Mrs Algernon's in hospital with a broken shoulder and the chauffeur has a sprained wrist—would you believe it! Goes to show you, you need eyes in the back of your head to keep safe these days!"

"Joseph, how dreadful!" exclaimed Jen. "There, Tony, you think I'm too cautious but we have to be wary these days."

Joseph smiled his lopsided grin. "To change the subject, Saturday night can't come too soon for my wife and me—we'll finally hear you sing *Boheme*, Mr Amato, thank you again for the tickets, such good seats! You are always too generous to us."

Tony looked down at the shorter man in sincere puzzlement, laying his hand on the doorman's arm. "No, Joseph, I am not—I am surprised very much when people say such a thing to me. I think they don't understand that without all of you, I—we singers—how shall I explain to you—we don't exist. The voice, it belongs to the audience, and the singer, he belongs to the voice."

Joseph listened attentively to this, the words serving to reinforce even more his private reasons for believing that Antonio Amato was just a little lower than the angels.

As Jen and Tony went up in the cherrywood panelled elevator, Jen remembered Carlo's invitation. "I've good news and bad news, Tony love. Which do you want first?"

"Bad. Then you will make me happy with the good." Tony replied, as she knew he would.

"The bad news is that the Caruso *Aida* score you wanted so badly has been found."

"How should this be bad?"

"Because Carlo has it."

"*Cielo*! He always gets there first! I will change my dealer—I am tired of Carlo always beating me."

She put her hand on his arm. "The good news is that we're to go to the Paolis for supper in March to see it. Darling, don't look so thunderous. You did get the stickpin first, after all."

Tony's temper was fast and fleeting. He grinned at her as the elevator door opened on the fifteenth floor, where their feet sank silently into the grey hall carpeting, deep and thick so that not a footfall might disturb the sleep of the insulated inhabitants. They entered their apartment, tiptoeing across the shine of black marble in the entry hall so as not to waken their children and the Scottish nanny Mrs Burns.

Jen and Tony passed the spacious library-music room, untidy with everything from a score-strewn grand piano, to children's books, to well-thumbed volumes of such subjects as English and Italian poetry. They pushed open the bedroom doors to look in on their sleeping children. The curious, bittersweet smell of childhood asleep greeted them. Seven-year-old Anton lay on his back, arms akimbo and mouth open, a miniature of his father, looking for all the world as though he were onstage singing a note *forte, forte, fortissimo.* Janina, breathing noisily, was curled into a ball, her dark hair spread out on the pillow, at three perhaps a little old to have her thumb so firmly in her mouth.

Jen turned to Tony with a whispered, "Aren't they beautiful?"

She hugged him conspiratorially, holding him tightly so he would not see her sudden tears. (*Gianni. Oh my dear dear Gianni! Why do my arms feel so empty, when I still have these two beautiful children? I long for the feel of you in my arms, like a broken bird you were, light, light, nevermore, oh Gianni!*)

After a long moment they continued on tiptoe down the black marble-floored hallway to their bedroom. Tony often thought that was his favourite room in all the world. He longed for it when his punishing schedule gave him insomnia in some far off place, although he was usually so happily tired from rehearsing or performing that sleep came fast to him regardless.

But this bedroom was so many things to him; he found there joy, refuge, refreshment. The walls were covered in a subtly sensual rose watered silk. A faint scent of roses from Jen's potpourri permeated the room. The outsize four-poster bed was massed with pillows, the Porthault prints making of it a bower of Arabian Nights colours. That was tonight's theme, thought Tony indulgently. The artist in Jen loved interior decorating, and Tony enthusiastically supported all her talents. Indeed, he encouraged anything that gave her pleasure, especially now since Gianni's death had, to Tony's dismay, almost extinguished her innate *joie de vivre*.

They had shared their lacerating grief as they watched Gianni's evanescent life slowly whisper away on a sigh. Afterwards, as the sad days tripped painfully over one another, Tony began to long for—to need—Jen's usual optimism. He relied so on her cheerful strength. She was both his compass and his keel, and he felt it was she who kept him from foundering on the rocky, dangerous, unforeseeable shoals of the operatic world.

So Tony was relieved that Jen had recently revived her interest in the decor of their apartment. These days their four-poster bed had several personalities, one being a white lacy bridal bed with an almost impossibly virginal aura; another being this lascivious orgy of Arabian Nights. Tony preferred the Arabian Nights decor, partly because Jen had painted an impressionistic watercolour which she hung in the bedroom whenever the bed was in this Middle Eastern mode. She was given to creating art which matched certain decors, or vice versa, and she often painted specific works to create certain effects in a room. Tony enjoyed never knowing what he would see hanging on their walls. But he considered this particular painting the most remarkable work of art she had yet done.

"You will stop soon illustrating the children's books and you will do this other serious art, yes?" he said. "The books done by Jenetta Amato, I feel always proud, but this makes me a so real emotion. Are you listening, Jen?"

"Darling Tony, everything makes you a so real emotion. That's part of being a great singing actor, yes?"

Tony scowled. "You are making fun of me. I do not want to make jokes. You have such a talent."

But Jen, apparently not in the mood to discuss her artistic future, retreated into the shower. In a few moments Tony opened the frosted glass door and stepped into the steamy cubicle with her. Her smile was welcoming. As the warm water flowed in voluptuous rivulets down their bodies, Tony cupped her breasts in his hands and bent to kiss the nipples. He was always aroused by her lavish breasts. Her body moved him deeply, even more now than before, now with the terrible scar from the emergency Caesarean section that had saved her life.

Jen's body at thirty-seven was just beginning to show age, a tiny loosening here, a dimpling there, and Tony to his secret surprise loved her all the more for it. These were the tangible signs of her spending herself unstintingly for him, for their children, for her art. He would always try to be there for her, but he prized her understanding and self-reliance when he wanted to be in one place and the voice had to be in another.

As the water swirled around them, Tony ran his hands down her back, down to the softness of her round buttocks. He pulled her hips hard against him. Now her open lips sought his, mouth against mouth, tongue seeking tongue. Entwined, they stepped together from the shower.

As he was drying her he was again stricken with remorse. The towel fell to the carpet as he stared at her face. How could he make her understand that she was the better part of himself— that his passing interest in other women had nothing whatsoever to do with his love, his addictive need for her?

"What, what, my dear?" Jen asked uneasily, reaching up to lay her hands on his shoulders.

"Sometimes ... tonight ... with Mia ... it means nothing, you know really it means nothing..."

He sat down on the edge of the bed looking stricken and penitent. She stood, irresolute, her hands still on his shoulders, and then in spite of herself she began to laugh. He looked up at her reproachfully.

"Tony, Tony, you're making an opera out of it as usual. If it means nothing I don't know why you bother, but I don't let myself take any of it seriously."

"But sometimes I am really afraid; what if I lose you? How should I live then? I think I ... I don't deserve you, Jen."

She looked at him reflectively. "I have the solution—less attention to the Sacred Trust, and more to me—show me why it's worth my while to stick around, my darling impossible tenor!"

He pulled her down onto him and showed her why it was

decidedly worth her while to stick around. Afterwards, they slept, happily entwined around one another.

Five

The day after the testy Carlo Paoli and his decorative wife Diana attended the new play starring the great British tragedian, Sir Mallory Mancroft, that actor himself was reclining sulkily on the green velvet chaise-longue in his cluttered dressing room. This silly little comedy, as he called the play in his private moments, was no stretch for his acting talents. He could sleepwalk through it and the audience would still think they had seen an inspired comic performance. He was bored bored bored.

He needed a challenge. What he really wanted, he thought sadly, was to play *Hamlet* again, as he had done often enough in his youth to make it feel like his own exclusive role. But he could see that he looked too old to be a convincing *Hamlet* even with the cleverest makeup tricks. He thought maybe he could still play the role in a film, as long as the close-ups were filmed through gauze or vaseline on the lenses, or did they have a new and better method these days? All this modern electronic gadgetry... something called computer enhancement, whatever that was ...

Would anyone bankroll a *Hamlet* of his now? Once, the financiers had fallen over themselves throwing money at such projects. But now, would even Sheldon Wasserman bankroll him to play *Hamlet*? God knew Sheldon was rich enough, with his recent inheritance from his uncle, not to mention his lucrative conducting career.

Sheldon and I are—correction—were such good friends, he thought. And then castigated himself. I'm bloody ridiculous. Do I think I can stop pain by renaming the truth? Shades of George Orwell and *1984*! Shel and I were more than friends. Call a spade a spade.

He smiled a wistful little half smile, remembering *Gwendolyn* in Oscar Wilde's play, *The Importance of Being Earnest*, who emphasizes the delicacy of her upbringing by averring that she has never seen a spade. Now *there* was a play! Sir Mallory had enjoyed the challenges of playing at various times both principal male roles. It was always a pleasure for a renowned tragedian to hone his comic timing, especially on the witty cadences of this particular script.

Sir Mallory sat up and peered at his reflection in the brightly lit makeup mirror. He decided that he was looking older all of a sudden. No point in deceiving himself. He must have just had what the French call *un coup de vieux*.

He thought, they've got it right, the French, as usual. People didn't age gradually; they had a sudden descent and looked that age for years and then had another sudden descent, and so on.

He examined his face minutely. Was it time for another lift?

He hated pain, and he was always terrified of the surgeon's scalpel, for hadn't old John Billingsley had one eyelid paralyzed by that supposed-to-be-so-good-but-reasonably-priced plastic surgeon in the suburbs of Buenos Aires? The lines around his eyes were tolerable. No performer who had laughed and cried a normal actor's amount could fail to have them at seventy, but oh, the drooping eyelids, and the telltale slackening of the jaw line.

Sir Mallory's thoughts turned abruptly to that young actor John Jerome, the new one playing *McRimm* and understudying the role of *Laughton*. Dear God but Jerome was beautiful. Sir Mallory stared at his own reflection. Life wasn't fair. Lonely, oh God! it was lonely; and unfair unfair unfair.

How could it have happened, how could Shel have left him after all those years in a relationship which had so nourished them both? A relationship they both vowed could never end?

Dearest Shel. How could he leave me for that pretentious tenor? That arrogant bastard Paoli with his fake Italian name. I think he never even wanted Shel. He deserves to suffer for the pain he has caused us... God! I wish he were dead, that damn tenor. I'd usher him out of this world myself if it would do Shel and me any good. I wonder if my darling capricious Shel has times when he hates Paoli? Shel must have got only pain from that affair. Does it do any good to phone that bloody tenor—anonymously of course—and tell him to get out of our lives? Dear God.

Never mind, he told himself. I am Sir Mallory Mancroft, the World's Greatest Shakespearean Actor. I am the drawing card for this little Broadway comedy. I was perhaps the greatest

Hamlet of the century, although I must say Gielgud, Olivier, and Burton must be somewhere up there near me...

The thought gave him pause.

Well, I am certainly the greatest *Macbeth*. Oof, that was close, I almost said *"Macbeth"* out loud. Two hours to curtain time and I almost said it out loud. I could have brought bad luck on this play.

Mallory rose heavily from his chair and walked across his dressing room. The most important dressing room, although they had given one almost as big, and furthermore newly decorated, to that confounded upstart, that soap opera adornment, Pollock Braun.

Mallory stroked the exquisite leather binding of the volume lying on his small inlaid wood table. How long ago it seemed, the evening Shel had offered Mallory a first gift, that book of poetry about love and death. Mallory poked a finger into the Lalique bowl beside it, stirring his patchouli scented potpourri. The odour wafted upwards, reminding him agonizingly that patchouli was Shel's favourite.

Why do I do this to myself, he wondered, not for the first time.

He squinted at the reviews tacked to his bulletin board, the now pockmarked sheet of cork encircled by a gilt frame which had once belonged to John Barrymore. Mallory had carried this framed bulletin board from dressing room to dressing room for more than twenty years. It had been a gift, so long ago, from his dear Shel, who had encouraged Mallory's fascination with Barrymore. The frame brought Mallory luck, he was certain of it. If he didn't stroke the smooth arc at the top of the frame before each performance, who knew what might happen? He stepped back from the board to try to read some of his reviews, and then, sighing, took a narrow wine-coloured Cartier case from his pocket, drew out his glasses and put them on.

This damn little play. The critics are at least kind to me, but then they've always been kind to me. Of course they would be, wouldn't they? I am the greatest *Macbeth*—oh God. I need this job. I've been such a snob about the live theatre, I've said "no" too often to television and films, if only I had realized, and now it's late, late in the day. I thought the theatre work would always be there, would always make money for me. Why didn't I make better financial plans? One can be the greatest stage actor, and yet—what is happening to theatre these days?

Sighing, Mallory opened his dressing room door and leaned against the doorjamb, peering into the badly lit corridor just as John Jerome strolled past. Seeing Sir Mallory, he stopped.

"Sir Mallory, sir, I've been wanting to ask you all week, ever since I was hired, whether you think I should bring some of my own interpretation to *Laughton*? Did you know I'm going on to-morrow? They just told me Pollock has to go to his grandfather's funeral. Do I have to do it exactly like Pollock or ...?"

Mallory thought, he knows the answer to that question. He's just making up a reason to talk to me. God, what eyes he has!

Mallory fixed John Jerome with his famous unblinking gaze, and watched John's glance waver, his long black lashes screening the almost peacock blue eyes. Mallory saw the sudden wash of colour suffuse John's face. All thoughts of old age vanished from his mind.

"Did you see me at the back of the theatre during the

understudy's rehearsal this morning?" Mallory asked. "I thought what you were doing with Laughton was brilliant. Most amusing, your business with the revolver. I've considerable experience with guns—target shooting is a little hobby of mine—but I confess I could never have thought up a bit of business as clever as yours. If I were you, I'd do it just that way tomorrow night. It doesn't matter what Pollock is doing. Do it your own creative way."

"Sir Mallory, sir, praise and advice from someone like you means so much to me."

Mallory put his hand on the younger man's shoulder and squeezed it encouragingly. He was moved to see the flush of colour wash again over Jerome's fair-skinned, beautiful face. With his usual impeccable timing Mallory turned back to the dressing room, leaving Jerome dazzled, he hoped, by the Great Actor's attention, help, kindness.

What sensitivity Jerome has! I'm glad I took the trouble to go to that understudy's rehearsal, thought Mallory. He judged John Jerome's version of *Laughton* to be much more convincing than Pollock Braun's superficial reading. But Polly was a star, a big hit in that ghastly soap opera, *Beautiful People*. Of course teenagers and excitable women would enthuse over someone like Polly Braun. Braun didn't like the name Polly. "Pol, if you don't mind."

Mallory peered again at the *New York Times* review. Odd that the Times had sent Jamie MacTavish to review Sir Mallory's comedy. But MacTavish had definitely written the best of a good bunch. Impaled on Mallory's bulletin board with bright pink tacks, it read; "Of course Pollock Braun, the well-known television star, can only aspire from way down to reach the acting heights of his fellow actor, Sir Mallory Mancroft. Nobody can help a good co-star look better than Sir Mallory, whose brilliance and generosity on stage are legend. But the corollary is that nobody can make a bad co-star look worse, if only because of the invidious comparison. Thus it may be said that Pollock Braun is unfortunate, although he cannot have thought so when he accepted this role. As a stage actor Braun is not only pedestrian, he is offensive in his tedious posing. Handsome in a macho way he is, no doubt, but he would do well to ask Sir Mallory for a bit of coaching in the art and craft of stage acting. Age has diminished nothing of Sir Mallory's effectiveness—always an athletic actor, his movements are beautiful to watch, and of course the voice, that exquisite voice, would be worth crossing the Atlantic to hear."

Sir Mallory drew himself up, and confronted his image in the mirror. He saw what he hoped John Jerome had seen, a tall, slender, elegant man still at the summit of his profession. He raised his hand to his throat, and stroked the massive gold Saint Christopher medallion which hung on a thick chain around his neck. For just a moment, as he basked in the glow of his encounter with his young fellow actor John Jerome, Mallory forgot the inscription which nowadays gave him such pain, "Forever, S.W."

I am The Drawing Card for this effete little play, he thought, and nobody better forget that.

Six

On a cold Valentine's Day morning, Hanne arose and prepared herself lovingly for this long-anticipated day, which, she was sure, would be the most thrilling of her life. She knew her interpretation of the messages was correct: the time had come at last.

Tonight was once again opera night. The previous opera in her series had been *La Bohème*, six weeks ago, when she met Antonio Amato. But tonight, tonight Carlo Paoli was singing in *Aida*. And Hanne's ouija board had finally—finally! told her this was the auspicious night for her to meet him again. That was the ultimate message, the one which set the seal on all the others.

In Hanne's tiny bathroom she splashed cold water on her face, wincing as she bumped her left elbow yet again on the wall. She unfolded her pink washcloth and, filling the little chipped sink, soaped herself all over with the translucent rose-scented soap she had found on sale last month. Carlo had worn a rose in his lapel in that photo from the December *Vanity Fair* magazine, so Hanne knew he loved roses. And the very same day she bought the magazine she had serendipitously found the soap. Carlo would be so pleased with her when he knew.

Hanne refilled the sink, rinsed herself, and towelled dry with the rose-coloured bath towel which, along with the washcloth, she had found in a "seconds" bin. She dressed in her work uniform, the grey skirt and white blouse favoured by her employer at *Les Classiques*, the record shop where she had worked for the past twenty-five years. She didn't much like her work uniform, although she had to admit as she gave herself one last glance in the mirror, that the plainness of the garb served to accentuate her splendid auburn hair.

Mr. Chansan had hired her a quarter of a century ago, when she sought full-time employment after realizing that no matter how earnest her efforts, she was not going to be able to finance her degree in music. Her singing talent had not been great enough to win her the scholarships she needed, and there would not have been enough time to spare, what with practicing and studying, for a job that paid well enough to keep her at the university.

So *Les Classiques* had been her solution, and Hanne realized as the years passed that she could have found worse substitutes for a musical career. This job enabled her, even forced her, to be knowledgeable about classical music, the subject most dear to her heart.

She sat down to a proper breakfast, one that her poor dead parents would not have been embarrassed to serve to the hired men on their bleak North Dakota farm. Orange juice, one fried egg with three strips of crisp bacon, (more likely slices of smoked venison back home, as all her family had been skilled game hunters, and she, to the disgust of her two now dead brothers, had been the best shot of them all), two slices of brown toast with molasses, and a cup of good strong coffee with cream and two sugars. Hanne had been taught that a person needed a nourishing breakfast so as to be able to work competently all day. And she prided herself on her efficiency.

She double-locked her apartment door and ran to catch the bus. At the bus stop she pulled out of her handbag a pen and her obligatory read-on-the-bus book, a battered paperback volume of poetry. Once seated, she read and annotated as she was driven down the bustling Avenue of the Americas to her intersection in Manhattan's Financial District. There she alighted and, buffeted slightly by the usual heterogeneous hurrying crowd, she walked to the shop. Its narrow store front was misleading; it concealed a surprisingly large brightly lit interior packed with classical music records, tapes, compact disks, videos, laser disks and books.

Mr. Chansan, dapper in his uniform of grey suit and white shirt embellished with a grey brocaded silk tie, greeted her with his usual phlegmatic, "Good morning, Miss Crasmann. You will be happy this morning; we have a new compact disk of your favourite, Paoli, singing German Lieder, not his usual thing at all but lovely. Wait till you hear the Schubert, exquisite, exquisite. Do put it on the public address system for nine o'clock, won't you?"

Hanne slipped off her raincoat and examined the package for the new CD. This picture of Carlo on the front seemed special to her; she deduced immediately that he had been thinking about her when it was taken. Look at the way he was holding his right hand cupped just so; she knew he had been dreaming it held her breast just as the photographer snapped the picture. And Carlo's eyes, the way they stared into hers from the photograph, what was he telling her? "I love you, Hanne, I love you, I can hardly wait to see you. I owe you so much. Why have you taken so long to come to me?" Tonight, tonight she would at last do more than stare from afar; she would truly be with him.

"Miss Crasmann! What are you thinking of, it is already five minutes past opening time. You haven't opened the doors, there are two people out there, and I don't hear the music from the new CD. Come now, this won't do, it won't do at all."

Hanne did not bother to respond; today she knew she was invincible. Nothing Mr Chansan could do or say could hurt her. Carlo would never allow anything bad to happen to her today. Not now when at last she was going to speak with him. In these awkward job situations she usually tried to defend herself, but today no cross words could pass her lips; she was too happy for that. So she murmured quietly, "I'm so sorry, Mr Chansan. It won't happen again."

Hanne hurried to open the door to the two customers. One was a regular, little grey-haired Mr Finch, the flautist who play-ed for Broadway musicals. The other was a new customer, a woman in a handsome tweedy coat, with her matching sandy hair cut in a short no-nonsense style. She asked Hanne to show her the latest compact disc recorded by "the world's greatest tenor, Antonio Amato."

Hanne felt herself flushing; certainly Amato was good, and since she had met him she could confirm the press reports of how gracious he was, but the world's greatest tenor? Nobody but Carlo could be described that way. "Surely you mean Carlo Paoli, who really is the world's greatest tenor."

"Of course not. Paoli makes lovely noise but to interpret music properly singers must have some acting talent. Amato is such a wonderful actor."

Hanne bristled. Her resolution to be happy all day was crumbling. "What has acting to do with singing? I am a singer; that is to say I was a singer, and I've been in the music business all my life. I can tell you that Paoli produces the most exquisite vocal sounds of any singer alive. Of course he has maturity going for him; Amato must be at least fifteen years younger. But Amato just can't touch him yet. You must listen to Paoli's latest CD."

"I did not come in here for a lesson in taste. I came for one specific CD. If I can't buy what I want here without a lecture I'll go elsewhere."

Mr Chansan's spicy after-shave lotion wafted around them as he stepped out from behind a pillar to say, "Miss Crasmann, I'll see you in my office. Madam, allow me to show you Antonio Amato's latest CD, and if you want I would be delighted to make you a gift of his earlier CD, *Love Letters*, if you don't already have it?"

The brisk customer looked somewhat mollified, and allowed herself to be soothed by the well-honed merchandising tactics of Mr Chansan—and by the gift of an Amato CD.

Hanne, waiting in Mr. Chansan's office, began to feel anxious as she saw him approach. Closing the door behind him, he said sourly, "Really, Miss Crasmann, do you think we can

The Otello Omen

afford to alienate new customers just because they don't share our musical tastes? I've never heard you do anything like that before. I hope it's not the beginning of a trend. I wouldn't like to lose you, but there are lots of energetic young people out there looking for positions like yours."

Hanne's heart thumped painfully. What had possessed her? What difference could it make to her if some opera lovers preferred one tenor, some another? Carlo was the best in the world, and no-one could take that from him. Or from her. And today he was waiting for her. Her, Hanne, his beloved. But she wanted, needed this job in this store so she could spend some of her working hours in Carlo's musical company, in addition to the hours she spent in his company at home. Preoccupied with her worries, she nodded half-heartedly at Mr. Chansan, who watched her leaving his office with an expression of fastidious distaste on his face.

Seven

Except for the little difficulty with that misguided woman this morning, thought Hanne, the day had gone well so far. Even the sun shone unusually brightly as she sat on the little wall surrounding Trinity Church cemetery, lunching on carrot and raisin salad and a bran muffin. She felt a profound sadness for those buried under the old gravestones in the churchyard—sad for them because they could never hear Carlo Paoli sing. She looked up at the sky.

Before the sun reappears tomorrow in exactly that place, thought Hanne, I will have spoken to my dear Carlo. Carlo!

Back at *Les Classiques*, Hanne's afternoon crawled by until it was time to go home and to dress for the opera. With, of course, The Jacket, the one blessed by Carlo's touch. She would wear exactly what she had worn for her rehearsal with Antonio Amato.

Amato had been kind to her. He was not the world's best tenor, no, but he had been kind to her all the same. He had looked right at her and had listened when she spoke. He had believed the lie she had told about him touching The Jacket. He had smiled at her. His handshake had been firm and warm. Altogether it had been a happy experience. But of course nothing like the bliss tonight would bring her.

Hanne opened her tiny refrigerator to take out the stew she had made with that bargain beef she had found on special at Gunther's Meat Mart. But looking at it made her realize that tonight she was so excited she could scarcely swallow her own saliva, let alone the stew. She put it back in the refrigerator, poured herself a glass of filtered water from her special filter jug, and forced it down with her vitamin pill which, taken on an empty stomach, soon made her nauseated.

Oh God don't let me be sick, she thought in panic. It's tonight I meet Carlo, don't let anything happen to spoil it, please dear God please!

Swallowing repeatedly and taking deep breaths, she forced herself to dress in the grey panty hose, the rose and grey dress, the black patent shoes, and of course The Jacket. She looked down at her right hand. Tonight he would touch it! She brushed her glorious hair, her one great vanity. Then she glanced anxiously at herself in the mirror. Would Carlo see the secret beauty she knew she possessed, that beauty dedicated only to him? Carefully she locked her door, and hurried down to the street where she waited for her bus on that now surprisingly warm February evening.

She very nearly missed her stop, so bedazzled was she in a galaxy of thoughts. Excitement and apprehension jostled each other for pride of place. To Hanne, opera was the ultimate art form, comprising all the others—music, acting, the visual arts. This beauty created for her an alternate verity, truer and more lasting than the realities of her daily life. And she knew from working in the field of music that many opera aficionados shared this feeling. The commonplace events of life would come and go. Personal tragedy and triumph, those two imposters, would come and go. But for her and her fellow opera lovers, opera would make meaningful, make extraordinary, make mythic much that in life might otherwise seem ordinary.

Hanne climbed the stairs towards Lincoln Centre from Columbus Avenue, approaching the Metropolitan Opera's famous facade of five illuminated arches. Through the vast expanses of glass, Chagall's two huge luminous paintings welcomed her. Each time she saw this vista, she moved into her unique realm of absolute truth.

And tonight, absolute truth had an added dimension— tonight was the ordained night, when she would speak with Carlo!

She was so excited she almost forgot the crucial first step, to go to the artists' entrance before the performance, to add her name to the list of people wanting to meet with Mr Paoli after the opera. Hanne made her way through the well-dressed crowd in the lobby and descended the stairs. She walked quickly through the double glass doors and down the harshly lit corridor to the artists' entrance, where she wrote Carlo's name and her reason for wanting to see him—"To say thank you"—on the piece of pink notepaper handed to her by an amiable uniformed black man.

He explained what she already knew. "You come back here after the performance and we'll tell you if Mr Paoli is seeing people and if your name is on the final list. He likes meeting y'all, so keep your hopes up." He peered closely at her. "You okay, Ma'am? "

Hanne, so excited she felt ill, tried to smile. "Just—just a bit breathless," she half whispered. "I must have walked too fast."

"You sure now? Y'all can sit down here until you feel better if you like," said the black man.

Hanne was touched. There was love all around her. Carlo was sending her a message of concern through this lovely man. Because people could do that, couldn't they? And of course Carlo would see fans after the performance tonight. Nothing could stop Hanne's momentous adventure. Carlo was waiting for her.

....

Backstage in his dressing room, Carlo was warming up his voice, singing half-tone scales and arpeggios at varying volumes. Tonight's performance was *Aida*, and the role of *Radames* was one his public particularly loved to hear him perform, although Carlo knew it was not one of his best. His voice always felt more comfortable in the lighter lyric roles. He usually regretted his infrequent forays into the spinto-dramatic repertory, which were so much more of a strain with a lyric voice like his. That damned difficult aria, *Celeste Aida*, was so close to the beginning of the opera, well before the voice had a chance to warm up. His voice had cracked on a high note recently, while he was rehearsing that aria.

Happily for him, he had been singing at home and only Diana had heard him. She had stared at him with irritation and said, "Don't tell me you're going to start that, Carlo. You'd better see to it, hadn't you?"

He had not seen to it, and it had not happened since. The voice had seemed fragile, but it hadn't cracked again. Yet tonight the voice felt so damn tight. He was sure it was from the tension of receiving those strange disagreeable phone calls. Whoever could be doing this to him? It had to be another tenor trying to unnerve him. A tenor would know the special terror, that the voice may suddenly crack on a top note, the one the audience has waited impatiently to hear. And Carlo knew how easily that built-in musical instrument, the voice, can be affected by tension, by health, even by climate ...

Carlo thought, every tenor is jealous of me, they're jealous of my high D; even my pal Tony Amato. But it could never be Tony ... could it?

"Fifteen minutes," came the call over the loudspeaker.

Carlo hoped the machine which misted the stage to put down the dust would be working efficiently tonight. He cleared his throat softly and adjusted his wig, the dark curly one that reminded him of Tony's hair. He examined his face carefully in the mirror. He preened a little; the makeup and costuming for *Aida* became him. He had impressive legs, muscular and well-formed, and the Egyptian tunic showed them to perfection. Furthermore the design of the tunic rather cleverly concealed his increasing girth. *I'm a fine figure of a man. Fifty-two is the prime of life.*

....

Upstairs Hanne hurried through the red lobby and down the long aisle in the auditorium, to her seat in the front row of the orchestra section. This marvellous seat was the one great luxury she allowed herself; she had reserved it each year for many years. What did it matter that to afford such an extravagance she had to buy most of her clothes second-hand? The clothes were presentable, after all.

Almost any economy was worthwhile as long as she had enough money to afford this seat. She had occasionally spoken to the woman seated on her right, an elderly dowager who was accompanied by two clones of herself, all three dressed in a style which reminded Hanne of photographs of elegant women of the nineteen-fifties. Hanne noticed with some awe their large jewels in antique settings. Yet Hanne regarded these women with puzzled scorn, for they committed the incredible *faux pas* of dozing throughout most operas.

With a shiver of aesthetic pleasure, Hanne turned in her seat and looked up to admire the crystal starburst chandeliers. These constellations of light seemed to symbolize her own radiant, explosive joy. Once again she felt how appropriate was the Metropolitan Opera's decor for heightening the abundant emotions engendered by opera: rich African rosewood walls, gold leaf ceiling, gold fronted balconies, gold silk curtains, all juxtaposed against the dark rubies of carpet and upholstery.

Now Hanne heard the chimes ring, summoning those not already in their seats to make their way into the vast auditorium, to experience the enduring reality that is music, that is theatre, that is opera. *Aida* was about to begin.

....

"Overture starting, beginners on stage," came the call backstage.

On the set, Carlo waited behind the great doors through

which, in a few seconds, he would make his entrance onstage. He closed his eyes as he tried to meditate his way into the role, but instead he found himself remembering inconsequentially how Tony Amato looked just before performing. At those moments Tony seemed to Carlo to be in a trance, before exploding onto the stage in one of his brilliant bursts of characterization.

Oh damn Tony Amato, thought Carlo. Let the voice be okay tonight. Please. Please.

At his musical cue he strode through the doors into the stage setting just below one of two huge Pharaonic statues, and sang his preliminary dialogue with the High Priest. A few phrases later, Carlo launched into his big opening aria, *Celeste Aida*, and by the time he sang *trono*, he knew he was in vocal trouble. A moment of panic, and then he reined in his bolting emotions and thought, I am the greatest tenor in the world. I have a superb vocal technique. I'll get through this and then I'll see the otolaryngologist, and my coach...

And so, with a major effort, Carlo set forth to show the glittering Metropolitan Opera audience, and to show himself, that with intelligent vocalizing and impeccable technique he could get through the opera *Aida* without unhappy incident and still excite the audience.

He feared that the high note might break, and cut it short so thrillingly that the audience outdid itself applauding him at the end. The audience could not discern that he was in trouble, but his *Aida*, Mia Mitsouros, who knew him only too well, certainly could. Not once did she tease him onstage during that first act. This made him feel worse. He knew she teased Jose and Luciano and Tony and Placido. Did she only bait her fellow singers when she knew they were feeling secure? Oh God.

After the first act Carlo came off the stage wringing wet, panting and unhappy. The mischievous Mia walked with him to his dressing room, holding his hand and saying nothing. At the door she said, "It'll be okay, Carlo. I know you're having trouble, but with your technique hardly anybody will know the difference. They'll think they've had the operatic experience of their lives. But for heaven's sake do something about it after tonight. I don't want to have to stop kidding you onstage, but I will, just for tonight, I promise."

And Carlo's assistant said admiringly, "I've been watching from the wings, and I've never seen you better theatrically, Mr Paoli, you conveyed such depth of emotion." (Terror, more likely, thought Carlo miserably. Good thing my assistant read it wrong. I hope everyone else here did the same.)

Jamie MacTavish the critic thought, there are some voice problems here, and what's more I can't figure out whether Paoli is just worried about the voice or whether he's finally going to learn to act. Interesting. And what do I put in Sunday's review? We'll see how things go for the rest of the evening. Mia sounds great as usual.

Meanwhile Hanne, in her front row seat, was in a state of nerves. Her dear Carlo was in vocal trouble, and maybe she was the only person in the auditorium to know it. But of course she and Carlo were so close. What one of them thought, the other intuited. Ever since that evening at the Met so many years ago when their bodies and souls united... So now she was frightened, for what if he were ill? What if he were going to die? How could she bear a world in which he was not?

Unhappily she contemplated this art she loved, operatic singing, which requires such great stamina to make the unamplified human voice permeate a large theatre and soar over the sound of an entire orchestra. What if the effort were one day too strenuous for Carlo? Hanne could bear it if he lost his voice, because with or without his singing he would still be her dear adored one, but what if he had a heart attack and died?

....

As the opera dragged on for him, Carlo found himself wishing fervently that he could die suddenly onstage like the great baritone Leonard Warren. Warren had collapsed and died at the Met in 1960 during the second act of *La Forza del Destino*, just after he had sung with his usual brilliance the aria *Urna fatale del mio destino*. Carlo had been among the horrified spectators in the audience that night. After the initial shock, he wondered whether such a fate might be what a singer would long for towards the end of a career—to drop dead on stage immediately after being acclaimed by an appreciative audience.

Tonight, when Carlo was on stage but not required to sing, he could feel himself sliding out of character and wondering whether the rest of his career—if there was any left after tonight—would be made up of performances like this one, during which terror would alternate with despair.

Onstage Mia whispered in his ear, "Quit making an opera out of your problem, Carlo darling. You're doing just fine. Only one act to go now."

Carlo finished the opera without obvious mishap, by transposing some of his high notes, saving his voice so he would be able to thrill the audience when they absolutely expected it.

His strategies worked; the applause they all received after *Radames* and *Aida* had died in the crypt was a joy to hear.

Is this my last ovation, Carlo, never one to make light of a situation, wondered despairingly?

And Mia the all-knowing (all things considered she should be all-knowing, at least about me, Carlo thought) answered as though he had spoken aloud. "Carlo, love, it's not the end of the world. Or even the beginning of the end of your career. One bad night is just one bad night."

In his dressing room, he slumped into a chair, exhausted, frightened, nauseated. Robert, his assistant asked, "Are you seeing the fans tonight, Mr Paoli?"

Carlo snapped, "No, I haven't got a thing left to give to anybody. They devour me, Robert, they devour me."

But Robert was used to being snarled at by Carlo. He persevered. "There's even more than usual on the list tonight. You may not think much of your performance, but they seem to. You're really going to let them down, are you?"

Carlo hurled himself out of the chair and dashed into the bathroom where he vomited. His assistant started to call out the door, "Cancel Mr Paoli's—" when Carlo surprised him with, "No, hell, I'm okay, Robert, this is just a tension reaction. I used to do this all the time when I was a kid. Damn fans. They want to see me, let them see me."

Trying to relax, he showered slowly, and dressed in a tweedy brown jacket and tan trousers, the British country gentleman's casual look. As he tucked a green paisley ascot into his collar, he told Robert he would be in the Green Room shortly, and to tell them at the door to start letting the line in.

....

Her chest aching with apprehension and excitement, Hanne rushed to the stage door as soon as she was free of the noisy, restraining crowd. There to stabbing disappointment she learned that no, Mr Paoli was not receiving, oh, one moment, there was a change, yes he was, and yes, her name was on the master list and would she line up here please.

Mr Paoli was receiving in the Green Room. Hanne found herself at the end of the long line, which was strung along the left hand side of the extended ivory-painted corridor. There were lockers on the right wall; it rather reminded Hanne of her old high school. The waiting line of fans moved slowly, so that Hanne was forced to listen to the conversations of those in front of her.

"Oh, Paoli's very generous with fans, once I went backstage and he actually kissed me!" exclaimed a nubile blonde well a-head of Hanne in the line.

"I've never met him myself, but I've heard that he loves to talk to his fans," said her companion, a slender man wearing a dangling earring.

Only a very few people were in front of Hanne now as she neared the corner. As far as she could discern, the system was the same as the one with Antonio Amato. Four people at a time were allowed into the Green Room to see the star of their choice. Hanne wondered who her three companions were, these three older women just ahead of her in line who would share her greatest moment. Of course it didn't really matter who they were. Carlo was waiting for her. So he kissed other fans? But that was just politeness, the air-blown greeting kiss of the upper classes. He talked to other fans? Of course, for wasn't he the best, the kindest, the most thoughtful of men? Carlo. Dearest, dearest Carlo.

Her moment had come. Hanne turned the corner and was ushered with the three women into the Green Room. Hanne's eyes swept over the room, for she must remember everything about tonight, everything, and something might have been changed here since she spoke to Antonio Amato. No, all was the same, from the boring, acoustically tiled ceiling to the open door behind Carlo. Then the tall woman in front of Hanne shifted slightly, and at last she could see him. Carlo.

Oh, he looked wonderful, but tired, Hanne thought with a lurch of her pounding heart. Such a beautiful man. The first woman to reach him grasped his hand and seemed to Hanne to grip it forever. Hanne heard her telling Carlo that he was a great singer, and could she have his autograph? Carlo smiled graciously as the woman produced her programme of *Aida* for his signature. She fumbled about, and dropped her handbag, which Carlo bent to retrieve. (Carlo's gorge rose as he bent over, and for one panicky moment he thought he would vomit again, a disagreeably theatrical public spectacle.)

"You have a pen?" Carlo asked.

"No, I thought you—"

Carlo, who usually carried a pen for these predictable moments, searched his pockets but tonight produced nothing. The second woman dug deeply into her handbag, and brought out a chewed-looking pencil, which she reached across to hand to Carlo.

"Oh, not in pencil, how will I keep it?" the first woman

asked petulantly.

Carlo sighed noticeably, glancing past the woman with only partially concealed impatience.

Of course, thought Hanne. He knows I am coming. He can scarcely wait for me to take his hand. Look how pale he is, look at the perspiration on his face, he can scarcely wait for me!

Carlo autographed the programme with the battered pencil, since no other writing instrument was forthcoming. Woman number one thanked him with an expression of adoration on her face, and ceded her place reluctantly to woman number two.

Woman number two appeared to be struck dumb. She grasped Carlo's hand, opened her mouth to speak, and uttered a tight little croaking sound. Thinking ruefully that he was not the only person tonight with voice problems, Carlo put his arm around the temporarily mute woman and bent way down to kiss her on the cheek; woman number three tremulously raised her camera and photographed them.

"I got that, Margaret, I got that! What a thrill! Thank you so much, Signor Paoli, thank you so much, may I shake your hand? Margaret, can you take a picture of Signor Paoli and I together?"

There was much shuffling of handbags, umbrellas, coats and programmes, as Carlo held the hand of woman number three who apparently was not going to let go until Margaret had taken the picture. Carlo thought he'd better kiss this woman too, and urgently wished they would get the photography over with, because he knew he was going to be sick again. With relief he saw there was only one woman left; he hoped he could hang on.

As he bent to kiss fragile elderly woman number three, she said, "Signor Paoli, you are absolutely the second best tenor in the world, only Amato is better than you."

Carlo's gorge rose precipitately. Second best? Second best? Of course Amato never breaks on his high notes, damn him, damn everybody, I've got to get out of here.

Hanne had heard the words "second best". Her Carlo? Second to any tenor who had ever lived? He looked so weary tonight. He needed her comfort, needed her love desperately.

Now it is my turn, thought Hanne. My turn! She looked up at her beautiful Carlo, this big man who alone among men made her feel petite, feminine, desired, and her heart opened to him. She held out her hand to grasp his at last, flesh to flesh, warmth to warmth. He would of course kiss her, he would know, he would know as soon as they touched.

Her hand touched his. To her surprise, his was hot and sticky with perspiration. She began her carefully rehearsed, "Thank you so much, Signor Paoli, I know you sang *Celeste Aida* just for me."

Bugger *Celeste Aida*, thought Carlo, I couldn't sing that damn note, will I be able to sing it next week, oh Lord, I need a bathroom fast. He dropped Hanne's hand as though it had seared him, and ran from the Green Room towards his dressing room without a backwards glance.

Hanne stood still, looking down uncomprehendingly at her hand. Then she lifted her head, unseeing, as a well-dressed older man stepped forward to say to the little knot of fans still waiting outside the Green Room, "That will be all for tonight, ladies and gentlemen. Signor Paoli thanks you for coming back to see him. This way out, please."

But there must be some mistake, thought Hanne,

bewildered. That can't be all there is to our first meeting after so long. He was waiting for me, I know he was waiting for me ... wasn't he? Wasn't he?

She walked back down the corridor towards the exit, unseeing, trying to determine what message he had conveyed to her through the touch of his hand. She knew there had to be a message. She was sure something significant had happened, must have happened. She passed through the doors to the receiving area, where a black Cadillac limousine purred, its uniformed chauffeur, an enormous blonde man, smoking and waiting for his employer.

Of course! thought Hanne. Carlo wants to speak to me privately, not with that bunch of crazy women. Second best tenor, how could she say such a thing? Worse than that woman in the store this morning. Carlo wants to speak to me out here, where there are no fans to bother us; well, not many anyway. Just that little group over there, I don't remember seeing them, they must have been in a line to see someone else, maybe Mia Mitsouros, I wonder if she has gone yet? I'll wait here for Carlo. Oh I'm so excited. Now we will share our feelings at last. Here he comes, here he comes! Who is that with him? Must be a bodyguard. What an ugly man, of course everyone looks plain beside Carlo.

Carlo, pale and perspiring, had almost reached the limousine. Hanne stepped towards him, her hand outstretched, all quivering love and hope as she opened her lips to start once again her speech, "Thank you—"

But he did not take her hand; he looked right through her and climbed heavily into the limousine, followed by the ugly man. Hanne had a glimpse through the open car door of an exquisitely pretty, beautifully dressed woman, whom she recognized even in her confusion as Diana Paoli.

Hanne stood transfixed. A wave of frosty cold descended from her head downwards until she felt immobile, as though encased in ice. Carlo had not spoken to her. He had not squeezed her hand in conspiratorial tenderness. He had not listened to her words, had not understood her message of deep, all-encompassing love. He had not even so much as looked at her.

How could he do this to her, after her years of devotion? He had led her on; surely he had imagined he was holding her breasts in his cupped hands when he was being photographed for that last CD package. Hadn't he led her to believe he loved her, hadn't he demanded loyalty throughout the best years of her life, through all his messages? Now at the ultimate moment, when she should have been rewarded for her unswerving devotion, he had betrayed her.

Had she been so wrong about him? Maybe he was not the wonderful person she had thought him. Would a good man have treated her love so shabbily? She was offering him the greatest gift she had to give; herself, forever. And he had not even taken time to listen to her carefully composed speech of gratitude, let alone kiss and hug her as he had done to those other ridiculous women. Ridiculous women!

She stood where she had frozen, in the covered automobile pickup area of the Metropolitan Opera, her only companion now a uniformed guard at the double doors which led into the lower foyer. She looked down the garishly lit corridor where Carlo had walked, white-faced and unsmiling, just a few minutes ago when there was still a vibrant, life-giving hope in her heart.

And now, thought Hanne, I am dead. Dead. Carlo has killed

me.

Suddenly she imagined she saw Antonio Amato, with whom she had rehearsed for her meeting with Carlo. In her vision he was coming down the corridor smiling and chatting as he had that other evening. He had been kind to her.

Hanne's experience of the occult caused a tiny surge of hope. Could Carlo have sent her a message through Amato? Could Carlo in some mysterious way have used Amato in order to tell her he cared about her? Surely such things could happen, couldn't they? Couldn't they? She remembered with dazzling clarity the night she lost her singing voice forever. A mystical, magical, fevered, inexplicable night. If what happened that night could happen, why not this?

Buoyed by her surge of hope, she moved, put one foot ahead of the other, made her way to busy, noisy Columbus Avenue where to her surprise something good happened; the first taxi she hailed stopped for her and took her home.

Home. She locked the door to the street and started to climb the stairs to her apartment when from under the stairwell a man appeared. Hanne's throat closed in terror, then relaxed when she saw who it was. Lawrence Smythe, her neighbour from across the hall—she categorized him as a "remittance man". She deduced that he must have independent means, for though he had no regular employment, he kept himself well dressed, and his apartment, which she saw through the often open door, was clean and tastefully furnished.

"Nishe night," he volunteered.

Hanne recognized his habitual problem—he was yet again slurring his words, pathetically drunk. His hair, carefully dyed dark brown, had fallen about his face; his tweed jacket, usually so neatly pressed, was crumpled and a dark wet stain adorned the left lapel.

He looked at her appraisingly. "If ever thou shalt love, in the sweet pangs of it remem ... rememember me..."

"Goodnight, Mr Smythe," said Hanne, continuing up the stairs.

"Don' go away, Miss Crasmann—I watch you so often, I don't talk to you enough—I want to know you better, you know, would you care for a drink, in my apartment? Shakespeare says, he says, "What's to come is still unsure, in delay there lies no plenty, then come and kiss me, sweet..."

He put his hand on her arm and looked imploringly at her. Hanne did not know much about him, except that, drunk or sober, he quoted Shakespeare and Congreve, Dickens and Milton to her in a splendidly upper-class Bostonian accent. They shared a love of good literature at least. She had not thought much about him, being so involved in her dream life with Carlo, yet she had found Smythe pleasant enough whenever they met and whatever his condition.

Maybe he was the messenger from Carlo? Surely there had to be a message, tonight of all nights? Surely? Maybe it was through this man that Carlo was going to tell her something.

"Why don't you come up to my apartment, Mr Smythe?"

"That would be delight—delightful. I'll get my bottle, I have some great brandy."

They climbed the stairs together; he went into his unlocked apartment and reappeared almost immediately with a bottle of Armagnac. Hanne unlocked her door and stood aside to let him enter.

"After you, dear lady, after you."

They entered the apartment, and Hanne thrust all her bolts home amid a feeling of mounting excitement. This man had messages for her from Carlo. She was certain of it.

Smythe looked around her sitting room in some puzzlement. "Who's this fellow? Lots of pictures of him, he looks familiar, this fellow, is he your husband? I haven't seen him here, have I? I don't remem—rememember—I thought you were a widow?"

"No, no, I've never been married, Mr Smythe. This is a very good friend."

Mr Smythe remarked with satisfaction, "Friends, wonderful thing, friendship, I used to have a lot of friends, a friend should bear his friends' infirm—infirm—ities, don't you think so? Will you bear mine?"

"I'm not sure what you mean."

They sat down on either side of a small table. Hanne had produced two glasses, and Smythe was unsteadily pouring Armagnac into one of them. He spilled some onto the doily her mother had crocheted during her last illness. Hanne put her hand on his to steady it, and at her touch he leapt up faster than she thought even a sober man could move.

He pulled her brusquely out of her chair with a strength she should have foreseen, for he was a big man. He clamped his sour-tasting lips firmly on hers. For a moment she felt only disgust; then, realizing that of course this was Carlo sending her a message through Smythe, she responded to his kiss in a way she hoped did not reveal her inexperience.

His reaction amazed her. "I've wondered if you cared for

me, I've wondered often when we talked, I've watched you come and go and I thought you might."

His hands were alternately unbuttoning her dress and caressing her, as he forced his mouth again and again on hers.

"What—what do you think you're—what are you doing?" Hanne cried. Was this the message from Carlo? What could it mean? "You're—you're hurting me—please—oh—please—stop—"

Hanne pushed him with all her considerable strength. His face twisted abruptly into an expression which made him unrecognizable, as he grabbed her hair with one hand and her throat with the other.

"Spitfire, are you? Well, I like a spitfire, I do, I do, and I know you want me, you kissed me, you kiss so well."

He squeezed her throat. She remembered she should knee him in the groin. She quickly raised her knee, but he was surprisingly fast for a drunk man.

"Oh no you don't. You promised me love, you'll give me love. Understand? I'll hurt you, I'll hurt you badly if you don't give me what your kisses promised."

His grip on her throat tightened until she could no longer breathe. She realized that she could not retreat, that she was compelled to submit to whatever he wanted, or else he might hurt her more, or even ... even ... kill her. She forced herself to smile in acquiescence. He loosened his grip on her throat. She wondered if she could talk to him, make him understand, at least ask him to be gentle, for it was her first time, her first time ever, and this was Carlo making love to her through him, wasn't it? Wasn't it?

But Smythe suddenly became uncontrollable. He tore at her clothes, tore at her underwear, and when she cried out, covered her mouth with a powerful hand. He grabbed her left arm and twisted it hard behind her back; then he alternately squeezed and kissed her breasts until she thought she would faint with pain. But she didn't know what agony was coming, she didn't know how her body would be cleft by his thrusting penis ripping into her, tearing her virgin hymen into bleeding weeping shreds.

Yet that pain seemed as nothing compared to the real anguish, the torture of knowing that the message Carlo had sent through Smythe was this, this knowledge that Carlo despised her, was happy to hurt her. In no way was Carlo grateful that she had saved her virginity for him. He had not taken her with the exquisite tenderness she had hoped for, longed for, dreamed of. He had—she must put the word to it, she must have the courage to put the word to it, he had raped her.

Carlo the beloved. Carlo the rapist.

She felt a terrible sickness, a weakness, and then mercifully she felt nothing at all.

Dawn was already seeping through the windows when Hanne regained consciousness. The light hurt her eyes, and whatever was she doing lying on the floor? She tried to turn her head to look around her, but her neck was so stiff she could barely move it. A glass had overturned onto the floor, and a wet yellowing stain seeped into her carpet. Her smallest table lay on its side. What had happened? Slowly Hanne recollected the events which had led up to her lying there. Physical pain and psychic agony warred in her as she struggled up to lock her door, which Smythe left open leaving her apartment. Then she sank weakly to her knees. Oh dear God. What could she do, what should she do? Who would avenge her? Who would even defend her?

The best photograph of Carlo with his real autograph on it, for which Hanne had purchased an expensive antique silver frame, lay on the floor, its glass cracked. There was a long diagonal scratch across the print of Carlo's wide, handsome face. A sob escaped Hanne's throat as she looked at Carlo. Then in spite of her desire to hold back, her aching body convulsed in painful, grinding sobs. She picked up the photo of Carlo and threw it across the room. The glass shattered, and the frame itself came apart. Rather satisfying.

Still sobbing, Hanne looked wildly around her. From a big picture tacked on the wall Carlo stared smiling at her, a smile she had known was a love message until he betrayed her, until he raped her. She half crawled across the room, stood up slowly, tore the picture free from its tacks, and threw it across the room to join the other one. The next picture she threw made a splendidly gratifying crash as the glass and the flimsy wooden frame splintered.

Slowly gathering strength despite her aching limbs, she found herself indulging in an orgy of vengeful fury as she mutilated each of her lovingly collected pictures of Carlo Paoli. Her sobs changed to little screams, then moans, and finally as she surveyed the satisfying revenge she had begun to take, to laughter.

Across town, Carlo, all unknowing, lay awake, his stomach aching with the fear that his career might be ending, that last night's *Aida* had been the first painful step down from his pinnacle.

Eight

On the first evening of March, Jen and Tony Amato walked up Fifth Avenue on their way to Carlo Paoli's apartment for supper and to view the Caruso *Aida* score. Tony only sporadically followed the advice of his security company that he should be accompanied by an aide-bodyguard when he mingled with the public. He enjoyed moments of anonymity, although with his growing fame such times became increasingly rare. Tonight he and his wife strode along briskly as the wind whipped at their similar beige raincoats and ruffled their hair, the dark and the honey-coloured heads close together as they talked.

When Jen was unable to put her impressions immediately on canvas, she remembered them with an interior monologue. On her right she noticed once more the elegant stone and brick facades of some of New York City's most prestigious apartment buildings. Graceful wrought iron protected ground floor windows, with matching balconies above adding a touch of lacy charm. From above each beveled glass doorway, canopies stretched to the curb. Uniformed doormen stood just inside, to open doors, summon taxis, telephone inhabitants, and otherwise smooth life's path for the residents of their buildings. Fifth Avenue was crowded with New York's generic yellow taxis, endlessly cruising for passengers. The yellow cabs were spots of cheerful colour interspersed with a pride of limousines, black, white, navy, oversized, ostentatious, some even conservative.

Those passers-by who recognized Antonio Amato had several reactions. It seemed always curious to Jen the way people's perceptions of the famous were distorted by the fame itself; for to her the illustrious were so often quite ordinary people with one extraordinary gift and the courage to exploit it. Some of the strollers on Fifth Avenue did a classic double take on Tony, after which they either gaped or looked away discreetly. One astrakhan-hatted elderly man stepped in front of Tony to shake his hand, saying , "Thank you for the great pleasure you keep giving your fans. Take care of your voice, whatever else you do. Aren't you taking a big risk, singing *Otello* so young with a voice like yours?"

"Why does everybody think they know better than me about my voice ?" muttered Tony irritably to Jen.

Outside Carlo's brick apartment building Tony noticed a tall big-boned woman, plain of face but with magnificent red hair. She stood near the curb, arms crossed, hands stroking the sleeves of her rosy jacket, staring at the door of Carlo's building with intense concentration.

"Who is this woman, Jen, somewhere I have seen her, if she can keep such a look on her face for long, they could hire her to be a witch in *Macbeth,* no?" Tony murmured.

"Tony, she'll hear you," whispered Jen, distressed.

"No, no, she is in a trance maybe?"

The large head with its cap of flame slowly turned towards Jen and Tony, glazed eyes focussing slowly. Recognition dawned in them, and she took a step forward, hands outstretched. "Mr Amato, you remember me, of course you do, I saw you backstage recently after *Boheme,* I remember how you sang *Che Gelida Manina* just for me."

Tony prided himself on his memory. Now he recalled the occasion when he had met this woman. "Naturally I remember you. It is a pleasure to meet you again."

He felt Jen's arm, linked through his, tighten against him as the woman clutched convulsively at his sleeve.

"Mr Amato, maybe you can help me, I need..."

Tony interrupted her. "Please forgive us, we are going to supper and we are late."

The woman clutched his arm with such force it hurt him. Firmly he opened her fingers, disengaging them. He smiled his little-boy smile, not without awareness of its effect, and took a step back, talking soothingly all the while, "Naturally I am happy you appreciate the singing. Please, we must go now to supper."

The woman gradually seemed to succumb to the not inconsiderable charm being directed at her. The corners of her downcast mouth twitched into a smile. "Of course, Mr Amato. I understand. I am so pleased that you will be singing *Otello* here at the Met, and not just in Paris. I would like so much to hear you in that role. Thank you, thank you, I enjoy hearing you sing very much."

Jen and Tony escaped into the foyer of Carlo's building, a green *trompe l'oeil* bower. In the elevator Jen said in a shaky voice, "That woman scared me, Tony."

Tony shook his head and, putting one arm about her shoulders, gave her a reassuring hug. "She is not harmful. Poor ugly woman, she likely makes sexy fantasies about opera singers."

"Likely fantasizes about you at any rate, from the way she grabbed you. Do you suppose she's hanging around here because she knows Carlo lives here? She probably wants to grab at him too."

The special elevator took them directly into Carlo's suite, where with expansive handshakes, hugs and a more than welcoming kiss for Jen, he greeted them.

Two hours later, Tony, Jen and their hosts sat in the Paoli's formal yellow drawing room, blissfully drowsy after a splendid supper. Of course the Valencian paella which was Carlo's culinary specialty had been the *piece de resistance*. Leah, the cook, was always exasperated when Carlo took over her kitchen. She felt sufficiently competitive with her employer that she outdid herself preparing a sherried *consomme* with mushrooms, and a raspberry-dotted *creme brulee*. Tony, trying to relax on Carlo and Diana's hard gold silk sofa, said contentedly he would have cancelled his Paris *Otello* in order to eat that *creme*.

"You shouldn't be singing *Otello* anyway, Tony. You know Caruso said no tenor should sing *Otello* before he's fifty," was Carlo's unasked-for advice, to Tony's intense displeasure. "You don't have the vocal depth," Carlo continued. "You'll lose your flexibility, no more *Rodolfo,* no more *Alfredo,* you're a fool."

"Thank you very much, Carlo. But you shouldn't be worried about me; so far both of us are doing fine, yes?"

Diana stared at her long rose-coloured fingernails. "Don't pay any attention to him, Tony. Carlo criticizes everything. Do you wonder I never learned to cook? Everything I tried in the kitchen when we were newlyweds, he criticized, criticized."

"Not everything, Di. I remember we had the softest brown carpet in our first kitchen, it tickled my back when—"

Diana gave her husband a look of distaste as she interrupted with, "Carlo, must you always be vulgar?"

Tony glanced at Jen, who raised her eyes almost imperceptibly heavenward. He read her thoughts; what subject could they introduce that would deflect the often-battling Paolis from their usual collision course? Carlo and Diana were notoriously one-tracked once they started.

Jen tried diversion with, "Carlo, what do you think of the roster for the Met AIDS Gala in April—you are singing, aren't you? Tony was surprised this morning when he heard more details. The programme isn't just music. Sir Mallory Mancroft has been asked to perform, doubtless he'll do his Shakespeare thing as usual, and..."

"Mancroft?" interrupted Carlo. "Can't stand the man. Do you know him? Conceited, irascible sonofabitch. The first time I met him we sat beside each other on the Concorde and he attacked me for absolutely no reason. He seems to have a hate for tenors. He said disagreeable things about you, Tony, and about Pavarotti. He even dredged up something nasty about Domingo. I don't know what's the matter with Mancroft. I could

understand professional jealousies, especially when you get to
his age, but what possible threat can tenors be to him?"

Carlo glowered at the recollection.

"But we should talk about the gala, Carlo," Tony interjected.
"Mancroft's not the problem. They are making such an unfoc-
ussed programme, they should know better what they want. Are
they wanting music, or music and classical theatre, or what?
They have even invited Pollock Braun to perform."

The bored Diana evinced some interest. "You mean Pollock
Braun who's on *Beautiful People*? I love that soap opera. I never
miss it. I even tape it when I have to be out. I wonder what he'll
do at the gala? Actually I think asking Braun and Mancroft and
people like that is a brilliant idea. I mean, it's going to be tele-
vised, isn't it? You'll get a whole different audience than you
would if it was just classical music."

Carlo slouched further into his down-cushioned chair, the
one comfortable seat in the Louis Quinze room. "Oh, for
Godssake Diana, what do you know about programming? Stick
to your expertise, whatever that is. Good God, I wouldn't have
agreed to do that Gala if I'd known people like Pollock Braun
were performing. Alongside me? What can Braun possibly do?
He certainly can't act."

"No, but he is looking very handsome," Tony interjected. He
jumped as the sleek yellow phone on the ormolu table beside
him rang shrilly.

Jen laughed. "Tenors! What nervous systems you have!"

"Answer it, Tony," Carlo said. "Get rid of them for me, whoever they are. It's time to make you envy me and my *Aida* score."

Tony snatched up the receiver, cleared his throat, and said

hoarsely, "Hello."

There was a silence, then a harsh whisper said, "Carlo Paoli? Keep looking over your shoulder, for soon you die. Bullets will tear your throat out."

Tony instinctively clutched at his own throat, at his vocal cords. His expressive face registered first astonishment, then anger. "Who are you? What are you talking about? I am not Carlo Paoli. This is a not funny joke. Who—" but the receiver clanged down and the dial tone mocked further questions. Tony held the receiver away from his ear, frowned at it, and said, "Crazy friends you have, Carlo, this is a strange kind of joke. This person is saying you die soon and—"

The expression on Carlo's face stopped Tony. Never a good actor, to his great sorrow on stage, Carlo was now showing genuine terror. His voice shaking, he murmured, "This isn't the first threat, Tony. First it was anonymous phone calls, sometimes I could just hear breathing and sometimes crazy whispered messages I could only half hear and didn't understand, but last week I got two calls that seemed like real threats. What did he— could you tell if it was it a he?"

Tony frowned. "I do not know. It was a—like a whisper, hoarse, in the throat? I don't know if it is a woman or a man, how to tell?"

"Go on, what did he—they say?"

"They say, look over your shoulder, you will die soon." Tony, about to continue, was suddenly unable to tell his friend about shots tearing at the throat. "Carlo, you maybe should be calling the police now?"

"I've already called them. They say they can't do anything.

Even though something else has happened—I got three anonymous letters. They each started with lines from poems, and at the end the first one said, 'I want you to suffer'. The next one ended with, 'I want you to go away' and the last one said, 'I want you to die'. When I talk to the cops, they just say to be a bit careful. But apparently unless I'm actually attacked nobody can do anything ... I talked to my security people, they say the same thing. Bunch of maggots feed off each other, the police and the Goddam bodyguards ... Tony, could someone really hate me that much? Why would anyone want me dead? What have I done to anyone that they would—"

Diana began incongruously to laugh. "It's likely your mother, Carlo, doing her nut number again. I mean, I don't blame her for being angry at you, you don't treat her any better than you treat me. She has likely dreamed up yet another diabolical way to punish you. She's good at it. She knows you so well, she knows this will really get to you."

"My *mother*? Are you crazy? Why would my mother want to hurt me? I'm not mean to my mother, Diana, or to you either, for Chrissake. You of all people know what my schedule is like. When do I have extra time for my mother? You show me. If we're ever lucky enough to have children, you'll know mothers don't hate their kids, not like that. Anyway I'm going to invite my mother to go on a cruise with us next summer. You know, that cruise to Alaska we want to go on, that one out of Canada."

"That's what you said last summer."

Tony glanced quickly at Jen. He said, "Maybe you could show me those letters, Carlo?"

"Why not? You might even have a helpful idea."

Carlo strode into his study and brought back the three letters. Each was made with words cut from a newspaper and glued on to a sheet of grey stationery.

Tony studied them incredulously. "*Dio*, Carlo, this is a bad business."

Carlo nodded, deep frown lines between his eyes. "Do you think what I think, that the phone calls and letters are from the same person?"

Tony examined each page, then abruptly dropped them onto the ormolu table as though they burned his fingers. "I don't know ... I only know we all have the little *nemico* ... the enemies. These are not important. But enemies that write 'I want you to die' and then say on the phone they want to kill you with bullets? Who would make such threats to you?"

"It's a tenor." Carlo looked guardedly at Tony. "I'm sure it's another tenor. Whoever it is can't really want to kill me, they just want to upset me so much it ruins my singing. They're jealous, Tony, you know they are, even you are jealous of me. Every tenor in the world would kill for my high D. If I couldn't sing any more, their high Cs would sound better because they wouldn't be measured against my D. Maybe you sent the letters." Carlo's mouth abruptly laughed. His eyes did not.

"But Carlo, I just answered the phone, right here in front of you. I cannot phone here if I am here already, how to do this?" He grinned, realizing Carlo must be joking. "You don't believe such a thing, you know it is not me. You know there is not a rivalry between us, except for collecting Caruso's stuff. Is only in the head of the journalists, our rivalry, is for selling magazines. But the opera world is big, you know there are not enough tenors to go around these days, and there is plenty of room for us two big—very big tenors."

Tony looked ruefully down at his girth and then up at the heavy-set, ever expanding Carlo. Slowly, almost reluctantly, the two singers began to laugh.

"You Italians always have a nice turn of phrase." A silence. Then, sombrely, "Only maybe Lennon's assassin waits outside the Dakota for me."

Tony was impatient. "He is in jail, Carlo. Anyway, you're not Lennon, and you don't live in the Dakota."

"Well, no, it was just a manner of speaking. Mind you, sometimes I do visit there..." mused Carlo defensively.

"Do you?" Diana interjected. "Is that where she moved to, that awful Mitsouros woman?"

"Mia is not an awful woman," Tony said. "She is a great singer. When we are singing with her, she is making us sound even better, yes, Carlo? And already we are sounding pretty good. But if you are talking about crazy fans, like who killed Lennon, I think opera fans are different ... your fans must be the same as mine? Mostly nice people, polite, they always appreciate the singing, of course sometimes women are wanting to go to the bed. Always the women, sometimes the men."

"Well, that too, of course, but—"

"But what, Carlo? Who should hate you? There is no reason anyone should hate you, you don't do anything for someone to hate you, you just sing, it makes people happy. These phone calls and letters are maybe somebody's idea of a joke. Okay, is a stupid joke, but you are making maybe too serious a drama from this theatrical—this—this—*assurdita*—nonsense."

"Takes one to know one, Tony," Jen said. "You make a drama out of lots of things. Carlo has good reason to be upset about this. It's hardly theatrical nonsense."

Tony was taken aback by this public conjugal contradiction, but his quick anger dissipated as common sense took over. "You are right, Jen." Tony looked at Carlo. "She always says to me, Tony, don't make the opera out of whatever I am making the opera out of. I apologize. *Mi scusi.*"

Carlo seemed oblivious, immersed in thought. "I can't think of anybody who could hate me that much. I mean, we all have our little enemies, but surely that's not enough to ... Maybe Di has a point. Maybe my mother is pretty annoyed at me. But hate me? Enough to threaten to kill me? It's not possible. I just can't believe that. As a matter of fact most of the time I can't believe any of this. Could I really have a dangerous enemy? Maybe you're right, maybe this is just a stupid sick practical joke."

But Carlo's face, pale and perspiring, belied his words.

Nine

The following morning, Carlo's manager phoned to say there were problems with the recording session of *Paoli Loves Puccini* because conductor Sheldon Wasserman had been delayed in Milan, and that instead of being held that afternoon, the session would have to be rescheduled.

Carlo strode into the bedroom to address Diana, who, as was her habit, was luxuriating over breakfast in bed. This morning it irritated him to see the exquisite detail she insisted on. One perfect red rose in a Daum bud vase ornamented the silver filigree bed tray. The Irish linen cutwork serviette and matching tray cloth were enhanced by a Belleek cup, filled with steaming black coffee, and by a matching plate with two slices of whole wheat toast cut diagonally and spread with low-calorie margarine and artificially sweetened raspberry jelly.

"Well, Diana, just to prove to you one more time that I try not to neglect my mother, I'm going to visit her this afternoon. I'll see if we can't arrange that cruise we've talked about."

"What a thrill. A cruise with your mother."

"You were the one who was after me last night about ignoring her, what's your problem now? I'll call her right away."

He grabbed the delicate blue telephone from the bedside table and dialed. "Mother? I'm coming to see you this afternoon about two. Oh, uh, if it's convenient."

Katarina—Kate—Pauling, had a beautifully modulated speaking voice. In her youth it had been a crystalline coloratura soprano, good enough to have taken her into a singing career had not destiny intervened in the form of Carlo's father.

"Carlo! How nice of you to call. Of course it's convenient. I'll cancel what I have on, because I haven't seen you since the afternoon of December twenty-ninth. As a matter of fact I haven't even spoken to you since the evening of January seventeenth. So it will be a pleasure to put my arms around you, dear boy."

She's trying to make me feel guilty again, thought Carlo. How can she not realize how little time we singers have to ourselves? I know I should make her a higher priority in my spare time; what spare time, that's a laugh. If people only knew how much of our lives we are forced to give up for our singing ...

Carlo decided to drive himself, and after lunch his limousine driver brought him to the garage, a mile from his apartment, where he parked his new red Jaguar convertible. Carlo eased his bulk behind the wheel, preparing to enjoy the drive upstate, the rare moment of solitude in his car, and the oddly spring-like feel to the air. His spirits lifted with every passing mile; surely these letters and phone calls were just a sick joke; surely his recent vocal problems were over. Why should his up-to-now charmed life start to go wrong? He even began to look forward to seeing his mother.

Kate lived with her housekeeper in a large Victorian "gingerbread" style house on the edge of the town of Westport. Carlo knew how fortunate he was that there had been money in her family for generations. Certainly when it was discovered that he had an exquisite lyric tenor voice, funds for his singing training were ample. Not for him the desperate financial struggles that beset the beginnings of certain other singers, such as his friend, American mezzo soprano Dolora Zajick, who had even slept rough in Central Park during the time of her early vocal training.

As the Jaguar pulled into Kate's driveway, she opened the front door and stood in its frame. She was a tall, heavy-set woman. Her mass of white wavy hair, drawn back into a complicated chignon, framed a face whose features were aging well. There was a certain resemblance to her son, but in Carlo another influence had modified the soft beauty to give him a chiseled, classically handsome aspect.

"Carlo, dearest boy, do come in and have tea, Gertrude has it all ready."

She put her arm around his waist and mother and son went into the drawing room together. It was furnished with antiques and artfully chosen reproductions which perfectly enhanced the Victorian style of the house. On the grand piano in a rococo gilt frame stood a large photograph of a remarkably plain fair-haired man, Charles Pauling, Carlo's father. Kate had been married to him only a few months before he was killed, one of those brave, reckless young pilots in the battle of Britain who would never "grow old as we who are left grow old". Charles never saw his son, never knew Carlo would become a world-renowned singer, never knew that the son named for him would find it expedient to capitalize on his mother's Italian-American background and Italianize his name.

Carlo was constantly amused by his mother's determination to surround herself with real and imitation Victoriana. He had been fascinated to learn that even the revolvers which she kept for protection, and which like all members of her country-gentry hunting family she shot with skill, were at least outwardly replicas of English guns of the 1880s.

Kate sat down on a red velvet love-seat decorated with carved wood, and patted the seat beside her for Carlo to sit down.

"It won't hold us both, Mother," he said, impatient and annoyed that she would thus obliquely criticize his weight problem.

"Of course it will, dearest boy. It's our own special place, you remember from when you were little?" She called, "Gertrude, Gertrude, you may bring tea now."

The stolid whey-faced Gertrude, only slightly younger than her mistress, appeared immediately with a silver tray bearing its heavy silver burdens of teapot, hot water jug, cream pitcher and sugar bowl. Carlo noticed his mother's best Royal Doulton cups and plates, and her sterling silver comport laden with his favourite cakes and cookies. Kate pushed aside the open volume of poetry lying on the coffee table, to make room for Gertrude to put down the tray.

"You shouldn't have gone to all this trouble, Mother."

"Darling boy, it's no trouble. What else have I to look forward to except your visits? When we heard you were coming today, Gertrude and I set to work to bake all your favourite things. Of course I'm a bit tired now, but nothing is too good for when my precious boy decides to come to see me."

Oh, Lord, here we go again, thought Carlo.

"So give me your news, Carlo. We talk so seldom, thank goodness for the newspapers and magazines or I would hardly know what you are doing. I was going to phone the Met for tickets for your *Aida* but my arrhythmia played me up so I didn't. I think I'll phone for your *Traviata*, maybe on Saturday afternoon; it's easier for me to get up to New York on a Saturday."

"Mother, you know you don't need to phone the Met for tickets, I can always get you good seats, all you have to do is ask. And I've told you I'll send a limousine any time you want to come to town, for any reason."

"I don't like to intrude on your life, dear. You are always so busy, no time for family life I shouldn't think and certainly no time for your mother. To what do I owe today's pleasure? What was cancelled, dear, so you could find an hour for me?"

Carlo took a deep breath. "If you must know, Mother, it was a recording session. But I've been wanting to come to see you anyway. Of course I'd like to see you more often."

"I wish I could believe that, dear, but I haven't noticed much evidence of it."

"Mother, please. Now, Diana and I have an idea; what we would like to do is—"

"And there's another thing. Diana. My only son, and my

only daughter-in-law, Carlo, and I still get more attention from your first wife than I ever have from your second. I try to understand that you are too busy to pay a lot of attention to your mother, but what about Diana? Couldn't she phone me more often, doesn't she realize how lonely I get for you both, my dear children? Of course she herself wouldn't understand a mother's loneliness, having no children of her own, but she might be a little more empathetic."

"Mother! I've come to invite ..."

"Must you shout, Carlo? Must you spoil our little visit? Naturally I understand that a bit of temperament is *de rigueur* for an opera singer, but you needn't bring it home to me. I put up with quite enough of your temper when you were living at home."

" ... to invite you to go on an Alaska cruise next summer with Diana and me."

"Well, Carlo, that's very nice, but who knows whether I'll even be alive next summer? I really can't plan that far ahead, and in any case the last time you and Diana invited me to go on a holiday with you, you had to cancel it, and I was so disappointed. You remember, afterwards I was so ill with 'flu, the doctor was afraid I might not recover, I never told you that, Carlo. I would never want to worry you. But the doctor felt that my resistance was lowered because of my great disappointment when the trip was cancelled."

"Actually, you did mention all that, Mother, at the time."

"Did I? I must have lost my judgement temporarily from the illness, otherwise I would never have worried you, Carlo, you know that."

"You haven't answered my question."

"What question, dear?"

"Would you like to come on a cruise to— "

"I thought I was answering it. Well, I do thank you, dear, but I must say no, my health won't stand the suspense. Perhaps just before you sail, if you haven't had to cancel, you might be able to get a last minute cabin for me, I wouldn't mind even an inside cabin, just to be on the ship with my dear children."

Carlo, upset, wondered suddenly if maybe it was his mother making the strange phone calls and threats; maybe she wanted him to retire so she could see more of him ... no, that couldn't possibly be, could it? Not his mother!

"Mother I can't stand this martyr number you lay on me all the time. What do you want me to do, retire? Then I'd have time to visit you all you want!"

"If you insist on shouting, dear, I shall have to ask you to leave. It's too upsetting for me. Of course I don't expect you to retire. How can you forget all the sacrifices I made so you could train as a singer, all the expense of getting the best teachers, the best coaches. Why ever would you think I would want you to retire?"

Kate fixed her eyes on the portrait of her husband. "That would make a mockery of my life's work, which was bringing you up all by myself, to be the great success you are now. Of course, it never crossed my mind when I was making all those sacrifices of money and time, not to mention my own career, that once you reached the pinnacle of your profession, you would leave me behind."

"I apologize for shouting, Mother. But what are you talking

about, leaving you behind? If I have, what am I doing here?"

"That's a good question. I might as well be living in Hindustan instead of an hour's drive from New York; I would likely see you as often. You might be interested to know that in the past six months I have seen you twice not counting today, and we have spoken on the telephone five times, four of those calls instigated by me."

(Not to mention, Kate thought, when I can't bear my sadness any longer and I make those phone calls when I say nothing, just to hear your dear voice, to know if you are home, but still not thinking of me, not calling me ...)

"You're keeping track, Mother?"

"Of course I'm keeping track. Each contact with you is so precious to me that I write it down in my special diary. Just a moment, I'll show it to you."

"I don't want to see it."

"I thought you'd like to know I keep loving records of every contact we have."

"Loving, my ass."

"Carlo! You certainly never learned that language from me. I can't stomach that sort of crude vulgarity. Please try to have some consideration for my feelings."

Carlo glanced surreptitiously at his watch. His dinner reservation for that evening was in two hours, but by the time he arrived back home through the early evening traffic, he would barely have time to change.

"I have to go, Mother. It's been nice seeing you. I'll call soon. Think about the Alaska trip, we were considering early June, we could book two deluxe staterooms now and we could always cancel one if you didn't care to come at the last minute."

"I'll think about it, Carlo, I'll have to talk to my doctor of course, and I'll let you know. But my answer will likely be no." She stared at him, unsmiling, as he rose. "It was good of you to come, Carlo my dear, please try to come again soon."

Kate tendered her cheek for a filial kiss. She walked with him to the door, and waved good-bye as he drove away in his sleek Jaguar, the top still down despite the encroaching coolness of the dusk.

As he pulled out from Kate's long driveway onto the highway, Carlo was pleased that he had once more done his duty. And he had actually got through a visit to his mother without losing his temper too often. Did he really see her so little? She didn't make visiting her any easier, when she acted as she had today. How much tension did she think he could stand on top of what he already had? Ah well, one more visit over with, and he had made the offer about the cruise. She should feel better about him for at least a little while.

But Kate was far from feeling better. Carlo would have been stupefied if he had been able to read his mother's thoughts at that moment. She stood for a long time in her open doorway, watching his car diminish and disappear.

She thought, I never dreamed when you were little, Carlo, that I could feel this way towards you. I know I'm hard on you, but you have hurt me so deeply for so long. Can selfishness be in the genes? Did you get it from your father? He was in and out of my life so quickly. But before he left he did commit that one act of such appalling selfishness that my life was forever changed. Did you inherit that tendency? Oh Carlo. Love you? Oh dear no, not love, Carlo. My feelings for you veer closer to hate. I am horrified to realize that sometimes I wish you were dead, so that I would not have to tell myself each night that one more day has passed without you calling me.

Ten

The week after his visit to his mother, Carlo had begun rehearsals for a new Met production of *La Traviata*. Despite the tension caused by the arrival of another anonymous letter whose message — "Look your last on all things lovely" — seemed to Carlo even more upsetting than the previous ones, he was relieved to find his voice behaving well. And he had been somewhat comforted by the remarks of a longtime friend to whom he had shown the last message.

"Carlo, you ass," this English professor had said affectionately. "This is just a quotation from the poem *Fare Well*, by Walter de la Mare. If this is the worst you get, threats by poetry, I wouldn't panic too much."

Carlo's role, *Alfredo* in *La Traviata*, was lyric, much more suited to his voice than *Radames*. The vocal problems he had suffered during the performances of *Aida* were, he hoped eagerly, gone for good.

That night, the Paolis had actually slept together in their

huge bed, an event which invariably gave Carlo more pleasure than it did Diana. Carlo loved their bed. It felt to him like sleeping on marshmallows, his favourite candy as a child.

Diana was convinced that singing *Alfredo* made Carlo more randy than usual, not that she felt he needed any encouragement. She kept a mental list of the roles she believed stimulated Carlo sexually, so she could devise convincing reasons to be away from him when he was performing them. Of course that was not always possible, but she would do anything to avoid pregnancy. Just the thought of becoming pregnant was enough to give her a migraine, so frightened was she.

Diana wakened that next morning with a savage headache. When she emerged from under the eider-down duvet and dizzily stood up, she was astonished to find she barely had time to get to the bathroom. Carlo heard her being sick, called out, "Are you all right?" and without waiting for an answer bellowed joyously, "Di! You're pregnant! Oh God, that's marvellous! At last all those doctors and treatments have paid off!"

Pale and shaky, Diana emerged from the bathroom. "Carlo, please, don't get your hopes up, I don't see how I ... but wouldn't it be ... I'd better go see Dr. Healy today."

Carlo strode across the room and picked her up as easily as though she were a kitten. He kissed her tenderly and exclaimed, "We are going to have a baby, I'm sure of it! Oh Diana this is the best news!"

Diana extricated herself from his enthusiastic embrace. "For goodness sake, Carlo, calm down. It may just be those oily specialties you love to cook. Who knows? I'll see what Dr. Healy says."

Still, the smile stayed on Carlo's face long after he had left home that morning to consult his business advisors at the World Financial Centre.

Diana phoned for an appointment with her gynaecologist. Then she slipped out of the blue silk and lace negligee and hung it in the section of her spacious closet which she, with a little brass plaque, had labelled Nightwear. She moved along to the Suit section to chose her outfit for the day. That pink wool crepe suit with the cutwork on the jacket and the paler pink silk blouse made her feel so feminine and look so guileless. It satisfied her mood. Something about her gynaecologist Brian Healy made her always want to look her vulnerable best for him. Thank God there was no way she could be pregnant. Was there? She sat down at the dressing table to select her makeup. One couldn't be too careful with makeup; it could so easily be the wrong shade for the outfit.

Her pretty face embellished, she smoothed back her gold-glinting brown hair (what good work her new hair colouring specialist was doing for her!) and slipped into the pink outfit. Satisfied with her image, she phoned to the chauffeur of their limousine to ensure he had returned from driving Carlo to his appointment. Ever punctual, he was already waiting for her in the street below. Diana swept out of her apartment and into the elevator.

That new man, the tall Egyptian, was operating the elevator. Diana was gratified with the appreciative look he gave her, before he resolutely turned sideways so as not to appear to stare. She observed him taking advantage of his peripheral vision to watch her. Feeling an obligation to be pleasant, she made small talk. It would never do for Carlo Paoli's wife to appear snobbish, even though she felt she had many reasons to imagine herself above the common crowd.

She glided gracefully into the black Cadillac limousine; the chauffeur shut the door behind her. She was grateful for the smoked windows which hid her from what she thought of as menacing crowds. She wished she could see as little of the people on the streets as they could see of her. What possible good could it do her to have to look at all those hurrying crowds, and at that terrible corner where so many homeless squatters had set up makeshift sleeping arrangements? What was the use of her looking at that? Of course she was sorry about it all; wasn't everyone? She encouraged Carlo to do benefit concerts and all that sort of thing. As his wife and helpmeet, she felt as though she too contributed something to charity by sharing Carlo's life and running his home efficiently. She also felt it a necessity to be decorative, so Carlo would never be stressed by not being proud of her.

All this came under the category of keeping Carlo happy and healthy so he could work hard and well. And, thought Diana, so that he would have energy left over to perform at those benefit concerts, with the gratifying result that she need not feel guilty about the unfortunate. But of all her wifely duties, she particularly enjoyed her obligation to be decorative. "Diana Paoli, beautiful wife of Carlo Paoli, the great Italian-American tenor, at the Gala for ..." the blurb had read under the photo in the magazine she had glanced through this morning.

The massive car stopped on Madison Avenue outside an ornate grey stone building that would not have looked out of place in Vienna. The chauffeur emerged from behind the wheel to open the rear door and Diana slid out, instructing him to wait for her, or to come back for her immediately afterwards if he received a call to pick up Carlo. She descended one of those half-stairways so common in New York, which took her to the office, according to a large gleaming brass plaque, of "Brian Healy, M.D., F.R.C.O.G., F.A.C.P., Obstetrics and Gynaecology." The blonde receptionist with the nasal voice—Diana was unusually conscious of voices— told Diana to have a seat, and that Dr. Healy would be with her "momentarily".

Diana barely had time to sit down before a tall sandy haired man in an expensive grey worsted suit opened his office door. This was Diana's gynaecologist Brian Healy. He beckoned her in. She brushed against him in the doorway, giving him a whiff of her exotic scent as she entered his well-appointed office. It was as elegant as its occupant. To her it seemed more like a lawyer's office than a medical office, especially since many of the reference books neatly arranged in glass fronted oak cabinets behind him were custom bound, as legal tomes often are, in beige leather, with titles embossed in gold.

Never particularly curious about other people, she still wondered whether he included that series of literary classics she discerned among his medical books, in order to give an illusion of intellectual tastes, or whether he actually read them. She watched him ease his slender body onto the deep green leather of his wing-backed chair, moving gingerly as though his back hurt him. During her frequent consultations he occasionally complained of painful back spasms. She was astonished by her unexpected urge to hold him, to comfort him.

He leaned forward, folding his arms across the top of his cherry wood desk. His pale ascetic face softened as he looked at her. "How are you, Diana? You look well; are things any better for you?"

She glanced away, tears coming all unbidden as she said, "Oh, Brian, I don't like what I'm becoming, what he's turning me into. A cheat, a liar. I wasn't like this before I married him, I swear it."

Brian stared at her. Her beauty fed him, sustained him. He wanted to believe,(so far with little overt evidence,) that she was as good and kind as she was beautiful. Was it possible he might one day get what he wanted? Folly, he thought, the gynaecologist who falls in love with beauty.

"How are things between you?" he asked.

"Just the same. He'll never stop harassing me, you know, not till I either have a baby or I'm too old for it. He wants a child so badly. If he knew what I'm doing ... I threw up again this morning so I assume these new birth control pills don't agree with me. Brian, if he knew I'd been taking these pills all through your supposed tests and infertility treatments, he'd, well, I was going to say he'd kill me. That likely sounds a bit strong, but opera singers do have operatic-sized emotions. Who knows?"

Brian felt an irrational, uncontrollable fear. He could only hope that opera singers' spouses learned their operatic-sized language of emotions from living with the singers. Surely she was exaggerating. But what if she were not? His doctor's training enabled him to speak calmly.

"If your husband knew, he'd likely try to sue me for lying to him. So it's in both our interests to keep quiet. But just in case, I mean, these pills are not one hundred per cent foolproof so we'd better do a pregnancy test to be sure."

Diana was ushered into another room where the pregnancy test proceeded. The results, to her intense relief, were negative. When Brian told her that she was not pregnant, she wept soft pretty tears of relief.

This woman is incapable of ugliness, he thought. Even when she weeps, she is lovely.

"I'd go mad if I ever had to endure childbirth," she whispered. "I just couldn't stand it. I have such nightmares still , about... oh Brian, will I ever be able to talk about it? You know, that terrible experience I told you about. Tried to tell you about, when I was ten and my cousin and I were stranded and ... oh, I want to talk about it so badly but every time I try ..."

Diana stood up, covered her face with her hands, and began for the second time that morning to weep softly. She looked up at him with her enormous green eyes, and what he saw was a little girl lost. Now a doctor has to help his patients, doesn't he?

Now. Now, finally, thought Brian Healy as he rose quickly from his chair and went around the desk to put his arm around her, convincing himself that he was keeping her from hurting herself, possibly from fainting. All in a doctor's mandate, of course. When she seemed recovered, he gently let her down into the patients' chair, and returned reluctantly to his position on the doctor's side of the desk.

"You're my last patient this morning, Diana," he said gently. (And knew himself for a liar.) "I think it would do you good to try to talk about your experience. I know the bare bones, you did tell me a little when you tried to explain why you would never have the emotional stamina to go through pregnancy and child-birth. And seeing the effect that just mentioning the experience has on you, I concur fully in your opinion. Otherwise I would not have gone along with your deception."

(And you really are a bloody liar, Brian. You would do anything for this woman, anything. How can her bastard of a husband not feel the same way? How can he not understand the unbearable tension he puts her under?)

"So why don't we go to lunch somewhere quiet—I've got a good hour and a half at least—and you tell me the details of what happened when you were ten."

Brian Healy tried to look gravely professional, hoping that not a trace of his excitement at the prospect of having lunch with Diana showed through.

Diana inclined her lovely head in acquiescence. "Yes, yes, I'm free too; should I dismiss my chauffeur?"

"You might as well, we can go to L'Aureole, it's just around the corner."

Diana went out to the curb to tell her waiting chauffeur he could leave and that she would summon him later when she needed him. Brian meanwhile instructed the nasal-voiced recep-tionist and his nurse to deal with the three appointments he still had on his books for the morning, as well as the impatient patient hovering in the oak-panelled waiting room. His two dis-gruntled employees glowered at his retreating back.

While she waited, Diana hastily pulled out her Cartier compact, to make sure she looked as good as she wanted to, for her first lunch with Brian Healy.

Eleven

iana and Brian went down the few stairs into the entrance of the well-restored brownstone. The rooms of L'Aureole were long, narrow, embellished by bas relief decorations on high walls. Soon ensconced with Diana on a curved banquette in a corner, Brian broke an awkward moment of silence by commenting on the floral arrangements, comprising three imposing bouquets several feet tall in huge dark potiches. He told Diana that one of the restaurant's owners spent a day each week creating these exotic floral focal points which added drama to the otherwise minimalist pastel decor. One huge, delicately coloured spray greeted customers at the door; another graced the landing for those who wished to dine upstairs, and the third was beside Diana.

Brian suggested a drink, and after ascertaining that Diana liked champagne, he ordered a bottle of Taittinger Brut. Not for Diana Paoli the little sparkling Vouvray he often ordered; for her, only the best, the most expensive, would do. Together they looked at the menu, which Diana laughingly averred was a sensual joy just to read, and they ordered seafood salads. Presently salads that were visual works of art were set before them. After saying what a shame it was to eat them and spoil the aesthetic effect, Diana and Brian proceeded to do just that.

Brian led the conversation, unwilling to force Diana to speak of her experience until she was relaxed and ready. They made small talk, fascinating to him because it revealed some of her interests, some of her peccadillos, in short, some of her. Eventually, he covered her hand with his, and said gently, "Now, Diana. It's time. You were ten years old, visiting relatives, where again?"

Diana took a deep breath, holding it, Brian felt, as though she were about to dive into deep waters.

As indeed in many ways she is, he thought. I hope I can help her. I can't bear to see this sweet vulnerable woman suffering. I wish her opera singing oaf of a husband would at least try to understand.

"I was ten years old," Diana began her story in a rush, "and we—my family and I had gone from Boston to North Dakota to spend Christmas with my mother's family on the farm. She came from a farming community there, lots of brothers and sisters and aunts and uncles and cousins, you know the sort of thing. Although I must say I never knew how many relatives I had until I married Carlo. I've even got people inventing relationships with me; you wouldn't believe how many, Brian, just so they can say they are related to Diana and Carlo Paoli."

"You're straying, Diana."

"I know. This is—this is hard to do. But I'll try ... It happened on a Christmas Eve, a beautiful clear windless night, and my cousin Anna wanted to go into town to see a Christmas pageant she had helped organize. Anna was a primary school teacher. But everybody else was having such a good time at the farmhouse, trimming the tree, wrapping gifts, cooking, you know all the fun things that go with Christmas when the family is large and everyone gets along pretty well.

"I was a typical ten year-old girl, shy, awkward, and I wasn't comfortable with this big family who knew each other so well. I felt left out, though when I look back, I realize everyone was trying to make me feel like I belonged. But I didn't share their in-jokes, I didn't know many of our traditional family stories and I thought it was all a crashing bore. So when Anna asked if anyone wanted to go with her to see the pageant, there was no great enthusiasm, but I thought I'd like to go and get away for a little while from all that noise and good cheer.

"I really liked Anna. She was twenty-six, recently married, very much in love, and seven months pregnant. Her husband was doing his military service, I forget now where he was stationed, but anyway he wasn't with her and she was feeling lonely for him. Well, I missed my Boston friends, and she missed her husband, and we were miserable together. In retrospect I realize that she was good with me because of her teaching training, she got on so well with children. Of course I didn't think of myself as a child at the time.

"I remember Uncle Harry, her dad, telling us to take the Jeep, it would be the best car for the snowy roads, he said. A lot of good it did us, in the end, but still ...

"So we went off together to the Pageant, and that part of the evening was like a Norman Rockwell Christmas. First the drive with a full moon shining on the snow, stars twinkling like on a Christmas card, one bright star that I imagined was the star of Bethlehem reincarnated. I told Anna this, and she didn't laugh at me; she almost made me believe that I was right.

"The Pageant was in one of those old village churches, with the stained glass window as a backdrop for the Nativity story. Oh Brian, I'm not sure I can talk about this, not really, when I start to think about the Nativity, and the birth of ... and then, how it all ended, except it's not really ended, not for me."

Brian poured out the last of the champagne. He picked up his champagne flute, and raised it to Diana, toasting, "To your courage."

She slowly raised her flute, in response to his toast. "To my courage, such as it is."

She drank the champagne down in one long draught and continued her narrative. "After the Pageant, there was a reception in the Church basement. At first I was stupid and snobbish about tea and sandwiches in the basement, but soon the warmth and Christmas spirit infected me too, and I remember that party as one of the best of my life, isn't that strange? I mean, let's be frank, Carlo and I are invited to some of the most sophisticated parties around, and yet that funny little Christmas Eve in a church basement in North Dakota stands out in my memory as something very special, very lovely. Maybe in retrospect I want it to have been special, for her, for poor Anna, for what came after.

"When we came out of the church at midnight, bundled up

and ready for the two hour drive back to the farm, the weather had changed. Not a star was in sight, and the terrible cold felt even worse because the wind had come up. I remember one of the ladies, who had been in charge of the wonderful food, inviting Anna and me to stay the night with them in the town because the weather looked so threatening. But Anna said we'd be fine; she had the Jeep, and she was used to driving on these roads, and anyway she didn't want to miss the traditional Christmas morning family festivities. You see, we opened our gifts Christmas morning, savouring each gift one by one; it was so lovely, it was one of the customs my family had kept up in Boston. Carlo and I do it to this day.

"I remember the lady seemed worried, and said something about Anna driving in her condition. I remember her looking sideways at me, I guess I wasn't supposed to know about babies yet, for heaven's sake, but since I had five younger sisters and brothers I knew something about them. You do figure it out after a while—Mom gets fat, Mom goes away for a few days, Mom comes home skinny with a baby in her arms.

"Anyway, we started out. After we'd been driving for about half an hour it started to snow, which made it hard for Anna to see the road. All that snow swirling in the headlights. Then Anna asked me if I was too warm; was it hot in the car, because she said she was hot and felt wet and sticky all over. I felt fine. I remember I was really happy. I thought the snow was so beautiful, and I was never allowed out so late, what an adventure this was.

"After another little while, Anna stopped the car. She said she felt a bit sick, and she was just going to get out of the car for a minute and stretch her legs. She opened the Jeep door, and of course the car light went on. She stepped out, and I was horrified to see that where she had sat her beige coat was covered in something dark and wet. So was the seat of the car.

"I remember crying out, 'Anna, what's on your coat?' She looked down and said, 'Oh Lord Di, I'm not perspiring, I'm haemorrhaging. We've got to get some help. Let's see, where are we, who's the nearest farmhouse?' She was quite calm still, but just as she started to climb back into the Jeep, she gasped and clutched her stomach. After a minute her pain passed, and she was able to climb into the car, which was pretty cold by now what with having the door open. The blizzard was on us in earnest; you could scarcely see anything but the snow.

"'I, honey, this may—do you know anything about birth?' Anna managed to get out before she clutched herself again in pain. I said I knew her baby had to come out one day from her bottom.

"'I don't think it will be one day, honey, I think maybe, soon now ... oh, Di, I'll start the car, it'll be all right, we're not far from the Friesens' place, and if they're not there, the Schmidts are home for sure this Christmas.'

"She had to stop talking again for a minute. 'I'll start the car, but I may not be able to drive it by myself. I'm not sure I can work the gas and the brake. This ... I hurt so much, oh Di honey I'm so sorry. Do you think you could work the gas and the brake and I'll sit in the passenger seat and steer? My legs don't want to ... I'm not sure ...'

"Anna turned the key in the ignition. The engine turned over once and stalled. She tried again. Same thing. She tried a third time. A fourth time. Over and over she tried, but the engine was dead, absolutely dead. I remember when she realized the car wasn't going to start, she turned to me with the most terrible look on her face. Then she tried to pull herself together as best she could. She said maybe someone would come along, but even I knew that was unlikely—you couldn't see the front of the car from where we sat, who would drive on such a night?

"She told me they always carried blankets in a box in back, in case of a stall in the cold, and she said there was a First Aid kit back there too. She said she had put a thermos of hot chocolate into the Jeep before we left, and some Christmas cookies, just in case we got held up. She told me to get the blankets, and for us to get into the back seat where we would be a bit more comfortable and we could wrap the blankets around us and try to give each other warmth. By this time I was gulping back tears, aware that we were in trouble but just mature enough to know I should not upset Anna any more than she was already.

"I got the blankets, and the thermos and food. Anna was in terrible pain, but trying so hard not to show me how bad it was, so as not to scare me. Partly I think because she cared about me, and partly I was the only help she had, and I wouldn't be much good to her if I was scared helpless.

"Between her contractions, we managed to get into the back seat. We huddled up together under the blankets. She tried to explain to me what I would need to know if she gave birth in the car with only me as her helper. Oh Brian she was so brave. She must have realized that what was happening to her was not normal. She was haemorrhaging severely, although because we were bundled up in blankets neither of us could see the blood at that point, but she must have felt it. And she must have felt herself weakening. She didn't want to traumatize me; she knew what a hideous experience it might turn into. But I don't think she realized yet what was going to ..."

Diana closed her eyes tight, and took in a long shaky breath. She sat for a long moment, her lovely head bowed. Brian's sympathy for her was so acute it felt like pain. He took her cold hand in his two warm ones and held it for a long moment. She slowly, reluctantly withdrew hers.

"I poured some hot chocolate for us," she continued. "I thought it might help us keep warm. I guess she hoped so too, for after I had drunk mine, she put her cup to her lips, sipped, and then, making a face, drank it all down. For a minute she seemed better, she actually smiled at me. Then she began to shudder. I've never seen anyone shake like that since. Then I got really scared. For a little while she seemed to rest, but then she opened her eyes, got a surprised look on her face, and then she lost control. She started to scream, terrible screams, mixed with coughs and grunting noises, and then she said, 'the baby, I think it must be coming, the baby, help me ...'

"I struggled to get her swung around so her legs were facing me, up on the seat. She was alternately groaning and screaming. When I got her into the position she had told me about, and started to try to loosen her clothes like she had told me to do, so the baby could come out, I was surprised at how much blood there was everywhere. But she had told me there would be blood, and pain, and that she might not always be in control, so although I was terrified, I didn't realize that all this was not just a normal birth. I didn't know anything about the baby being premature, I didn't know anything about haemorrhaging, I'd never even heard the word before that night, let alone know what it really meant.

"She was pushing by this point, and her screams were louder than I ever want to hear again. After a bit, I could see the baby's head. It looked awful to me, the hair all covered in blood. She pushed and pushed, there was blood everywhere, and then the baby came right out. I had my hands underneath it, but as it came out I could see that there was something terribly wrong with that baby. It had a hump on its back, and instead of arms and legs, it had stumps. I felt so sick, looking at it. But then I quickly wrapped it in a corner of the blanket, because I didn't want it to get cold. I didn't know what to do about that cord thing, so I just left it alone and tried not to pull on it when I handled the baby.

"Anna was sort of panting, and she said between gasps, that I should turn the baby upside down and spank it. I didn't know how to do it, but when I turned it upside down it gave a sort of little cry, like a kitten. I looked at Anna, and she was actually smiling.

"Then she whispered, 'Is it a nice baby, Di? What is it, a boy or a girl?' I didn't want her to see how—how deformed it was, and I hadn't even looked to see what sex it was. I peeked under the blanket, and told Anna that it was a little boy.

"She whispered, 'Adam will be so pleased. We'll call the baby Adam David, like his dad. Oh Di, honey, show me his face.'

"I held him up, tightly swaddled in his blanket so she

wouldn't see his deformities. She tried to reach towards him, but her arms fell back, and the last thing I heard her say that night was, 'Beautiful, so beautiful, my baby son born on Christmas Day.' And then she was quiet. I thought, she's worn out, she must need to sleep. But I hoped all that bleeding would stop soon, there seemed to be so much.

"I held little Adam tightly against my body, to try to keep him warm. He made odd little mewling noises for a while and then seemed to fall asleep. After Anna's screams, the howls of the blizzard seemed gentle, though I can never listen to that kind of wind now without horror. I drank some more hot chocolate. That poor baby and I huddled against Anna, trying to keep warm through the long cold night. I remember wanting desperately to cry, and not being able to. I remember my throat hurting terribly. Then gradually I realized that Adam didn't seem to be breathing. I uncovered him and put my hand on his little chest, to feel if he was breathing. Nothing. Only he felt oddly cold.

"In a panic I thought, but he's going to die and he's not baptized and he won't go to heaven, I have to do something, oh dear God what do I do? I can't baptize him in hot chocolate, what else do I have? Then I thought how stupid I was, I could just melt a bit of snow in my hand, there was enough of it. So I opened the window and took a handful of snow, and when it was melted I made a cross on that poor baby's forehead, only I didn't realize then that he must have been dead already, and I said, 'I baptize you Adam David Harrison, in the name of the Father and the Son and the Holy Ghost, and dear God please take this poor baby back to Heaven if he dies, he won't have a very good life the way he is, maybe You can fix him up.'

"Oh, Brian, isn't that a ridiculous prayer?" Diana asked, her eyes filled with tears, her face registering her desperate hope that it had been all right. By this point, Brian would have acquiesced to anything to help Diana, but it happened that he thought it was a lovely prayer indeed. He said so, gently urging Diana to finish her story.

"Well, I kept holding Adam, and he got colder and colder. Anna was still asleep, I thought, and I was relieved that I didn't have to cope with telling her about her poor little Adam. I didn't realize yet the enormity of what was happening.

"After what seemed like an eternity, it began to get light. I was getting pretty cold, but there was still a bit of hot chocolate left and I sipped it slowly and ate one of the cookies. That made me a little warmer. But as the brilliant prairie sun came up, for the blizzard had ended sometime during the night, I saw with horror just how much blood there was everywhere inside the Jeep. I looked at my sleeping cousin, and I suddenly needed to wake her: I needed reassurance that she was all right, that I had done the right things.

"Her face was buried in a fold of the blanket. I pulled the blanket away, and was shocked at Anna's appearance. Her face was a sort of grey colour, her lips parted, her eyes half open. I thought she was waking up. I reached over and touched her cheek. It was icy. With mounting terror I called her name, shook her, touched her cold hands—and then the full import of what had happened hit me. Anna was dead. Adam was dead. I was alone with two dead people in that bright wilderness, on a snow-blocked road, in desperately cold weather, my clothes cold and damp with congealed blood. I was ten years old, and I was sure I would die there too. Nobody had come to help us, nobody would ever come, I would die there with that poor baby and his mother.

"In my confusion and despair, I put poor Adam beside Anna, and got out of the car. The sun was blindingly bright. I couldn't believe the sun could be shining so cheerfully when in the car everybody was dead. Maybe I was already dead too. I remember starting to cry. Then I heard the faint sound of a motor. It got louder and louder. And there came the snow plough, blowing snow off the road. I remember the plough coming up to us, and the driver, he was my aunt's neighbour, Mr Jenkins, getting down off the plough with a cheery, 'Merry Christmas. You folks okay? They've been terrible worried about you up at the farm. What's ...' and then as he came closer he caught sight of the blood all over me.

"'Oh my God,' he said as he looked into the jeep. I remember saying, 'Everybody's dead...' and then I remember nothing until I woke up, they tell me it was two days later, in my bed at my aunt's place. Everybody was crying, or so it seemed to me.

"And what I know, and how desperately I do know it, is that I could never face a pregnancy, Brian. Never. I'd be too afraid that I might die like Anna did, or bear a poor deformed baby like Adam." She wiped a tear from her cheek. "Well, you wanted to hear it. There it is."

Brian Healy looked down at his long, beautifully manicured hands, those hands that had delivered so many children, mostly wonderfully healthy babies to splendidly healthy, often wealthy women. And he wondered how he would have done at age ten in a terrible situation such as the one Diana had so painfully described.

He took her hand. Deeply moved, and thankful for the professional training which helped him not to show it, he said, "I do thank you for having the courage to tell me your story. I understand why you never want to think about it, let alone talk about it. Surely Carlo doesn't know the whole story; no decent man could ask a woman to go through pregnancy after an experience like yours, if she didn't want to."

"Oh yes, Carlo knows. I told him—as much as I was able to talk about without falling apart—before we married. I didn't think it would be fair to him—or to any man—for me to marry him without telling him I could never have children."

"And?"

"And he agreed that I need never bear children; he said he loved me so much that I would fill his life completely. But that was before we married. After a while, when we'd been married a few years, he began to talk about having children. He got more and more enthused about it, until it seemed to me like an obsession. He insisted that my fears were nonsense, that what happened to Anna and Adam was a fluke, that he could afford the best doctors in the world and that I need fear nothing. Only it's not that simple."

"But you do have some say in the matter, don't you?"

"Do I?" Diana looked at him sadly. "How can I explain? You see, Brian, sometimes it's—it's very enjoyable being Carlo's wife. A lot less now than before, but—it has its moments. I mean, I was a little stenographer from nowhere who happened on this wonderful job as Carlo's assistant's secretary, and *voila*, Carlo fell in love with me. He's likely no worse as a husband than other high-powered men. They're not often known for being tender loving homebodies, are they? Anyway, I finally realized it would be wiser to pretend I agree with Carlo, that I want children and that I'm trying hard to conceive."

"What do you mean, wiser?" Brian's intense dislike for Carlo was growing. There was something here he had long suspected and now needed to know.

"Well, there were, how shall I put it, disagreeable consequences when Carlo was insisting on children and I was still saying I couldn't bring myself to go through a pregnancy."

"Like what?"

"Like ... well, you must try to understand the operatic temperament. Opera singers spend their professional lives portraying extremes of love and death and violence, and it seems to me that some of them have trouble separating that make-believe world from their real lives."

"What are you saying, Diana? That Carlo has threatened you with violence if you didn't ..."

Diana looked down at her empty plate. She had certain fears, but she was unprepared to go much farther in her explanations to Brian. Still, she was faintly ashamed of her next realization, that it wouldn't do any harm if Brian imagined a bigger threat to her than actually existed. It would help keep him enthusiastically on her side in the pregnancy issue.

And she would have her way, must have her way. She did not wholly understand herself, not being given to deep self-analysis. But she did know that, as a consequence of her hideous lesson about the fragility of life, she had resolved to get everything she wanted, using whatever means were necessary, before a malevolent destiny prematurely snatched her away too. It had not taken her long to discover that she had formidable weapons with which to accomplish her objective—her rare and exquisite beauty, and an ability to manipulate others by the giving and withholding of herself.

She knew perfectly well that the recounting of her prairie trauma, hard though it had been for her to do, had brought the sympathetic Brian Healy more firmly under her influence. Diana looked up from her plate at Brian, and the welcome thought crossed her mind that he was falling in love with her.

And Brian thought, how could that opera-singing oaf even consider laying a hand in violence on this lovely sensitive woman? He had thought he hated Carlo before, for the way he treated Diana, but now—they should invent a new word for this feeling of murderous hatred.

From the restaurant, Diana telephoned for her limousine to pick her up at Brian's office. Then she and Brian walked together in silence back to his neo-Viennese building. Brian asked her to come in so he could give her a prescription for different birth control pills, ones he hoped would not nauseate her.

Once in his office, with the door closed, the enormity of the tragedy she had lived through in her recollections flooded over her again, and a shuddery sob shook her slender body. He turned towards her, and put his arms gently around her.

Trying to pull out of her sad memories, she looked up at him for the second time that day like a lost child. Only he was the one who was lost then, utterly lost. Against all his better judgment he bent down and kissed her, softly at first and then with the passion he had been trying to fight for the three years she had been his patient. To his intense joy she responded, with a hesitant warmth that promised later to equal his. But then he recollected his situation as her doctor. He drew back, and slowly walked around the desk to his chair. He sat down. Diana sat also, rather abruptly, as though her knees had given way.

In a shaky little voice, Diana returned to their professional conversation. "Thank you for understanding. What if I hadn't found a doctor to help me like you have?"

"That's just a 'what if'. You did find me and I am only too glad to help you. I don't even feel as though I have betrayed my Hippocratic oath, because you are my patient, not Carlo, and your well-being has to be paramount. I know I'm supposed to be objective ..."

He didn't finish the thought.

Soon she left his office, glancing back with a warm smile just before she closed the door behind her. For too long a time, considering the patients fidgeting impatiently in his outer office, Brian stared unseeing at the closed door, engrossed in thought. Then he shook his head as though to clear it, and wrote an entry in Diana's medical file, after which he unlocked the bottom drawer of his desk to remove his unofficial medical file on her—the one in which he wrote details of her birth control pills, among other things. When he had brought the unofficial file up to date, he put it back in the drawer on top of an alligator leather case which held two guns he had recently purchased for his collection of small revolvers. He carefully locked the drawer.

Then all Brian's medical training reproached him for the thoughts that went through his mind each time he saw Diana.

What would happen if the Paoli marriage could not stand the strain of Diana's deceptions? Or if that singing oaf dropped dead? They do sometimes, these heavy middle-aged singers; opera is such hard physical work. And what if Diana were free ... would she ever consider ... would she consider ... marrying him?

He knew he would be unable stop his phone calls—mostly from phone booths so the number could not be traced—to the Paolis, hoping Diana would answer so he could hear her lovely voice say "hello" before he hung up. Unfortunately so far the only person who had spoken into his silence was Carlo.

Twelve

Carlo's large black Cadillac limousine turned onto Fifth Avenue and glided to a stop outside the building where he lived. Carlo emerged alone from the limousine, opening the door himself. He bent down to speak to his chauffeur, who then drove away. He straightened and stood unmoving under the canopy, enjoying the mellow air of a surprisingly quiet night. Across the street a lone, androgynous figure clothed in unrelieved black, stood partly concealed by a tree trunk, seemingly staring at Carlo. Why, Carlo wondered, should he notice that particular figure?

Damn threats. I'm getting paranoid.

He saw the figure begin to tug at something in a greatcoat pocket.

A car sped up the Avenue, swerving, tires squealing as it arrived at Carlo's intersection. Carlo's head swivelled towards the car as bullets missed him by a hand's length, crashing behind him as they hit and shattered one of the glass entry doors.

Carlo ducked as fast as a big man could when he heard the tinkling sound of glass shattering behind him. The rotund doorman, who had just stretched out his hand to open the door for Carlo, was staring down at blood pouring from a deep cut across his palm. Pale and trembling, he muttered something to Carlo, and then as his knees gave way he sank down on the sidewalk, his back against the brick wall of the apartment building. The other man on duty in the lobby pulled himself from his transfixion to dash out across the shattered glass.

"Signor Paoli, what on earth was that? Are you hurt?"

"For Godssake call the police!" Carlo shook with rage and fear. "Can't you see I've been shot at? And do something about your colleague, I don't think he can stand the sight of his own blood."

Carlo glanced with distaste at the pale doorman still sitting on the sidewalk, bleeding all over his green trousers from his cut hand.

Carlo, trembling, strode furiously into the lobby, his shoes crunching on the glass shards of what had been a beautifully beveled door. "Isn't anyone running the elevator? Can't you people do your jobs? I'm going up."

"But Signor Paoli, there is no-one else, you said to call the police and—"

"Oh all right all right, I'll take myself up."

Carlo stepped into the elevator and soon was struggling with unsteady hands to insert his key into the lock of his apartment door. Eventually he accomplished this, but not before he had gone through some of his spectacular repertoire of profanity.

Within a few minutes the police were in Carlo's apartment. They tried to reassure Carlo that since they were investigating a report of young men in a car shooting randomly along Fifth Avenue, this particular shooting was not directed deliberately at him. Therefore, it could not have any connection with the threats Carlo had been receiving. Nor with the shadowy figure Carlo spoke about, who had seemed to be struggling with something in a pocket.

That ass Sergeant Donlevy, as Carlo privately thought of him, assured Carlo, "Look, Mr Paoli, if everybody pulling something out of his pocket was after a gun so he could shoot somebody, we'd be in big trouble. Let's not get crazy here. Hey, don't worry, Mr I mean Signor Paoli. Like I said before, lotsa celebrities get this kinda stuff, letters and phone calls and so on all the time, doesn't mean a thing unless there's some follow-up."

"You don't call this follow-up?" bellowed Carlo in a voice whose magnitude only years of training could produce.

"Look, Signor Paoli. Of course I'd call this follow-up if it was an isolated shooting. But a bunch of other people got shot at too. We'll let you know if we think you should take extra precautions. You said you sometimes use bodyguards, well, what more can you do? Just try to relax."

"Relax! You're out of your mind! Why don't you catch these hooligans, these cretinous jerks who are ruining this city? Why don't you cops do your jobs properly? I tell you, if I did my job as badly as you people do yours, I'd be covered in rotten eggs and tomatoes every time I sang. Oh, go away, get out of here. I can't stand the sight of you."

Sergeant Donlevy turned away, rolling his eyes heavenwards for his partner's benefit. "Okayokay, goodnight, Signor Paoli, you try not to worry."

The two policemen left the apartment and Carlo locked the door firmly after them. He then hurried across the living room to an antique Chinese cabinet remodeled to hold his liquor supply, and shakily poured himself a triple Scotch. No soda, no ice, just a large quantity of Scotch. He plumped down heavily in his one comfortable chair and gulped the drink, hoping it would dull his fear.

What Sergeant Donlevy said probably made sense, didn't it? Didn't it? So why was he so frightened? How could he be expected to sing well when his life was so full of these tensions? He stared through the open French doors into his study, where his etching of the stag at bay glowed with reflected light from the living room.

Where was Diana when he needed her? Bad enough that he should get shot at, without him having to worry about his wife not being home at midnight in New York City. Carlo had used the limousine all evening, so what was she doing? She hadn't told him she was going out. Had she?

He heard a key in the lock, and rose quickly from his chair to greet her, or rather to accuse her of disappearing just when he needed her. And where had she been, anyway? She rushed in, her face a mask of concern, crying, "Carlo, they told me downstairs what happened, are you all right?"

As she rushed towards him, her quilted Chanel handbag caught on the door handle, the fragile clasp snapped open, and the contents spilled onto the floor. Diana ignored this in her haste to reassure herself that her illustrious spouse was unharmed. Carlo, who occasionally remembered that he had been brought up to treat women in a chivalrous manner, bent to retrieve the bits and pieces for her. With the wallet and cosmetic pouch was a small white paper bag stapled closed with a pharmacist's receipt. Carlo saw the name of the pharmacy, and said, "What's wrong, Di? Are you not well? Are you ill and not telling me about it because you know what a bad time I'm having lately?"

As he tore open the paper bag and looked inside he was saying, "That's unusually considerate of you ... what is this stuff?"

For Diana had blenched visibly and was trying to grab the package from his hand.

Carlo was surprisingly fast for a big man. "Just a minute, just a minute, what is this stuff, Di?"

Diana quavered in what Carlo recognized as her I'm-terrified-but-I'd-better-not-show-it voice, "It's nothing, Carlo, honestly. Just give me the bag. It's absolutely nothing to worry yourself about, would I lie to you?"

"Damned if I know, Di, would you?"

Diana continued her frantic but ineffectual attempts to snatch the paper bag from him. Holding it out of her reach he removed a package in the form of a green cardboard circle, with a number of yellow-coloured pills embedded in tiny pockets around the circumference. He turned the green circle over to read the instructions, which said, "Ortho-Novum. Take one tablet daily beginning on the fifth day of the menstrual cycle, for twenty-one days ..." With a sick feeling he tried to remember his ex-wife's medications.

Carlo looked at Diana incredulously. "I don't believe this. These are ... these have got to be ..."

He rushed into her bedroom. If he could find more pills he would know. Dear God, let him be wrong. Could Diana have betrayed him about this, about trying to have a child, something he wanted perhaps more than anything else? In a frenzy he emptied her drawers and cupboards, throwing lace and silk and cashmere in soft heaps on the thick carpet, as she, by now sobbing in fear and anger, begged him to stop. And then he found what he feared. Another package, same company, different dosage.

Dear God.

His Ilona had taken this last type.

Birth control pills.

Birth control pills!

Grey-faced and shaking with rage, he waved the package in front of her. "You bitch! You castrating bitch! How could you do this to me, Di, to us? You know how much I want a child—I thought we were trying— you made me go and have a semen count, for Godssake. It was damn humiliating, bugger you, Diana!"

In this moment of panic Diana's uncertain control deserted her. "Must you? Must you always be vulgar? Sometimes you disgust me, Carlo."

That was the second blow. She had betrayed him, and now she told him that he disgusted her. His middle hurt so acutely he had to will himself not to double over with pain. With his huge hand he slapped her across the face, sending her staggering across the room onto the bed. She struggled up, one side of her face scarlet, her eyes wide with terror. "I didn't mean—"

"Oh yes you did, Di," and he hit her again. And once more for good measure. Now she lay on the bed, curled up in a ball, gasping and sobbing. Without a backward glance Carlo strode coatless from the apartment, though icy fury chilled his bones. He asked the replacement doorman to get him a cab. He knew exactly where he needed to be. In the cab he said, "The Dakota, please," before he realized that his dear friend Mia Mitsouros was in England singing with Tony Amato in *La Fanciulla del West*. He couldn't conceive of any other place he wanted to go, so he told the cab driver just to drive. Anywhere. He needed to think.

Thirteen

On the Friday in March just before her tenth wedding anniversary, Jenetta Amato had an unusually disturbing day. She was scheduled to leave New York Saturday to join Tony in London, to hear his last performance of *La Fanciulla del West*, at a Sunday matinee. After, they planned to celebrate their anniversary at dinner in the Dorchester Hotel, where Tony had given Jen her engagement ring all those years ago. Monday, they were to go to Paris for the rehearsals preceding Tony's *Otello* debut.

She hoped this celebration, this change, would lift from her the shadows through which sometimes she could see only Gianni, the child she had held but twice, had never nursed, would ever mourn. She knew she had to let him go, let light penetrate this darkness, for her living children and for Tony who so needed her strength and joy. So why did she let Gianni call her with his tiny piteous cries? Call her ... to go ... to come ... where? Sometimes the beckoning darkness became terror.

"The best laid schemes o'mice an' men gang aft a-gley," thought Jen, agreeing with Robbie Burns, for today everything was 'ganging a-gley' with a vengeance. Murphy's law. If anything else can go wrong this day, it surely will. As if she needed any more reminders of Gianni, she was having new physical symptoms which, given her own recent brush with death, would have to be seen to before she could travel. So she made an urgent appointment with her gynaecologist Brian Healy.

But what was more distressing to Jen than her own health problems were those of little Janina who had become ill with chicken pox. Jen felt wrenchingly unable to leave her, especially as the little girl, normally deeply attached to Nanny Burns and resigned to her parents' periodic absences, now could not bear her mother out of her sight and cried forlornly each time Jen tried to leave the sickroom.

Under the watchful eye of Mrs Burns Janina had fallen into a restless sleep, and Jen at last could retreat for a moment to her bedroom. In solitude she wept into her lacy white pillow. Here we go again, she thought. In the ten years of her marriage to Tony, career and familial demands had kept them apart for more than seven years.

Tony laughed when he heard friends complain about telephone bills. "You should see mine and Jen's; it is each month bigger than the Italian national debt, I am telling you!"

Jen sometimes wondered whether one reason their marriage remained such a success was that they had little chance to tire of each other. But that theory did not always hold, for she knew how often the separations necessitated by careers such as Tony's led to the breakdown of marriages. Instead of holding an absent spouse in imaginative longing, tense lonely performers far away from home frequently yielded to the need to hold someone real. Propinquity took its toll.

"Sometimes I wonder why you stay with me, Jen," an exhausted, jet-lagged Tony had said to her two years ago, despairing about making a marriage work when one of the spouses is such an absentee partner. He had arrived in New York from the Orient at one in the morning and had just climbed wearily into their bed and put his arms around her, burying his face in her hair.

"We married each other for better or for worse, Tony love," she had said to him, holding him tightly to ward off the demons of depression that beset him at those rare times when his considerable stamina was spent. "We made vows, remember?"

"Of course I remember. But you could not know then how much of 'worse' there would be for you."

"There's a lot of 'worse' for you too, Tony love. Of course there's a lot of excitement—all that applause and adulation, not to mention the money!—but look at you tonight. This is the reverse of the coin; this is what people don't see." She caressed his hair softly. "The loneliness, the fatigue—and you can't even take a couple of days off to rest, because you have to sing in four countries on two continents in the next three weeks..."

She had stopped, because he had fallen into a dead sleep in her arms. She had held him, gently caressing his face, knowing that she would never give up easily on anything as hard-won and valuable to her as their union.

So on this particular morning it seemed cruel to her that after all their efforts to keep their marriage inviolate, and after their recent tragedy, she and Tony would even miss spending their tenth wedding anniversary together.

But soon she wiped her eyes and, lying back among the massed pillows, she telephoned to Tony in London. Trying to sound more cheerful than she felt, she told him why she would be late for their celebration. To his urgent questions, she answered with assurances that she would get to Paris for at least some of the *Otello* rehearsals and of course for the premiere. Unspoken was the caveat, "If Anton doesn't come down with the chicken pox too ..." No point in worrying Tony unnecessarily.

And now it was Friday afternoon and Jen, depressed and impatient, sat half undressed in Brian Healy's examining room on his high, narrow, uncomfortable table, with the modesty sheet covering her naked lower body. Doctor Healy seemed to her to be taking an unconscionably long time getting to her; he was not given to making his patients wait, although he did have the knack of making each feel that he was spending a special amount of time just with her. Some genius of scheduling, Jen thought. Only today something had gone awry.

As she waited, she heard someone go in to Healy's office, just a thin wall away from this particular examining room. Healy generally did not use this room if he could avoid it since it was inconveniently small, but a plumbing problem in his usual large bright examining room forced his patients into this one just for today. Jen realized, as Healy began to speak in his office, that there was another good reason for not using this room. The soundproofing between the two rooms was non-existent.

She heard Healy say in a tight voice totally unlike his professional tones, "What on earth happened? You said you'd fallen, how could a fall do all that to you? How—where—"

Then a woman's voice, choked and husky. "It was the stairs, on the stairs in—" The voice paused.

Jen thought she was not the only one in this office who was upset today.

Healy's voice, higher-pitched than usual, betrayed his tension to Jen. "Tell me the truth, Diana; that's not what happened. What are you trying to hide?"

Diana? Diana who? wondered Jen, half curious and half wishing herself elsewhere. Did she know that voice?

Then Jen heard the woman called Diana burst into sobs, which she had some difficulty in controlling. After a long moment of tears, there was a little silence. Then she spoke. "Oh, Brian, I didn't want to have to tell you. But I didn't know where to turn—you're the only doctor I trust. You see, Carlo ... oh, I feel like such a traitor..."

Carlo? Diana Paoli? What is this? Jen wondered uneasily. Now she urgently wished herself elsewhere; a deeply private woman herself, she did not want to be made privy to her friends' secrets unless they themselves confided in her.

Then came Healy's voice, almost hissing. "What did that bast—what did Carlo do to you? Did he do that to you? Tell me, tell me, Diana."

Another silence. Then, "He found my birth control pills. It was after the drive-by shooting, you know, he was so upset; you must have heard about it; it's been all over the news. I came home late, just after he was shot at, and my purse opened accidentally and the pills fell out and ... oh, Brian, he was like a madman. And I said something I shouldn't have said ... and then he just went crazy. He hit me over and over, and he's so big, and ..."

"He beats you?"

"Never before ... at least, never like this. But I've felt he was capable of it; he's got a terrible temper and so many things trigger it, but not ... oh, Brian, I haven't really loved Carlo for years, but now I ... I think I hate him..."

Another silence and then Healy's voice. "I'm being anything but professional to say it, but I don't think I hate him, I know I do. My God, Diana! Can you just wait here a minute, I won't be long, I've only one patient waiting, and then I'll examine you to see if he's done any serious damage."

There was a breeze blowing through the slightly open window in the examining room where Jen waited uncomfortably. The door between the small room and Healy's office was not, she realized, completely closed. The breeze caught the door and opened it slightly.

Through the crack Jen saw Brian Healy put his arms around Diana Paoli. They embraced in a kiss that was obviously mutually enjoyed. Then Healy put his hand against Diana's bruised and swollen cheek in a caress of infinite tenderness. As Diana sat down, Healy straightened his dark tie, brushed a hand across his greying sandy hair, and opened the door to enter the examining room where Jen waited, surprised and unhappy, her mind swirling with the convolutions of the problem she had just witnessed.

In his usual warm professional voice he said, "Well, Mrs. Amato, I didn't expect to see you today. I'm sorry you're still having problems. It seems to me the experience you had was traumatic enough without you having to be reminded of it with symptoms like this. Now let's just have a look."

But as he held her arm and helped her to lie down, he glanced once at the now closed door separating them from Diana Paoli, and the distressed Jen saw that his composed professional face was ashen.

Fourteen

In London two days later, on the Amatos' wedding anniversary, cars on the Strand were densely packed and unmoving, for as far away as Tony could see. He fidgeted worriedly with the fringe on his scarf as he sat in the idling limousine hired to bring him to the Royal Opera House, Covent Garden.

Tony needed to be in his dressing room for at least an hour and a half before singing *La Fanciulla del West*, so he could be made up and in costume half an hour before the overture started. At that point before any performance, he craved solitude and a piano, to warm up the voice and to concentrate as the mood and motivation of the character he was portraying penetrated until it felt like part of himself. Without that time alone Tony felt as though he were going naked onto the stage. He had to fight for that precious half hour, against his fame, against all the people who believed he and his time belonged to them.

Fumes from the traffic increasingly invaded the tightly

closed car. Tony's throat felt constricted, sore. A moment of panic electrified him before he could control it. He asked the driver, "Is there anything to do? The performance starts at two, it is already a quarter of one."

Limousine driver Jack Smallwood could scarcely contain his excitement. His first customer on the company's new contract with the Royal Opera House was actually the famous Antonio Amato. Although Jack knew nothing about opera, Amato sang other music as well, and Smallwood's wife was enchanted by Amato's sentimental approach to love ballads.

Jack wondered if he could get up enough courage to ask for an autograph on the package of the compact disk he had bought this morning for his wife's birthday. *I Send You My Love* by Antonio Amato was Tony's latest recording of contemporary songs. The quasi-operatic interpretation was not to Jack's taste, but he knew his wife would love it.

"I can't do anything, Mr. Amato. It would likely be quicker for you to walk. I'm really sorry." Jack had wanted this drive to go so well.

Tony weighed his options. The limousine had been purring, motionless, for fifteen minutes. All around him on this foggy day he could hear sirens howling, so doubtless the unusual traffic congestion was worsened by an accident somewhere near. If they sat immobilized much longer he risked being late, risked not getting his precious, irredeemable half hour. But if he got out and walked, the voice would be hit full blast by air pollution, the traffic fumes undissipated in a windless, mist-shrouded London. *Dio!* His throat did feel scratchy.

This afternoon was the last performance of *La Fanciulla del*

West, and Tony's role of *Johnson-Ramerrez* required considerable vocal and emotional stamina. He decided to risk the pollution, to gain his pre-performance concentration time.

"I will walk."

Tony opened the limousine door and put one foot onto the pavement. In a sudden surge of courage, for Jack might never get so close to Antonio Amato again, he slid open the panel dividing the driver's seat from the passengers, and asked for Tony's autograph. "You must get sick of signing autographs, Mr Amato, if it's too much bother..."

"It is not too much bother, my friend. We singers, we need people like you. You love the opera, yes?"

Jack looked disconcerted, and Tony knew then he was merely after the autograph of a famous person. But that was fine with Tony; maybe Jack would be sufficiently intrigued by the CD and by his contact with Tony to explore further the world of Tony's music. And if Jack explored far enough, inevitably he would be led to opera. That mattered to Tony. He wanted as many people as possible to share with him the joy and power and beauty of this art form.

Tony emerged from the limousine and, head well down and scarf warming throat and chin, he began to walk north towards Bow Street and the Opera House. He was alone, since his aide from the London security company was ill, and Tony had not bothered to find a replacement. There were times when constantly having aides with him in public destroyed his concentration—times when he was content to gamble. It did not feel like much of a risk, since nothing untoward (other than female strangers occasionally seizing and kissing him) had ever happened to him in public, so he believed the fuss about aide-bodyguards was overdone.

The thought crossed Tony's mind that he had seen this scene—the swirling fog blurring the edges of everything in his sight—many times in mystery films. He pulled his cashmere scarf higher across his chin and mouth. Hoping nobody would recognize him, he began as he strode to go over the mental drills he tried always to use before performing. *La Fanciulla del West* was not one of the composer Puccini's most popular operas. But Tony shared with his fellow tenor Placido Domingo a great liking for the role of that complicated character, *Johnson-Ramerrez*. Though not a long role, its musical and psychological complexities present exciting challenges to an actor-singer.

At ten past one, Tony arrived at the imposing, classically pedimented facade of the Opera House. He smiled his way past the doorman on Floral Street, who said with some relief in a broad Yorkshire accent, "Oh, good, Mr Amato, you're here, they were beginning to wonder where you were; you usually arrive earlier than this."

As Tony hurried down the corridor, he decided to tell Maestro Sheldon Wasserman that he had arrived, to ease Wasserman's tension as he prepared, quite unexpectedly, to conduct today's opera. Wasserman had flown to London from New York Friday, on his way to Paris to start conducting rehearsals for Tony's *Otello*. Wasserman had expected to be a member of today's audience, but instead had been pressed into service to replace a suddenly flu-stricken Sir Colin Davis. Tony made a detour towards the conductor's dressing room. The door was pushed to, but not closed.

In his pre-performance reverie, and without realizing he had not knocked on the door, Tony pushed it open. He started to say, "Maestro ..." but stopped abruptly at what he saw, and with embarrassment closed the door, muttering frantically, "*Mi scusi, per favore, mi scusi.*"

What he had glimpsed surprised and saddened him. Sheldon Wasserman stood in his dressing room in splendid white tie and tails, being embraced by a distinguished looking, grey haired man who Tony recognized as Sir Mallory Mancroft. And Mancroft was weeping as he embraced. He held Wasserman as tightly as a drowning man clutches a plank, but Wasserman, his arms firmly clasped behind his back, showed no emotion.

Tony, upset, had heard that their affair was over years ago. He tried to recollect what someone had told him about Wasserman and Mancroft. But Tony had no memory for gossip. What was that story? About Wasserman leaving Mancroft for some new love, only the love was not returned, whatever was that story? And Mancroft never getting over it ... Tony decided to ask Carlo when they next met, if he remembered. Carlo always knew the latest gossip.

At one fifteen the makeup man began his work on Tony. That done, the dresser helped him slip on his costume; thank goodness the costume for this role was uncomplicated. At one-fifty Tony was ready to go onstage for two o'clock. Just then his newly hired British agent William Anderson arrived at the door of the dressing room with, "Can we talk? You've got ten minutes before you go on."

Tony's famous public equanimity (perhaps only Jen knew

his carefully concealed tensions) suddenly deserted him. Ten minutes. Ten minutes to warm the voice in the still painful throat, and to pull the character of *Johnson-Ramerrez* into and around himself.

"Is enough now!" he shouted, to his agent's astonishment. The agent had heard only good things about the temperament of this particular tenor. "Out! Out! Everybody wants pieces of me, sharks, crocodiles, out!"

"I'm sorry, Mr Amato, I had no idea," babbled a dismayed Bill Anderson, backing away from the dressing room. He looked so distressed that Tony forced down his fury and tried to explain something he felt most people did not understand.

"Bill, I need quiet before I sing, everybody should leave me alone. You stand outside the door and you see nobody comes in, ten minutes, *cielo*!"

Anderson, contrite even though he only half understood, took up his position outside Tony's dressing room.

"Overture starting; beginners on stage," they soon heard from the loudspeaker.

Although Tony's entrance came halfway through the first act, once the opera began he immediately became, emotionally, part of the action on stage. And if the character of *Johnson-Ramerrez* was not already around him like a cloak when the overture began, he feared he would not give a good performance.

Mia Mitsouros, singing the part of *Minnie*, finished her complex aria about love's longing, with its impossibly difficult attacks on the high notes. Now Tony opened the door at the back of the set which represented a saloon during the California Gold

Rush, and exploded onto the stage singing his first angry phrases. Soon his voice began to feel big and secure and marvelous. Mia was, as usual, singing splendidly. It was going to be a triumphant afternoon after all.

For once, as the curtain calls continued unabated after twenty minutes, Tony found this enthusiasm a bit excessive. He had impulsively decided to surprise Jen by arriving in New York tonight for their wedding anniversary, since she could not come to him. The success of his plan depended on his being able to catch the Concorde to America this evening. As he bowed for what seemed like the hundredth time to an audience with cast-iron hands—he was sure of it—he decided if this went on much longer Mia would have to go on bowing without him.

Jen would be astonished to see him in New York tonight. That was not what she expected, since she knew he was due to be in Paris tomorrow morning for his *Otello* rehearsals. He knew her too well; though she had tried to hide from him her sadness during their phone call on Friday, he was a highly accurate reader of voices—how could he be otherwise? Now, he would try to lighten her melancholy mood with his surprise visit. In any case, he was feeling unsteady about his immediate future; he admitted to himself that his need for her tonight was perhaps greater than hers for him.

Tony was almost sure the timing was right for him to sing the difficult role of *Otello*, despite various baleful predictions including those of *Otello*'s conductor, Sheldon Wasserman. Tony had weighed the risks of singing—or forcing his voice into—that long heavy role, if his voice were not sufficiently mature. Not only might his voice lose the flexibility needed to sing the lighter lyric roles, but there was an even graver risk. By pushing themselves to sing roles too heavy for their voices, singers can haemorrhage into their vocal cords or lose their singing voices forever. But the ambitious Tony was prepared to gamble.

Tony wanted Jen with him when he was rehearsing a difficult new role, especially one as controversial for him as this. Wanted her with him? It was much more than that. He craved— he fed on—her cheerful strength. She shared in perfect empathy, as only another artist could, the moments of great exaltation his art brought him, and only she knew how to pull him out of his dark times. Tony knew very well that he was addicted to his wife.

So yesterday he had phoned Audra, Jen's New York editor and friend. "Audra, you don't tell Jen, but I have made reservations in your name at the Rainbow Room for eight tomorrow night, I will surprise her for our wedding anniversary. Only I need you to do me a favour. You invite her to supper, you say you are sad it is our anniversary and I am in London and Janina is sick, and you get her to the restaurant. Then, when you are at the table, I will sneak on the stage, I will sing to her with the orchestra, then I will come to the table and you will go home."

"Tony darling that's the nicest invitation I've received in years!"

"No, it is not nice, it is awful, *mi scusi*, Audra. I will make up to you next time, we will all go out to dinner, but this time you will do this for me, yes? It will make Jen happy I think."

"Yes, Tony, it will, and of course I'll do it for you. I think it's a great idea. You opera singers are so romantic! Speaking of opera, though, what's happening about Paris? Jen said the other day that you were to be in Paris Monday."

"I am. I will. I come back Monday. I come only to New York for one night. It is worth it, I make Jen happy, I make me happy, for once the voice can be where I want to be."

"You'll kill yourself, Tony. I don't know how you people live at such a pace."

"I don't know sometimes too. But we do, it is just how the profession is, and it is a good profession, you know? Audra, *grazie, molte grazie.* I will see you Sunday night, the short visit, yes?"

"The very short visit, yes, Tony darling. If something comes up and I can't get Jen to the Rainbow Room, I'll call you at your hotel before your performance tomorrow afternoon."

So all had been arranged.

The applause for *Fanciulla* showed signs of weakening slightly, just as Tony said to Mia, "I have to stop now, Mia, I have to catch the Concorde for New York, it is our wedding anniversary today."

Mia was sufficiently astonished to stop in mid-bow and stare at Tony. "New York? I thought we were to be in Paris tomorrow."

"I will be, don't worry, or for sure I will get there Tuesday."

Now behind the curtain, Tony grinned at her and indicated with a movement of his head an impeccably dressed man staring fixedly at Mia from the wings.

"I see your faithful British lord is still around, he has very much the passion for you, why don't you marry him, Mia? Take away his affliction, he looks always so sad."

"Are we going back for another call? No, looks like it's over, thank God, I'm exhausted, Tony darling. And I need some energy for 'my' lord, as you call him. He's worth a bit of energy."

"Marry him, Mia. Why not?"

"Because he's married, more or less, and anyway I'm wildly in love with you, Tony darling."

"Sure, sure, and Pavarotti tells me you say to him the same thing."

"Well, you know, you're tenors. I love tenors."

Tony laughed, and ran to his dressing room to take off his makeup. There he found Bill Anderson, his agent, still urgently needing to get in his few minutes of business conversation.

"*Dio*, Bill, you come to the airport, we will talk on the road, the car after will take you home, yes?"

Part of this sentence was muffled in a towel as Tony frenziedly scrubbed off his makeup. Bill, still uncomfortable after their earlier incident, agreed.

The limousine was waiting as Tony, accompanied by Bill, dashed from the Royal Opera House. Bill would attend to sending Tony's luggage from the London hotel to the Paris hotel.

Jack Smallwood thought this was really his lucky day. Twice in one day to be chauffeur to Antonio Amato! Jack thought Tony might not remember him from earlier. He had been told by a sour fellow driver that these artistic people were so into themselves they wouldn't know a limousine driver they'd only seen once, especially with the caps which made them all look alike.

But Tony surprised him. "Hello my friend, is you again, are we having better luck with the traffic this time? This is even

more important than the opera, it is my wedding anniversary in
New York, I mean, is my wedding anniversary everywhere, but
my wife is in New York, tonight I will surprise her, I even will
sing to her, if I can catch the plane."

Jack Smallwood was happy that his colleague was wrong,
and that these big stars weren't always full of themselves. This
one seemed like a regular fellow. "You'll make it, Mr Amato, if
we have to hopscotch over the traffic!"

Tony leaned his dark head back against the seat and closed
his eyes for a moment, just as Bill Anderson began, "That was a
splendid performance, Mr Amato. I was so concerned, I should
have known better than to come to your dressing room just
before the performance. I have a lot to learn."

Tony had been so concentrated on *Johnson-Ramerrez* and on
catching the Concorde that for a moment he couldn't remember
what Bill was talking about. Then he recollected that he had
perhaps unfairly lost his temper. "It is okay, Bill. You don't do
that again, I promise I will find always time for us to do our
business. But anybody could make such a mistake. It is hard for
people to understand." Tony reflected a moment. "And you call
me Tony, yes?"

While Jack Smallwood skillfully guided the limousine
through the crowded, still fogbound streets to suburban London,
Bill and Tony talked. At one point Tony commented on the fog,
and Smallwood interjected to tell Tony that this was nothing
compared to what Londoners used to call the 'London
particular'.

Tony watched the clock in the panelled partition ticking
inexorably towards departure time. He was certain he would

miss his plane. His mood darkened, although he tried to conceal it, knowing the chauffeur was doing his best. They arrived in the noisy, seemingly impenetrable melee of people, cars and buses that surround London Airport, a scant half hour before the Concorde was due to leave.

Tony tipped Jack Smallwood generously. He shook both his and Bill's hands quickly, and refused Bill's offer to see him to the departure gate, on the theory that one person could thread through the crowds faster than two. He ran across the crowded concourse, dodging people as he went. The heads of a few travelers snapped around to stare as they recognized the tenor Antonio Amato looking only too human as he ran, curly hair disheveled and jacket flapping, towards the departure gate. He arrived at the Concorde waiting area where a British Airways official anxiously scanned the crowds.

"There you are, Mr Amato! We were beginning to think you might miss the plane. If you'll just come along with me. No luggage, I see?"

"No luggage, I go just for one night, I have the apartment in New York so I have there the toothbrush and the clean shirt, you know?"

George Pendrell, the official, smiled faintly. "How amusing for you, Mr Amato. I hope you will have a good flight. Er, might I ask, that is to say, my wife is so fond of opera, er ..."

Tony grinned. This was obviously not a man accustomed to asking for autographs. "Do you have a piece of paper, I'm happy to give you my autograph. Who do I write it to?"

"Er, to Daphne Pendrell."

Daphne's husband fumbled ineffectually for a pen. Tony

finally produced his own, and then when no paper was forth-coming either, he found one of his business cards to sign.

I would autograph something with my blood, thought Tony as he hastily signed his name, just so I get on this plane.

Finally Tony dashed down the ramp and into the waiting Concorde. He was going to make it.

Fifteen

Tony slipped into the last vacant seat on the Concorde. Always a bit claustrophobic, this graceful silver tube. But its supersonic speed made it invaluable to singers like Tony, since the quality of their performances depend on remaining physically fit despite their constant hopscotching from city to city across the operatic world. Tony fastened his seatbelt, and remarked to the seatmate whose averted grey head was all he could discern, "Oof! I have almost missed this plane. I am so happy to be here!"

His seatmate slowly turned to scrutinize Tony, who was startled to recognize Sir Mallory Mancroft. Sir Mallory, the greatest Macbeth of the century, the former lover of Sheldon Wasserman. Sir Mallory, whom just a few hours ago Tony had unwittingly glimpsed weeping while embracing an impassive Wasserman.

Tony, tired from his performance, was not in the mood for pleasantries with Mancroft. He wished he could sit beside someone with whom he would not need to chat.

In his famous mellifluous voice Sir Mallory replied distantly, "I'm glad you're happy, Signore. It is Signor Amato, is it not? Allow me to introduce myself. I am Mallory Mancroft. May I compliment you on your usual splendid performance this afternoon. I left just after they put the noose around your neck. I expect the opera was well received."

Tony held out his hand, and received an abrupt, hard handshake. "It is for me so much a pleasure to meet you, Sir Mallory. Yes, we were well received this afternoon—there was applause for almost thirty minutes. For once I am wishing for less applause. But I am worried I will miss my plane. We are in the same business, you and I, it is not often we wish for less applause!"

Mancroft's voice cut across Tony's like a blade. "We are not, let me assure you, in the same business. As for me, I have always appreciated my audience. I would never feel that I had given them too much satisfaction. They may applaud me as long as they wish; I should never dream of complaining."

"No, no, you have not understood, it must be my English, I have meant to say it is the anniversa—"

"Signor Amato, it is an honour for me to meet such a great singer. But if you will excuse me, I am feeling very tired. I do not wish to converse further." Mancroft turned away to stare out the minuscule window.

Tony felt the sting of Mancroft's rebuff, and wondered how in so short a time he had managed to offend this celebrated actor. "*Mi scusi,* I do not intend to offend you ..."

"You have said and done nothing offensive, Signor Amato.

On the contrary. It is just that I prefer not to speak with you. Please do not give my whim another thought."

But Tony was suddenly grinning. Sir Mallory stared at him. "I was unaware that I had said anything even remotely amusing."

"Oh, you did not, it is not you makes me smile. It is just me remembering about Carlo Paoli sitting with you one time on the Concorde and that you—" Tony faltered. He had suddenly recollected the rest of what Carlo had said, that Mancroft seemed to have a virulent hatred of tenors.

Mancroft glared down his long aristocratic nose at Tony. "I can imagine what that man would say about me. Well, he's a fool, Signore. A fatuous, conceited fool. If he believes I dislike him intensely, he's quite correct."

Tony was taken aback. He had not wholly believed Carlo when Carlo had described Sir Mallory's attitude towards him, and towards tenors generally. But now, with Sir Mallory's last phrase hanging in the air, Tony's opinion of Carlo's accuracy was improving.

"Carlo is my friend, Sir Mallory. I wish not to offend you, but I will not listen that he should be insulted."

"Oh for goodness' sake, Signor Amato," Mancroft said, the beautiful voice dripping with contempt, "Stop sounding like you're in an opera. I have not impugned either your honour or Carlo Paoli's. And if I do say something further about Paoli that displeases you, what do you intend to do, challenge me to a duel? What are your weapons—swords, pistols? Oh, of course, I know, high C's. You tenors are quite ridiculous."

At this, Tony felt his temper rising. He tried to hold it in check, realizing that Sir Mallory's attack on him could have no personal cause; he had said and done nothing offensive. Tony recalled that earlier this afternoon Sir Mallory had gone through an experience upsetting enough to make him weep. By this time the Concorde was airborne, and its usual clamour was making conversation more difficult.

Tony finally replied, his hands moving eloquently to emphasize the passionate sincerity of his words. "Maybe tenors are to you ridiculous, but we have very much in common with you all the same. Like you, we have a special work to do, it is not an easy work, but when we do it well, it is so satisfying, maybe the best feeling there is, because it gives joy to so many people. And like you we want to be in one place when the voice has to be in another place. Like you we go on stage when we are scared or sick or sad, as long as we can make the voice work. Tell me, Sir Mallory, are we really so different, you and me?"

Tony stopped, hoping Mancroft would answer. But Mancroft's response was a silent, haughty stare. Tony continued, "Would you maybe rather be in London tonight but the voice has to be in New York? Me, I am supposed to be in Paris to-morrow, to rehearse for my first *Otello*. But my wife, you know maybe Jenetta Amato the artist? She is home in New York, she planned to come to London but our baby is sick with the chicken pox, so now I go to my wife. I surprise her for our tenth wedding anniversary. Then I will go tomorrow to Paris, I will be only one day late. Yes, it is exhausting, but what else could I do?"

Tony smiled his famous little-boy smile, and watched the expression on Sir Mallory's face soften slightly.

Sir Mallory looked down for a long moment, then turned

and fixed Tony with the well-known unblinking gaze. Each of these performers unconsciously used, in conversation, well-honed stage business which had become part of their real-life armoury of charm. Or was it the charm that had become part of the stage business?

"Signor Amato, I ... this is difficult for me, but ... I feel I must apologize for my rudeness. It was inexcusable. It's just ... that I've had a ... difficult time in London. Like you I've stolen time, two days out from my play, to try to ... if there is any excuse for my rudeness it is that I am deeply grieved about a personal matter."

With his peripheral vision Tony could see that Mancroft's hands, held together so poised in his lap, were shaking. For only a second Tony debated whether he should plunge in: then he took a deep breath and dived.

"I know, Sir Mallory. It was I who opened ... I was late before *Fanciulla* and the doorman told me everybody was worried, so I thought I would tell Maestro Wasserman I had arrived. I did not realize; I was in such a hurry I forgot to knock."

Sir Mallory looked at Tony, his actor's face expressionless. "You're saying you saw Sheldon and me. We did wonder which of you it was. We knew it had to be either you or that fellow singing *Rance*, because the man who opened the door apologized in Italian."

"It was me. Whatever it ... whatever has made you this sadness, I am truly sorry."

"How very curious."

"What do you mean, curious?"

"I mean, I believe you. How very odd. I don't have a lot of

faith in the sincerity of sympathy, but for some reason I believe you really are sorry for my sadness."

Suddenly the handsome, fine-boned elderly face crumpled, as Sir Mallory again lost his self-mastery, but this time, instead of indulging in sarcasm, he began to weep. Tony, disconcerted, was unsure of what his next step should be. Had Sir Mallory been Italian, Tony would have been more sure of what to do.

"*Mi scusi*, please forgive me, I should not have told you I saw you, I do not want to make for you more sadness, is there anything I can do? To help, I mean?"

The square, erect shoulders shook, and then the superb acting training took over, and Sir Mallory controlled himself. He breathed deeply several times while Tony looked away tactfully, and finally he was able to say to Tony, "I owe you at least the rudiments of an explanation. I realize I have been insufferable to you, while you have done nothing to provoke my behaviour except to live up to your advance billing."

"What advance billing?"

"You have a reputation for kindness, Signor Amato. Not always the case among celebrities, as you undoubtedly know."

Sir Mallory stared at his finely manicured hands, as Tony, covertly watching his face, saw his desperate attempts at self-discipline. Human misery never failed to move Tony. Unlike people who see suffering around them and feel happy because their own problems pale by comparison, the unhappiness of others never cheered Tony. It only added more sadness to whatever he was feeling himself.

Finally Sir Mallory spoke, his voice trembling. "I have a ... I have a need to test your reputed kindness, Signor Amato. May I trust you with my confidences? I fear a breakdown, I fear I will begin to weep and be unable to stop, if I don't talk to someone. I can no longer bear this pain. Oh damnation, whatever makes me think I can trust a tenor?"

"Whatever makes you think you cannot? What did tenors do to you that is so terrible?"

"One of you—I mean you tenors—has—has indirectly ruined my life. I know I should be broad-minded enough to realize that just because there's one rotten apple in the barrel they're not all rotten."

Tony's grasp of the English idiom was always vague. "Why now do you talk about apples? I thought we were talking about tenors."

"Yes. Tenors. You saw me with Sheldon, perhaps you saw me weep, perhaps you saw his response. Or rather lack thereof."

Mancroft stared for a long while out the small window. Then, slowly, he continued in a monotone as though he thought if he put emotion into the words he would shatter.

"Signor Amato, there is no way you can have missed the gossip in the media about me, just as I have not missed the rubbish often written about you. But I have to tell you that in spite of the nonsense about me lately, it is Sheldon Wasserman who is the true love of my life. We met when I was thirty-five, and despairing of ever finding someone who could reciprocate the love I knew I was capable of giving. We met at a shooting party; it was on the estate of the Duke of—oh, what does it matter? Odd; I remember Sheldon's first words to me were 'Good shot!' What useless trivia one's memory throws up at times."

Sir Mallory mused for a moment. "Sheldon was a revelation to me, all I had ever dreamed of. We spent twenty-seven beautiful years together. We pledged to stay together forever. I knew no-one could ever be to me what Sheldon was ... is. And then one day Sheldon met someone else. Something about that person apparently reminded Sheldon of me, as I was when my relationship with Sheldon was young. And Sheldon fell in love, in love at first sight, can you believe it? I thought nothing could happen that would ever separate us."

The stewardess came down the aisle with champagne; both Tony and Mancroft accepted glasses.

"This other man," Mancroft continued, "there were rumours that he would entertain advances ... he was married, but one heard that he was ... that on occasion ... only that seems not to have been true. Sheldon, not knowing, planned his campaign carefully. When he confessed his love to—to this other man, Sheldon was told that his feelings were not returned. But Sheldon was deeply enamoured of his unrequited love, and that infatuation came between us. There were scenes, quarrels, and then Sheldon left me."

The old actor bowed his head. He did not notice the tear that fell into his lap. "I've been alone now for eight years. Well, not wholly alone, there have been *passades*, there are always *passades*, are there not, Signore, but never anyone who even remotely... This last while I have been particularly unhappy. Is it not curious, Signore, that I, the greatest living Macbeth, did not understand despair until I was sixty-two years old and my lover left me?"

The stewardess passed caviar canapes. Tony and Mancroft

both declined.

"Recently there have been articles and pictures of Sheldon's other love everywhere, I cannot get away from him. I couldn't bear it—I was compelled to ask Sheldon one more time if we could try again, if we could be together in these our mature years. What's the point of living, of striving, if you can't share it with someone you care about? Sometimes life gets so lonely, is it worth even trying to go on? But Sheldon said no, he was not ready to come back to me.

"Sheldon has been in New York for the last little while, and I was able to control myself and not contact him. It will sound strange but I am always oddly comforted when he and I are in the same city, even though there is no communication between us. Then he left for London on Friday, and suddenly I could not stand the loneliness any longer. So I booked a flight to London and went to him, I begged, I abased myself before him, and he refused me."

Mancroft's voice had faded to nothing. He cleared his throat. "Sheldon says he knows it is futile, carrying a torch for this other man who will never love him, not as I love him, but he will not come back to me until he has exorcised that man. I've thought lately if that bloody tenor were just removed from the face of the earth, Sheldon and I could get back to the way we were. I would do anything to get him back, and I would forgive him anything."

Mancroft pulled out a handkerchief and rather noisily blew his nose. After a long pause he said, all his doubt in his voice, "Am I going to be sorry I confided in you, Signor Amato?"

"If you are afraid I will gossip, you don't have to be. When people tell me secrets, I keep them. I don't want to—to injure somebody. Life hurts everybody; it is not up to Antonio Amato to hurt everybody even more. Please, Sir Mallory, don't be worried. You can trust me."

"Signor Amato, I do believe you. Isn't it odd that I should feel better because of a tenor?" Sir Mallory was silent for a time. Then he continued, "I do have friends, you know, but I can't bring myself to talk to any of them about this; there is the matter of pride. I can't bear the thought of people feeling sorry for me. I would feel too vulnerable if they knew how much I miss my dear Sheldon. So you see, in my personal life I'm acting, just as much as on the stage. But I don't need to tell you this. As you say, we're in similar professions."

Sir Mallory stared at his well-manicured, blue-veined hands. "May I thank you for putting up with this undoubtedly tedious tale of an old man's sorrows? Talking to you has helped me."

He stopped abruptly, and seemed to Tony to be waging a painful inner struggle. Finally he said, his voice tentative, "Could we meet occasionally? I've no one to whom I've dared to talk like this, and now that I have actually broken the ice and confided in someone, could you bear further confidences, should the need arise? God knows I needed help tonight. I will be totally frank with you, Signor Amato; I was contemplating putting a final end to my sadness."

Tony was horrified. He made his living by singing operas filled with various forms of love and death, death by all sorts of means like murder and suicide, but when he met such things in real life he was non-plussed. He could not yet imagine sorrows so great that even the possessing of an enormous talent would not ward off the desire to end pain.

"Of course we could meet, Sir Mallory. What are we in the world for, if not to help other people? Please, talk to me any time. I do travel very much, but I will be happy to meet you when we can. We will shake hands on this."

Sir Mallory grasped Tony's hand in a long, firm handshake, nodding wordlessly. Then the two men fell silent, and a short while later when the stewardess passed their seats, she noticed them both fast asleep, Mancroft's head tipped back, his mouth open, while Tony's head rested at an angle against the seat back, his dark curls dishevelled. She concluded, not for the first time, for she had seen many weary performers, that the theatrical life must be an exhausting one.

And the Concorde flew arrow-like through a never-changing dusky sky towards New York.

Sixteen

Jen's friend and editor Audra realized she was beginning to sound shrill, and with considerable effort lowered her pitch, so that Jen would not suspect how frustrating this telephone conversation was becoming. Audra was so enchanted with Tony's romantic surprise for Jen, that she couldn't bear to have it spoiled because of any lack on her own part. But with Tony already on the Concorde on his way back to New York, whatever was Audra to do now? This was her third phone call to Jen, her third attempt at persuasion since yesterday.

"Audra, you know I'd love to have dinner at the Rainbow Room," Jen was saying. "It would cheer me up no end, but I just can't leave Janina. She cries every time I'm out of her sight. And she's so uncomfortable, poor little soul, I would feel selfish taking pleasure for myself when she wants me so badly."

"And where is the redoubtable Nanny Burns? I mean, what's the point of having an expensive highly trained nanny if you can't leave your children with her for an hour or so?"

"Oh, she's here; she's not redoubtable—actually, the children adore her."

"I'm glad to hear it. She scared the hell out of me when I met her. I felt like I was being interviewed by the Queen of England."

"I know, she does have that British upper-crust manner. It's interesting, actually, how loving she is with the children when she's so starchy with the rest of us. Maybe that's how they're trained at Nanny School—Nanny School?—to keep their employers at arms' length. Mrs Burns trained for two years for her profession, she has worked at it for twenty years, and she makes it very clear to us that she's in no way our servant."

"And costs you a fortune, no doubt!"

"That too." Jen said.

Audra judged the moment propitious to try yet again. "So! The doctor says Janina is over the worst. And since that paragon of warmth, love and nursing skills, the expensive Nanny Burns, is there," (Jen laughed, a good sign, thought Audra,) " what harm can there be in you taking a couple of hours to have dinner with me at the Rainbow Room? You're only five minutes away from Janina. Come on. I've made the reservation, the music is always delightful; if you won't come for yourself, will you come for me? I mean," (and here Audra had a sudden inspiration, given Jen's personality,) "I didn't say anything earlier, but I really need to talk to you."

"Is something wrong?" Jen asked quickly.

Audra realized she had better not make Jen think her company might be depressing, as Jen seemed depressed already.

"No, not at all," Audra said. "It's just that I have to make an important decision, Jen, and I value your advice so much." (And

The Otello Omen

if that doesn't get Jen to the restaurant, nothing will, except of course the truth.)

"Well, all right, if you put it like that, I'll come. Why don't you drop by here for a drink and then we'll walk? It's not far, and I could do with a breath of fresh air. Audra, I must be desperate when I call the air of Manhattan fresh!"

Audra hung up the telephone, happy that she hadn't yet lost her powers of persuasion.

Jen told Nanny Burns she would be going out for dinner after all.

And that was how she, attired in full skirted pale blue silk, and Audra, dressed in what Jen thought of as "editor's ink black", found themselves being ushered to their table in that elegant example of Art Nouveau, the Rainbow Room at Rockefeller Centre.

Their table was on the edge of the circular parquetry dance floor, opposite the bandstand where a pianist and five violinists serenaded the guests. At each place setting, laid on silvery tablecloths, was one of the famous red, black and rainbow hued plates, echoing the name of the room. Jen's eyes swept the scene before she sat down, happily taking in once again the floor-to-ceiling windows with their incomparable views, and the rainbow within the Rainbow, the varied hues of gowns surrounding her.

For a large room, Jen thought, the atmosphere here is always surprisingly intimate. The artist in her subconsciously stored up the effect of the colours, lit as they were by a peach glow from ceiling lights concealed in two large sculpted circular recesses.

Audra and Jen ordered cocktails, eagerly read the menu and

160

chose appetizers, Audra ordering pressed duck, and Jen choosing smoked salmon with capers. They made small talk until Jen began to wonder why Audra was taking such a long time finding the words to tell her what she had come to say.

"So, Audra, are you going to divulge this big event that you want my help with?" Jen looked suddenly disconcerted. "Big event? Audra, you haven't decided to—I mean, I know you've toyed with the idea of having a baby and not waiting any more for Mr Heavenly to come along—"

"Well, you know what my problem is with waiting for Mr Heavenly. The only one I want is taken."

Jen smiled. "You wouldn't like being married to Tony. You want somebody who's going to be around a lot more than he will ever be. He can't help it, of course, but for instance, look at me tonight. It's our tenth wedding anniversary, and I'm all alone."

'Thanks a lot. Here I've been thinking all this time you were with me."

"On my tenth wedding anniversary you barely count," Jen said, though the warmth in her voice belied her words. "Anyway, Audra, back to you, what's going on? I'm expiring of curiosity. Now you're going to tell me I have to wait for the main course before you divulge. I swear I won't eat until you reveal all—I wasn't right about a baby, was I?"

(*Tony, Tony, where the hell are you? It never crossed my mind you might be late*), Audra thought frantically. What could she think up to tell Jen, something important so Jen wouldn't realize Audra was dissimulating? And then Audra remembered something she had long been curious about, a question she kept forgetting to ask Jen during their too infrequent meetings, the answer to which might preoccupy Jen right through the meal, if that became necessary.)

"No, I won't tell you yet, my news is the *piece de resistance* of our dinner, so you'll have to possess your soul in patience, as my grandma used to say. But we've got a couple of uninterrupted hours for once, and I can ask you a question I've been curious about for ages. Very apropos, since it's your anniversary, and I think your mind should be firmly on Tony. Tell me, I'm dying to know how you two met? Where do paths first cross for people with such different interests—a Canadian watercolour artist and an Italian opera singer? On a plane, I bet."

"Oh no, nothing as trite as that for Tony and me," Jen answered. "You know Tony, everything that happens to him seems to be larger than life. We met in a maze, more or less."

"You mean those tree puzzles? So tell me already! In a maze, I can hardly wait for this—are you kidding me?" (*I hope this is a long story and that Tony gets here before it's done!*)

"Our paths first crossed," began Jen, happy to reminisce about Tony because that seemed the next best thing to having him with her, "to use your phrase, at Glyndebourne, you know, the opera festival in England, seven months before we married. Well, not exactly at Glyndebourne, but after one of Tony's performances there, at a dinner given by Thomas Graham Lanville, you know who I mean, the elderly industrialist who is such an opera buff. He has become a great friend of ours since. Lanville had bought a lovely chateau years before and had restored it for his wife. The grounds were gorgeous—there was a famous maze—the place was delightful."

"I was living in Montreal then, but I had come to London to give a short series of lectures and seminars on watercolour at the National Gallery. I was thrilled to have been asked, especially since I was only twenty-seven; it was a great honour. My life was coming together; my career was well launched and I was even unofficially engaged to Alain Bonenfant, you know, the French-Canadian set designer and director? Although I must admit I was having some doubts about that. You'll see why when I tell you more."

"You can't be serious!" exclaimed Audra. "However did you meet him? I've come across him once or twice at cocktail parties; he's a fascinating, complex man, but I don't see you two as a couple."

"Well obviously in the end, neither did I. But we met at a very arty party in Montreal, and discovered that we had art in common, although not of course the same kind. He was fascinated by the ethereality of water colour, something he's not good at, and I was interested in the creation of stage effects, something I'm not good at. When I think back on it, our art was almost all we had in common, but it was enough to intrigue us almost long enough to get us married." Jen stared for a moment unseeing into the vast, attractive room. "People do set out to marry for daft reasons."

"Go on, go on, this is getting good."

"Alain had come to England from New York," Jen continued, "to design the *Tosca* sets for Glyndebourne that summer. A tenor whose star was rising fast was making a Glyndebourne debut in that *Tosca*, singing *Cavaradossi*. He was an Italian whose name I had not heard before—Antonio Amato.

The Otello Omen

"Opening night was to be a glittering affair, formal dress of course, with royalty present, the Duchess of Kent, and afterwards an intimate dinner at Thomas Graham Lanville's chateau, including of course the Duchess, but also including the principal singers and Alain—and me as his fiancee.

"Alain was becoming rather well-known by then, but he was still terribly impressed to be invited to this exclusive little soiree. He was eager to make a good impression, since Lanville was an important financial figure in the theatrical world. He wasn't above using people, and he even felt it was good for his career to be seen with me, since my star was rising too.

"Alain insisted on helping me choose my dress for that occasion. He always insisted on me having a particular look. He was fascinated by what he called the 'ice-fire look,' and he thought I did that look very well.

"For that party he chose for me a pale pink dress with short puffy sleeves, a very low neckline and a slim skirt—he called it an irresistible mixture of the seductress and the innocent. I have to admit I thought I looked great."

Audra laughed. "You've never been one for false modesty!"

"Thanks a lot. Anyway, the day of the performance Alain was already at Glyndebourne, and I had hired a car to drive myself down from London after my seminar, to get there in time for the performance and the dinner. Well, I had a series of small disasters. First my zipper stuck and I had to be sewn into the dress at the last minute by my obliging landlady; then an accident on the road held up traffic for almost an hour; then I had a flat tire and had to wait for help as the hired car had no jack in it for me to change the tire, and anyway I was hardly

164

dressed for automobile mechanics.

"The result was that I missed the performance entirely, and arrived at Glyndebourne in time to be directed down the road to Lanville's estate where I hoped the dinner would not have already begun. I was tempted to turn back, but I knew—or rather I thought—that Alain was counting on me. So I decided to go on, and to make a funny anecdote out of my adventures to tell my fellow diners.

"So, there I was in my pale pink finery driving up the circular driveway to the chateau. A butler—if he had been cast in the role he could not have looked more suitable—met me at the door, and told me in the haughtiest way you can imagine that dinner had already begun; however, he would inform Mr Lanville that I had arrived. By then I was getting quite uncomfortable, but Mr Lanville himself came out and was so gracious to me, laughing at my tale of misadventures, that I felt I had been right to come even though I was so late.

"'Take my arm, my dear,' he said and he escorted me through the great hall, which was heavy with gloomy heraldic tapestries and suits of armour. We went up a staircase that looked straight out of a Gothic film, *Jane Eyre* maybe, and entered a dining hall that likely was new when the first Elizabeth ruled England. It was such a thrill for me. A chamber music group, dressed in Elizabethan finery, was playing music that sounded Mozartish to my relatively untrained ear. At the end of the great dining hall, tables were set in a U-shape to accommodate about thirty people.

"Mr Lanville announced to the group that the lost was finally found, and took me first to the Duchess, where I made my apologies. Then Mr Lanville accompanied me to my chair beside Alain, and as he pulled it out for me he said to Alain, 'Well, Mr Bonenfant, here is the late but not unlamented Miss Maclean. I will leave you to do the honours; I must get back to my other guests.' And he left us to return to his seat at the head of the table.

"I smiled at Alain, I remember, being pleased to have finally arrived, and excited now by the ambience and the company, but he looked at me so angrily I could hardly believe my eyes.

"'Where the hell have you been?' he said to me, none too quietly.

"I started to tell him my little story, when he continued, 'You shouldn't have come, Jenetta. You've embarrassed me unbelievably.'

"I remember looking around at our dinner companions to see who had heard this, as Alain was not exactly whispering. To my right was a man engaged in conversation with his neighbour, obviously oblivious so far to Alain's comments. Across the table ...'"

Jen stopped, smiling at her memory. "I remember that I looked up and there was this dark man staring at me with eyes, how can I describe the effect his eyes had on me? It was like time stopped, like I was drowning. I remember the thought flashing through my mind that my feelings were like the heroine's in the only romance novel I have ever read. I looked at Alain expecting him to introduce us, but he just went on eating and drinking, mostly drinking.

"The man across the table held out his hand to me, smiled that irresistible little-boy smile of his and said, 'I am Antonio

166

Amato.' I must have murmured my name; he took my out-stretched hand and held it for much longer than necessary, before he raised it to his lips and kissed it. I thought feebly, 'Italians ... '

"'Don't make such an ass of yourself, Jenetta,' Alain hissed. Antonio Amato just kept looking at me. I knew he could hear Alain's remarks, and I was mortified. I thought I would stop Alain by starting a conversation with Amato. So I told him how sorry I was to have missed his debut, and recounted to him my amusing misadventures, piling adjective on adverb in order to prolong the story and to try to make Amato laugh. All around me my dinner companions were amused by my tale, except of course for Alain whose fury I could not understand.

"Antonio Amato smiled a little at my story but didn't laugh like the others. When I came to the end of the story he did that little-boy grin again and said, 'My English, very small.'

"I burst out laughing, and rejoined, 'My Italian, even smaller.'

"He said, 'Is *competizione?*'

"I looked at this lovely man, and thought I could never compete with him for anything; I could only be part of his team and cheer him on. The thought surprised me, and I replied, 'No, it's not a competition. Not with you.'

"Well, the dinner progressed, and Alain kept either humiliating me or ignoring me, and Antonio Amato kept staring at me, and I got more and more rattled, until during our last cup of coffee Alain, who by now had drunk far too much, positively hissed at me, 'Not only have you mortified me, Jenetta, but you have ruined my little surprise. I was going to give you an engagement ring at the theatre during the performance tonight, and I was going to ask Lanville to wish us well from the stage, and to propose a toast to us at this dinner. I had it all planned; it would have been memorable.'

"Finally I couldn't stand it any longer. I said, 'It would certainly have been theatrical, Alain dear. Maybe not romantic, and maybe not intimate, but definitely effective. Undoubtedly great publicity for you. Did it occur to you to ask me whether I would accept your ring?'

"I must say that stopped him. We had spoken of marriage, but we had no definite plans. Alain's opinion of his charms was pretty high; I think it never crossed his mind that I might have second thoughts. But I had been humiliated by Alain on one too many occasions; this episode confirmed my already serious doubts about him. I realize now, and I guess I realized then, that a lot of our problems were caused by Alain's drinking, but still ...

"All through this I kept glancing across the table at Antonio Amato, who never took his eyes from me, as far as I could make out."

Jen fell silent, her eyes seeing not a famous New York restaurant, but a young Antonio Amato staring and staring at her.

"Go on, please!" urged Audra, surreptitiously glancing at her watch and hoping there was a lot more to this story.

"Tony's English has improved a lot, Audra. So much better than when I first met him. Anyway, at that point Alain did an unforgivable thing to me; he grabbed my thigh with his hand— he's very strong—and squeezed and twisted it so hard he really hurt me—I had a bruise for weeks. And Antonio Amato knew, I could see those eyes widening; he made a move to get out of his chair.

"I was mortified and in pain. I was nearly in tears; I excused myself, and left the banquet hall as quickly as I could. When I got to the great entrance hall, I dashed for the door, looking for somewhere to hide for a few minutes, somewhere to weep necessary tears before I pulled myself together and returned to the banquet.

"Once out the front door, I could see bright lights to my right, so I walked along to the side of the building, and there I saw the entrance to the maze. There were floodlights lighting the tops of the trees, so I knew I couldn't get lost if I simply wandered into the maze a little way, because I could follow the lights above me and get out again. So I started in, intending only to conceal myself long enough to cry a little, before I returned.

"What I didn't bargain for was that the floodlights were programmed to go off every night at a particular time. So after I had wandered a few moments in the maze, certain I knew how to get out again, two rights and three lefts, suddenly the lights went off and I was plunged into darkness.

"It was an overcast night, so no light from the stars or the moon reflected on the trees to help me find my way. But I thought I would be all right; I would just feel my way and turn my two rights and three lefts and I would be out. So I did — except that when that didn't work I realized that I should have gone the other way, that those were the turns I had made coming in and I should have reversed them — so I tried to get back to where I had begun my exit, but soon I was hopelessly lost.

"I'm a claustrophobic. As long as I thought I knew my way

out I was able to control myself, but now I knew I was lost, and nobody knew where I was. Alain would not look for me because he would assume I had taken my hired car back to London in a fit of pique. He would tell anyone who enquired that I had to leave; he would likely say I had felt unwell. As it turned out, that was true, for by now I was becoming so panicky that I did feel ill.

"Honestly, Audra, I felt like Snow White in the forest with all the trees viciously clutching at her—remember that scene? I was terrified out of all proportion to what was really happening. I mean, what was the worst that could happen? That I would be there all night, and that I would be a bit chilly without a wrap. But it was summer; it was not particularly cold; rain was not forecast; obviously I was not in any real danger. And come the dawn, if I couldn't find my way out, I could call until someone heard me. It wasn't like I was lost in the Canadian tundra.

"But when you are phobic, the terror is out of all proportion to the peril—if any! So I was terrified. I began to cry, and to wander frantically through the maze, feeling my way along until my hands and arms were scratched and bleeding. I must have been sobbing when I heard someone coming quickly through the maze, with what I assumed was a flashlight glimmering through the dense trees. Then I heard, '*Signorina* Maclean, is you, yes? Is all right, I come, I promise.'

"'Mr Amato?' I called out.

"'You call me, I find. You keep call me.'

"So I kept calling, until a bright light a little way in front of me showed me I'd been found. I covered my eyes to protect them from the sudden glare, when I heard him stumble and the light went out. The voice said, '*Il diavolo*, I break him the light. *Signorina*, where are ...'

"I heard him feeling his way towards me down the narrow channel. I walked hesitantly towards him, feeling my way along the bushes at my side; he must have been coming with his hands held in front of him because I suddenly found myself up against his chest, my face against his dinner jacket. I put my hands on his shoulders and hung on for dear life and burst into sobs mixed with apologies for being so ridiculous.

"He wrapped his arms around me and held me.

"He said, 'You so cold, you shiver, yes? No—*piangere*—not to cry, please not to cry, I stay with you, I never leave you.'

"I remember thinking he'd better learn English better than that or he'd often find himself being sued for breach of promise.

"Then he said—oh, Audra, I shouldn't try to mimic what he said but his English was so small and the speech was so charming and I remember it so well and it went like this: 'I not understand ... *amico*, how you say? Oh yes, you friend. You go away a long time, I say to him, where you friend, she sick? He say, who cares, and he go drink with Lanville. I *inquieto*, I worry on you, I ask the butler, he say you in the garden. Sudden I know, if I be you, where I go, I go in the maze, be sad, cry maybe, *privato*. So I look in the garden, but is not the light in the maze. I say to the butler, he say, the light program to go out at night. I ask him the flashlight, say I need walk in the garden, he looking like he think all the singers crazy. But I know you here, I know you sad, I think you lost, I have to find.'

"'You've found,' I said, still hanging on tightly.

"'I know.'

"I lifted my face, and he kissed me very gently. Then we were both trembling. And he kissed me again. Not quite so gently. Then he said, 'You take my coat, you so cold.'

"He took off his dinner jacket and put it around me. He told me, 'I drop him the flashlight, he break. But we get out, I know this maze, I sleep in this ... this *castello*, these nights for when I singing *Tosca*, you know? Yesterday I walk in the maze, tonight I know to get out.'

"Together we felt our way out of the maze. When we were safely at the door of the chateau, Tony said, 'What you do now? The party it is finish.'

"'I have a hired car, and a reservation at Horsted Place, do you know it?'

"'I know, is good, is having the restaurant very nice, how long you stay?'

"'Why do you ask?'

"'You know why. We have to see us again. I want see you always.'

"I was confused by his limited English, not sure whether he knew the weight of what he was saying. As it turns out—well, as it turns out, he did. I was to have gone back to London the next morning although I had no seminar to give until the following day, so when Tony asked me to spend the afternoon with him and have dinner at Horsted, what could I do but say yes? And Audra, by the time that dinner was over, we were both so wildly infatuated we would have married on the spot had anyone been there to perform a ceremony. And as you can see, what I firmly told myself then was infatuation turned out to be something deep and beautiful and, so far, lasting..."

"Jen, what a great story! I've never read one thing about that in articles about you and Tony, but what great public relations that story would be!"

"Thank God I can trust you, Audra, because that story is going nowhere. There's not much that's private for Tony and me, and it's getting less so all the time, but that, that belongs just to us. So you keep this to yourself, y'all hear?"

They laughed together, sharing the trust that is the rich soil on which all good friendships grow. They fell silent, enjoying the romantic music which was curiously appropriate as background to Jen's story.

The small orchestra continued playing a nostalgic medley of songs by Irving Berlin, George Gershwin, and Cole Porter. Then the pianist, a woman in a tasteful but cleverly revealing black dress, announced that the next song was a request, in celebration of a wedding anniversary. She gave no further details, waiting quietly as one of the violinists tuned his instrument.

Jen smiled warmly at Audra. "That's sweet of you. I bet I can guess what you chose—your favourite love song, *La Vie en Rose?*"

Jen wondered at the odd grin on Audra's lips as the orchestra played sixteen chords of an introduction.

"Lehar?" queried Jen, astonished. "You chose a song by Lehar? I didn't know you'd ever heard of him, let alone shared my liking for—"

Offstage a tenor began to sing very softly, "*Dein ist mein ganzes Herz*"—"Yours is my heart alone." The voice rose, all honey and gold. Jen clapped her hand over her mouth, then whispered "Tony! Oh, Tony!" as the tall dark-haired man in the navy blazer emerged from behind a glowing partition and slowly descended the stairs, singing as he came. He stepped up onto the small stage, his unique glory of a voice filling the room with exquisite sound. Jen could not restrain tears of surprise and joy as he finished the song and moved to the microphone to speak.

"Ladies and gentlemen, I am Antonio Amato. This beautiful surprised woman,"—Tony gestured in Jen's direction—"Stand up, Jen, let everybody see you—she is my wife, we are married ten years today. Tonight I surprise her, as you can see, because she thinks I am in London. I say in front of you all, I have a big emotion today because I am so lucky to have this wonderful wife. Happy Anniversary, Jen. That song is for you. This one is for me." And he launched into *Because You're Mine*.

Jen was moved and joyful and amused all at once, amused because people's heads at surrounding tables swiveled as though they were at a tennis tournament. First to Tony, then to her to see her reaction, then back to him.

Tony's arms spread wide as he sang the last "mine", and the dinner guests applauded this unexpected, sentimental little concert with spontaneous pleasure. As Tony stepped off the podium and walked to Jen, the diners began to tap their glasses in the way they do at wedding receptions when they want the bride and groom to embrace. Jen turned her head to share her pleasure and faint embarrassment with Audra. Audra was standing, scooping up her small gold handbag. She kissed Jen quickly on the cheek, hugged Tony as he arrived at the table, said "Happy Anniversary, darlings," and, grinning hugely, took herself away. The diners were risking shattering the glasses, so

Tony took Jen in his arms.

"We must not disappoint our audience, must we, Jen?"

And for the next few delightful moments, nobody in the Rainbow Room appeared the least bit disappointed.

The orchestra fulfilled Tony's anniversary request by playing *The Anniversary Waltz*. Tony emerged from embracing Jen to ask, "Madame, will you dance?" He bowed in the exaggerated gesture of an eighteenth century courtier, Jen laughingly gave a charming if understated curtsy, and he twirled her around the floor as only a good dancer whose style had been perfected by stage training could dance.

Jen's skirt flared as she and Tony twirled and twirled, a well-matched couple, lovely to watch, thought their audience. The crowd reacted with delight, first applauding, and then simply watching, dreaming of romance, of old films, of opportunities taken, of opportunities missed.

The waltz over, Tony and Jen sat down to the accompaniment of more applause, after which their fellow diners, perhaps recollecting their own past celebrations, left them alone, though with many surreptitious stares, to the enjoyment of their anniversary.

The celebrants held hands across the cutlery. A waiter hovered attentively, as Tony ordered first a bottle of Dom Perignon champagne, and without looking at the menu said, "Please, I will have roast chicken, just plain, baked potato, vegetables ... you always do this very nice, thank you."

As the waiter left, Jen said, "Tony, Tony, what a fantastic thing to do for me."

"I do it also for me. I want to be with my family. Is Janina better?" At Jen's quick nod, Tony continued, "I wanted to be with you tonight. Correction, I needed to be with you tonight."

He raised her hands to his lips and kissed them in a charmingly old-fashioned gesture. They stared at each other, he serious, she with a gentle smile. He did not return her smile.

"Are you all right?" Jen asked, scanning his face, reading him like a favourite poem. She could see that he was happy and tired, as always after giving himself totally in an operatic performance. But there was something else. Was it fear?

"Tony, it's all right. It's not too soon for you to be singing *Otello*. Wasserman's wrong this time."

"Here is why I need you tonight, you know all of me. I don't even need to tell you, you know already why I worry. Only, how can you be so sure, Jen, this *Otello* doesn't hurt the voice? Sometimes even I am not sure, and it is my voice."

"Because there's so much voice there, Tony. And your vocal technique is so secure. You know yourself you've rehearsed and rehearsed *Otello* full voice at home, and what's happening? You're getting even better reviews for your lyric roles, so how can *Otello* be hurting you?"

Tony stared at her a long moment. "You are right. You are always right. Jen, *per favore*, you say Janina is better, so you will come with me tomorrow to Paris, yes?"

Not for the first time in her marriage Jen felt her spirit cleaving in half. The part of her that was mother needed to be with poor itchy uncomfortable little Janina, and the part of her that was mother and wife needed to go with Tony. She knew he needed her to be—to use his terms—his compass as he navigated the rocky physical and emotional shoals of singing his first

Otello…

By now Jen knew only too well that opera singers sing on the edge. Always there is the fear that the voice will disappoint the audience which has waited with orgasmic anticipation to hear it. The brain of any opera singer may give all the right signals to the vocal chords, but for innumerable physical and psychological reasons, the vocal chords may not give the right response.

To the outside world, Jen knew, Tony seemed controlled, calm. A few people close to him understood that he was not impervious to the stresses of his demanding career, but only to Jen was he able to show his real vulnerability. He, like her, was too private a person to burden others with his concerns.

So Jen knew that if she was not with him in Paris he would share his worries with nobody. And that could only add to his tension, for he was facing perhaps the biggest stresses of his career.

With a lightness she did not wholly feel, she replied, "Of course I'll come with you tomorrow to Paris, Tony love."

"Good! Now I know I will be okay. So. Let us really celebrate this anniversary."

He reached into his jacket pocket, and his hand emerged concealing something small. "Close your eyes, give me your hand. Your other hand, Jen."

She felt him sliding a ring onto the third finger of her left hand, where she wore a thick, sculpted gold wedding band and a simple emerald cut diamond solitaire.

"I am the most lucky man, and I need you to remember this always. Open your eyes."

The Otello Omen

On her finger was an antique diamond "eternity" ring, the setting designed in a "u" shape, which framed her solitaire on one side. She knew the ring would have a story, for Tony gave thoughtful gifts. It often surprised her that he would take the trouble to seek out such presents, constrained as his time was by the demands of his career.

"It's marvelous, Tony. You are a lovely man. How did I ever get so lucky?"

"You don't take it off, you keep it there all the time. I need you, Jen. I want you always to know this. I will tell you a story about the ring." Tony was grinning, not the famous smile but a cat-that-stole-the-cream grin.

"The ring belonged to John Marin, the artist, that I am always telling you when you do the serious arts it is reminding me of his works. I had my dealer who is finding my Caruso memorabilia, looking for a jewel from a painter for you, for such a long time. And finally! Just in time for our anniversary!"

And so the dinner progressed, with intimate talk and shared laughter, until after each of them had finished their meal with two cappuccinos Jen finally said, "Tony darling, if we are going to Paris tomorrow, maybe we should go home and get some sleep."

"Among other things," agreed Tony with a little grin.

If it hadn't been for those other things, Tony and Jen might not have been so sleepy the next morning. And Jen might not have automatically turned off the radio alarm clock whose raucous signal was to help them get to the Concorde on time. And they might not have missed the plane, nor had time to look over the *Sunday New York Times Arts Section* of the day before.

Nor been there for Carlo's disastrous visit.

Seventeen

While Jen and Tony revelled in the unexpected joy of being together for their anniversary, a few blocks away Hannelore Crasmann, in her narrow bed, awoke suddenly to the realization that she was weeping, sobbing again from the effects of one of her recurrent nightmares. Not this time the re-creation of her rape by Carlo inhabiting Smythe's body, but an older misfortune. Troubling, this particular dream. Not always so troubling in the dreaming, but in the awakening and trying to know whether any part of the dream was fantasy or whether it was all a recollection of reality.

Hanne disentangled herself from the sheets she had loosened in her flailing, and sat up in bed. She turned her head towards her old electric clock to see the time, but was greeted by darkness. More electrical trouble in the building, she thought. She felt her way to the kitchenette where she kept candles and matches for this increasingly frequent occurrence. She found a fat stub of decorative pink candle, felt for the matchbook beside it, and lit the candle which she set down in a saucer on her small table.

She walked over to her closet and pulled out her navy dressing gown, which she put on over her white flannel night-dress. Now she was shivering—she seemed never to be the right temperature recently. She drew hot water from the hot water tap and made herself a cup of decaffeinated instant coffee. Then she sat down to think the dream through, to try to exorcise it so she could go back to sleep. Tomorrow—today, actually, was a working day.

Hanne stared past the candle flame into the middle distance of her room, into the middle distance of her past, towards that night twenty-three years before when it had ended; when it had begun.

Tonight she had awakened dreaming that she had just awakened in the hospital, waking from a dream of waking from a dream. But the nightmare had not begun like that.

It had actually begun with the man who appeared one morning at her bus stop all those years ago. After waiting for the bus with her every day for a week, he had struck up a conversation with her. The common point between them was their red hair, hers a splendid deep auburn, his the colour of flames.

He was even taller than she, thin and freckled, with a gentle charm and a lovely wide grin. He was new in the city, having just started work as a book-keeper for a brokerage firm in Wall Street. He dreamed of returning to university part-time and becoming a chartered accountant, he told Hanne, and to this end he was saving his money.

He was kind to Hanne, kinder than most men were. She was painfully aware that men did not find her attractive. She had never been out on a date, not a real one, in all her twenty-two years. But he—his name was Hubert—spoke to her every morning, asked about her, sat with her on the bus until she descended at her stop to go to work at Les Classiques.

She began to think about him when she was not with him. She wondered whether he might one day ask her to go out with him, for a cup of coffee maybe, or even for a walk on a Sunday afternoon. But the weeks went by and the relationship remained unchanged, confined to the amiable morning chat.

In those days Hanne still sang seriously. She practised faithfully every day; scales, lieder, arias, and she sang in the choir of a Lutheran church in Brooklyn which had advertised for soloists in a music oriented newsletter which came regularly to Les Classiques.

Recently she had read about a much-heralded new tenor, an Italian-American named Carlo Paoli, and she waited eagerly to hear his first records. When they came, she was stunned by his voice, by his technique, by the sheer beauty of the sounds Paoli made. Her whole being responded to his singing in a way she had not felt before, in a way that even she, virginally naive though she was, recognized as sexual.

It became her great dream that she might one day hear Carlo Paoli in person. She knew he was about to make his Metropolitan Opera debut singing *Alfredo* in *La Traviata*, and she enquired about tickets, but the price of any reasonably good seat was well beyond her means, and she did not want to hear him from up in "the gods". She wanted just once in her restricted young life to go in style; to reserve a good seat for her first time at the Metropolitan Opera to hear the incredible Carlo Paoli in person.

As she was pondering this, Hubert appeared at the bus stop one morning with a small blonde woman whom he introduced to Hanne as his good friend from "back home". It was clear to Hanne that Ellie was a good friend indeed, although Hanne still harboured hopes that Hubert's enthusiasm was prompted more by the pleasure of shared recollection with Ellie than by prospective future plans.

That day a faithful customer of Les Classiques, the elegant Frenchwoman Georgette de Couvreur, came into the shop with a happy smile on her long thin face. She advanced on Hanne purposefully.

"*Ma chere* Mademoiselle Crasmann, I am looking for someone to make 'appy, and I believe I should like it to be you. We were speaking only the other day, *oui?* of this wonderful new tenor, Carlo Paoli, and you said 'ow you would 'ave so much liked to go to his debut but of course the tickets are so expensive, *oui?* Well my dear, *devinez* what I am going to say!"

Hanne looked suitably bewildered.

"I 'ave tickets, two good seats *ma chere*, and my 'usband he says to me we are going instead to Martinique, so I am thinking I usually give tickets I can't use to my nephew, but he is so disagreeable lately. So then I am thinking, wouldn't Miss Crasmann like these tickets? So *ma chere*, I would be so 'appy to give them to you, you take a friend, maybe there is a special man, *oui?* But you are always so good, so attentive, that giving you these tickets would make me very 'appy."

Hanne was so overwhelmed she found herself wiping away tears of joy. A disapproving look from Mr Chansan soon stopped the tears, as Hanne repeatedly thanked her unexpected benefactress.

Hanne debated about asking one of her fellow choir members to accompany her to the opera, but decided that since her luck seemed to be in, she would invite Hubert. He had said he liked opera, and had been interested when she told him she sang. So the next morning when he reappeared alone at the bus stop she blurted out that she had been given two wonderful seats to hear Carlo Paoli and would Hubert like to join her?

Hubert looked astonished; clearly it had not crossed his mind that his relationship with Hanne would ever extend further than their pleasant casual conversations while going to work. But he thanked her enthusiastically, saying the opportunity to hear Paoli was irresistible.

Hanne was beside herself with feverish anticipation. After much indecision she chose to wear her bright green polyester dress, the one which looked almost like silk and which favourably accentuated her long, thick, splendid hair. She would not wear a coat even though it was winter, for her coat was a little shabby. She had a reasonably warm white acrylic jacket, with white piping across the lapels and down the front, that would do nicely.

On the morning of the performance, Hanne awakened with a headache so fierce she could barely get out of bed. From experience she knew that headaches like this usually heralded the onset of a feverish illness. A momentary panic set in, before she resolutely decided that she would swallow as many painkillers as necessary, and she would go to the opera regardless of how ill she became during the day.

As it transpired, she needed that resolve, for by evening when she was changing to go out, she felt hot and nauseated, with a pounding heart and a sore throat to go with her appalling headache. To her intense embarrassment she had to take Hubert's arm when they descended from the bus at Lincoln Centre, for a sudden sick dizziness assailed her.

He asked, with genuine concern for her, "Are you sure you're all right to go? You look awfully flushed..."

"Hubert," she averred, "I wouldn't miss this if I was dying!"

The Metropolitan Opera and *La Traviata* itself more than lived up to Hanne's expectations. There were no adjectives left in her repertoire to describe the effect Carlo Paoli had on the entire audience and on her especially. His voice left her amazed, stunned at its beauty, its quality, its power to excite her.

As the evening continued, Hanne's throat hurt her so painfully she was afraid it might be closing. At the first intermission when Hubert asked her if she would like a stroll with him in the lobby, she had only a croak left with which to reply, "No, thank you, I'll wait here for you." During the second intermission she had only a whisper with which to agree with Hubert's enthusiastic praise of the music; during the third intermission she could only nod her head gingerly, so hot and dizzy and ill did she feel.

During the last act Hanne began to see distortions, hallucinations as though the singers on stage were wired puppets being moved back and forth between the stage and her seat. But where were their wires? Why couldn't she see them? What were the performers swinging back and forth on? She wanted to ask Hubert, but her throat was too sore for even a whisper.

Her head felt light, then heavy, as she watched Carlo Paoli reach out over and over again towards her. He swung across the theatre to hover in the air just above her, then moved back to the stage, always in this position of entreaty. She wondered what he wanted of her, why he kept stretching his arms out towards her.

Her throat was afire, resonating with the music and with its own pain. The auditorium throbbed and pulsed around her, now thrilling, now fearsome, now menacing. Paoli stretched out a hand, and pointed it at her throat. Then Hanne realized what it was he wanted. She felt her throat, her vocal cords, her neck tear themselves bloodlessly from her body, and she saw them float unattached towards the stage, swathed in her misty ivory scarf. Hanne wanted to put up her hand, to feel what there was in the place of her throat, of her neck, holding up her head. But she found herself unable to move.

Her body ached terribly, yet at the same time felt exceedingly light. Were the lights flickering, she wondered? She watched in fascination as her throat, still prettily wrapped in the scarf, floated within reach of Carlo Paoli. He was singing, his arms outstretched towards this floating object, and when he was able to grasp it, he embraced it against the base of his throat with crossed hands. As Hanne watched, the neck in its diaphanous wrapping disappeared, somehow incorporated into the being of Carlo Paoli. He uttered an exquisite soft high note, the most lovely of sounds in an evening filled with beautiful sounds. Afterwards he finished the last scene, his tragic notes coloured even more heart-rendingly than before.

Of course, thought Hanne. Of course. He has my voice now.

Thunderous applause broke around her. She turned to look at Hubert, to see whether he had noticed that Carlo Paoli had taken her throat, had taken her voice. But Hubert was applauding enthusiastically, and Hanne could see his smiling mouth working as he turned to her, although she could not hear his words. She realized that she was not applauding, could not applaud, could not move her hands. Then, quite abruptly, she needed to stand up; she made an immense effort, as the grand auditorium of the Metropolitan Opera whirled more and more quickly around her.

She awakened some time later in a hospital bed. She was alone in the room. She found a summons bell pinned to her sheet, and when she pulled her wits together sufficiently to ring it, she was greeted by a masked nurse, who in response to her questioning, told her she had diphtheria, and that she had been in hospital for five days.

Hanne was hospitalized for three months. Hubert sent her a beautiful bouquet of a dozen yellow roses with a thank-you note, then two get-well cards, and then a note saying how sorry he was that she was still so ill, as he would have liked her to come to a party given in honour of his forthcoming marriage to Ellie. He said he had tried repeatedly to come to see her but the hospital had not allowed her to have visitors. Then he sent her a small nosegay of violets with a note saying he was going back to the mid-west to live, as Ellie had decided she did not want to stay in New York. Hanne never heard from him again.

She felt a disappointment about that, as she lay for what

seemed unending time in her hospital bed. But it didn't really matter much. When she enquired about her illness, they told her she had come close to death, with a raging uncontrollable fever. But that didn't matter much either. Because she remembered very clearly her adventures during that time. She remembered that Carlo Paoli had taken her voice.

After the performance of *La Traviata*, she knew Carlo had come to her, still dressed in his costume from the last act. She knew he had stood beside her bed that night when the nurses were at their station and everybody else was asleep. He told her he had seen her in the audience, and that he knew she had come to help him by giving him her singing voice to add to his. He told her that sometimes he was afraid his top notes would crack, but that because her voice comprised such exceedingly high notes, if he could mix hers with his in one glorious instrument, he would never have problems with his top notes again.

So he had taken her voice. He said he was sorry and he hoped she didn't mind. When she asked him if she would still be able to sing, he looked sad and said of course not, how could she sing without her voice? Then he had kissed her and thanked her for her big sacrifice. He said he would repay her, that she would never regret what she had done for him. He said he loved her, and that one day he would send her a message to come again to him.

Hanne was never able to sing again after her recovery. But although she forgot many details surrounding her grave illness, she continued to remember the episode with her voice, her voice which she had given to Carlo Paoli. When she read of his remarkable ability to sing a full-voiced high D, she knew he was using her voice to sing it with. And she knew that they were one person, he and she, and that it was only a matter of time until they were truly together.

A matter of time. The twenty-two year old Hanne was prepared to wait forever for that destiny Carlo had promised her. She knew, mysteriously, that their time together was foreordained, but that perhaps she must wait years, maybe decades, for the moment to be absolutely right. Meanwhile, she reveled in the certainty that he thought of her, dreamed of her, longed for the time when finally they would be one.

Now, twenty-three years later, Hanne sat with her empty coffee cup, her candle almost burnt out. Empty ... burnt out ...

The breath-stopping pain stabbed low in her abdomen, deep in the centre of her, that pain which had begun when Carlo in the person of Smythe had thrust away her carefully hoarded virginity. But Carlo had loved her—surely he had loved her—hadn't he? All those years when she had listened and watched for the signals of his love, they were there, unmistakably there—weren't they? She knew for certain that he had taken her voice, that the glory he had attained was in part due to her. She had been so sure that one day they would be together in person. But now what could she believe, what should she believe?

Hanne shook her great ugly head with its cap of flame, and slowly lowered it onto her arms. Her bony shoulders heaved, and she wept.

"Oh, won't someone help me ..."

And as she wept, all unbidden there came to her the memory of Antonio Amato.

It was not Amato to whom she had given her voice. But

surely, surely he had been singing to her when he sang *Che Gelida Manina* just before she met him? And the photograph on his latest CD, the one where he looked off into space so wistfully, surely he was looking at a vision of her, wondering when they might meet again, wasn't he? Wasn't he?

When? Where? Should she meet Antonio Amato once again?

Such pain ... such confusion ... what to do?

And then a great sob; "Carlo! Oh my love, my darling, my Carlo!"

Eighteen

The morning after their surprise anniversary celebration at the Rainbow Room, Jen lay in bed, in what she privately thought of as the envelope of Tony. His long hard legs were folded closely behind hers, his broad chest rested against her back, (all operatic tenors have chests like barrels, her mother long ago pointed out to her), and his left arm lay heavily across her shoulder. She could hear his breathing, deep and regular, as the strident alarm in their small white radio started to buzz.

She reached quickly over to the bedside table to switch the alarm off. She had set it to awaken her at five a.m., so she could pack and they could arrive at Kennedy Airport without rushing, in time to catch the nine-thirty Concorde to Paris. This would mean that Tony could be at rehearsals by Tuesday, only one day late.

Tony's breathing continued, rhythmic and unchanged, after the sound from the alarm was cut off.

Jen, luxuriating in the warmth of her husband's embrace, decided she would lie there for five more minutes, and then get up quietly so as not to waken him. How heavenly it would be to have him here every night of her life. Pointless to think of that, of course; it just made her feel sorry for herself, but when he was here she felt so safe... She closed her eyes, drifting. She mustn't let herself fall asleep.

Some time later, there was a firm knock on the bedroom door. Jen opened one eye, and groggily mumbled, "Yes? What is it?"

Nanny Burns, in her determinedly almost-upper-class British accent, called out, "I'm so sorry to disturb you, Mrs Amato, but what time is your plane? I understood you to say you were leaving early this morning."

"We are, Mrs Burns, what time is it?"

"It's eight o'clock, Mrs Amato."

Quickly Jen sat up in bed and looked at the clock radio. Tony sighed and turned away, then turned back towards her, opened his eyes and smiled the little-boy smile that had so charmed Jen the first time it had been directed at her. And just about each time since, she thought with rueful fondness.

Like most performers whose major work is done in the evenings, Tony awakened slowly, cheerful but never at his most alert first thing in the morning. He reached out for her and tried to pull her down to him. She resisted.

"Tony, I'm so sorry, I turned the alarm off and was going to get right up and pack, and now ..."

He understood the unspoken phrase by the stricken expression on Jen's face. "*Dio*, what is the time?"

"Eight o'clock."

"Can we make it to Kennedy? No, it is not possible, not in the morning traffic. *Il diavolo!*"

"Oh, Tony, I'm so sorry. This is the last thing I wanted to do to you."

She waited for his usual sharp explosion of temper. Always quick, always over equally fast. But it didn't come. He simply lay back against the pillows and considered her appraisingly.

She looked remorseful, on the verge of tears, her tousled blonde hair and small features giving her the look of a naughty child who has just been caught out. He smiled indulgently, his turn now to treat her like a contrite child.

"*Cara mia*, I will pardon you, on one condition ... since we have missed the plane, maybe we could ..." and he again tried to pull her down to him.

This time, she didn't resist. She only said, "You're incredible, you know that? Most husbands would throw a first class tantrum if their wives made a mistake like this."

He said, his mouth against her cheek, "Most husbands, how do you know what most husbands do? I am the only husband you ever had. And I better be the only one ever. What should I do without you?"

Jen kissed him, at first tenderly and then with an increasingly devouring passion. "You don't have to worry, my darling daft tenor, you'd be a totally impossible act to follow."

"Why are you talking now about acting?"

"Shush, Tony love, I'll tell you later..."

But somehow it remained unexplained.

Much later that morning, Tony telephoned to ask his

secretary to rebook flights to Paris and to contact Maestro Sheldon Wasserman, the conductor of *Otello,* so Tony could explain that he would be an extra day late arriving.

By noon Tony was sitting in his untidy book-strewn study with Anton, who was investigating the board game called Spy which Tony had brought for him from London. Tempting odours from a pasta casserole wafted through the apartment. The phone rang, and when Tony picked it up, Sheldon Wasserman's assistant asked for Mr Amato.

"Eustace, is me speaking. You are well I hope? Can you answer me yes or no, is Wasserman very angry?"

"Definitely yes, Mr Amato."

"*Dio!* Is this a good time to talk to him? He has had his supper? I will maybe be able to calm him down?"

"Seeing that it's you, Mr Amato," Eustace said, "there's hope. He's right here, I'll put him on."

"Okay, Eustace, grazie."

The conversation began acridly. But Tony had an advantage, that of being skilled at seeing other points of view. He honed his acting skills by observation, by trying to enter the psyches of others to see life from their perspectives, and to learn for future use the body-language and facial expressions with which they portrayed these outlooks. So he understood and empathized with Wasserman's agitation; already the rehearsal time was short, Tony was a debuting *Otello,* and reputations were on the line, enhanced or diminished by Tony's performance. By the end of the telephone conversation Wasserman was somewhat mollified, and Tony was more relaxed.

Jen called out from the kitchen, where she had been able to

hear Tony's part of the conversation, "Is Wasserman likely to survive?"

"Maybe. But it is a near thing. He is wishing probably he could fire me."

Jen came into the study, wiping her hands on a small red and white dishtowel. "Don't be ridiculous, Tony. Your *Otello* is the biggest thing at the Paris Opera this year. You'll enhance even Wasserman's reputation."

"Is what he is scared of."

Jen laughed. She sank into a chair, and picked up the *Arts Section* of the *Sunday New York Times*, which she had not read on Sunday as she usually did, because of chicken pox and anniversaries.

"I see Jamie MacTavish was in London for your *Fanciulla*. Do you think he follows Mia Mitsouros around? I get the feeling he writes one of those drooling reviews every time she emits a high C anywhere. Probably even in the shower."

"No, not in the shower. Not yet. But you are right, he likes Mia. Maybe he should make the application."

"Application? For what?"

"For to be her lover."

"What are you talking about? You have to make an application to be Mia's lover?"

"Well, it would make a long list, men who want to. MacTavish has to put in his name in advance."

"Tony, you're dreadful! I thought you liked Mia."

"I do, very much I like Mia. She is an interesting woman, she sings *molto bello*, maybe is my best soprano, but I have to call a shovel a shovel, you know."

"A spade a spade."

"What? What is the difference?"

"I don't know, Tony, I suppose it's idiomatic."

"I suppose it is idiotic, is what. Oh, speaking of Mia, have I said to you her English lord is still around, in London he was backstage every night and every matinee. He gives her a necklace, sapphires, diamonds, it is very beautiful. I tell her she should marry him, he seems a good fellow, and very much he is loving her."

"What does she say?"

"She says he is sort of married and anyway she cannot, because she loves me. Oh, and Luciano, and Jose; she says she loves all tenors."

"Must complicate her life."

"No, she is just talking."

Jen began to read MacTavish's review. Then she exclaimed, "Tony, this is terrible! What unscrupulous things to say."

"What now? MacTavish would not say a bad thing about Mia, and what is there to say bad about me? I sang fine in London, *Fanciulla* was good, everybody sang fine, what is his problem?"

"No, Tony, nothing bad about you, *per se*, it's about you and Carlo, and it's dreadful."

She handed the newspaper to Tony, who read the final paragraph with increasing dismay.

"So the operatic world waits eagerly for Mr Amato's first *Otello*, premiering at the Paris Opera's Palais Garnier in three weeks time. With the great American soprano Mia Mitsouros as his *Desdemona*, Amato will undoubtedly add Verdi's *grande oeuvre parmi ses oeuvres* to his list of sparkling triumphs.

"Amato has reached the top of the operatic world, stepping, one might say, into the breach slowly being vacated by Carlo Paoli. Paoli's increasingly strained top notes amply demonstrate the folly of pushing a medium-sized lyric voice too far into the dramatic repertoire. It is perhaps time that Mr Paoli took a well-earned rest from singing, in one of his several luxurious homes, in the hope that his voice might be restored to some of its former lustre. With Paoli on his wealthy way out, Amato's place is secure among the rarefied ranks of top tenors, of whom one can name perhaps ten in the entire world."

There was pain in every line of Tony's face as he said, "*Cielo,* if he had written so about me, I might never sing again. This is cruel, irresponsible. I will write to MacTavish; poor Carlo, this is too much to bear."

"You can't write a letter to a critic, not you, Tony, it just isn't done."

Tony looked distressed. "You are right. But this makes me very discomfortable. What should I do for Carlo? He is my friend, Jen. I could phone..."

"It's so difficult, Tony. What can you say to him? What can he say to you? Maybe you should just pretend you never saw the review. He must think you're in Europe and that I'm with you, so for him the likelihood is that you will never see this. Honestly, Tony, in your shoes I'd forget I ever saw it."

"I don't like it, Jen, but you are likely right."

Tony went thoughtfully back to his study, where Anton was now sitting on the floor cutting words from the front section of the *New York Times* and pasting them on a sheet of pale grey stationery. "Look, Daddy, I'm making my own game of Spy. You want to help me?"

"Why not?" said Tony, easing his tall frame onto the floor. He narrowly missed crushing a tower he and Anton had made with a Meccano set, retrieved by Anton from Tony's childhood toy box the last time they had visited his parents in Italy. Athletic and limber, Tony sat cross-legged on the rug with ease, as he reached for the scissors and began the serious work of cutting and pasting words onto pieces of paper. Tony's note said, "DO NOT TRUST ANYONE".

Anton's note was more blunt; "YOU WILL BE DEAD SOON ".

Breathing heavily, Anton bent over his page, earnestly trying to get the words straight on the paper. His red Italian wool sweater and matching shirt, a gift sent from Tony's parents, separated from his jeans, and on the soft olive skin of his back Tony saw a cluster of rosy spots. He called Jen; surreptitiously they examined the spots together, and at the same time looked at one another and mouthed the word "chickenpox". Tony sighed. He and Jen went into the kitchen, out of earshot of Anton.

"You better stay, Jen," Tony said in a low voice. "You come to Paris next week, by then we will be sure he is all right."

"Oh Tony, I'm so sorry. What about you?"

"I am a big boy. I will be fine, not to worry."

"But last night?"

"Last night was last night. I was only tired. You know how sometimes I ... but now I have seen you, I will be fine, and I will be so busy in Paris. Is better you are here for Anton for a few days, I remember I had the chicken pox, I was his age, it was not fun. I will feel better if you stay."

And like all good actors you're a convincing liar even though you don't like lies, Tony darling, Jen thought. But all the same she was grateful to him for not giving her more pain than she already felt about not going with him tomorrow.

Nineteen

At nine that evening, as Jen and Tony were finishing a late supper of poached salmon, wild rice with pine nuts and caesar salad, the telephone rang the special double ring that told them their call was from the lobby. When Tony answered, Joseph the doorman told him Carlo Paoli was downstairs and wanted to know if he could come up. Tony looked at Jen with surprise, and said to her "Carlo is downstairs, he wants to visit us, is odd, it is the first time he drops down." At her nod, he told Joseph to send Carlo up.

"In, in, Tony."

"In in what?"

"Drops in, not drops down."

"Never will I get it right this idiomatic idiotic language!"

Tony waited in his open apartment doorway as the elevator door slid open to disgorge an unusually disheveled Carlo. His red silk paisley tie was askew, and the row of buttons on his navy Burberry raincoat was pulled asymmetrically across his ample front.

"God, Tony, I'm glad you're in. I was just going for a stroll when some crazy redhead accosted me, I haven't figured out whether she loves me or hates me but she really manhandled me, look at me! This'll teach me not to go for a walk without my aide. But with him the walk kind of loses its charm. Fucking fans. 'Scuse me, Jen."

"*Cielo*, Carlo, come in, is good to see you, nice you should drop in, how do you know we are here?"

"I didn't—I just took a chance. I would have come into your building anyway, anything to get away from that woman, so if you hadn't been here I might have ended up visiting your housekeeper—if you have one, that is."

Carlo hung his coat in the vestibule and they went down the marble-floored hallway into the living room.

"You sit down, Carlo, you relax. You like a drink, Scotch on the rocks, yes? We don't have a housekeeper but we have a nanny. She would be happy to meet you. She likes your voice better than mine, I think; she plays many tapes of you."

Tony, Jen, and Carlo settled themselves on the comfortable pillows of the rose and ivory living room chairs.

"A prophet without fame in his own country, that's you, Tony."

"If you say it, Carlo, it must be true. So! You are looking tired, are you okay? How is the life?"

Carlo scowled. "The life is lousy at the moment. I was just reading the paper ..." (Jen glanced uneasily at Tony) "and then I decided it would be a nice day for a walk. I hadn't gone two blocks when I realize somebody is following me. When I turn around I see this wild-looking woman. She catches up and walks along beside me, by this time I'm at the end of your block, Tony. Then all of a sudden she jumps at me and grabs my arm and starts saying things like she's always loved me and do I love her, sounds like a bunch of crazy stuff to me."

Carlo took a long drink of his Scotch. "I'm trying to talk to her, trying to get her to calm down, but she just grabs my tie and talks louder and louder, finally I'm thinking I'd better go into one of these buildings, that'll get rid of her. So since I was at your building, I kind of shook her loose and came in."

"Sometime I have such troubles too. What does she look like, this woman?"

"Tall ugly woman, bright red hair."

"Red hair? Where I have seen such a woman?"

"You're thinking of that woman who was outside Carlo's apartment building," Jen reminded him. "It was the night we saw your Caruso *Aida* score, Carlo. She scared me, she was so persistent."

"I remember," reflected Tony. "I say to you she looks like she should be hired to play a witch in *Macbeth*. You say be quiet, not to hurt her feelings. They are peculiar, fans like that, I have also some, they sometimes hang around the door here, don't people have something else to do?"

"Speaking of something else to do, how come you're here, Tony? Shouldn't you be in Paris?"

"Yes, but I have come back for our wedding anniversary on Sunday, and then I missed the plane today. Tomorrow I go."

Carlo gulped the rest of his drink down quickly and Tony poured him another. He asked Carlo, "So, how did your recording of *Traviata* go last week?"

"Well, that's another thing, Tony, that bloody Wasserman, have you had any trouble with him?"

"How are you meaning, trouble? He is always very cautious with me, is Wasserman, I mean with my voice, for example he thinks I should not be singing *Otello* yet. Why he makes this his business I do not know, but I tell you, Carlo, he thinks I will ruin the voice but he does not back out from conducting my *Otello*. So. What kind of trouble do you have?"

"Not that, I don't consider that trouble, I mean, Wasserman's cautious with everybody. He conducted my first *Radames*, and he didn't think I should be going into that heavy a role with my type of voice, and who knows, maybe he was right. These days I ..." Carlo stopped, and drained his drink in one long gulp. "He's right that you shouldn't sing *Otello* yet, Tony. We've had this conversation already."

"No, Carlo, don't tell him that," Jen interceded quickly. "Tony knows his voice, and the decision is made. It will be all right, we're sure of it. So—"

"So back off? You're too damn polite, Jen. Don't you ever get mad?"

Tony looked at Jen and they both burst out laughing, a secret shared.

"She is lots more fire than she looks, I tell you, Carlo! But you are saying about Wasserman, what kind of trouble do you have with him? Mostly I enjoy to work with him, he handles the operatic voices with much consideration."

"Oh yeah, there's always that of course. No, it's the other thing."

"What other thing?"

"Well, he's homosexual, as you know."

Tony was puzzled. "I know, but how should that make you the trouble, Carlo? Wasserman is not interested in you in this way."

"You wouldn't think so, would you, but eight years ago, when he conducted my first *Aida*, which was the first time we worked together ... funny, you'd think our paths would have crossed before ..."

"Go on," said Tony, staring fixedly at Carlo, a question taking form in his imagination.

"Maybe I shouldn't be telling you this, but Wasserman makes me so damn mad; anyway, you're not going to repeat this, not that he didn't make gossip at the time acting like he did. I gather you never heard anything?"

"Eight years ago I sing mostly in Europe, I don't hear always the gossip from America."

"Ah. Well, when I started rehearsing with Wasserman, he and Sir Mallory Mancroft had been together for years, you know Mancroft, that rude sonofabitch, the one who hates tenors. Hey!"

Carlo, not usually—in Tony's opinion—one to make brilliant connections, stopped, a possible enlightenment dawning. "I never even thought, maybe he hates tenors because of me!"

Carlo stared pointedly into his second empty glass. Tony refilled it with less Scotch, more ice.

"Anyway, Wasserman stares at me all through the first rehearsals, and then he starts being nicer to me than to any of the other singers. You know how he usually is, careful with the voices but tough, tough. Except with me he was kind and gentle;

we all noticed it, and wondered. I thought, it's because he's concerned about me going into the heavier repertoire and he doesn't want me upset. More fool me."

Carlo ran a plump finger around the rim of his glass. "One night Wasserman asks me to have dinner with him, just the two of us at the Russian Tea Room, and there, would you believe it, he comes on to me. Me! I could hardly believe it. I mean, I had divorced Ilona and married Diana and God knows there was enough publicity about it all; where would Wasserman get the idea I would consider his kind of liaison?"

"I hate to tell you this, Carlo," interjected Jen, "but there was some talk about you at one point. I found it difficult to believe at the time and now I know you better, I realize it was just a lot of unfounded gossip. But maybe Wasserman believed it, and let's be fair, Carlo, you are an unusually handsome man."

Carlo preened. "So Wasserman kept telling me. He kept saying how I reminded him of some old friend of his. Anyway, I thought he'd stop once I'd said no, usually that's what happens, isn't it? But he didn't. He kept at me and at me, until he broke down and cried one day when we were having a piano rehearsal alone together. Can you imagine that uptight Englishman crying?"

Jen shook her head.

"I couldn't deal with it," Carlo said. "I told him where to get off, and I walked out of the rehearsal. Then Wasserman got mad as hell. Anything he could do to humiliate me, especially in public, he did. Except every once in a while he would phone and beg me to reconsider, and sometimes he'd even cry on the phone. It's all so damn disagreeable."

"So why did you say you would do the *Traviata* recording with him?"

"Tell me how to avoid working with Wasserman. Could you avoid him, in my shoes?"

Tony was silent, taking in fully the realization that Carlo was the tenor Sir Mallory Mancroft had talked about with such bitterness.

"Well? Could you?"

"O, *mi scusi*, Carlo. No, we could not avoid to work with him, he is on the top of the music world. So you say you have trouble again last week with him?"

"Yeah. He's getting worse with me. Seems like I couldn't do anything right for him in the recording sessions, he criticized nearly every note I sang. No-one can be more sarcastic than Wasserman. I know, I know, it takes one to know one. But in these sessions even the orchestra was squirming. I nearly walked out, except I didn't want a legal hassle over my contract. What a week. How do they expect me to sing well with all this tension, for Godssake?" Carlo sprawled in the soft chair, larger than life, with a larger than life dismay on his face. He opened his mouth, but no words emerged. Then he muttered, "Tony, did you see the *Arts Section* of this week's *Sunday Times*? I didn't get to it till today."

"I have seen it, Carlo, *Dio*, MacTavish is crazy, it is irresponsible, such writing..."

Carlo continued, "I never usually read reviews about me; I mean, what's the point? You do your best but if the voice doesn't respond, you know it; you don't need some damn critic to tell you. But I thought this was a review of your *Fanciulla* and I get a charge out of the way MacTavish oozes flattery every time our Mia gargles, but that last paragraph, my God, Tony, what am I supposed to do? I can't believe it's that bad, I'll grant you I've had a bit of trouble lately but ... " Carlo leaned forward and put his head in his hands.

Jen and Tony exchanged a quick, distressed glance. Carlo finally looked up and, seeing his hosts' anxious faces, he said, "Don't worry, I'll be okay. I'm just having a lousy day, is all."

He sighed heavily and stared with distaste at his almost empty glass of Scotch. "Of course it's those bloody phone calls, Tony, and those letters. I'm sure all that tension is causing my vocal problems. I wish I could get the police to do something. But they still think it's either a harmless fan getting his jollies this way, or a friend's practical joke."

"What kind of cruel friend would do such a thing, Carlo?"

Carlo shrugged. "No doubt you heard I got shot at last week. The cops said it's a bunch of hopped up types joy-riding but I'm sure I'm the real target. I saw somebody across the street who looked suspicious, just seconds before the shooting, but the cops won't even listen to me. Maybe whoever it was that shot at me organized the other shooting—the kids in the car—to cover up that they were really shooting at me."

Carlo rubbed his forehead and covered his eyes with his hand. After a moment he continued. "Or is all this making me crazy? Am I getting paranoid? And ... and then just to top everything off that MacTavish wrote this review ... oh God."

Jen and Tony exchanged a glance of acute misery. Tony launched into an embarrassed tirade against MacTavish, his English deteriorating rapidly as his passion rose.

"If they would write such a review about me, I would not be able to sing, so much I would be upset. What is he trying to do, MacTavish? If he wrote on some soprano I would understand. Because he is so crazy for Mia he maybe thinks destroying her competition will get him in Mia's bed. He is wrong, Mia sleeps with only who she wants. I don't know why I am telling you this, Carlo; you know all about Mia. But why should MacTavish write so about you and me? What is my career having to do with yours? Is nothing he can want from me, what can he want from you? You did not fight with him, no?"

"Not at all. Any conversations I've had with MacTavish have been pleasant enough, but there haven't been many. I thought he was reasonably fair as critics go, except of course over Mia. Funny actually, the way he writes about Mia, like you I figure he has a crush on her, except he seems such an asexual fellow."

"Maybe he finds out about you and Mia, maybe he is jealous?"

Carlo shook his big head slowly. "It's not possible. Mia and I are old news; we've been more or less finished for years. Mia and I are friends, we always will be, I don't think she makes enemies. Except for the odd soprano. No, I can't understand why MacTavish would write a thing like that about you and me. I mean, these days there aren't enough good tenors to go around anyway, why would a critic risk destroying the ones there are?"

"More fool he, Carlo," Jen said. "It's easy for me to say, but maybe you shouldn't take what he wrote so much to heart. You all get bad reviews once in a while; maybe MacTavish feels he has to show he's still able to be tough, to contrast with his delirious ravings about Mia."

Carlo mused morosely, a big man looking curiously shrunken. Tony admired Jen's ability to be supportive, to find something plausible with which to bolster Carlo's sinking morale in this impossible situation. And his perceptive Jen could well be right in her analysis of MacTavish's motives.

"You sure you didn't put MacTavish up to this, Tony?" Carlo suddenly blurted out.

"Carlo!" Jen flared. "How could you even think it? You should have seen how upset Tony was when he saw the review. I had to stop him from writing a letter to the *Times*, and he wanted to phone you right away; he's your friend, he thinks you're his, what kind of a friend are you if you can't trust him?"

Carlo bit his lip hard, as if to stifle words. A silence fell among them. Then Tony, distressed and uncomfortable with the souring atmosphere of this visit, had an inspiration.

"My antique dealer, he just found for me the cufflinks, they think Caruso wore these when he got off the ship coming to America for the first time, there is a photograph ... You want to see them, Carlo? You feel so bad today, I will give them to you, it is a present, to bring you luck. I have faith in you that the voice is okay, maybe you take a little time off from the singing as soon as you can, you will be fine, I am sure of this."

Carlo shook his great head in disbelief. "You're something else, Tony. I won't take your cufflinks, though I'm tempted! But let me see them just the same."

The two men walked down the hallway to the constantly untidy study. Carlo stood waiting by the massive, well-used oak desk, while Tony opened the antique curio cabinet which over the years he was slowly filling with Caruso memorabilia. He took out a small black jewel box, the corners slightly worn, and opened it worshipfully to show the intricately scrolled Italian gold cufflinks inside.

Carlo reached towards the box, Tony let go of it, and it fell, the cufflinks scattering and coming to rest under the desk. Carlo bent down to retrieve them, grasped one, then knelt to seek the other which had bounced further under the desk. He scooped his hand across the rug under the desk, retrieving the cufflink. Still on his knees, he examined it admiringly, and noticed that a bit of paper had stuck to his hand. He looked more closely. It was a word, "Danger," cut from a newspaper. He bent down lower to look under the desk.

Tony stood beside him, waiting to take the cufflinks and replace them in their case. But Carlo, on his knees with his head down almost to the rug, was scrabbling about with his arm under the desk, and when finally he stood up, he had two sheets of grey stationery in his hand. Glued on the sheets were messages made up of words cut from a newspaper. One message said, "DO NOT TRUST ANYONE", and the other read, "YOU WILL BE DEAD SOON".

Carlo's face was ominously flushed. "Goddam you all to hell, Tony, you ... you ... I knew it was another tenor, I knew it!"

He dropped the notes on the desk and swung surprisingly fast with his huge clenched fist. Tony, younger and faster, avoided the first blow and blocked the second. Carlo backed into the desk, knocking over an antique Tiffany desk lamp which missed falling on the carpet and hit the oak floor, with a crash of breaking glass.

"Tony? Are you ... what's going on?" called Jen as an overturned chair hit the floor. She appeared in the doorway to see Carlo flailing furiously while Tony, still unwilling to hit his friend, tried to block the heavyweight Carlo's blows. Carlo had backed him against the wall, dislodging a large watercolour of Jen's which hung absurdly crooked.

Jen did not hesitate. Grabbing one of Carlo's arms, she levered herself between the two men. This was not as brave as it looked; she was quite sure Carlo would not hit her, however terrible his reputed temper and however angry he was—at what?

Carlo lowered his arms, breathing heavily. "For Chrissake Jen, get out of my way. I'm going to kill him!"

He tried to shake her loose but by now she was holding onto both his arms, her entire weight against him.

"Carlo, Carlo, stop it, what are you talking about? Kill Tony? Why? He's your friend!"

"Not ... any ... more."

Carlo spread his arms and Jen could restrain him no longer. " Move, Jen, I'm going to kill him."

"Move, Jen," panted Tony. "This is between Carlo and me."

Tony tried to push her out of the way but she stood firm, understanding only one thing, that Carlo was angry enough to murder Tony, and that she was going to stop him.

"First you'll have to kill me, Carlo. What is this? What happened?"

Breathing heavily, Carlo stared malevolently at Tony. "Bugger you, Tony. I've got a better way to get you. You won't get away with this. I'll ruin you. I'll bloody sue you down the drain. I can't wait to tell the police I've found out who's writing these letters. You get such great press all the time. Just wait till the media hear about this. You think your public will accept such a thing from dear Saint Antonio? The world's love affair with you is about to end. I'll make you box office poison. Just watch me."

"Carlo," asked Jen, utterly bewildered, "What are you talking about?"

"You see those?" Carlo grabbed the two sheets of grey stationery with their fatally damning words cut out from a newspaper. "They're identical to the ones I've been getting. Don't you remember, Jen? You were there the night I showed the first ones to you and Tony, more fool me..."

"But Carlo, at your apartment I answered the phone, remember?" Tony said wildly. "How can it be me making the threats when it is me who gets that phone call? I cannot phone myself and answer too."

"Yeah, Tony, yeah, I do remember. I wonder how ... you fucking sonofabitch, how did you do that? Come to think of it I only have your word for it that whoever was on the phone was threatening me. And ... and anyway how do I know you didn't hire somebody to phone and make those threats? Hell, that wouldn't be hard to do, you just tell somebody you want to play a practical joke, you bastard, how could you do this to me?"

"But I don't do it to you! You have known me so long a time, how can you believe I would treat a friend so?"

"Easy, easy, you bastard, you're not explaining away these notes very fast. All you can say is you didn't do it. Think fast, think fast, how you gonna explain these?"

He waved the offending papers in Tony's face.

"Carlo, this is only a game I am playing with Anton! Is a game called Spy, a children's game, I will show you; when you see, you will understand and you will be sorry, you will apologize."

In deep and measured tones Carlo replied, "I? Apologize? Are you crazy? Do you think I'm so naive I believe you? Oh no, Tony, no way. Spy, for Chrissake. Show me your stupid game, do whatever makes you happy, but don't expect me to believe you. You have too good a motive for wanting me out of the way, even MacTavish sees that. If I'm not singing any more, your place in tenor ranks is secure. That's what he said, wasn't it? Without my D, your high C sounds great. Sure, Tony, sure, Spy, my ass. I'm going to ruin you."

"You think I am so stupid I make these letters to send you and I invite you into the room where you can see them?"

"They were under the desk. The desk is pretty low to the ground. Almost no risk I would see them. You're guilty as hell, Tony. No way you can get out of this one."

Jen said, common sense coming to the fore, "But Carlo, just ask Anton. He'll tell you himself what he and Tony were doing."

"Only if I can get to him before you can coach—"

Carlo snatched the grey sheets of paper from the desk and charged down the hall to Anton's bedroom, with Tony and Jen rushing behind him. Carlo thrust open the door of the boy's room. The hall light illuminated Anton, asleep, his face flushed with the feverish beginnings of chicken pox. His dark curls were wet with perspiration, and his head moved from side to side on the pillow as he muttered in a nightmare, "No, run, Daddy, run..."

Carlo grabbed Anton's shoulder and shook him roughly, saying, "You! Anton! Tell me the truth now! Did you..."

Tony struck Carlo full force with his body, dislodging his hand from Anton's shoulder. Anton opened his eyes and stared, frightened but not wholly awake, not wholly grasping reality.

"*You ... don't ... touch ... my ... son ... ever!*" Tony stood now beside the bed, one arm around the shoulders of his son, who was sitting up, utterly bewildered.

Carlo waved the grey sheets of paper at Anton, his voice getting louder with each word. "Did you make these? Did you and your Dad make these, as some kind of goofy game? Don't you dare lie to me, tell me the truth!"

Anton, feverish and frightened by the animosity swirling about him, shrank against his father. "Daddy, daddy, what does Mr Paoli want?"

"I want you to tell me if you made these papers!"

Anton burst into tears. "What do you want me to say, Daddy?"

Carlo looked triumphant. "There's my answer, Tony. He won't tell me the truth, he'll only say what you want him to say. Right, you little brat?"

Anton began to sob wildly. Nanny Burns flung open the other door into the bedroom, disheveled grey hair matching her hastily tied wool worsted dressing gown. "What on earth?"

Tony, breathing hard, said in a tight voice, "You get out, Carlo, before I do something I am sorry for. You have no right ... Anton is just a child, he is sick; you get out. I tell you I don't send the letters, if we are not good friends enough so you trust me, I don't want this friendship. You go, before I lose ..."

Jen put a restraining hand on Tony's arm. "You'd better go, Carlo," she said urgently, forcing her voice to be calm. She knew Tony well. His imperfectly controlled rage was about to explode.

Carlo looked down at the still weeping Anton. "They should punish you, kid, for not telling me the truth when I asked for it. Oh well, you poor little beggar, I guess having Antonio Amato for a father is punishment enough."

Tony took a quick step towards Carlo. Carlo backed away fast, then turned and ran down the hall and out the door, not even taking time to collect his coat, as Jen caught Tony's arm in what she hoped was a restraining grip. She said, "Let it be, Tony, let it be, he'll get over it."

Tony, white-faced and panting, did not reply.

Twenty

Carlo snarled at Joseph the doorman to get him a cab. In his fury he forgot to tip, an omission which only served to reinforce Joseph's opinion that Antonio Amato was not only the best tenor but also one of the best human beings around.

Carlo directed the cab driver to take him to his apartment, where he ordered the driver to wait. Carlo strode to the elevator.

"Can't you see I want to go up? Get in here and do your job, don't hang about the lobby for Godssake," snapped Carlo at the second attendant. The doorman raised his eyes imperceptibly heavenwards at his colleague, and hurried to the elevator to attend to Carlo. Carlo was unaware that he was impatiently humming a Mozart aria as the elevator crawled upwards.

Once in his apartment Carlo stomped to his study. From the desk drawer he snatched out his few threatening letters and slammed the drawer shut. There was no risk that his noisy foray might awaken Diana; two days after he had discovered her birth control pills, she had decided to visit her elderly parents in Boston for a while. Good riddance, he had thought furiously when he had found her note telling him where he could find her. So far, his desire to do so was minimal.

Back in the cab, Carlo directed the driver to go to the closest police precinct.

If I'm lucky, he thought, I can get charges laid right now, tonight. I hope I can talk to that ass Donlevy. I'll show him who's got the brains around here, that damn know-it-all.

Inside the dingy station, unusually noisy and busy for such a late hour, he learned from the young black policeman on the desk that Sergeant Donlevy had left for the day. This was scarcely surprising, since it was now nearly midnight.

"I am Carlo Paoli," Carlo said, drawing himself up to his imposing height, "and I must see Sergeant Donlevy right now. This is very important, it's an ongoing case, and he needs to know I've solved it and who the culprit is. Tell him I need to talk to him immediately." Carlo paused, realizing the officer being addressed looked skeptical. "You do know who I am of course? I want action—now!"

The policeman at the desk looked acutely uncomfortable. He was about to reply when Carlo continued loudly. "Can I talk to someone who knows something? Right now!"

The young officer hastily summoned his superior, who had some notion of the importance (or at least self-importance) of this noisy complainant. He had enough experience to sense the yeast of trouble starting to work. He told his young colleague to call Sergeant Donlevy.

After what seemed to Carlo an insultingly long time,

Donlevy appeared. His expression was anything but agreeable; he had endured an unusually difficult day, even for a New York City police sergeant. He had looked forward to the evening with his family watching television, (cop shows were his favourites—the quintessential busman's holiday) and then going early to bed. He had not anticipated being interrupted in the middle of lively sex with his plump and pretty wife.

Now at the station he viewed Carlo Paoli with distaste. "Yes, Mr Paoli, what can I do for you that I couldn't have done just as well in the morning?"

"I want to speak to you privately. Can't we go into your office?" demanded Carlo.

With bad grace Donlevy led the way into his office. When they were seated in a small cubicle lit by one dangling green-shaded bulb, Carlo announced triumphantly, "Since you so-called detectives are incapable of detecting who is threatening me, I've done it myself. So, here's your solution, Sergeant Donlevy, if you happen to be interested. I did some serious analyzing," here Carlo preened at the delicious sound of this impromptu lie, "and I've found out these bloody letters were sent by a man I thought was my friend."

Carlo paused for effect.

Donlevy was uninterested in this theatrical timing. "Can we get on with it, Mr. Paoli?"

"Of course. The culprit is my so-called friend, Antonio Amato."

Sergeant Donlevy whistled in astonishment. "Are you sure? He doesn't seem the type, if you believe what you read about him."

Carlo leaned forward in his chair. "He wants to destroy me, that's the type he is. Now I want you to lay charges, I want you to throw the book at him."

"But ... but Mr. Paoli," said Donlevy, the grin slowly widening on his pleasant broad Irish face as he deduced that he had been right about this case all along, "obviously this is a joke."

"Joke? Joke? What are you talking about?"

"Come on, Mr. Paoli, you can't lay charges that easily. Everybody knows you and Antonio Amato are friends, obviously this is a practical joke. I admit it's a kinda bizarre sense of humour, but as you pointed out to me on several occasions, you're opera singers. I mean, no reason you guys can't like practical jokes same as anyone else, but you live in a kinda dramatic world, so likely your jokes would be more, how should I put it, theatrical than mine would be?"

"But—if you can't do anything, I'll—I'll go to a lawyer; I'll sue!"

"You haven't got a hope in hell, Mr. Paoli, believe me. Don't waste your time and money. You'll never find a lawyer who'll take you on. For a practical joke yet, for God's sake!" Donlevy laughed heartily. "Well, anyway, congratulations on your detective work. Now I'm going home to bed, I'm glad you've solved your problem, you don't have to worry any more, right? Have a good night's sleep; it's been interesting getting to know you."

....

Carlo spent a wretchedly restless night—the few sporadic hours of sleep he was able to catch punctuated by nightmares of masked figures chasing him with long sharp scissors. Finally he abandoned his marshmallow soft bed and staggered half asleep through the dark and silent apartment into his study. He sat heavily down at his desk and brooded inventively over his agenda for getting revenge.

The Manhattan morning traffic was already roaring many stories below his window before Carlo decided on his next step. He needed to do this wily bit of public relations on his own and not through his public relations people who might try to talk him out of it. Or would they? If he could publicize the malicious cruelty he believed was behind the sending of these letters, surely Tony's reputation would be damaged, and the enthusiasm he generated in the operatic world would be diminished. And that would be good public relations for Carlo, would it not?

If Saint Tony becomes a lot less popular than he is now, the sonofabitch, it would leave all the more room for me. I'll destroy that treacherous bugger, thought Carlo.

As soon as he thought there would be someone at work to answer his call, he dialed a number, ostentatiously announced his name, and asked for the editor of *People Magazine*. After Carlo had explained why he was calling, the editor promptly sent over a photographer and a journalist.

Carlo gave what he believed to be the juiciest short interview of his career. He was posed by the photographer against the backdrop of his impeccable study holding his menacing letters. Carlo stood with pride in front of his oak bookshelves with their leaded glass doors, not a book out of place. (One of the journalists to whom the picture was shown before publication commented that the books looked like they were bought by the yard, strictly for show. He was surprisingly close to the truth.)

Pleased with his tactics thus far, Carlo was totally unprepared for the tone of the item which appeared in the next edition of *People*, on a page devoted to news about the famous and/or talented. Under a flattering photo of Carlo, which showed him smiling slightly and holding the letters, was the headline, "Humour, Opera Style".

The item read, "Here's an interesting question; what kinds of practical jokes do opera singers play on each other? Tenor Antonio Amato recently played one on his friend and fellow tenor Carlo Paoli which almost backfired. Amato made threats in the form of anonymous phone calls and unsigned letters, which Paoli took seriously enough to report to the police. Just as Paoli was believing his life was in danger, Amato 'fessed up, and now everybody's laughing. We hope."

This was not at all what Carlo wanted; couldn't the journalists get anything straight? This business was far more serious than he had been able to make anyone understand so far. He would have to find another way of getting back at that sonofabitch Amato. Only, how?

He sat brooding in his quiet sitting room in the one comfortable armchair, drink of Scotch in hand, a larger than life man grappling with what he believed to be a larger than life problem.

Twenty-One

Jen had already awakened before the alarm went off at five. She turned to look at Tony, at last deeply asleep. Reluctantly she put her arm over him, and whispered, in an attempt at lightness, the English pubkeepers' end of the evening pronouncement. "Time, gentlemen!"

Tony opened his eyes, blinked hard several times, and shook his head quickly in an urgent attempt to wake up.

"Have I slept?" he asked hoarsely. "It can't be time to go yet."

"I don't know whether you've slept, love, but it is, unfortunately."

Jen's heart constricted as Tony turned on the light and she saw his face more clearly. Deep lines of fatigue were etched around his eyes and mouth, and she had a premonition of what he would look like as an old man; if, she thought, he survived the murderous pace of opera superstardom long enough to grow old.

Jean Dell

They had talked for a good part of the night. Jen was intensely concerned about what this episode with the furiously threatening Carlo would do to Tony. Would he, facing the enormous challenges of preparing his new role, be able to retain his hard-won emotional equilibrium if Carlo carried out his threats? Tony's creed, so obviously different from Carlo's, was never knowingly to hurt anyone, even when he might thereby gain an advantage. So she was determined to be cheerful for him this morning, especially since his next words were, "I have to prove to Carlo I would not do to him such a thing. This is not bearable, Jen."

"When did you decide that? I thought you were asleep."

"Not much—I am thinking, thinking, how to find who sends the letters?"

"Tony love, you have to put it all out of your mind and keep yourself in good shape for your *Otello*. A little misunderstanding with a friend isn't worth compromising that for."

"It is not so little, but you are right. Oh Jen— I will be happy when you come to Paris."

While Tony hastily showered and dressed, Jen scrambled eggs and made toast and coffee, but when he dashed into the kitchen to join her for breakfast, he toyed with his food and drank only half a cup of coffee.

"You're not sick, are you, Tony?"

He grinned, the little-boy grin that Jen—and how many others?—found so irresistible.

"Maybe a little bit sick, is not serious, I promise you. I can live on not so much sleep, you know how little, but—I cannot live with this Carlo business, Jen. He says he will ruin me but

223

surely he cannot do such a thing, can he?"

Jen reached across the table and mutely took his hand. Finally he said, "I know, I know, I am putting it out of my mind, right now."

Tony shrugged into his blazer, and, grabbing his navy trenchcoat, prepared to leave with a speed born of long practice. Jen was not far behind him. The limousine they had ordered was already waiting in front of the building, and Joseph, who had just come on duty, held the door for them.

"You going to Paris now, Mr Amato? I think it's wonderful that you're going to do *Otello*. Good luck, or rather Break a Leg."

"You know I cannot answer or I lose the luck," Tony said, smiling.

"Oh, I know, Mr Amato, these theatrical traditions are so interesting. Well, I'll be reading the reviews, I know they'll be wonderful, I hope you record it so my wife and I can hear it. See you soon, Mr Amato."

And it seemed like a very short time until Joseph was opening the door to an unusually somber Mrs Amato, back from Kennedy Airport by herself.

On the Concorde, Tony sat staring at the small window, seeing nothing, his psychic pain over Carlo's betrayal of their friendship transmuting itself until even his bones ached.

Twenty-Two

"**W**irginal, wirginal, Miss Mitsouros, how many times I haf to tell you?" stage director Otto Zimmer shouted above the rehearsal pianist's graceful accompaniment to the love duet.

Mia, in Tony's arms, looked at him and raised her eyes heavenwards. Under her breath she muttered, "Virginal, virginal, isn't he tiresome?"

"Vat? Vat you said, I haf not catched that, Miss Mitsouros," Zimmer lowered his voice, as the accompanist stopped his cadenza.

"I said I'm trying, Herr Zimmer."

"Vell, try harder, Miss Mitsouros."

Mia was rehearsing with Tony, conductor Sheldon Wasserman, Zimmer, and Georges the pianist in a high ceilinged, spacious rehearsal room on the second floor of the old Paris Opera House. Elegant molding on the ivory painted walls and graceful coving between walls and ceiling reminded them that this building was conceived before the era of the pre-cast concrete brick.

Through open windows they could hear the dull, persistent roar of traffic. For Tony's momentous premiere in the role of *Otello*, special galas had been planned, and it had been decided that the Palais Garnier, rather than Paris' new Opera House, would be the sumptuous venue for the five performances.

Maestro Sheldon Wasserman, very tall, stooped and wire-thin, leaned against a wall stroking his grey goatee. The great Austrian designer-director Otto Zimmer was an almost comic antithesis to Wasserman, being very short, relatively rotund, and with a fair, smooth complexion. Zimmer appeared as young, fresh, and naive as Wasserman appeared old, fragile and gentle. Both appearances were deceptive. The two men were perhaps ten years apart in age, still vigorous and at the summit of their professions. They had not arrived at these peaks by being either naive or gentle.

Wasserman said, "Shall we start the love scene again, Georges. Now, Mr Amato, if you please, I know you want to put your own stamp on *Otello*, but you don't need such tenderness that the audience will have to strain to hear you."

"Nobody complains before, Maestro," a jet-lagged Tony snapped, his mood as cutting as his headache. "Everyone is hearing me fine. There is nothing wrong with my projection. But I keep telling you, I see *Otello* very much tender and vulnerable, and I must do this with the voice as well as with the acting."

"Well of course if you had arrived in Paris when you were scheduled to, we would have all this ironed out by now, would we not, Mr Amato. All right, take it again from when you lie down beside *Desdemona*. Can we try for more *sostenuto* on the top please, Miss Mitsouros."

"And wirginal, not to forget please," urged Zimmer.

In the rehearsal room, plain wooden structures were stand-ins for the furniture that the singers would eventually use on stage. For the bed that would be used in an unusual staging of the love duet, there was a raised wooden platform padded with its usual layer of foam and the two layers of exercise mats which Mia had insisted on after the first day.

"Darlings, you can't expect me to rehearse lying down on that thin layer of foam, it's fine for Tony, he has some padding, don't you Tony love, but look at me! I'm all bones!"

The men in the room at the time had looked appreciatively at Mia, whose description of herself was accurate only in certain respects. What they had seen was a slender woman with an uncontrollable mass of curly dark brown hair, and round turquoise eyes which gave a perpetually surprised look to a face of unconventional beauty. It was no wonder that the diva Mia Mitsouros was regarded as one of the most splendid ornaments in the operatic world.

Tony, singing, gradually let himself down onto the "bed" beside Mia as directed. After a long period in which Tony felt his voice portraying exactly what he wanted of the emotions of the Moor, at a natural pause in the music Zimmer stopped them again.

"Please, Miss Mitsouros, wirgin!"

"But Herr Zimmer, I don't see her as innocent as all that. I see her as utterly faithful to *Otello* but very passionate."

"Be passionate wirgin then but be pure! Pure!"

Mia whispered in Tony's ear, "Passion I can do, but after two husbands and three children, I can't even remember virgin."

"You want to say something Miss Mitsouros," Zimmer expostulated, "please you speak up. Funny, your voice carries fine when you sing, how come all your projection you lose when you are talking? What did you say now?"

"I said, uh, I'll try to project virginity better."

Tony suddenly got up from the "bed", causing Wasserman to say, "No, Mr Amato, we're just continuing from where we were, starting with—"

"*Mi scusi, momento, mi scusi*," Tony muttered as he dashed out the door to take a painkiller. Like all opera singers he dreaded the advent of a headache, because when he sang with one, certain notes resonated so agonizingly in his head.

Zimmer looked questioningly at Mia. "What now? First he does not here come until two days after we need him and then he so our time wastes, every five minutes rushing off. We do not need this, such a nervous-wreck tenor."

Mia got up from the makeshift bed and went over to link her arm through Zimmer's. "Otto darling, Tony's not a nervous wreck tenor. You know that. There's no-one more professional than he is. You said yourself you were amazed at how fast he took your direction and remembered it. No, he'll be fine, I think he's not feeling well today, that's all."

"All? All? You hear that, Wasserman, now we haf a sick tenor. *Lieber Gott*, we do not for this haf the time. Next he will be wanting time away to recover."

"Oh no, not Amato," interceded Wasserman, a hard man but a fair one. "I've even known him to rehearse when he had a concussion from playing soccer; it was in Milan, I remember. Actually it was a highly impractical idea, because he passed out in the middle of the *Giulietta* act of the dress rehearsal of *Les Contes d'Hoffmann*. But I have to say in his defense he went on to sing the opera on opening night two days later, and he was superb. I wish I could say the same for the rest of us—we were wrecks thinking he might pass out again."

Wasserman smiled his odd, corners-of-the-mouth-turned-down smile, as Tony came back into the room.

Mia started to laugh. "I was *Giulietta*, do you remember, Maestro, and when Tony passed out he was singing lying more or less on top of me. They had an awful time getting him off me, he was absolutely out cold, and Tony's a big man. I thought I'd never breathe again!"

Tony, grinning, added, "I remember this, Mia, and on opening night when I am singing to you in the same position, you whisper to me if I am going to faint again, please to roll away first. You make me laugh, you almost spoil my aria, this aria always gets the most applause. Come to think, you do this to me often."

Laughter filled the rehearsal room. Then Wasserman, scrutinizing Tony, asked, "You all right, Mr Amato?"

"Fine, Maestro. Well, maybe not so fine, but soon I will be okay."

The rehearsal continued. At the end of the day, Zimmer apparently decided it was time for praise; he had been harsh enough earlier, but he seemed to think his principals were coming along very well.

"Miss Mitsouros, you are getting more wirginal, thank you

wery much. You haf the right kind of eyes for wirginal. And Mr Amato, you so quick, we haf not worked before together, but I know already before what a good actor you are, just I never believe you can be learning so quick and such a memory if I for myself haf not seen this. It is a pleasure to be directing you both."

Mia linked her arm through Tony's and said, "Come on Tony darling, let's have supper. You look exhausted; let's just go to our hotel coffee shop."

And she laughed mischievously, for the coffee shop was one of the most famous restaurants in all Paris, perhaps in all the world; the Grand Hotel's Cafe de la Paix.

"How come you are not eating with your English lord? He is here with you, no?"

"He was, but he had to go back to London for a meeting, he's chairman of Ridlo Consolidated Industries, you know?"

"Marry him, Mia. He can afford you."

"I keep telling you, he's sort of married. Anyway, I can afford myself! I don't need to marry for money; if I lost my voice tonight and could never sing another note, I'd be financially secure for the rest of my life. You too, I'm sure. Unless you spend it like it's going out of style."

"I would be fine too, I support my family, even without Jen's paintings. But what kind of talk is this, to lose the voice and never sing again? I don't want to think about when this happens."

"Then don't, Tony love. Neither of us needs to worry about that, not for a long time. And when it does happen, we can always teach. Anyway, you're right, let's not think about it."

By now they had crossed the nearly gridlocked street across which lay the Cafe de la Paix. From the entrance they were led by the *maitre d'hotel* through the ornately decorated restaurant to the corner table they had requested. Parisians and tourists sitting at the tables glanced up as they went by, and then stared with frank enjoyment at the spectacle of two of the opera world's superstars walking past them. One table of expensively dressed Americans even burst into applause as Tony and Mia passed their table. The singers rewarded these appreciative fans with their best stage smiles.

Once seated, Mia scanned the menu avidly, saying, "I'm starved, aren't you? I'm having the Steak Tartare, I'll have Salade Maison to start, what about you, Tony?"

Tony looked dispiritedly at the menu. "You don't mind, Mia, I am not so hungry. I will drink the mineral water, maybe Vichy Celestins."

"I say, you weren't kidding when you said you weren't feeling well. The only time I remember you ever stopping eating was when your wife was so ill and your poor little boy died— Tony darling, should you maybe see a doctor? I hate to say this to anyone because it never helps, but you do look awful."

Tony laughed. "Thank you, Mia, here I am thinking I am such a handsome fellow."

"Don't be an ass, Tony, you know what I mean. Is it—are you worried about this *Otello*? You mustn't, you know, your voice sounds wonderful. I think we're on our way to a major triumph. Did you see the last review by that MacTavish? He thinks we're on our way there too."

"That MacTavish, he is maybe in love with you, Mia?"

"I don't know—I can't figure him out, actually. His reviews of me are incredibly prejudiced, I mean he writes as though I am some sort of soprano absolute, *la soprano assoluta*, darling, but whenever I've met MacTavish, he's tongue-tied. He just stands there looking at me like I'm some fascinating specimen under his microscope. It's beyond me. But I won't look that gift horse in the mouth; he's such an influential critic."

"What do horses have to do with it?"

Mia, her mouth full, exploded with laughter. She patted away the ravages with her large white serviette. "I forget that sometimes the idiom escapes you, darling. It means if someone gives you a wonderful gift, don't question it, just accept it."

"Is difficult, English idioms, especially for an Italian."

"Don't complain, Tony darling. So many things are easy for an Italian."

Tony raised an eyebrow at her. "I did not know women can leer. But you are leering, Mia."

"Finally he recognizes it! I give you an E, for Excellent Effort So Far, Tony darling."

"What are you talking about? Why 'so far'?"

"Because we'll see what happens later."

Tony stared at her, and then shifted his gaze to the window and to the passing Parisian parade. He was silent for a disturbingly long time.

"Nothing happens later. Even if we want, nothing happens later, Mia."

"So you say, Tony darling. We'll see. Anyway, we've got other things to talk about. MacTavish's review, it was great for you and me, but what about for Carlo? Do you know if he saw it? You two are pretty good friends, except of course when you both try to win out on collecting the most Caruso memorabilia."

A shadow of concern flitted across Tony's face, not unnoticed by Mia. "Uh oh, what have I said, has he just beaten you out on something of Caruso's you really wanted?"

"No, not that, Mia, it is just that I … no, better we not talk about it." The pain in Tony's head was almost blinding him. No use worrying Mia about that. He felt for the bottle of painkillers which should have been in his pocket, but didn't seem to be. He'd go to the washroom and search further, or maybe the washroom attendant could give him something. He rose from the table. "*Mi scusi, momento*, I will be right back."

He quickly made his way through the restaurant and up the stairs to the Men's Room, brushing off a young woman who rose from her table intending to ask for an autograph. While she was complaining in astonishment to her parents that he wasn't as nice as the press made him out to be, Tony returned, stopped at the table and, smiling the famous smile, said, "*Mi scusi*, you want to say to me something?"

Beaming, the young woman told Tony how much she loved his latest CD of love songs, and held out the first available piece of paper, a menu, for Tony to autograph. Later she found herself in an argument with the maitre d'hotel, with regard to purchasing the signed menu, which she now considered hers. She won, and the framed menu now has pride of place on a wall in a frilly bedroom in Pittsburgh.

Tony wended his way through the room full of staring patrons, and sat down again opposite Mia, who was now devouring Peche Melba.

"Tony darling, what is going on? You seemed more or less okay, then I mention Carlo, and all of a sudden you turn even paler—I mean, you're looking lousy, darling—and rush off yet again. There's something going on here, and it's nothing to do with jet fatigue or *Otello*. Come on, darling, tell all to Mia!"

"You are too smart, Mia. I wish I could tell you, but it is confidential."

After a long reflective moment Mia slowly began to speak. "Darling, I know I have my faults, but haven't you noticed I have a lot of real friends? I don't mean just theatre friends. Do you think I keep them by being indiscreet? Have you ever heard me divulge anybody's secrets, even to you, and God knows you and I are good friends?"

Silence fell between them. Tony weighed his need for privacy with his need to share his burden. Without Jen to talk to, he found his fears about Carlo growing sickeningly. He made a decision. He had known Mia for a long time. He had no reason to imagine that he could not trust her discretion.

"You are right, Mia. Broadcasting secrets is not your thing. There! I got an idiom right!"

"So you did, Tony darling. But if it would help to tell me your troubles, for goodness sake talk to me. We've got to pull a triumph out of this *Otello*, and if you're going to be uptight and unwell, what happens to the voice?"

"Good question. You finally finished eating your supper? We will go upstairs, you come to my room, we will talk. I have a bottle of beautiful Napoleon Brandy, do us good, well, do me good, anyway."

So Mia and Tony found themselves sitting together on the

cherry red couch in Tony's glamourous suite at the Grand Hotel. They sipped brandy from huge etched snifters, the liqueur warming them both, but particularly Tony who had eaten very little for several days.

"You promise you don't tell anybody. This is not a happy story. Do you know about the anonymous phone calls and letters Carlo gets lately, they threaten—"

"Oh sure, everybody knows about those phone calls and letters; Carlo never stops talking about them these days. Knowing Carlo like I do, I've wondered if he wrote them himself to generate some publicity, except he's in such a state about them, and we do all get a few crazy letters. The media would have to run special sections just to list all that craziness, let alone print the contents. Anyway, what about it?"

"Carlo thinks I made the phone calls and wrote the letters."

"What? But what would give him such an outrageous idea? And what does he imagine your motive is?"

"I will tell you, Mia. It is an almost unbelievable story." Tony shook his head and ran his hand across his dark hair. "Carlo comes to my apartment in New York last Monday night. That day I play a board game called Spy with Anton, and after a while he wants to make his own game, so he cuts out words from the newspaper and glues them on writing paper. We make these threatening messages together."

For a moment Tony forgot why he was telling Mia this story, as he remembered his pleasure that afternoon with Anton. How lonely he was for his family whenever he was not with them. He had once hoped he would get used to the loneliness. A futile hope. Time, as he thought so often, time is the enemy.

Had he had any choice about his all-consuming career? Could he have stayed in one place, been a professor of music in a great university as his father was, had time to enjoy every aspect of family life, been present for his children's first words, their first steps?

He would have been there with Jen when she went into dangerous premature labour with Gianni, instead of being summoned urgently in mid-performance in San Francisco. He never would know that the stage-manager and Tony's aide had argued bitterly about whether to tell Tony immediately and risk ruining the opera, or to wait until Tony had sung the one remaining act. Tony's aide had won; Tony was told during the final intermission. Tony's aide had already organized Tony's immediate trip back to New York; a friend was readying his own private jet which would be serviced and ready to leave after the opera was scheduled to end. So, summoning his self-mastery and his fortitude, Tony agreed to continue singing the opera.

Tony had needed all his self-control to finish the last act of *Boheme,* at the end of which his stage beloved dies. He had always forced himself to ration his overpowering flood of emotion when performing, in order not to lose control over his singing technique. This night he came perilously close to losing it; his anguished cries over *Mimi's* dead body were altogether real. The San Francisco critics had raved about Amato's acting talent; they had not known how true his emotion was.

Immediately after the performance and with but one group curtain call, Tony flew back to New York, wondering despairingly whether Jen would still be alive when he arrived.

Now, Tony's conclusion was that he had never had a choice

of profession. Once he had understood the joy and inspiration he could give with his singing, personal considerations paled besides his need to give the voice to the world to which it belonged.

Mia, waiting for him to continue, cocked her head quizzically to one side. Tony emerged from his reverie and went on. "It was a happy time for me, those two days. We have not enough time with our children."

"No, unfortunately. It's the price of fame and fortune, Tony darling. But go on with your story. I think I see what's coming."

Tony told Mia about Carlo's arriving at his apartment disheveled and upset, and about their conversation regarding MacTavish's review. "Jen and I say to Carlo this review is so irresponsible, why should MacTavish do this?"

Mia was thoughtful. "A lot of people don't like Carlo, you know. He's not like you and Luciano and Jose and Placido, just about everybody loves you. But you know how Carlo is, he has that terrible temper, and he holds grudges, and I think he's made quite a few enemies along the way, what with one thing and another."

Tony remembered vividly how Carlo had given him no benefit of the doubt once he found the notes; not a moment had he allowed Tony for explanation. Once he suspected Tony, Carlo had immediately hit out like a furious child bursting into a tantrum.

"You are right. He is sometimes a hard man to keep a friendship going with. So Carlo finds the letters Anton and I made to go with the Spy game, on the same kind of paper as Carlo's letters, everybody has this grey paper, you can buy it anywhere. Then Carlo ..."

Tony paused, reluctant to betray Carlo further by telling Mia the next part of the story.

"I can guess, Tony; I know Carlo too well. He did his instant rage number. Tantrum first, think later if at all, that's Carlo. That's why I didn't stay with him long, actually. But what possible motive did he think you had?"

"I tell you, Mia, but like I say, this is a pretty crazy story. From the beginning Carlo suspects it is another tenor making the threats. He thinks every tenor is jealous of his high D, he is probably right, he is lucky to have this note in his voice. So he thinks if he cannot sing any more, other tenors sound better because they are not compared any more to him. So he says some jealous tenor wants to destroy him."

Tony stared morosely into his brandy snifter. "Carlo thinks the jealous tenor wants to make him nervous so he will not be able to sing well; then Carlo will have to retire and leave the field to the other tenors. So now he thinks the jealous tenor is me."

"But that's ridiculous. You're not really in competition with each other. But even if you were, it's not as if there's a surplus of great tenors. There's plenty of room for you two and lots more. You're hardly vying for the only operatic job around."

"I know this. You know this. Carlo does not seem to know this. And is making me very upset that he believes I could do such a thing. He is so angry, he says he will ruin my career. I think he cannot do this, but who knows? If people are thinking I can do such a cruel thing, maybe they don't want to hear me singing any more. I am telling you, Mia, I don't eat, I don't sleep;

not since our Gianni died and my Jen almost, have I felt so."

Mia mused for a moment. "This isn't like you, Tony darling. I think of you as someone who doesn't let his personal life interfere with his professional life. When you sing, your art rides over any other consideration. Yet in the time we've known each other, you've had plenty of personal problems."

"I know, I can mostly put everything to the side, and concentrate on the singing, on the acting, they are so important to me. This is why the Carlo business bothers me so much. What if he really does hurt my career? What if nobody wants to hear me any more, what will I do then? I wish Jen could be coming before Monday. She makes always so much sense."

He reflected silently for a time. "What should I do now? Maybe this worry will ruin the voice for *Otello*, and then it will be even easier for Carlo to hurt me."

He leaned forward on the couch, and put his head in his hands. "I think I am doing what Jen always says, I am making an opera out of this. Only this time, it seems to me I have the good reason to make an opera. *Dio*, I feel terrible."

Mia moved up against him on the couch, and put her arm around his shoulders. "Darling Tony, but you've been singing better than I've ever heard you. You look awful, but you sound wonderful. You've got to stop worrying; there's no way Carlo can ruin you, you're far too well-loved."

She hugged him warmly and put her cheek against his as her perfume, Chanel Number Nineteen, wafted over him.

"I want to believe, Mia, but how do you know?"

He drew back, looking at her as she said, "Don't you read your press? The public adores you! You and your famous smile,

Tony; sometimes even I am jealous of the great press you get! Carlo can maybe make a blip in your career, but it's his word against yours, and he may also make himself look petty and paranoid, suspecting a good friend of such malice. Tony love, please don't worry any more. I'll weigh in on your side, I promise you, and if it comes to a feud, who knows? That might even be good for your careers; in some ways it would make excellent publicity."

"I would hate a feud."

Mia, her face close to his, paused for effect as only an actress knows how to do. Then she spoke, her voice husky. "What would you rather have, darling, instead of a feud with Carlo? An affair with Mia, maybe?"

He turned to her, so that their lips were almost touching. Mia, never one to let a glorious opportunity pass, put her hand on his cheek, turned his face completely towards her and kissed him even more warmly than after their *Boheme*.

He responded with a passion fuelled by brandy, by fear, by the loneliness which every great performer knows too well. He put his arms around her, as his open lips sought hers. She unbuttoned his shirt, caressing his chest. He kissed her again as she, laughing delightedly, began to unbuckle his belt.

At which point Tony thought of Jen.

Gently but firmly he took Mia's shoulders in his hands and held her away from him. "I cannot do this, Mia. So much I would like to, but I love Jen, I need her. *Per favore*, I don't want to hurt Jen ... or you ... or anybody."

Mia looked at him silently. For the first time in their friendship he could not read her face. He said unhappily, "Mia, I am ...

I want always to be your friend, I trust you, we are so good together. Sometimes when I am with you I feel ..."

Tony stopped. Some things are too perilous to express. He breathed deeply and continued. "But this ... this is impossible for me, even with a so desirable woman as you. Is hard maybe for you to believe, and sometimes is even more hard to do, but I have been for ten years faithful to Jen. It is not just because I should be; it is because I love ... I need her, it is like I am not a whole person; she is the other half of me."

Mia stood up, her expression still inscrutable to Tony.

"*Per favore, mi scusi*, I should not have let this happen."

At last she smiled. "You didn't let this happen, Tony darling. You're no fool; you have to know I've been looking for an opportunity for months. I asked for this, with my eyes wide open. And your reaction only makes me want it more."

"You are not angry?"

"Of course not. I'm a big girl, Tony darling, and I'm not likely to react like an outraged 'wirgin'."

She turned and walked to the door, with him behind her. She opened it to leave, and closed it again. Drawing his un-resisting head down, she kissed him very softly on the lips. And said, "Dear Tony, I've liked you, I've respected you ever since we first worked together, but I've never admired you more than right now. You're quite extraordinary."

She bit her bottom lip reflectively. "I almost wish I'd found you before Jen did. Ah well, *c'est la vie*, as they say here in France. Get some sleep, my dear, everything really will be okay. And anything I can do to help out, you can count on me. You've got yourself a better friend than you know, Tony darling."

The Otello Omen

Mia went out and shut the door quietly behind her.

Tony went back into the living room and sat heavily down on the couch. Hunched forward miserably, he sat with his head in his hands, staring at the abstract pattern in the rug for a remarkably long time.

Twenty-Three

While waiting at Kennedy Airport for the plane to take her to Paris, Jen had an inspiration. Making her way to the phone in the Concorde waiting area, she dialed the international operator and asked to be put through to the Paris Opera House, to Sheldon Wasserman. She knew she should not interrupt the busy conductor, but Tony was uppermost in her mind, and she could not at the moment think of anyone except Wasserman who could help her accomplish her purpose. After Jen had listened to all the appropriate and necessary bells and whistles, she heard a female voice on the line.

"Il repete, Madame. On ne peut pas l'interrompre," came the chilly Parisian voice.

"Il est assez urgent, Madame," explained Jen.

"Madame," continued the Parisienne in French, "unless it is a life and death matter, one does not interrupt Maestro Wasserman in the midst of a rehearsal. If you would care to leave a message, I will of course see that he receives it."

Oh dear, thought Jen, I dislike taking out the big guns, but I guess I will; I must get this surprise right!

Jen forced her warm speaking voice to sound cool as she said, "I am Madame Antonio Amato, and I am calling from Kennedy Airport in New York City. I would like to speak to Maestro Wasserman now please, about a matter of some urgency. And I would appreciate it if you did not tell my husband I called."

There was a momentary pause. Then, "*Oui Madame, ne quitter pas, un instant s'il vous plait.*"

Jen held the line for what seemed an unconscionably long time, until eventually the measured British tones of Sheldon Wasserman, irritation held almost in check, came on the line. "Sheldon Wasserman here."

"Maestro Wasserman, this is Jenetta Amato speaking, Antonio's wife."

"Of course I know who you are, Mrs Amato. How pleasant to speak to you. To what do I owe this?"

Jen's laughter bubbled over the telephone. "This interruption? Please do forgive me, Maestro Wasserman, but I know you are rehearsing Mia Mitsouros this afternoon and that you will be with Tony this evening."

"That is correct, but surely you haven't called to let me know that you are aware of my schedule?"

"No, no, of course not. I've phoned to tell you that I am supposed to be coming to Paris today, but I—"

Wasserman's voice changed perceptibly. "You mean you are not calling from Paris? This idiotic woman told me there was an urgent call from you, she did not say from where. Are you not able to come here today? This is disappointing news, Mrs Amato."

"It's gracious of you to say so, Maestro Wasserman. But you mustn't—"

"No, not gracious at all. It is only that I am—we are all somewhat concerned about Mr Amato, and we were hoping you would soon get here."

"Concerned, why? Is something wrong? What's wrong with Tony?" Jen's words tumbled over themselves in unreasoning fear.

"No, no, do not alarm yourself unduly, Mrs Amato. It is simply that he seems tired and preoccupied, although when I asked him if something was wrong he said he was likely suffering from jet fatigue."

"Tony hardly feels jet fatigue, Maestro Wasserman, I'm often envious of his ability to function so well when he travels. Maybe what's bothering him is *Otello* itself. He was quite confident the role wouldn't hurt his voice, and he ignored all opinions to the contrary until you told him it might."

There was a long pause. People considered carefully before making controversial remarks to Maestro Sheldon Wasserman, one of the most revered yet feared conductors in the musical world. Finally he replied, "Mrs Amato, I scarcely need tell you I am not often wrong in my musical judgments. But in this case I believe I am. I was passing on to Mr Amato received wisdom, but his vocal technique is so excellent that I now believe this will not harm his voice."

"Have you said this to Tony?"

"No, I thought I might say something tonight when we have our rehearsal, especially if he continues being ... doing what he is doing."

"Which is what?"

"As I say, the voice sounds as beautiful as ever, but his effort to produce it is far too great. This is not the Antonio Amato I am used to, with his usual seeming ease of vocal production. He'll not sustain this, he's going to run out of stamina. I've worked with him several times as you know; the only time I've seen him like this before was when you lost your—when you were so ill recently, Mrs Amato. I was—did I express to you my distress when, er— "

"You sent me lovely flowers, Maestro Wasserman, dahlias, as I remember, which took pride of place next to Tony's. I appreciated them and your note."

Wasserman was once again grateful for his remarkable assistant Eustace, who did this type of thing with such aplomb.

"Mrs Amato, I hope you will come to Paris as soon as you are able. I remember how Mr Amato picked up and was his usual professional self when he knew for certain you were out of danger. You obviously share something very special. He would seem to need you."

For a long moment Jen could not speak, her voice strangled by a rush of emotion. Then finally she was able to say, "That's what I'm calling you about. You see, Tony thinks I'm coming today, but I've left a message at his hotel saying I can't arrive until tomorrow. Actually I'm in the Concorde Lounge at Kennedy waiting to take off for Paris shortly, and what I want to do is surprise him. He loves surprises, and he gave me such a wonderful one by appearing in New York for our wedding anniversary last week."

"Which was why he was late for the rehearsals here in Paris."

"Well, yes." Jen paused. "I was phoning to ask you a small favour, but now I'm having second thoughts. If you think it would be better for Tony if he knew I was arriving today, I'll gladly give up my surprise."

Wasserman reflected only a moment. "No, I think you should go ahead with it. He needs something lighthearted to buoy him up."

"In that case, here is my request. I know you are rehearsing with Tony tonight. I want to be waiting for him in his suite when he finishes the rehearsal. I was hoping you could phone me at the hotel tonight, and let me know Tony's on his way. Or if he's going somewhere other than back to the hotel, could you find out and tell me? Just so I can get my timing right? I want this to be a really good surprise!"

Wasserman began to laugh, a sound rarely heard, a sound like dry twigs rustling. He had never been known for his rollicking sense of humour.

"My dear, I would be pleased to do this for you and Mr Amato. Anything I can do to improve the condition of our tenor, I will most gladly do. I am very happy that you are arriving today. I look for great things from you."

"Thank you, Maestro Wasserman. I'll hear from you tonight then."

"Good-bye, my dear. *A ce soir.*"

The passengers were starting to board the Concorde as Jen

hung up the telephone. Then, both joyful and worried, she took her seat, and, working to master her acute claustrophobia in this surprisingly small cabin, was soon on her way to Paris.

Twenty-Four

This was the seventh day that Tony had virtually no appetite. Increasingly tired and insomniac, he, the consummate professional, was still able to produce the quality of singing and acting that directors, conductors, colleagues and the operatic world expected of him. But how long he could go on doing it, he did not know. He was not rehearsing with Wasserman until this evening, and as he had just received a disappointing message that Jen could not arrive today, he decided to have a massage, a sulphurous bath and a throat treatment at the Thermal Baths in the suburb of Paris called Enghien les Bains.

He phoned the Thermal Baths office to make an appointment, only to be told that there were absolutely no appointments available for a week.

Tony thought, I don't like to take out what Jen calls the big guns but I need this today.

"*Ici* Antonio Amato," he said in his Italian accented French.

Tony shrugged, smiling to himself as the receptionist at the Thermal Baths found that he had misread the schedule and that there certainly was time available for his massage, his bath, and his throat treatment.

Tony, gloomily wanting solitude, dismissed the idea of taking an aide, and called downstairs for a limousine. Soon he was being driven through the normal Paris traffic jam, past the Porte de Clignancourt where in the nearby flea market Tony occasionally searched for precious Caruso memorabilia that might have been overlooked. So far in vain, he thought wistfully. Then the limousine made its way through the narrow streets of St Denis, surmounted by its great basilica where so many of France's early kings and queens lay entombed.

Sic transit gloria mundi, Tony reflected sadly. Never one to minimize a problem, he thought, when I die they will not put me in so illustrious a place, not for all my hard work. Probably I will be buried in an anonymous grave, my life ruined by Paoli.

They drove past the pretty little artificial lake at Enghien, ornamented by its three white buildings: its casino, its hotel, its thermal station. The limousine stopped at the door of the treatment centre and Tony stepped out, stared at by three patients leaving the building.

They each had a similar thought: if Antonio Amato is treated here, this must be highly effective therapy.

Tony moodily endured rather than enjoyed his massage, his sulphurous bath, his throat treatment. Afterwards he morosely pushed roast chicken around his plate at a small restaurant he had previously enjoyed, La Venise on the Avenue d'Enghien. The thoughts that he had been avoiding all day emerged, buoyed to the surface by the Dom Perignon champagne he had ordered for himself in the hopes it would stimulate his appetite.

"Dio, am I going to lose everything? I am tired ... very soon I will not be able to sing well. Then Carlo can make me much bad publicity, and soon I don't have a career left. Cielo! And ... what if Mia and I had ... what if I lost Jen too? How would I live then?"

Jacques the headwaiter hovered nervously around his illustrious customer. "Could we offer to Monsieur something else perhaps? A little veal *paillarde*? The chicken seems not to be to Monsieur's satisfaction."

"Non, non, merci, it is not the cuisine, Jacques, it is always delicious, it is just me today. *Mi scusi, per favore,* I will come back when I have my next spa treatment this week, my appetite will be back then, I promise."

Tony left a lavish tip to make up for what he feared was an offense to the chef and the headwaiter. He climbed wearily into the limousine and was whisked back through the darkening streets of his usually beloved City of Light, to his evening rehearsal with Wasserman.

I never before thought Paris could be such a dismal place. Even this room is depressing, Tony thought, as he entered the third floor rehearsal chamber in the Palais Garnier. He was early, as he liked to be, so none of the others—Georges the rehearsal pianist, Bruce Grey the baritone singing *Iago*, and Maestro Wasserman—had arrived. Tony sat down at the piano, and began to play a melancholy Chopin Nocturne.

Long before it was discovered that he had a voice, he had dutifully but unenthusiastically obeyed his parents' edict and had studied piano in his native Italy. The athletic Tony had actually been hoping for soccer and tennis lessons. But he still played—both the sports and the piano—the latter now with pleasure and a certain amount of skill.

As he played tonight he thought about Chopin, resting forever in Paris in the Pere Lachaise cemetery, a grave where grateful music lovers still left flowers every day.

Tony wondered whether he would have even one tribute remotely like that, for the second time that day contemplating his own death. No, he thought, he would likely have nothing but a modest headstone in an obscure cemetery.

Wasserman flung open the door, to let Georges in. The pianist said teasingly to Tony, "Don't play any more, Mr Amato. You make me nervous. A little more practice and you'll have my job."

"If Maestro Wasserman is right about what *Otello* is doing to my voice, I maybe need your job," answered Tony.

Wasserman took a deep breath. He had very little experience in admitting he had been mistaken. "Mr Amato, I think I may have been hasty." He paused. "No, that's not what I want to say. What I want to say is, I surmise I ... I've been wrong. I've heard you singing *Otello* for nearly a week, and I believe it's going to be all right. Your vocal technique is very secure."

"You're just saying this because you want to keep up my spirits. You don't believe this in your heart."

"Of course I want to keep your spirits up—up where, by the way? I haven't noticed them soaring since you got here. I want more stamina, Mr Amato, this isn't like you at all."

"So you tell lies about the voice to me, so I will sing you an okay *Otello*."

A momentary expression of outrage flickered across Wasserman's face, and then his habitual icy reserve gained ascendancy. He reminded himself he was dealing with a member of that notably volatile clique, tenors, and that this particular tenor seemed to be struggling with some private demon.

So Wasserman measured his words with care. "I don't tell lies, Mr Amato. We have worked together several times now, and you know I care very much about the vocal health of my singers. I am a hard man, I know that, but I think I am a just man too. I will compliment my singers when they deserve it, I will encourage them when they need it, I will chastise them when necessary. I will do what I must to look after them. But you have never known me to tell a lie, nor will you."

Tony flicked at the piano with his fingers, staring at the black and white keys. He finally admitted, "You are right, of course. I should not have said this about lies. *Mi scusi*, I apologize." He smiled his little-boy smile. "Then, since you say you are not lying to me, you must really believe I am not hurting the voice with *Otello*. I have already believed this before, but now if you think so too, I will be okay. I hope."

Bruce Grey came noisily into the room, a stocky British singer of utterly insignificant appearance, but with an acting talent and a baritone voice so impressive that he was swamped with bookings from the world's major opera houses.

If I had been born a baritone, I would not have to worry about these high C's, not ever, thought Tony wistfully.

The rehearsal began with what Tony considered the fiendishly difficult second act. It was going very well, Tony thought; he liked what his voice was doing, when without warning it broke, not on a high note, but on an A. He tried the phrase a second and a third time; the voice broke again and again in the same place. He unfortunately caught Bruce Grey and Wasserman exchanging a quick, panicky glance.

"Enough for tonight, Mr Grey, Mr Amato," Wasserman said, his voice tight. "Mr Amato, I'll cancel your rehearsals for tomorrow, we'll work with Miss Mitsouros and you, Mr Grey, and I suggest, Mr Amato, that you rest the voice for twenty-four hours. Don't speak at all. But especially, not to worry. This is just a fluke; you know it, I know it, let's not worry. Are you going right back to the hotel?"

Tony could feel his heart pounding in his throat. Of course this was just a fluke. Was it not? "Yes, I will go to the hotel, I will rest now. Believe me, I will not use my vocal cords before Wednesday when I come in the morning. And—*grazie*—for what you have said of me singing *Otello* — you maybe want to take it back now?"

"No, Mr Amato. Absolutely not. Whatever is bothering you, I feel certain it's not *Otello* that is hurting your voice. Now go, get a good night's sleep."

In an unaccustomed gesture the reticent Wasserman put an arm briefly around Tony's shoulders and gave him a gentle, almost affectionate push out the door. Then he went across the hall to a small office, from where he dialed Jen, by now waiting in the Grand Hotel across the street.

"He's on his way, Mrs Amato. I'm counting on you to help him; now the voice is in trouble. He broke three times tonight— on an A. I haven't myself heard Amato breaking before, although of course every singer does, occasionally. I—I hope you can help him pull off the triumph we all want."

Twenty-Five

Jen bit her lip worriedly as she hung up the phone. Then, after turning out the lights in the richly furnished living room, she slipped into the bedroom and climbed into the king-size bed. She moved her body voluptuously in her silk and lace gown, loving the feel of it against her skin. It was new, a lacy pale turquoise which quite by chance matched one of the colours in the flowered sheets on the bed. She had bought it yesterday in New York especially for tonight and Tony.

Soon she heard a key in the lock. Her heart betrayed her with its pounding as she tried to lie quietly. Through the half-open bedroom door she saw Tony's tall figure silhouetted in the glow from the corridor as he reached for the sitting room light switch and locked the door. She expected him to come immediately into the bedroom, but instead he slowly walked through the sitting room to the built-in cabinets, and took out the bottle of Napoleon Brandy she had earlier noticed there. He poured some into one of the immense snifters, and, turning off the light, sat heavily down on the couch.

He was illuminated for Jen by the street lamps, radiating subtly through the long sheer-curtained windows. She remained motionless. She could see him drinking the brandy, and then reaching for the phone. He asked the hotel operator to call his home in New York. Jen knew from the flat, tired sound of his speaking voice that he was deeply troubled.

No-one answered the telephone in their New York apartment, and Jen heard Tony mutter to himself as he hung up the phone, "Where are you, my Jen?" The urge to get up and run to him was overwhelming, but knowing how he loved surprises she decided to continue with her original plan. Gingerly she moved a little, hoping he would not hear her.

Tony poured himself a second brandy and sipped it slowly. Jen saw him put his head in his hands, and she heard a sound that was something more than a sigh, something less than a sob. He rose slowly from the couch. That is how he will move when he is old, she thought, if the world lets him get old. He came to the bedroom, pushed the door open all the way and flipped the switch which controlled the rose lights just behind Jen. He was looking down despondently, when he sensed a presence in the room and snapped his head up.

"Jen!"

He seemed not to touch the floor; he flew across the room as she hastily sat up and responded to his rib-crushing embrace with one of her own. Then she held his drawn face between her hands, saying, "Oh my dear, what are they doing to you? You look so tired."

"Not that tired," he grinned, the little-boy smile taking on a distinct leer.

"Right! I should have known. Never the connubial headache for you! But what's going on, Tony?"

"What do you mean, what is going on? Who have you talked to?"

"Well, Maestro Wasserman, to start with. He told me he was wrong about *Otello* hurting your voice. Has he told you?"

"Yes, tonight he tells me, and then something terrible happens ... the voice breaks, three times it breaks, Jen! Not even on a high note, on an A. How can this happen? It is not happening to me since I was so young ..."

Jen stopped his phrase with a kiss, her mouth open against his. With an insatiable hunger for one another they kissed over and over.

"Come to bed, my darling tenor. We'll talk later."

Tony rapidly shed his clothes into a pile on the carpet, and climbed into bed beside Jen, laying his hand on the curve of her stomach where the life-saving incision had left its terrible scar.

"This is a beautiful gown, I like it. Is it new? Now you take it off."

"I can see how much you like it."

"No, really, it is very pretty, but you don't need it to be beautiful, you are in all the world my most beautiful..."

He covered her lips with his, tongue thrusting against hers, as he slowly raised the gown. She arched her back, then he drew away and she sat up while he pulled the sensuous pale silk over her head.

Now with his lips he caressed her, from her eyes down, down to her throat and her splendid full breasts, down to her stomach, down, down. His hands touched her ripe body, almost ready to receive his. She ran her fingers through his hair, and sucked at his nipples until they were as erect as hers. Now he was a pillar, now between her legs, like a Roman God, she thought, with his tight unruly black curls, his big beautiful body, his heavily muscled limbs.

Now she needed him, the secret place shivering with longing. He was hard, ready, superb. He entered her, entered her secret place, and together they crossed the boundary which would lead them to their shared and private magic land.

He brought her to orgasm first, because he had long since learned how many she was capable of. As the first delicious pulsing waves raced through her, she, moaning, thrust her tongue again and again into his mouth, meeting his. When she was panting with exhausted joy, he came himself, with a shout of exultation followed by groans of pleasure.

Then they lay spent in each other's arms, their breathing slowly coming under control.

"Oh my Jen, I love you so much." He lay quiescent, his eyes closing in spite of his efforts to stay awake. "Maybe ... maybe I will even sleep tonight, I have been awake very many nights, but now ..."

His voice drifted off, and his breathing became slow and regular. Soon Jen heard the welcome sound of his gentle snoring. Various parts of her were tingling and numb, being caught up under various parts of Tony, of which there seemed a great many, all very heavy. Slowly, so as not to disturb him, she extricated herself from all but the welcome arm across her breasts. And then she fell asleep, a long sleep in which she dreamed, she dreamed that she was Sleeping Beauty, and that Tony had just leaned over her bier and had kissed her awake.

Twenty-Six

There are days which change a life forever, although they are rarely recognized as irrevocable turning points at the time. Such a day was this, unsuspected as yet by the two people involved.

Kate Pauling lay on her back in her heavy mahogany bed, her head twitching on the white lace-and-embroidery pillow slip. She murmured like a Biblical supplicant, "Manna, manna." Her breathing was irregular, and perspiration had formed a film over her still surprisingly smooth skin.

With a sudden shake of her head she came fully awake and sat up in bed, breathless and unhappily aware of the erratic beating of her heart.

Frightened, Kate forced herself to lie back quietly in her bed, willing her heart to slow down, to resume once more a regular beat.

Today, she thought. I had better do it today. I've waited long enough. Too long, perhaps. But some decisions are so difficult that it takes a harsh jolt to make the mind up.

She reached for her medication. *This arrhythmia—it doesn't get better—it will kill me, perhaps soon.*

She forced her mind back, going over one more time the events that began what today at last she would finish. Or was what she would do more of a continuation? That day which had changed her life was long ago, yet so fresh in her memory.

It's time. But can I really come face to face with him and stay rational? Maybe I should write a letter, and leave it in the safety deposit box with my will. Only, what if he dies before I do? Doesn't he have the right to know? I must find the courage to tell him now, viva voce. And he can do with the information what he will.

Her gilt rococo bedside clock said seven-thirty. The morning paper should be on her doorstep by now. She slipped into her fur-lined slippers, and, standing up slowly so as not to succumb to dizziness, she descended the stairs and opened the front door to glimpse the paper girl riding off on her bicycle. A cold March wind blew the newspaper across the porch towards Kate who bent to pick it up. She took it into the living room and, sitting on her love seat, she opened the paper to the theatre directory. Yes, there was a matinee today.

Kate ate her usual breakfast of oatmeal, laced with raisins and brown sugar and topped with a banana and cereal cream, and drank two cups of strong black tea. Then she phoned the limousine service and requested a car to take her to Manhattan for lunch and for the theatre.

How the memories flooded in now that she had opened the dam! Now she remembered that on the fateful day so long ago she had worn a lemon-yellow dress with a white Peter Pan collar and her beautiful new strand of pearls. She went upstairs to her clothes closet, buoyed by a sudden inspiration.

She had a lemon-yellow Givenchy wool dress, long sleeved and with a white collar and cuffs. And of course she still had the pearls, a long valuable strand of large rosy beads which her wealthy parents had given her when she graduated from high school and embarked on her singing studies in England.

Kate dressed with great care, swirling her thick hair into a complicated chignon. She put on her usual light touch of mascara, of lipstick, and perused herself in the mirror with a critical eye.

Could he possibly recognize her, after fifty-odd years? She knew what time had done to him by the photographs, but he had no way of knowing what the years had done to her. Of course she looked older, but, she thought, not bad, not bad at all.

Later that day, in Manhattan, Kate lunched alone in the red, ivory and gilt Palm Court of the newly refurbished Plaza Hotel. She decided she preferred the decor before, before that woman whose name escaped her — oh yes, Ivana Trump — decorated it in this style. Kate had enjoyed its previous aura of slightly worn gentility.

Then, dismayingly aware that her heart had resumed its abnormal, erratic beating, she told the waiting limousine driver to take her to the theatre.

....

Sir Mallory Mancroft was having a good day. It was Pollock Braun's day off, and Sir Mallory was enjoying the pleasant experience of acting with the beautiful and talented John Jerome. Onstage Jerome was a delight, an unselfish actor with a riveting stage presence. Sir Mallory watched him, to his own surprise wanting now only to be a mentor to John, and wishing for nothing more from him.

It was a satisfying day, and not a time for questioning, or for being profound. It was a day to enjoy being alive, being an actor, playing in an amusing little comedy in front of a receptive crowd. Audiences were loving this play, and reviewers continued to be effusive in their praises. It looked like a long and lucrative run. Which Sir Mallory needed, since his chosen lifestyle was not inexpensive.

The matinee that afternoon ended with even more applause and curtain calls than usual. Sir Mallory was finally able to leave the stage and sink gratefully into a comfortable chair in his dressing room. He began slowly to peel off the false mustache, and to wipe away some of the greasepaint. It was not worth taking it all off. He would have to put it on again in two hours. He would just take off enough to be presentable. He intended to go out in the sunshine for a while on such a lovely day.

....

Kate's heart was doing a wild dance as she went to the stage door and spoke to the doorman. She asked whether she might go to the dressing room of Sir Mallory Mancroft. She wanted to surprise him, she said. She was an old friend of his and she did not wish to be announced.

The doorman looked skeptical. "What name did you say? I can't let everybody who comes along get in here just because they say they're old friends of somebody in the cast. Who did you say you were?"

Kate drew herself up, knowing she looked regal. "I am Kate

Pauling, and as I've said, I am an old friend of Sir Mallory's, but you might know me better as Katarina Pauling, the mother of Carlo Paoli."

The doorman scrutinized her closely. "Yeah, you do look alike now you say so. You're an old friend of Sir Mallory's, you say? We-e-ell, okay, you can go in, down this corridor, first turn to the right, after that, the first door on the left, it has Mancroft's name on it."

Kate followed directions, and found herself outside a dressing room door on which a name was emblazoned in large important looking letters, "Sir Mallory Mancroft". Her heart felt as though it were seizing up, as she raised her hand and knocked. She heard footsteps, and then Sir Mallory opened the door, and, unsmiling, said, "Yes? What may I do for you, madame?"

"Sir Mallory Mancroft," she said. "What a lovely sound that has. I've waited a long time to tell you how pleased I am that your career has been so successful."

"How kind of you to say so, madame. It was good of you to come backstage. I always appreciate it when members of the audience take the trouble to tell me they've enjoyed some of my work. Now if you'll excuse me I ..." He stopped. He peered into her face. "Do I know you? You look familiar ... and your voice ... say something more."

Kate smiled, and the years fell away from her attractive face. She said, "Oh yes, Sir Mallory, you know me. In more senses of the word than ..." She felt a sudden dizziness, and, faltering, reached out to steady herself on the door jamb. Quickly Sir Mallory put his hands under her elbows to support her, saying,

"Here, let me help you, do sit down, I'll get you some water. I'll call someone."

He helped her into a chair and poured her a glass of ice water from a crystal water jug on his dressing table. She sipped it slowly and then looked up at him and said, "Thank you, you were always kind, even when ... thank you, Manna."

The actor's training suddenly disappeared and Sir Mallory stood undefended before his memories. "Manna? Only one person has ever called me that ... your voice ... oh my God, it's you. Kate, my dear Kate. How ever did you ... why are you ... this is so unexpected. I think I'd better sit down too; are we getting old, my dear friend?"

"We do get old, Manna. My Manna from Heaven I used to call you, do you remember? I was so in love with you when I christened you that."

"Yes, yes, I do remember. Some memories are too ... some should be left buried, don't you think? I'm not proud of ... but are you ill, Kate? Should I be calling somebody? Do you need a doctor?"

"Oh no, Manna, not now. Not yet. Not until I ... I've come because there is something I never told you, and the more I think of it the more I realize you should know, before I die, before the secret is lost for both of us."

"What is it, my dear Kate?"

"In a minute, Manna, let me catch my breath. This ... it's not so easy to tell you; I have to lead up to it in my own way. It has to do with ... you remember the one night we, you ..."

Kate faltered, her voice husky.

"Is it easier if I say it?" Sir Mallory said gently. "The night we made love, the night you gave me your virginity, the night I knew my experiment was a failure, that I was proudly homosexual, had been and would be all my life. I did a cruel thing to you, Kate, using you as the subject for such an experiment. But do you know, oh, you must know! that in my own way I did love you. You had everything I would have wanted if I ... You were so splendid, so talented, such a good person. Maybe that will be a little comfort to you, because God knows I hurt you enough."

He stopped momentarily, his voice strangled by memories. "I didn't come away unscathed, you know, even though you thought I did. I remember leaving you sobbing on the bed that night, after I had told you the truth. You shouted after me that I was a ruthless, unscrupulous bastard, I can still hear you shouting those words, after all these years. You were right, of course, I was. I've tried not to be those things since, though not always successfully, I must confess. Of course man can dream of perfection but he cannot achieve it. That is his tragedy, is it not, Kate."

"That is his tragedy, Manna."

"And you, dear Kate, you went on to more disaster; you met that pilot Charles Pauling; at least you got over me quickly because you and he married very soon after as I remember, and then he was killed and you went back to the States and I lost you completely. Until today. I had heard you were expecting a child when your husband was killed, but it seems to me someone told me you had a miscarriage. Damn sad, all of it. I'm so sorry, Kate."

"You've got it almost right, Manna, except that I didn't lose the baby. I would like to be able to say thank God for that at least, but my son has turned out to be only a partial blessing. He's something less than a loving, attentive son to me. Of course he has a career as demanding as yours, so I can't expect undivided filial attention, but still ..."

"Career? Am I being obtuse, Kate? What are you trying to tell me?"

"Several things. You really haven't made the connection, have you, Manna. My son changed his name; he's ridiculously convinced that in his profession an Italian name brings more prestige and success. He calls himself Carlo Paoli."

Sir Mallory's eyes opened in such classic astonishment that even in this difficult situation Kate was forced to laugh. "You do have a wonderfully expressive face, Manna. You always did. You were absolutely right to leave singing and concentrate on acting. Why is the fact that I'm Carlo's mother so astonishing? Somebody has to be his mother; I was a singer, the genes are there. It's not all that surprising."

"It's not that, it's just ... Carlo Paoli ... I can't seem to take this in ... I have reason to dislike Paoli, and it seems ironic that I would dislike a son of yours."

"Yes, Manna, all things considered, it does seem strange."

"But Kate, you said you came to tell me something before we both die. Was it to let me know that you forgive me, despite the cruel thing I did to you? What a kind thing to do. I wish you had done it sooner; it might have eased my conscience. I have had pangs about you, I freely confess it."

"Maybe I didn't want to ease your conscience before, Manna."

"Well, you certainly had justification to want me to suffer. If it's any consolation to you, your Carlo has been the unwitting cause of the most terrible suffering of my life. I know it's not his fault, but I have hated him all the same."

"Whatever has Carlo done to you?"

"I'd rather not talk about it to you, Kate. In any case, it's not really what he has done, it's what he caused someone else to do."

"Good. Because it would grieve me to think Carlo deliberately managed to make both his parents suffer. One is bad enough."

"Both his parents? What are you talking about?"

"The terrible night that you made love to me and left me, you didn't only leave me hurt and angry. You left me pregnant."

Sir Mallory's face had taken on a grey colour. At the word "pregnant" he flushed. "Go on, Kate."

"You can guess the rest, Manna. Carlo is your son."

"*My* son? Paoli is *my* son? Are you absolutely sure?"

"Absolutely sure. Six weeks went by before I met Charles, and we were another month before we married and made love. I am absolutely sure."

"But ... but I have hated Paoli! Hated him! Wanted him to die! How could I feel that way towards a man who was really my own son?"

"Dear Manna, I am ashamed to admit that even I have felt that way towards Carlo. He can be such a cruel man."

"Were you about to say, like his father? Does he know I'm his father?"

"No, Manna, no. If you want him to know, I want it to be

you who tells him, not I. I haven't protected you all these years just to blurt it out now. I felt I had to tell you this in person and in secret, because you've been so courageous, you've done so much to promote understanding and acceptance of homosexuality, and I thought you might never want to acknowledge publicly that you had ever had a liaison with a woman, let alone fathered a son. That's why, though I considered telling you about Carlo in a letter, I was afraid that knowledge might fall into the wrong hands."

Kate reached out and took Sir Mallory's hand. "Oh Manna, I do hope this was the right thing to do. I mean, in many ways Carlo is a son to be proud of."

Kate stopped, breathless once more. She fought for control. "What do you think you will do? Do you want Carlo to know? Do you want everybody to know?"

"I ... I don't know. I need to think ... It's come so out of the blue, it's been such a ... such a shock to me. I can't quite take it in. I feel a bit like the world has come to an end, or is it just beginning ... Oh God, what's the time? I have to have a bite to eat, I'm on stage again soon and I can't go on without a meal, I haven't the stamina any more. Kate, will you come and have a little supper with me? It seems to me we have a lot to talk about."

Twenty-Seven

The morning after Jen's surprise appearance at the Grand Hotel in Paris, Tony awoke to the sight of her dressed in a peacock blue silk dressing gown, standing in the doorway of the bedroom watching him.

"*Buon giorno, cara mia*, I see the sun shines, have you eaten breakfast, I am really hungry!"

"Shhhh, Tony love, you're to have a silent day, remember?"

"*Si, cara mia.* I do remember. We order breakfast first, yes? I am starving, we will talk just a little over breakfast, then I will have the silent day."

Tony stretched luxuriously as Jen sat down on the edge of the bed and picked up the phone to order breakfast. The Room Service manager demurred when breakfast was ordered at eleven in the morning, but he found Jen's voice and her French so charming that he eventually acquiesced, having used only a few snarls out of his vast armoury. And when the actual order was placed —cheese *omelette* with *petits pains, croissants,* butter, jam, *cafe au lait* and grapefruit for two, plus bacon and sausages for one, he turned away from the phone with a shrug and complained to his assistant that *les Anglais* were a very strange people.

"How are we supposed to understand a people who insist on ordering the breakfast at eleven o'clock in the morning, then when I finally agree to do this, they order the lunch instead? *Sacre nom de dieu*, and now we are joined with them by the channel tunnel, this is a disaster, you will see, *petite*."

"While we wait, Jen," murmured Tony, and didn't finish his phrase. He simply untied her sash of peacock blue, and lifted his head from the pillow to kiss the aureole of her breasts revealed by the open gown. Then he pulled her down to him.

Enough time elapsed so that when Room Service rang the doorbell, Jen and Tony lay entwined together, their breathing slowly coming under control. Jen snatched up her gown from the floor, slipped it on and hastily tied the sash; then she opened the door to Claude, an experienced Room Service waiter who, when he returned to the kitchens, recounted with many a wink that singing did not take up all of Antonio Amato's energies.

"*Et la belle femme qu'il a, mon Dieu*, he's a lucky man, that one."

The lucky man sat at the table in the sitting room with his *belle femme*, and for the first time in a week found that food had flavour, and that he was able to eat his usual sizeable meal.

He grinned at his wife. "Have I told you I need you, Jen?"

"I think you may have mentioned it. Darling, are you going to stop talking now?"

"Soon, soon, but we need to talk a little about Carlo. It is such a worry for me that he might hurt my career. Mia says he cannot, but I think really he can. *Dio*, I cannot believe we have worked so hard and sacrificed so much all these years, for Carlo to ruin it all now."

"I don't see what he can do to hurt you, unless you let the tension affect your singing."

"But he says he will sue me, he says he will go to the press, this can be making for me a very bad publicity."

Jen got up from the breakfast table and went to the bedroom, where she opened her luggage and from deep inside pulled out a *People* magazine. "I didn't know when would be the best time to show you this, but ..."

"What do you mean, best time? Stop treating me like a child, Jen, I don't need you to protect me."

(Don't you, my dearest love?) "I know you don't, Tony; I apologize. But look at this. If *People* takes this line, no other magazine is likely to take the threats more seriously."

Jen opened the magazine to the short item about Tony, Carlo and the so-called practical joke. Tony read the caption, a scowl deepening on his face. "I do not like this at all, it is making me look so cruel, not *gentile*, how you say, not—nice."

"I know, but it's written lightheartedly enough that I doubt anyone will take it seriously. It's one of those, 'oh for heaven's sake don't opera singers have more important things to do than that,' items. I've spoken to your agent, and your publicity people, and our lawyers, about all this."

"What for, our lawyers?"

"Frankly, I was looking for some good news to bring you. I needed to be sure Carlo didn't have grounds for a lawsuit against you. The lawyers say he doesn't. First, Carlo has no proof you made the threats, and he can't get proof, since you never did make them. And second, since the press and the police are convinced that it's all just a practical joke anyway, Carlo hasn't a hope of a lawsuit. As a matter of fact our lawyer wonders whether you might have a lawsuit over this interview Carlo gave to *People* magazine. If anyone's character is being defamed, it's yours."

"This is supposed to make me feel better? You know I would not sue a friend, Jen."

"Yes, I do know, Tony. But right now the important thing is your *Otello*; nothing must take precedence over that. I brought you the magazine and the lawyer's advice because I figured they would help get your mind off Carlo. Tony love, now you are going to stop using your vocal cords until tomorrow noon's rehearsal. What shall we do; would you like to go for a walk in the woods at Fontainebleau? Shall I order a car?"

They stood up, looked at one another, moved towards each other, and found they had something urgent and enjoyable to do together before they went walking in the Fontainebleau Woods.

Twenty-Eight

Carlo Paoli snatched up a grey envelope he found lying beneath the mail slot on his entrance hall carpet, and strode into his study. With his antique letter opener he slit open the crumpled envelope. As he drew out the single page it contained, he realized with incredulity what it was. This latest message, slightly longer than the others but in all other ways similar, said, "Not a practical joke. You will die. Say your prayers now, soon it is too late."

Carlo wiped the perspiration from his forehead in a gesture of stunned disbelief. "Why would that stupid bastard Amato send me another letter when he knows I know it's him? And how did he send it? The Amatos are in Paris. Does he have an accomplice? Another bloody tenor? He must have given the letter to somebody to mail on ..." Carlo perused the postmark, "... March 24th. Bugger Amato. I'm going to Paris to stop this at the source. And if I can, I'll throw a spanner into his bloody *Otello* while I'm there."

He grabbed the telephone, and dialed his secretary. "Get me on the Concorde for Paris tomorrow; book me into the Plaza Athenee or the Ritz. No, I don't give a damn about that Red Cross Gala, just cancel." He listened with impatience to her expostulations. "Hell, Zelda, they were lucky I accepted at all. Don't get your shirt in a knot. And don't think they won't ask again. But right now I have bigger fish to fry. Well, you'll just have to wait and see."

He marched into the master bedroom, and took from his enormous walk-in closet a Louis Vuitton suitcase. Snatching various garments from hangers and drawers, he stuffed them haphazardly into the suitcase. After all, any hotel he could afford would have a more than adequate pressing service. It surely wasn't up to him, Carlo Paoli, to worry about mindless details like packing a suitcase properly. He had more important matters to attend to.

He pressed down on top of the suitcase and locked it shut. Straightening up, his eyes fell on the photographic portrait of Diana, the one by that fellow who photographed all the models—what was his name again? Oh yes, Richard Avedon— which made Diana look like the most beautiful woman who had ever existed. He sighed, then shrugged, realizing unhappily that her exquisite beauty had lost its power to move him.

Twenty-Nine

The dress rehearsal of a major operatic debut is a tense electrifying time. Jen was with Tony in his dressing room as he put on the blue caped and armoured costume designed for his first entrance, just before *Otello's* great cry of *"Esultate"*, and the brutally difficult short aria after it. That aria, sung before the voice has had a chance to warm up, has frightened many a tenor away from even attempting to sing *Otello*.

But Jen could feel no fear emanating from Tony this night. Since Jen's arrival and Tony's day of silence his voice had responded to all his demands on it, and barring unforeseen disaster, everyone involved in the production anticipated a major triumph. Tony was bringing to the role of *Otello* a riveting interpretation, one which owed more to Placido Domingo than to Jon Vickers; not a majestic raging paranoia, but a vulnerability which made the Moor's jealousy and bewildered pain even more profoundly moving.

"Break a leg, Tony," Jen said, her lips against his cheek, her arms tightly around him, as the call came that the overture was starting. But she knew he scarcely heard her. He had gone into his private realm; he was *Otello,* just as he had been *Rodolfo* and *Cavaradossi* and *Radames,* when he had first interpreted those roles. And so, bathed in the light of the dark stars that illuminated his *Otello,* he walked, hand in hers, to the stage set up for the storm at sea, to make his entrance.

At such times, Tony experienced the joyous exaltation of his art, a moment of transcendence when all his work and thought about a role came together into an infinitely satisfying whole. Just this one confirming rehearsal, and Tony's carefully crafted, deeply felt interpretation was ready to be shared with the world.

Jen planned to watch from out front, so she passed through a side door and crept into a centre aisle seat, seven rows up from the orchestra pit. The dress rehearsal was closed, a privacy conductor Sheldon Wasserman nearly always demanded for major debuts like this one of Tony's. So Jen shared the huge, ornate interior of the Palais Garnier with the singers, the orchestra, the chorus, the crew, and others involved in the production. There were only three other people in the theatre who were not involved in producing *Otello,* one being Mia's English lord, and two men Jen did not know.

"*Esultate!*" Tony's voice rang out. As Jen responded again to the sound of his voice, she wondered if other people had orgasmic thrills from hearing Tony, or whether this was something she brought to her listening because she was Tony's wife. Whichever it is, she thought, I won't dissect it, I'll just relish it.

Singers often "mark" in a dress rehearsal, not singing out in full voice, saving their vocal cords and vocal strengths for opening night. But tonight Mia and Tony marked very little. Now they were beginning the love scene, kissing and caressing in an ornately embellished Italianate bed, singing some of the most moving music ever composed to express love's ecstatic passion, its exquisite tenderness.

At this moment there was a loud noise at the back of the theatre. An attendant said in French, "No, *monsieur*, you cannot come in; this dress rehearsal is closed."

And then a male voice, projected as only an opera singer can project, said, "There is not an operatic rehearsal anywhere in the world that is closed to me, *monsieur*. I will enter, or heads will roll, most notably yours."

Wasserman glanced around irritably but continued to conduct the last part of the love scene. The speaking voices continued, with the quieter voice insisting that the intruder must leave, and the intruder loudly ordering everyone out of his way.

Wasserman snapped down his baton, silencing the orchestra. Mia peered into the darkened house, but Jen could see that Tony was so consumed by his characterization of the Moor that it would take more than this noisy interruption to disturb him.

Maestro Wasserman said in measured, carrying tones, "I will have silence! What is going on out there? Restore silence immediately!"

There was the sound of a scuffle, and Jen saw a big man erupt down the aisle from the theatre entrance. As he approached, to her astonishment she recognised Carlo Paoli. He walked up behind the podium and addressed Sheldon Wasserman.

"Good evening, Maestro, it is I, Paoli, and I will believe I am not welcome at a dress rehearsal when I hear it from the conductor. May I add I have never heard it yet. I had no intention of disrupting your rehearsal; my apologies to you all. I never dreamed that ass of an attendant would make such a fuss."

He snarled something Jen could not hear over his shoulder at the distressed attendant. Then he spoke again to Wasserman. "I may stay, of course, Maestro? I have come to learn from Amato. Who knows, I might want to sing *Otello* myself someday, so I could hardly miss the auspicious debut of the great Antonio Amato, now could I?"

Given what Jen knew of the bitter relationship between Carlo Paoli and Sheldon Wasserman, she was appalled by Carlo's effrontery. But she was even more shocked when she saw the expression on the face of Sheldon Wasserman as he turned fully to address Carlo.

If hate can be personified by a look, she thought, that is Hatred. And the artist in Jen subconsciously took note, in case she might need to use such a look one day in her increasingly frequent forays into portraiture.

"Mr Paoli, I am totally unaccustomed to such behaviour at my dress rehearsals. However, since you are here, you may stay. I would not deny someone of your stature the pleasure of hearing the dress rehearsal of a work that promises to be a major triumph. I do expect silence from you, however. Any further disturbance and I shall be forced to ask you to leave. And incidentally, you don't have the voice to sing *Otello*, even now in your vocal maturity. Stick to your usual repertoire; you do it quite well."

Wasserman turned magisterially back to his score, picked up his baton, and said, "We start ten bars before the '*un bacio*' please. Mr Amato, Miss Mitsouros, just come in at '*un bacio*' itself."

Jen looked up at the stage. To her consternation Mia Mitsouros, who had a well-deserved reputation for being unshakeable on stage, was actually looking uneasy. But Tony was the Moor, his concentration unbroken by the Carlo eruption.

He's incredible, thought Jen. If I know my husband, there's almost nothing that fool Carlo can do between now and opening night to break Tony out of his concentration. If Carlo thinks he is going to hurt Tony's *Otello*, he doesn't understand Tony. Carlo is too late ... I hope!

The dress rehearsal ended without further interruption. Those in the production not needed for this last act had stayed to listen, moved by what the principals were doing with this deeply tragic ending. They erupted in applause as *Otello* passionately sang "a kiss—*un bacio, un bacio ancora, un altro bacio!*" and, too weak to take that final kiss, fell dead across the body of his beloved *Desdemona*. Jen was weeping again, moved one more time by Verdi's great work, and by this interpretation of it.

Before she could collect her thoughts, Carlo had come up beside her, saying, "That bastard of a husband of yours, he had the nerve to send me another letter, would you believe it! What's the point, now I've found out it's him sending them? I thought Tony was supposed to be so smart." He watched as Mia hurried up to them. "Hello, Mia, great *Desdemona*, as usual."

"Carlo darling," she trilled, giving Jen a quick conspiratorial glance. "What a treat for us all that you should be here, so supportive for Tony and Bruce and me. It's always good to have friends around at such times. Of course it's not my debut, I've done *Desdemona* many times, as you know. Carlo darling, have you met my good friend?" Mia turned to include the impeccably dressed, quietly attractive man who had come up behind her. "Cedric, I'd like you to meet Carlo Paoli; Carlo, this is Cedric Tyhurst, Viscount Ridlough."

Like most Americans, Carlo was deeply impressed by titles. He forgot his mission of vengeance just long enough for Jen to get away to join Tony, and then was caught by Mia saying, "We're going out for a late supper at Le Pre Catelan, Carlo darling, and I know Cedric would be thrilled to have you join us. Cedric is such an opera buff."

Cedric looked somewhat less than overjoyed at this prospect, but, being a man of irreproachable manners, he averred (truthfully, as it happened) that he had been hoping for many years to have the pleasure of meeting the great Carlo Paoli, and of course Carlo was most welcome to join them at supper.

"Well, if you'll just wait for me out front," continued Mia with a convincing show of enthusiasm, "I'll take some of this makeup off and be with you in a few minutes. Ta-ta, darlings, see you shortly."

Mia rushed backstage, leaving Carlo with Cedric, who began to ply him with flattering questions and comments about opera as a career.

Mia knocked frantically at the door of Tony's dressing room. Jen opened the door and embraced Mia in a congratulatory hug. "Come in; you were marvellous, Mia, but then you always are. The electricity between you and Tony makes for great theatre. I still haven't recovered, it was such bliss. Tony's in the shower. He's so wrapped up in *Otello* he has scarcely realized Carlo is here."

"Carlo's here for nasty mischief, if I know him—and I do. He's a vengeful man, Jen, and this is a bad business between him and Tony. I'm going to see to it he doesn't get near Tony before opening night, if I can."

"Carlo would have trouble disturbing Tony's concentration at this point, you know. Tony *is Otello*, and he's not likely to come out of character any more than necessary between now and opening night. He's going to do his best to have two days of peace before Friday's opening, so we'll be pretty well sequestered except for a few interviews tomorrow afternoon and a couple of TV interviews the day after."

Mia raised her eyebrows questioningly. Jen responded to the unasked question with, "You know Tony. He's unstoppable, and everybody wants pieces of him, especially just before a debut like this. What can he do? Anyway, other than for the interviews, we're pretty well free. I've already told the hotel not to give out our room number to anyone and to put calls through to Tony's assistant to be screened, so Carlo won't get to us all that easily, unless of course he happens on us by chance."

"I'll enlist Cedric. He's a good sort, Jen, maybe Tony's right, maybe I should think about marrying him. He has just officially separated from his wife, more or less; don't ask me exactly what that means, I'm not sure myself; anyway I can't worry about that now. *Otello* takes priority! So I'll—we'll—see to it that Carlo is kept as busy as we can. We'll try to deflect whatever devilment he has in mind."

"Don't you need to rest up too?"

"Who, me, Mitsouros the Indestructible? Actually, yes, I do.

The Otello Omen

'Mitsouros the Indestructible' is a not quite accurate description dreamed up by the media. Of course *Desdemona* is not as taxing a role as *Otello*. Don't worry about me. I won't risk anything. I know I seem lighthearted, but believe me, my career—and my kids of course—are the most important things in my life."

Just then Tony came out of the shower in a red terrycloth robe, his wet dark curls tight around his head. He grinned at Mia, and not being one to believe that a good dress rehearsal presages a bad performance, said, "It was good tonight, I feel pleased. We pulled it together, I think it will be okay."

"Tony darling," said Mia, "I think it will be a triumph." She glanced at Jen, and continued, "Except we have to deal with Carlo. Cedric and I are taking him out to supper now. Wouldn't it be nice if he realized he's been an ass, and had come to be supportive? You don't suppose ..."

Tony interrupted her. "I don't suppose, Mia. He's here to make mischief, if I know Carlo. I hope he doesn't make mischief for you too. I will keep you away from him, Jen. You don't need this."

Jen and Mia exchanged a "who is protecting whom" glance, and Mia continued, "You're not going to let him get to you again, are you, Tony. You just can't let yourself ..."

"Not to worry. I am all right. I have to be thinking, the next two days, about *Otello*, about whether I am doing all I can to communicate this man, this emotion, this wonderful music, to the audience. I am not having time to think about Carlo. He stays out of my way, I stay out of his."

Thirty

B rian Healy had been apprehensive and troubled for some time. Had he been too overt, had he shown Diana Paoli too much of his feeling for her? She had come to consult him, hurt and afraid after Carlo had attacked her; by what right had he added to her concerns with such an unprofessional show of tenderness and affection? Now, as days turned into weeks and he saw no appointment with her on his engagement book, fear translated itself into back pain which grew more paralysing as time passed.

So it was with relief that today he finally saw her name on his book as his last appointment of the day. He was both annoyed with himself and faintly amused to realise that his back spasms became less severe as the afternoon progressed.

At last all his patients but Diana had left. He ushered her into the consulting room. Observing her pallor and the tell-tale puffiness around her eyes imperfectly concealed with a heavier-than-usual layer of makeup, he knew she had been weeping.

He thought unhappily, "What has that singing oaf done to her this time?" But what he said was, "How are you, Diana? I was wondering when I'd hear from you. You didn't come back as I asked you to, for a checkup after your incident with Carlo."

"I know, Brian. I couldn't. I've been in Boston with my parents. I needed to think. And I had to see what Carlo would do next."

"Which is?"

Diana rummaged in her purse for a tissue. "Which is that ... oh, Brian, this is all so hard." She wiped her eyes, smearing her mascara which made her look uncharacteristically dishevelled. "Carlo's gone to Paris to see Tony Amato's *Otello*, so we've only talked on the phone ... several times actually, since he ... since the ... and I think now that my ... my marriage is ... it's pretty well finished."

Brian looked at her silently for a long moment, trying to contain his hopes. "How hard can that be, when you've told me you don't love him any more?"

"It's still hard. Not because I do love him, or want him any more, although once—oh Brian, I did once love him very much. It's that this is the end of so many lovely romantic dreams, that won't ever come true now. It's too late."

"How do you know? Maybe you just dreamed them with the wrong man. Maybe this marriage was a learning process, a step on your way to real happiness."

Patient and doctor sat staring at one another, unwilling and perhaps unable to unlock their eye contact.

Try as he might, he couldn't stop himself. He blurted out, "I've been divorced twice. I know the pain, and it is terrible pain, even if you really want the divorce. Losing your partner that way can be worse than losing her—or him—through death, because if they die you can still go on loving them, without anything ugly interfering with your memories. But divorce—to see someone you've loved and maybe still love, become your enemy—that causes such grief. Maybe I'm a fool to think there could still be someone out there for me, someone right, but—"

He stopped speaking, struggling now with himself. Should he go on? Should he tell her how he felt? She certainly knew he was attracted to her; but had she guessed the depth of that attraction?

He decided to plunge in; he had very little to lose, and perhaps everything to gain. "Diana, I have to say this to you. You're the woman I see when I close my eyes at night. You're the woman I want to see when I open my eyes in the morning. I've tried not to make an ... I haven't made an issue of this, because you're my patient, and you're married. But if your marriage is over ... I ... I have to tell you how I feel. If there's no hope for me with you, then I'll terminate our professional relationship right now and recommend another doctor, because I can't stand to be in contact with you any more and know it's going nowhere. But if ..."

Diana was a decisive woman who invariably knew what she wanted. Doubt and irresolution had little part in her personality. She stood up. "Where do you live, Brian?"

"Up, upstairs, I mean here, in this building, but why?"

"I'd like to see where you live."

Brian's heart gave a sudden thump. A wild hope, like a forced bud, burst prematurely into bloom. "Come. You're my last patient. I'll show you my bachelor pad and we'll have a drink. It's not as lavish as your place, I'm sure; my ex-wives cost me a fortune, but it's still very comfortable."

They went silently together into the mirror-panelled elevator, not touching, not speaking. On the sixth floor they emerged, and Brian opened the door of an apartment decorated in a minimalist, modern, exceedingly expensive style.

"This isn't my idea of a humble little abode, Brian."

"Even for the wife of Carlo Paoli?"

"Even for the wife of Carlo Paoli."

He mixed icy dry gin martinis for them, and said, "Come see the rest of it."

The bedroom was done in black and white and mirrors.

"This is where I close my eyes every night, when I'm not delivering babies, that is."

"This is where you close your eyes and see ..."

"You."

He put his martini on an ebony chest at the foot of the bed, then took hers and placed it beside his. He bent towards her, kissed her quite gently, and then put his arms around her and unleashed his pent up passion in one eager hungry kiss.

She submitted to his embrace, then pushed him back gently and said, "Have you something I could put on, more comfortable than this tight dress?"

He could not conceal his joy. From his closet he drew out a bright green brocaded silk dressing gown, which, although it was his, might have been created for her, so closely did it match her remarkable eyes. Wordlessly she took it from him, and retreated into the guest bathroom. When she returned, he was waiting for her, in a similar dressing gown of maroon.

A long while later, he drew himself up into a sitting position on the bed, as Diana lay smiling beside him.

"How soon?" he asked eagerly. "How soon will you be free, how soon will you be here every night and every morning?"

She pondered. "I must stay with Carlo until after the big Met gala on the 24th, Brian. For many reasons—he's been having voice problems, and that's his last engagement before the summer; he's planned to take six weeks off after that, which will give him time to get over the marriage breakup before he has to sing any major roles again."

"I thought you didn't care about him."

"I do and I don't. To be perfectly candid, what I have to care about at this point is my own financial security. According to my lawyer, I'll get a good settlement and maintenance, though Carlo may be able to make trouble for me because I never wanted children and he did. But of course my future will be more secure the more money Carlo has, which means the longer he can go on singing, the better. I'm not going to jeopardize my security."

"You're right, of course. I mean, I can certainly support you well enough, but not like Carlo could. Eleanor and Lois and my kids take a lot of upkeep."

They lay together in a tender embrace, silent for a long while. Finally Brian said, "Penny for your thoughts."

"I'm thinking something I'm so ashamed of. I guess it proves that I don't care for Carlo at all any more. There was a time when even the thought of such a thing happening would have made me sick with fear."

Another silence.

"Well, are you going to tell me?" asked Brian.

"Promise you won't hate me. I even hate myself for such a thought."

"Diana, as a doctor I've learned that good people sometimes think terrible thoughts. And I've learned that good people are also capable of dreadful deeds, given the right circumstances. So, try me."

"I was thinking how much more money I would have if Carlo were to die. At the moment I'm his only heir; he made a final settlement with Ilona when he married me. Oh Brian, don't hate me for thinking such a thing."

"I don't. Do you want proof that I don't, my dear?"

They turned towards each other on the bed, and the night was soon punctuated again by soft little moans, and then by a long, intense, surprising conversation.

Thirty-One

The premiere of a superstar tenor singing his first *Otello* draws opera critics from all over the world. Jamie MacTavish of the *New York Times* emerged from his taxi and swept up the wide outer steps of the Palais Garnier, scrutinising the ornate facade so reminiscent of a sixteenth century Venetian palace. Arches, pillars, busts of great composers, pediments, famous sculptures such as the one representing Dance, are imposed and superimposed on one another in an effect MacTavish, an architectural minimalist, should have hated and could not.

Into the lavish marble foyer of the old Paris Opera House and up the vast staircase he went with the glittering crowd of opera-goers, the women gowned by the most illustrious couturiers, bejewelled by the biggest names in gems, coiffed with styles which had kept the most expensive hairdressers of Paris going without meals all that balmy Friday. Compared to the women in their splendour, the men in dinner jackets or white tie and tails looked understated, and MacTavish thought one more time that whoever designed men's formal wear must have done so with the idea of creating a becoming background for the colourful gowns of the women.

MacTavish realised he was excited and faintly uneasy—he, that most jaded of opera critics—except of course where Mia Mitsouros was concerned. But this debut of Amato's would, he knew, be either triumph or disaster; there could be no middle ground with Amato and *Otello*. Where his performances were concerned, Amato was prepared to risk all for the grand effect; the great moment of complete communication between himself, the audience, and the work of art.

Backstage in his dressing room, Tony was ready, in his dark makeup and costume for the first act of the opera. Watching him, Jen knew from long experience that he was not fully aware of her presence, as he moved even further into his own dimension, surrounded by his visions, protected and isolated by the parameters of the character he was creating. He was pulling into himself from his particular Muse all the strength and emotion he would need for his explosive yet tender portrayal of the Moor.

He was not her Tony, her "darling daft tenor" now. This man standing almost unseeing before her was the great Antonio Amato, who belonged neither to her nor to himself but to the world. She knew how deeply he felt the responsibility of the sublime voice that was both his bliss and his *raison d'etre*.

Jen left him to go to the stage, to peek out from behind the curtain at the scintillating audience, taking their seats amid a babble of anticipatory chatter. She came back to report to Tony, not in words, for she more than anyone understood his needs just before a performance, but with a thumbs up gesture which meant, "Everything's on course."

There was a gentle tap on the door. It was Mia, who had come to hug Tony and to say, "Break a leg, darling." She motioned Jen outside afterwards to say, "We've done it, Jen. Carlo's still around but we've succeeded with our damage control, as far as I can see."

"Absolutely. Carlo tried and tried to phone us, according to Tony's assistant, and he tried to find out what our room number was, but I assume even bribery didn't work. It makes me realize again how well-liked Tony is; even the staff at the hotel seem to dote on him. So don't give Carlo a thought, Mia, just 'break a leg' yourself. There's no way Carlo can hurt Tony tonight. The Opera House would have to fall in on him before Tony would notice that he isn't really *Otello*."

Mia laughed. "You're right of course. I've often kidded Tony onstage, just to see if I could put a chink in that armour of concentration. Wicked of me, I know. But he's impenetrable."

"*L'ouverture commence, mesdames et messieurs*," came over the backstage loudspeakers. Jen took Tony's hand, and together they walked to the stage behind the set, where Jen uttered the French version of a stage "good luck"–"*Merde*, my darling!" She bestowed one light kiss on his darkened cheek and dashed for her seat in the auditorium.

Time and time again throughout that exalted evening Jen found herself holding her breath at the sheer beauty of what she watched and heard. How splendidly Mia and Tony played off one another, she thought; the electricity between them was palpable. During the love duet *Otello*-Tony rose from the bed, clutching his chest, singing that he felt such overwhelming emotion he could scarcely breathe. His acting was so convincing that Jen had an involuntary flash of fear, and, quickly reasoning with herself, she thought nevertheless that if he were one day to have a heart attack, he would look just so. Then, as *Desdemona-*Mia rose to bestow on him the kiss he asked for, "*Un bacio, un bacio*", Jen wept tears of rapture before this almost unbearable beauty.

At the end, as a drained, unsmiling Tony took his first solo curtain call, the sophisticated audience stood and applauded with such vehemence that the sound actually hurt Jen's ears.

They were still shouting with joy half an hour later. Jen was now backstage, watching the principals acknowledging the applause over and over and over again. By now, Tony had emerged from his identity as the tragic Moor enough to smile; indeed he looked as though the famous little-boy grin would never leave his face.

All around Jen she heard the words, "A triumph!"

"A landmark in the history of this opera!"

"The most incisive portrayal of the Moor ever!"

And even the jaded critic Jamie MacTavish knew he had been privy to a performance he would remember with awe for as long as he had memory.

As the applause finally died away, Mia asked Jen and Tony, "Darlings, do you think we have time to celebrate *en famille* for a very little while before we have to go the big reception? I reserved a table at the Cafe de la Paix, it's so close by, what do you think? Just one private toast for us, and of course Cedric?"

"Give me a moment, I will get out of this dark paint, and we will be happy to come with you. Oh oh, here comes Carlo, what do we do with him?"

"Leave Carlo to me, darlings. I'll take care of him." Mia turned towards him. "Carlo darling! Where were you sitting? Now tell us, what did you really think? I'm sure you won't hold back, you rarely do."

"What do you expect me to think, Mia? You were superb, Bruce Grey was superb. Oh, there you are, Tony."

Carlo paused noticeably. Then, with a singular lack of enthusiasm he managed, "Congratulations. Good effort."

Tony and Jen exchanged a fast look. Viscount Ridlough moved up quickly beside Mia. He whispered to her, "No, don't invite him again tonight."

Carlo stood looking expectantly at Mia, who, mindful of Cedric's request, said, "It was so good of you to come to Paris to hear us, Carlo darling. So supportive of you. Now, if you'll excuse me, I have to take off my makeup. We'll see you at the reception of course. When did you say you were going back to New York?"

....

Tony felt so secure, so comfortable with his *Otello* the day after the premiere, that he finally responded to Carlo's repeated telephone messages and agreed to meet him for a drink in the Cafe Drouant. Jen insisted on going with Tony, smiling to hide her unease, although she was almost certain there was little Carlo could do to disrupt Tony now.

Once again customers in the restaurant were treated to the spectacle of two operatic superstars as well as a celebrated artist sitting in a corner drinking Kirs Royales. The celebrity-watchers at surrounding tables noted with gossipy glee that the meeting looked something less than friendly.

"Tony," said Carlo, " you don't deserve it, but I have to admit you've got a bit of a success on your hands."

"Why don't I deserve it? You know how hard we work for these things, Carlo."

"That's not what I mean, don't twist my words. I mean you're a sonofabitch. How could you be so stupid as to send me another letter? You bastard, I know you'd like me to quit singing—but your nasty little letters aren't going to make me, so you might as well save your efforts."

"He didn't write any of those letters, Carlo," Jen said angrily. "Why would he need you out of the way? He's on top of the operatic world. Your career makes no difference to Tony's."

Tony joined in. "You got another letter, Carlo? I think maybe you are really in danger. I think you should start to take some serious precautions with ..."

Carlo stood up, almost knocking over the small table, his ears rapidly reddening. With difficulty he kept his voice down. "There isn't one thing you can say that will convince me you didn't write those letters. So any effect they might have had on me is over." Now Carlo, ever inventive, began to improvise. "I'm talking to my lawyers; we're going to sue you into the ground. And I'm talking to *Vanity Fair* magazine; they're profiling me and they are very interested in what you did to me. If you're not sorry yet, just you wait, you cretinous bastard; you haven't even begun to suffer."

With that, Carlo marched out of the cafe, to the fascination of the diners seated near Tony's table who had overheard the conversation but, except for the few who had earlier seen and remembered the item in *People* magazine, had understood none of it.

Jen looked stricken in spite of her best efforts. But Tony quickly reassured her. "Is okay, I promise you. I cannot think of this Carlo business now. I think of *Otello* only, then I think of my one *Traviata* in London, on our way home. It is too much for me already to do, I have not the time to think about Carlo. I don't owe to him. I owe to the audience and to me. Correction. To us."

So the run of *Otello* finished as triumphantly as it began. Reviewers were unanimously ecstatic in their praise and adulation. And Tony's *Alfredo* in *La Traviata*, sung in London five days after the last performance of *Otello*, proved to be one of his most eloquent interpretations of that role. Sheldon Wasserman, who was in the audience, admitted again to Tony that he had been wrong to worry that *Otello* might hurt his voice for his lyric roles.

Carlo, fuming with rage and jealousy, read the reviews. "I'll ruin the sonofabitch, I will, just bloody watch me!"

Thirty-Two

B ack in New York on the evening of April 24, Carlo dressed in his expensive new lightweight evening clothes, and, pleased with his appearance, waited impatiently for the moment to leave for the Metropolitan Opera Aids Benefit Gala. Wandering into his sitting room, he gulped down three consecutive drinks of Scotch in order—he told himself—to relax his throat. Now feeling somewhat heartened, he rose and ambled aimlessly through the apartment, noticing to his surprise an envelope lying beneath the mail slot on his entrance hall carpet. Surely the last mail delivery had been hours ago? He snatched it up, and realizing immediately what it was, almost threw it into the waste basket unopened. He had received no threatening letters since his discussion with Tony in the Cafe Drouant, which confirmed his opinion that the letter writer had indeed been Tony. But to receive one now, tonight?

Holding the unopened envelope in his hand, he thought, of course it's Tony. We're singing tonight on the same stage, it's only the second time we've ever sung together, and he figures the critics will compare our voices. He's trying to make sure he comes off best. Dirty ruthless bastard, I'll show him. I'm going to sing better tonight than I have ever sung in my life. Now, do I open this damn thing?

His curiosity was too great. He slit the envelope open with his antique letter opener. But this time the sender had used a *New Yorker* magazine—Carlo recognized the print style—to create a message, not on grey paper, but on construction paper the colour of blood. The message said, "Tonight your blood flows. Say final prayers."

The paper slipped out of Carlo's fingers and dropped to the floor. He felt a sudden, fierce nausea. Then gradually his common sense took hold. He would of course be using his aide-bodyguard tonight, so what could possibly happen to him? Anyway the letter writer was just Tony, of course it was. Wasn't it? Wasn't it?

I'll confront that bastard Amato with this just before he sings. That should equalize our chances of singing well ...

Carlo stood for a long moment staring at the letter on the floor. He then shouted in a voice which, given his training in projection, carried through the concrete wall into the neighbouring apartment, to the astonishment of the stock-broker who lived there. "Diana, are you ever going to be ready, for Godssake?"

Diana had been sitting nervously on the edge of the marshmallow soft bed, apprehensive about her first public outing with Carlo since she had returned from the sanctuary of her parents' home in Boston. What behaviour to adopt? Hearing him indulge in his usual shouting, she concluded that the best and easiest way to act with Carlo tonight was to be the woman he knew—the one she had become during the last years of their marriage. With that firmly in mind, Diana, completely aware of her outstanding beauty, emerged from the bedroom, head high, arms held slightly out from her body in order to show off a new gown Carlo had never seen. It was a long-skirted sequined gown in bright red. His reaction, when she had expected his usual leer of approval, astonished her.

"My God, why are you wearing a dress like that, Di? It's the colour of blood! This I don't need tonight."

Diana decided not to explore this strange reference, but to answer as she would usually answer. "Don't be ridiculous, Carlo. It's a beautiful dress. You always say you like me to stand out in a crowd; well, I'm not exactly invisible in this, am I? I bought it to please you."

She stopped worrying about herself long enough to notice his unsettled demeanour. "What's wrong with you? Are you all right? You're perspiring but it's chilly in here."

"Nothing's wrong. It's just that stupid bastard Tony, he sent me another threatening letter. He's trying to unnerve me; what do I mean, trying? He's damn well succeeding."

"I don't see why another note should upset you. You saw *People* magazine, Carlo; it's a practical joke. He just doesn't know when to quit. Italians likely have a different sense of humour from Americans. I told you, Carlo, I told you I didn't like Tony and Jen. Now do you see what I mean?"

"You don't understand a damn thing, Diana."

She couldn't resist saying, "I do, Carlo, I do, I understand better than you."

She put down her large evening bag, filled with absolute necessities for tonight, and opened the door of the hall closet, taking from it an ankle-length sable coat. Shrugging herself into it with no help from her husband, she said, "You say you're ready; so let's go."

He marched out the door ahead of her, waiting by the elevator while she double locked the door. And it was just as well he was gazing blankly at the closed elevator doors as she turned to walk towards him, for the stare she directed at him was pure malevolence.

....

In their apartment a short way down Fifth Avenue, Tony was saying doubtfully to Jen, "I hope this is a good idea of Wasserman's that Mia and I should sing the love duet from *Otello* tonight. It is not right for this kind of Gala—is too serious, I am thinking."

"Leave it to the experts, love; they know what they want in the programme."

"How come I am all of a sudden an amateur?"

Tony and Jen were dressing in their bedroom, their huge bed in its virginal white lace phase. Tony was putting on his white tie and tails, and Jen had just slipped on a new gown with a low back and long sleeves, the entire top embroidered in mother-of-pearl paillettes and the long skirt a swirl of navy chiffon.

Tony examined his reflection in the mirror. "I think I lose some weight, this is fitting loose now."

"The slim Antonio Amato was a sensation tonight singing the love duet from—"

Tony laughed. "I wish!"

He took Jen's hands and held them out from her body, admiring her gown while at the same time he undressed her with his eyes.

"It is so beautiful a gown, you will be the most beautiful woman there tonight, my Jen. Now you are all dressed, I have for you the little present."

He went into the walk-in closet and brought out a thin jewel box, which he handed wordlessly to her.

"Now what have you done, my extravagant husband?"

She opened the box to find there a heavy chain on which hung a large gold pendant in an irregular shape, rough surfaced and with a small *pave* design in its centre, a design made of garnets, sapphires so dark as to be nearly black, emeralds, and one diamond. She looked at it more closely. The advertisements for Tony's Otello had shown a stylized profile of him as the Moor, wearing the green cape that had been his costume for part of the love duet. As she examined the pendant more closely, she saw that Tony had commissioned that profile copied in *pave*, but with such subtlety that only someone who looked very closely at the design would realize that it was not simply an artistic arrangement of gemstones. It was cleverly done, with the dark sapphires as his hair, the deep maroon garnets his face made up as the Moor, the emeralds for the top of his cloak, and one diamond for his bright eye.

"Tony darling you are clever, what a lovely gift. You could earn your living designing jewelry, you know. You really are good. And what have I done to deserve such bounty?"

"You cannot figure that out, you are dimmer than I thought,

Jen,"

Tony smiled, seized her in a hug that threatened to rip the dress, and whirled her about the bedroom in a happy waltz. They landed on the bed in a joyful heap, and eagerly sought each other's lips, before Jen caught sight of the bedside clock. She laughingly pushed him away.

"You're a bodice ripper, that's what you are," she said as she disentangled herself and straightened the fragile gown. "Now curb your fantasies, love, have you looked at the time?"

"*Cielo*! You are right, we better go now, did you check, is the car downstairs?"

"Should be. Now if you'll just do up this clasp for me; how well this pendant goes with my dress. Tony, I just had the oddest thought. You collect Caruso memorabilia; do you suppose one day in the future somebody will acquire this pendant, and they'll say this belonged to Jenetta Amato, Antonio Amato's wife; he gave it to her when he did his first *Otello*?"

Tony looked sombre. "I hope our children's children have this, but who knows, Jen? Anyway, maybe they will be saying this belonged to Jenetta Amato the great watercolour artist; she was married to some singer."

"Oh, Tony, I do love it, and you."

He put his arms about her and held her tight against his chest. "Without you, I could not have done the *Otello*. Maybe I could not do the singing at all. You must always remember this, Jen."

"I think you're wrong, Tony. You would sing no matter what. Your voice is a sacred trust—it has nothing at all to do with me. And you must remember that, whatever happens to me."

"What should happen to you?" Tony looked wary.

"Well, nothing, I hope, Tony; it was just a manner of speaking. Let's go, darling. Gala, here we come!"

....

Hannelore Crasmann excitedly slipped The Jacket on over her rose and grey opera dress. When she had received notice of tonight's Gala and had realized that season ticket holders to the Metropolitan Opera had the first opportunity to reserve their usual seats, she eagerly took advantage of the occasion. Antonio Amato would be performing and Hanne knew he wanted her—needed her—there so he could sing to her.

She felt she had been tragically misguided about her first love, Carlo Paoli, he who had stolen her voice, who had made her wait years for him and who had then rejected her so cruelly.

But Antonio Amato had been kind to her when they met, had held her hand for such a long time—she was certain she remembered that—so she felt quite sure he would be even more receptive to her tonight. After all, hadn't he sung *Che Gelida Manina* just for her, knowing she would be coming backstage to meet him after the opera?

As for Carlo, Hanne was absolutely certain God knew where to find the instrument to punish him for his sins. No sinner went unpunished, according to Jehovah. And Carlo was a great sinner. Hanne knew he would be performing tonight, and she wondered how she would feel, seeing him for the first time since the night he had taken Smythe's body and used it to rape her. She hoped for courage, but she was uncomfortable about the coming ordeal. She gathered up her outsized handbag, in which she had placed, among her other absolute necessities for tonight, a compact disk recorded by Antonio Amato. She knew he would be waiting for her after the performance, eager to autograph for her the photograph of himself that was featured on its cover.

Hanne anticipated an electrifying evening. She locked her door, and descended the staircase to street level, her knees unaccountably trembling.

....

Brian Healy had been until recently quite indifferent to opera as an art form. He preferred good jazz. But tonight he tensely prepared for an unaccustomed evening at the Metropolitan Opera. He dressed in his tuxedo far too early, and then had to kill time, drinking two large martinis and pacing his living room until the clock crawled to the moment of departure.

He went to his bedroom to examine himself once more in the mirror on the wall at the end of his bed. Just being in his bedroom gave him such pleasure these days, for he was either there with Diana, sharing their particular joys, or anticipating and remembering them in her absence. But tonight the pleasure was attenuated, mixed with an unpleasant apprehension that Brian did not dare analyse.

He tried to concentrate on his reflection.

It was not vanity, but objectively he found himself to be a good-looking man. No wonder some of his patients fancied themselves in love with him. And he, he was in love with the most wonderful, beautiful woman who ever walked the earth. Now if he just played his cards right, and did not lose his courage for what he must do, he would get her, and everything else he wanted along with her. Why was he so shaky? His plans were perfect, right down to the most minute detail. God, he needed another drink. No he didn't, he needed to be steady. Happiness was waiting.

He packed his absolute necessities for tonight in the small bag he sometimes carried, slipping in his silent pager so he could check it at intermission. He left his apartment, locking the door carefully behind him.

....

Sir Mallory Mancroft was more apprehensive about what he intended to do at the Gala than he had ever been in a life fraught with unnerving situations. But he knew with every fibre of his being that what he did tonight would determine the course of his future. It was necessary to get the timing right, in order for it to seem the most natural thing in the world that he should segue from one thing to the next. So no-one would notice what was really happening in between, no-one, of course, except one person.

Sir Mallory dressed in his white tie and tails, and, because he did not always trust the professional makeup people, he put on his stage makeup before he left home; he did not wish to appear washed out under the lights at the Metropolitan Opera. Since he was not a musician, this was the first time he had appeared on the stage of that theatre. If he had not decided that the deed was to be done this night or never, he would have looked forward to moving the almost four thousand members of the audience with Jaques famous soliloquy, "All the world's a stage," from Shakespeare's *As You Like It*. But he could not relax and let himself enjoy the performance, for he had to concentrate on how he would accomplish his other mission.

I'm a good-looking man still, he thought, examining his reflection. Oh Shel, my dearest, please!

He put into his slim yet capacious purse his absolute necessities for tonight. The purse felt unusually heavy as Sir Mallory locked his door behind him, before going down to hail a cab.

....

Kate Pauling's heart did its curious tango as she pulled a gold Victorian-style compact out of her large black alligator handbag, which held her absolute necessities for tonight, and looked at herself once more. Her rented limousine pulled up by the steps leading to Lincoln Square. The Metropolitan Opera building, its five-arched facade illuminated for the Gala, provided a brilliant backdrop. Kate tucked a rebellious strand of hair into place, shrugged her soft chinchilla jacket around her, and climbed out of the car.

She smoothed the skirt of her gown, a black beaded dress designed on empire lines, very expensive and quite old. Suitable for tonight, Kate thought. Tonight marked one of the few milestones in her quiet life. But those few had been big enough for her to trip over, to trip and fall and never stand up quite as straight afterwards. Tonight she would not fall. Tonight she knew what she must do.

She was nearly at peace, knowing Manna knew, knowing she had almost finished the tasks she had set for herself. If tonight she concluded that which must be concluded, everything would finally be as it should be.

Holding herself tall and regal in the night wind, she walked across Lincoln Square to the Metropolitan Opera building.

....

Sheldon Wasserman was alone in his dressing room, checking to make sure he had his absolute necessities for tonight. He was worried about several things, among them that he had not had sufficient rehearsal time with the orchestra, but he told himself he often felt under-rehearsed, and his conducting almost invariably went well.

Everything went so fast these days with the confounded jet planes—except of course when there was a delay like on his trip here. Anyway, what did it matter? It was a near miss, but he had finally managed to get back to New York on time, and there was little point in worrying now. Not about that, anyway. But the other ... he wished he could be sure it was not too late for what he wanted to do. Surely he shouldn't feel so paralysingly unnerved about something he had planned to do for so long. Should he?"

He glanced at his long, heron-like reflection in the mirror, trying to divert his thoughts.

Elegant, these new tails, elegant. He might as well look his very best for this crucial night. Taking a long, shuddering breath, he covered his face with his hands for one brief moment.

Thirty-Three

The Gala began with Maestro Sheldon Wasserman conducting the orchestra, which just for tonight's performance was on the stage rather than in the pit, in Rossini's overture to *William Tell*. The arrogantly handsome Pollock Braun waited in the wings to do an amusing monologue from his play, the comedy in which he reluctantly shared top billing with Sir Mallory Mancroft. Tony stood a little way from Braun, waiting to sing the *Flower Song* from *Carmen*, when Carlo strode up and grabbed his shoulder from behind, pulling him so violently he nearly lost his balance.

"What are you trying to do, Carlo, are you crazy?" exclaimed Tony in a low voice.

"No, you're the one who's crazy. How damn stupid are you? You really think today's letter is going to make any difference to me now? This joke is over, Tony. Stay the hell out of my way. God, I don't know why I don't put you out of commission for this concert, it'd serve you bloody right."

The Otello Omen

Carlo clenched his fists. Tony raised his arms towards Carlo, palms outwards, saying, "You don't try anything, what is the matter with you? What are you talking about, getting another letter?"

"Don't look so innocent. I know you can act, it cuts no ice with me. Of course I got another letter. Here, here, look at it, not that it will be news to you."

Carlo pulled the folded red letter out of his pocket and shook it in front of Tony's face. Tony grabbed the paper, unfolded it and changed colour as he read it.

"Carlo, believe me, it is not me sending this. I think maybe there is a real danger to you. You are using a bodyguard tonight?"

"No more than usual, just my one aide, why should I? What are you trying to do, ruin my singing and make me waste money on security too?"

"Carlo, *per favore*, listen, I believe you are really in trouble. You should be ... "

Carlo sneered. With a huge damp hand he patted Tony hard on the cheek. "With friends like you, Tony, I sure don't need enemies," and he walked away to stand as far from Tony as the large crowded backstage space would allow.

Pollock Braun's monologue elicited much gratifying laughter. Then it was Tony's turn. His aria was received with the usual adulation, although he was not pleased with the way his voice was responding. To Tony's dismay, he realised Carlo had actually succeeded in intruding on his concentration.

Now Sir Mallory Mancroft strode to the limelight, his mere presence on the stage filling the theatre so that he seemed a

310

Colossus. Sheldon Wasserman had come offstage and was standing beside Tony, his head bowed in an attitude of uncharacteristic dejection.

"What's the matter with Wasserman?" Tony whispered to Mia, who had come up on the other side of him. Mia glanced at Wasserman, then back at Tony. She shrugged eloquently, making her perpetually round eyes rounder yet to express her puzzlement.

With the famous velvet speaking voice Sir Mallory began *Jaques'* monologue. As he reached the phrase, *"Sans* every-thing," Mia quickly wiped the sudden tears from under her eyes so her makeup wouldn't be smudged. She whispered to Tony that there was not an actor alive who could speak that speech better.

"You're right, my dear Miss Mitsouros," interjected a solemn Sheldon Wasserman. As Mia turned to look at him, she noticed with amazement that he was trembling.

As the applause died down, Mia moved in front of Wasserman, ready to go on, but surprisingly Sir Mallory did not leave the stage. Mia and Wasserman looked at one another, puzzled, and then Sir Mallory launched, seemingly impromptu, into the Shakespeare poem about man's ingratitude, which ends:

"Freeze, freeze, thou bitter sky,

That dost not bite so nigh

As benefits forgot:

Though thou the waters warp,

Thy sting is not so sharp

As friend remember'd not."

As he came to the last three words, Sir Mallory turned his

noble head toward the wings, and stared full at Sheldon Wasserman. Tony looked quickly at the still trembling Wasserman, saw him glance away and then look up unflinchingly at Sir Mallory.

Waves of applause broke again, and only the technical staff involved with the production realized that Sir Mallory was so disconcerted by something private that he left the stage on the wrong side, thereby not having to go past Wasserman and Mia Mitsouros as they came onto the stage.

After Mia's aria, Carlo sang; then Mia and Tony did their love duet from *Otello* to excited applause. As they were bowing, the house lights were raised slowly to signal intermission. Tony had been hearing loud *bravos* from somewhere in the front row, and as he fixed his smile for yet another bow, he noticed the flash of red hair. The *bravos* were coming from a woman who Tony recognized, and, still bowing, he recollected the two occasions on which he had met her.

After the intermission, a renowned pianist was to play Chopin, then Carlo would sing again followed by Mancroft, then an orchestral solo and afterwards Tony and Mia singing the back to back *Boheme* arias from that opera's first act.

Tony listened with his usual interest to the Chopin. Scanning the audience, Tony could just glimpse Jen sitting in the front row at the far side. He had a much better view of the red-haired woman fidgeting in the front row, and was amused to notice her companions on either side, an elderly man fast asleep on her left, and on her right an equally elderly dowager trying to stay awake. But the dowager's head kept slowly drifting backwards and then snapping forward despite her noble efforts.

Good thing this wonderful pianist watches the keys, thought Tony. If he saw those sleepy people he would worry that he might be losing his touch.

Tony was increasingly fascinated by the red-haired woman. She seemed to have forgotten how to blink her eyes, as she stared fixedly at centre stage, motionless, both hands hidden in her lap under her large soft looking black handbag.

As the applause for the pianist died away, Wasserman and Carlo came up behind Tony. In a gesture that to anyone watching would appear amiable, Carlo hit Tony between the shoulder blades, but so hard that Tony lost his breath. Then Carlo walked to centre stage to sing the famous *Nessun Dorma* from *Turandot*, as Wasserman took his place on the podium.

Tony coughed, and angrily drew in a ragged deep breath, raising his shoulders and looking out over the audience just as Carlo sang his first phrase. The audience seemed to Tony to give an anticipatory sigh, knowing how splendidly Carlo usually sang the high note at the climax of this short aria. Suddenly Tony's eye caught an abrupt movement in the front row. There, between the two sleeping opera lovers, the red-headed woman pulled a revolver out of her handbag, and, expertly holding the gun in front of her with both hands, stood up and aimed it directly at Carlo.

"Carlo!" shouted Tony, but even his voice, trained to carry over the loudest of orchestras, could not penetrate the sounds from the singer and the musicians.

Tony was athletic and quick. The audience, waiting to thrill to one of Carlo Paoli's famous high notes, was astonished to see tenor Antonio Amato run onto the stage, gathering up speed as

313

he came, shouting—what? Wasserman's baton stopped in mid-air, as Amato hit Paoli with the full force of his tall, solid body. Both men tumbled heavily to the ground, as a different sound rang out over the orchestral music, the sound of gunshots.

In the front row the red-haired woman uttered a hideous wail, which mingled with the dying notes of the orchestra. A sturdy greying man sitting two seats away from her leapt up, and struggled with her for possession of the revolver she was waving wildly. He wrested it from her, and was about to throw it behind him and apprehend her when she seemed to fold in on herself. She sank back into her chair, covering her face with her hands and whimpering like a frightened puppy. The grey-haired man stepped back, almost tripping over Hanne's open handbag which had slipped to the floor. A battered paperback anthology of poetry had slipped from it.

On the stage, Paoli and Amato lay still, Amato lying face down across Paoli's ample chest. Clutching their instruments protectively, some of the musicians rushed off into the wings while others moved towards the front of the stage to get a better look at the fallen singers. A horrified Sheldon Wasserman knelt beside his soloists to see what help might be needed. Both singers seemed to be unconscious, with a pool of blood on Paoli's shirt widening gradually.

From the wings a spokesman came onto the stage with a hand held microphone. Although the shocked audience had not yet moved from their seats, their babble was increasingly hysterical.

"Ladies and gentlemen, ladies and gentlemen," the spokes-man shouted into the microphone, quieting the hubbub ever so slightly, "please remain calm. There has been an unfortunate incident, but the person with the gun has been disarmed, and there is no further danger to anyone. Please remain in your seats while we assess the situation. A further announcement will be made shortly."

The spokesman glanced into the wings at the assistant stage manager, who was calling out, "Ask for a doctor, we can't locate the house doctor ... " The spokesman continued, "If there is a doctor in the house will he please make himself known and come to the front of the theatre. Thank you."

While this speech was being made, the Metropolitan Opera's attendant nurse had rushed to the stage with her small bag. Wasserman got shakily to his feet and made room for her as Carlo slowly opened his eyes and, finding it difficult to breathe under the heavy weight of Tony, began to struggle to get out from under him. As Carlo pulled himself up to the sitting position, he and the audience were horrified to see that his white waistcoat was covered in blood. Now people from the wings were rushing onstage.

"I'm hurt! I've been shot! Help me! Do something, do something!" Carlo shouted hysterically. But when the nurse unbuttoned his shirt, no wound was to be found.

In those moments when it was believed that it was Carlo who had been shot, little attention was paid to Tony, now lying face down on the stage where he had been left when he was pulled off Carlo. But since the source of the blood was not Carlo, the nurse quickly turned to the immobile Tony. A pool of blood was slowly widening under and around him. She turned him over with the help of two strong stage hands. His eyes were half open, but he was beyond seeing, his face grey. There seemed to be blood everywhere. The nurse looked up quickly at a blenched, deeply distressed Wasserman, and bent again to look more closely at Tony.

At this point Jen, having fought her way through the hysterical crowd, ran on to the stage. It seemed to her that all her recent thoughts about Tony not attaining old age had been prophetic, though never in her wildest nightmares had she imagined she might lose him like this. She had always thought in terms of Tony's exhaustion, of premature illness and death as a result of being worn out by the demands of a greedy, adoring public and by his stringent demands on himself. But never had she imagined she might lose him to a bullet meant for someone else, although even in her terror she realized that it was typical of Tony to risk his life for a friend.

She reached Tony and looked down at him lying motionless, increasingly covered in blood. His grey face with its half open eyes seemed to her to be a death mask. Her worst fears were concentrated into unendurable anguish. She knelt beside him, and bent her face down to his. Cupping his face in her hands, she kissed him over and over, whispering brokenly, "Tony my love, oh Tony! I love you more than my life. Don't die, please, oh please live, live for me. If you die I will sleepwalk through all the rest of my days."

Vaguely she heard Mia Mitsouros say, "Jen, there's a doctor here, he was in the audience, a Dr Healy."

Brian Healy put his hand under Jen's elbow and helped her up. Seeing the agony in her face, he said, "Don't panic, Mrs. Amato; these things often look worse than they are."

He bent quickly over Tony. Mia put one arm around Jen's shoulders and held her. Jen was shivering, full of the tears that would come only later, but Mia, although she tried to use her formidable acting talent to hold back tears, did not succeed.

....

The ambulance had come and, sirens screaming, was now on its way to the hospital, carrying Tony, Jen, Mia and Brian Healy.

The police had come and were escorting a shrieking, fighting Hanne to the police station. When a police detective searched her purse, he found a last letter, addressed to a Carlo she supposed would be dead, and made up, like most of the other letters, of newspapers, glue, and grey stationery. It said simply, "Now I am free and you have paid for what you did to me."

"Well I'll be damned," Sergeant Donlevy exploded when he was told details of the attempted murder. "Now how in hell do they expect us to weed out the real threats from all the rest when we're so short staffed? Bloody crazies. It sure is a shame about Amato."

....

Some time later, little knots of distressed people still clustered around the Metropolitan Opera, both inside and outside in Lincoln Square. Near the stage, the group around Carlo was gradually dispersing. Diana, standing a few yards away from him, went over and put her hand on his arm. She realised with a surprising sadness that she now had no emotional alternative. She began to speak softly, almost regretfully.

"I'm sorry ... really sorry to have to tell you now like this, Carlo, but you and I are ... we're ... it's over. Because after the shooting when you got up and I saw the blood and I realized how little it ... how little I ... it would be just too hypocritical of me to stay with you, even for one more night. I wish we ... I wish I could say I'm sorry for ..." She stopped, as the unexpected relief of finally telling the truth almost overcame her. Then she continued, "I'll go home, Carlo, and get a few of my things and go to a hotel; you'll hear from my lawyers shortly. I don't imagine you'll miss me, not now."

Carlo looked sombre. "No, I don't imagine I will. There was a time when I ... but it was a long time ago. Go get your things, Diana. I guess this is good-bye."

Diana and Carlo looked at each other for a long intense moment. Diana wondered fleetingly what Carlo saw; for her part she saw him as through a film, and on that film was the image of the ascetic, attractive face of Brian Healy.

....

Now Kate Pauling had moved forward and was standing beside her son on the stage, holding his hand. She had no illusions that in future things would change much between them, but her horror and pain when she thought he was hurt, perhaps dead, revealed to her that she was still driven by her maternal instinct, much more than she had realized. As they stood wordlessly, she saw Sir Mallory Mancroft come hesitantly towards them.

Has he made a decision, she asked herself, almost afraid of the answer. She glimpsed Sheldon Wasserman half concealed backstage behind the corner of a set, finally alone.

No, Manna was not coming to Carlo. He was walking straight towards Wasserman. Kate saw Manna stop a few feet from Wasserman. For a long moment the two former lovers stared at one another. Kate thought, if anyone had ever looked at me with as much love as Manna is looking at Wasserman, I would have been forever lost.

As Kate watched, Wasserman slowly opened his arms, and Sir Mallory Mancroft walked into his embrace, home at last after eight long years adrift.

Thirty-Four

The ambulance pulled up outside the Emergency entrance of the hospital, tires screaming, sirens moaning, attendants rushing to remove the stretcher. Tony lay motionless, his face grey, his eyes closed, a small oxygen mask over his mouth and nose. He had opened his eyes once in the ambulance to stare unseeing at Jen who was holding his flaccid hand, and he had whispered, "Jen? Jen, where are you?"

"I'm right here, Tony darling, don't be afraid."

Tony murmured faintly, his voice muffled by the mask, "I am not afraid, now I find you ... I am thinking you are lost. I am looking for you ... but the lights ... they go out. Is so dark ... in the maze, Jen ... Jen? Are you still here ..."

Jen bent to kiss him as he drifted once more into unconsciousness. She gave a panicky glance at Brian Healy, who was sitting beside the stretcher listening with a stethoscope placed on Tony's bleeding chest. He put his hand on her arm and said to her, "Please, Mrs. Amato, try to stay calm. We'll know more when he can be examined properly."

Now the attendants had the stretcher ready, and they and Brian Healy, accompanied by three people from the hospital staff, ran into the hospital, pushing the stretcher with them. Healy called over his shoulder to Jen and Mia, "I'll get a message to you as soon as we know something!"

Mia put her arm protectively around Jen as they entered the hospital. Just inside the door Jen was astonished to see a portable television camera being aimed at her, and a trench coated journalist thrusting a small microphone at her.

"Mrs Amato, Mrs Amato, how is your husband? They say he may be gravely wounded. Have you anything to say to his worried fans?"

Jen flinched, shaking her head, as the cameraman caught her reaction in pore-revealing close-up. Mia abruptly went into her great diva routine. Drawing herself up to her full height of five foot four, she said magisterially, "Mrs Amato has nothing to say at this time. Undoubtedly the hospital will issue a statement later. Mrs Amato thanks you for your concern."

The journalist began to push past Mia to get still closer to Jen, when a large black doctor suddenly appeared at Jen's side. He said with all the authority that his position, his size and his deep bass voice could give him, "The public relations office is down that corridor. If you wait there, gentlemen, an announcement about Mr Amato will undoubtedly be issued in good time. Now please excuse us."

Firmly he ushered Mia and Jen into an elevator, saying gently, "There's a small private lounge on the third floor where you can wait comfortably. I'll take you there; and don't worry, there'll be no press appearing unexpectedly. Can you tell me how in God's name they heard so fast where Amato was being taken? We'll bring you news as soon as we know something, Mrs Amato, Ms ..."

Mia smiled. Her name was obviously not a household word in every home in the nation. "My name is Mitsouros. I work with Mr Amato."

"Are you a singer too?" asked the doctor.

"Yes, you could say that."

The doctor showed them into a small lounge, decorated in the obligatory hospital green with hard looking beige leather chairs and a coffee machine on one of three metal end tables.

"I'll be back as soon as I'm able. I hope the news will be good."

He hurriedly left them. A tense Mia said to Jen, "I'll have some coffee, I think ... would you like some?"

"No ... oh, maybe, yes ..."

Mia filled a styrofoam cup for Jen and one for herself. They sat down, sipping coffee in silence, each lost in her own disquieting thoughts.

Suddenly Jen squeezed her eyes tightly shut and made a face. "I don't think I should have had that coffee," she said, looking helplessly at Mia who moved beside her on the couch and put her arm firmly around Jen's shoulders. Mia thought mournfully that she specialized in sitting with her arms around stricken Amatos, trying to help them. She knew she had to try to keep Jen together—Tony would need her when he—if he—oh God, could Mia keep herself together?

Jen sat trembling, cold and perspiring at the same time. "A

fine example of grace under pressure I am. Tony always tells me he needs my strength to keep him afloat. So where is it when I need it?"

"It's there, Jen, you're doing fine, all things considered. It never crossed my mind that you weren't human."

Now for the first time since Tony had been shot, Mia saw Jen begin to weep, painful tearless sobs that left her gasping. Then the tears came coursing down unchecked, and Jen began having trouble catching her breath.

"Jen, you mustn't fall apart, not now. Tony needs you."

"He has needed me, Mia, past tense; what if he never needs me again?"

Mia was too much of a realist to utter soothing words such as "Don't worry, everything will be all right". She knew from having seen Tony lying bleeding in the ambulance that everything might well be all wrong. She tried to find something appropriate to say that would not be unrealistically optimistic.

Mia gave Jen's shoulders a little squeeze. "Let's not trouble trouble yet; let's just talk. It must be … it must be lovely to be needed by Tony and to need him… "

Jen gave Mia a long speculative look, as Mia, struggling ineptly to find a distracting topic of conversation, continued, "Do you remember the first time you realized you needed him? As distinct from loving him, I mean?"

Jen stared off into the middle distance of the small room, seeing her own visions. "Oh yes. Only needing him and loving him happened at the same time. It was the night we met. You heard what Tony said in the ambulance?"

"I did; I wondered what that was about."

"It's about the moment when I first knew I needed Tony... It's strange that his mind should take him there now."

Mia thought, "I'm on the right track; this may keep her occupied, keep her thoughts away from the present."

She said, "I'm a collector of how-lovers-met stories. What about you two?"

"It's a good story; my editor says it would make fantastic PR, but there are some things you cherish and keep to yourself. Of course, if you really want to hear it—"

"I do. I know you've been married ten years," Mia interjected, "because of your surprise anniversary dinner. Did you know each other long before you married?"

"Seven months. We married 'in haste', since we set our wedding date within days of meeting each other, but between then and the wedding everything conspired to keep us apart." Jen mused, "The rest of that saying is 'repent at leisure' ... oh, Mia, I've never repented for a moment; am I now going to grieve at leisure for the rest of my life?"

Jen bowed her head, rubbing her forehead with her hand.

Mia detoured around that question and continued doggedly, "So you met and immediately realized you needed him, go on, tell me ..."

"It was in the maze, that Tony remembered in the ambulance ..."

Jen began to tell her story. She stopped as a man in a surgical gown threw open the door of the lounge. He looked at them quizzically, said, "Sorry, wrong lounge," and closed the door again. Jen took a ragged breath.

"Oh God, Mia, they're taking so long. Maybe that's a good

sign. Surely if ... he must be all right, they must be working on him, don't you think?"

Mia knew all too well how hope triumphs over reason. She lied, "Yes, yes, that's very likely why they're taking so long ... but go on, Jen, tell me the rest."

Moments later Jen fell silent, seeing not a green hospital waiting room, but a young Antonio Amato staring and staring at her across an elegantly appointed banquet table.

"You know, I do remember now, hearing about your first meeting." Mia said. "It was during *Boheme* rehearsals, when the director was talking about portraying love at first sight. I told Tony I didn't think there was such a thing, and he said there was, and that it could become lasting love. I called him a romantic dreamer, and he said, 'No, Mia, I'm not, I know it lasts. Because when I first see Jen, is a magic spell, and now is almost ten years, and is magic still...' Sometimes Tony's words stick with me exactly, probably because his English is so charming."

"Tony's English is still sometimes small, isn't it, Mia? But so much better than when I first met him." She smiled at her recollections as she continued her story. "... and there it is, Mia; the first time I needed Tony. And I haven't been lost in a maze or anywhere else since, never until ... until tonight ... oh God aren't they ever coming?"

Jen had been staring into space while she reminisced about Tony. Now she turned towards Mia, and saw that Mia's face was contorted with weeping. The two women held each other in a tense, strained attempt at comforting.

"Maybe I shouldn't say this," Jen said thoughtfully, all defences down, "but I ... I know there are many women who want Tony, who would happily go to bed with him anytime, anywhere. He says he has been faithful to me, and I believe him, maybe because I want so much to believe. Sometimes I wish I loved him less. But I hope you will understand me if ... if I tell you that if he ever does have an affair, I hope it will be with someone who really values him as a person, and not just as an attractive famous man; someone ... someone like you, Mia."

Jen's face lit suddenly, her teasing, impish grin fighting with the tears. "That's not *carte blanche*, you understand!"

Mia wiped her cheek with the back of her hand and stared at Jen, understanding sadly why Tony treasured her so.

At that moment the big black doctor opened the lounge door to bring news to Jen. He was greeted by the sight of the two women, their arms about each other's shoulders, weeping.

Thirty-Five

Coat flying behind him, Carlo strode through the automatic doors of the hospital towards the unsmiling young blonde woman who sat behind the art deco information desk. Carefully chewing her gum, she watched him come.

"I need to see Antonio Amato. Where is his room?"

"Visiting hours are over, sir. Please come back tomorrow after two."

Carlo shifted a larger-than-life spray of twenty-four red roses from his left arm to his right, in the process almost dropping a fat square parcel wrapped in opalescent gold paper. Glibly he said, "Well, never mind, tell me where he is and I'll drop these off at the nursing station on his ward. Someone can take them in to him. I'll come back tomorrow night."

"Visiting hours start at two, sir."

"At two I'll be singing a matinee of *Butterfly*. I'm replacing Amato, of course."

"You're what?"

Carlo sighed irritably. "I'm singing ... I'm replacing .. Could you just tell me where to take these?"

The blonde parked her gum in one cheek and operated her computer, muttering as she typed, "Amato, let's see, he's in the private wing, 303, if you'll just take that elevator up to the third floor and turn left, the desk will be in front of you."

Carlo nodded and stalked to the elevator. On the third floor he turned left as directed, and moved unobtrusively past the nurses' station, where a stern looking middle-aged nurse was engrossed in filling out her charts. But moving unobtrusively did not come easily to Carlo, and the nurse looked up when his shadow fell across her work.

"Sir, sir, visiting hours are over. They are from two to eight every day. Please come back tomorrow."

Carlo sighed noticeably. "I've come to bring these gifts to Antonio Amato. I won't disturb him, I'll just say hello and deliver these and leave."

"Sir, visiting hours are—"

"I know when visiting hours are. But I'm here and I want to see Amato." Carlo smiled. "You won't send me away without letting me see him, will you?"

The head nurse was tired. It had been a long day fraught with emergencies. Making a great effort to be courteous, she said, "I'm afraid so, sir. If you would care to leave your gifts, I'll be happy to see that Mr Amato gets them. Please come back ..."

"Goddam it woman I'm here and I want to see Amato right now! He's in a private room for Chrissake; who do you think I'm going to disturb?"

"Just about everybody if you keep shouting like this. I suggest you leave, sir, or I 'll have to call security. I'm sure you don't want that kind of trouble."

"Do you know who I am?"

"I don't care if you're God. Kindly get out of this hospital."

She reached for the telephone.

Carlo drew himself up. His voice grew louder by several decibels. "While you're making phone calls, try phoning Dr Don Giordano. Ask him about me. The name, incidentally, is Carlo Paoli."

Her hand stayed above the phone. "Dr Giordano? The chief of staff? What's he got to do with anything?"

"He's my cousin," snapped Carlo, as he turned and headed rapidly down the hall towards room 303. As he marched he could hear the rapid beeps of the pushbutton phone as the nurse dialed.

Arms full, he backed through the half open door of Tony's hospital room, saying, "For Godssake they do fuss around here, so how are you feeling ..." and then he turned and caught sight of Tony.

Tony lay motionless in the narrow bed, his left chest and arm wrapped in bulky bandages. Carlo had been prepared to see that; it was Tony's face that arrested him. Only Tony's bright dark eyes, which he was opening slowly at the sound of Carlo's voice, gave his grey face any touch of its usual vivacity. Drained of life, expressionless, it looked to Carlo like death's portent. Carlo knew from having earlier spoken to Mia Mitsouros that Tony, though seriously wounded in the chest and arm, would likely make a good recovery. What would happen to Tony's singing, though, was anybody's guess at this point. But Carlo had been totally unprepared for this look of death on a face always so filled with light and life.

"*Buona notte*, Carlo," Tony said hoarsely, and then winced and squeezed his eyes shut tightly.

"Migod, Tony, what can I do? Should I get somebody?"

"No, is ... you not be worried, they just give me another ... how you say ... needle, soon the ... *dolore* ... stops. *Mi scusi*, Carlo ... the *droga* ... it makes my brain confuse ... I forget the English very fast."

Clearing his throat, Carlo tried for lightness as he said, "I should have learned to speak Italian when I decided to Italianize my name. I've said I was going to; it's been my next year's project for thirty years. Maybe this is the year. I'm likely going to have some free time now I don't have a marriage any more. You likely haven't heard—Diana and I have split. No, no." Carlo held up one hand to stop the sympathetic comment he could see was coming. "It's no big tragedy, Tony. Actually, I'm relieved it's over."

He shifted the flowers to his other arm. "I brought you this little bouquet. Coals to Newcastle, I see; looks like you could open a flower shop from here."

Carlo stood in the centre of the flower-filled room staring, a big man in a small space, awkward, uncomfortable.

"Please to sit down, Carlo."

Tony waved his arm to indicate the chair and flinched in momentary agony, drawing himself in against the pain. "Oof, if I can just remember not to use the hands when I talk I won't bring on the ... *dolore* ... what is the word I am wanting?"

"Pain. Pain, Tony."

For a few moments they looked at one another, until Tony exhaled deeply, saying, "There. Is better. I think it starts to work, the *droga*, is wonderful, I don't feel so much." And he smiled, a weak version of the famous little-boy smile.

"What made you do it, Tony? Why would you do it for me?"

Tony grinned. "Because you are always so nice to me, Carlo. Always give to me the ... how you say ... benefit of the doubt."

"That's right, twist the bloody knife, for Godssake. In my shoes you would have—anybody would have suspected you, Tony, if they'd found those letters under your desk like I did. You going to hold that against me forever?"

"Sure, Carlo, sure. That is why I—"

The door was opened suddenly to reveal a tall heavy-set man with a passing resemblance to Carlo, followed by the annoyed head nurse of the ward.

Unsmiling, the newcomer spoke. "Well, cousin Carlo, I see you're making trouble as usual. In theory I should call security and have you thrown out. What do you say, Mr Amato? Are you too tired for this visit?"

"I am never too tired for the visit," Tony said. "It is lonely; Jen goes home, here is nobody to talk to."

"All right, Mr Amato." Dr Giordano looked at his patient with sympathetic interest. "You're a lucky man to be here to talk at all, you know. A couple of inches to the right and you'd be ..."

Tony looked even more uncomfortable than before. "You don't talk to me about this. I am not ... died, I have to sing *Otello* soon. I will be fine."

"Well, I don't know about singing *Otello*, but ..."

"I know about singing *Otello*. Not to be worried, Dr Giordano. I will be fine , I will sing it."

"All right, we'll see, don't upset yourself. You can stay for a bit, Carlo, but Mr Amato is still weak; don't wear him out. It's a pleasure to see you looking better, Mr Amato."

Dr Giordano turned and left the room, followed by the still disgruntled head nurse.

"Where were we, Tony?"

"You were losing the temper as usual, Carlo."

"What the hell do you mean, as usual? Oh for Chrissake, you're right, there I go again. I'm sorry. I didn't come here to ..."

But Tony had closed his eyes. Carlo turned away, made room for the flowers and the parcel on the already crowded bureau, and sat down heavily in the blue tweed armchair beside the bed. He could see that Tony was desperately weary, and he knew he should leave, but there were things he still wanted to say. As he sat watching Tony, a tension he had felt in his throat for the three days since the shooting became tighter and tighter until to his horror he burst into tears. Real men, in Carlo's view, don't cry.

He pulled a tissue from the box on the bedside table and blew his nose quietly. But Carlo was not a quiet man, and the brief trumpeting sound woke Tony, who frowned for a moment in an attempt to remember where he was. Confused, he said, "Carlo? You cry? What for to cry? Is okay, I promise."

"I know. I guess that's why I'm crying. Because you promised ... I mean, not in words, but ... I get the feeling that ... that your definition of friendship is a kind of promise that everything will be okay for your friends if you can possibly make it okay."

Carlo loudly blew his nose again. "God, Tony ... I'd be dead if you hadn't ... they tell me that the Crasmann woman is a crack shot; she learned to shoot on some farm in North Dakota where she was brought up, and there's no way she would have missed me at that close range if you hadn't ... did you know they've got her in here for psychiatric evaluation? My cousin says she's mad as a hatter. I don't think she'll ever go to trial; she'll be committed for care and treatment."

"I hope they help her, poor sick woman."

"Saint Antonio." Carlo shook his head in disbelief.

"Now what are you talking about, Carlo? You say this to me before, I don't understand. What is it to do with that poor woman?"

"You don't even hate her, do you? God, you're not ... you're not even angry. In your shoes ... I don't have any idea what it's like in your shoes. Would I have done for you what you did for me?"

"Of course you don't do what I did, Carlo, you cannot run so fast as me!" Tony laughed, and winced again. "Is not a good time for the laughing."

Momentarily irritated by this teasing, Carlo for once fought his annoyance. "Tony, I don't apologize easily, but ..."

Tony tried not to smile. "No kidding, Carlo!"

"You think you're making this easy? Okay, okay, in your shoes I wouldn't make it easy either. Anyway, I ... I'm bloody sorry for thinking you wanted to hurt me. I'm sick about what I tried to do to you, Tony. I guess I'm paranoid, but I hated you; I was going to destroy you if I could ... and then even though you knew what I was doing, you risked your life for me. Can you imagine how I feel? For the first time since I was a kid I feel ... ashamed."

"You don't cry, Carlo. Is okay, I promise."

"But can you forgive me? Can our friendship get back on track? God, Tony, I don't have many friends, sure there are always lots of hangers-on, but they're not real friends. Not like you and Jen are ... were. And now with Diana gone, it's going to be damn lonely sometimes ... I need your friendship, Tony. Is it still there?"

"You are thinking I nearly die for a friend and then throw him away? You are crazy, Carlo, if you are thinking like that. Naturally the friendship is still there. You just have to ... how you say about the football ... pick it up and run with it."

Carlo took Tony's right hand in his and squeezed it hard. Then he remembered his other mission. "I almost forgot. I brought you a present."

"I can see, Carlo, the roses, they are *molto bello, molte grazie.*"

"No, not the roses."

He walked to the bureau and took up the square gold wrapped parcel. "I brought you this." He held it out to Tony. Tony took it, and lay it beside him on the bed.

Carlo, suddenly as excited as a small boy, said, "Aren't you going to open it?"

"How to open? I have only one hand to use. You want me to see it now, you have to open it for me."

Like a child at Christmas Carlo ripped off the carefully arranged gold paper to reveal a black box. He opened it, and drew out a fat sheaf of papers, slightly yellowing at the edges.

"Here!" He thrust the sheaf at Tony.

"I cannot see, Carlo, you hold it up for me so I can read it."

Carlo held up the first page.

"But ... but Carlo, this is your Caruso *Aida* score! You are wanting to give me your *Aida*? This is ... *meraviglioso* ... marvelous, I would be so happy... but no, I cannot accept, this is too important a present, you are so proud to own this."

"Without you I'd probably be dead. What good would owning this score be to me then? Put yourself in my place. I want you to have this. Please. If you accept, I'll know the friendship is still on."

Tony looked from the score to Carlo's face. He read there an urgent need. "Then ... of course I accept, this is a beautiful present. *Molte grazie*, Carlo."

Carlo realised he had been holding his breath. "I won't leave it here in the hospital, Tony, I'll deliver it to Jen tomorrow morning. But I did want you to see it. Uh ... will Jen still speak to me?"

"Of course, why do you ask so foolish a question?"

"Well, I don't know; Mia's spitting nails at me because of the way I treated you. And I've got to sing with her tomorrow in your *Butterfly*."

"Poor Carlo. When Mia she is angry ..." Tony made a quick throat-slitting gesture, and winced once more. Then, exhausted, he closed his eyes.

When pain awakened Tony two hours later, Carlo was gone. He rang for another needle, and when the young night nurse came with the drug, she found him smiling, despite drawing himself in against the pain. It hurt him to talk, so he whispered, "I am so excited, I have to tell somebody! Do you know Carlo

Paoli, he gives to me a present, his score which belonged once to Enrico Caruso! Is this not a wonderful generosity?"

The night nurse was not quite sure who Carlo Paoli was, let alone Enrico Caruso. Her idea of a great historical musical figure was John Lennon. But Tony's pleasure was so contagious that she shared it enthusiastically. She had just finished her rounds, and everyone on the ward was asleep, so she considered it her duty to stay and hold the hand that had convulsively clutched at hers in a moment of agony, before the painkiller took effect. Cherishing her admiration of this famous man, she wiped his forehead with a cool damp cloth and brushed back his sweat-soaked hair. And knew that in years to come she would say to her children and grandchildren, "I once nursed the great Antonio Amato—I actually spent quite a while just holding his hand one night when he was in pain. And do you know, in spite of being such a famous man, he was one of the nicest, kindest people I ever met."

Thirty-Six

Tony prided himself on not cancelling performances. If he could make his voice function adequately, regardless of how he felt, he refused to disappoint his audience. But when Tony's physician Albert Giordano realized that Tony had no intention of cancelling his upcoming Metropolitan Opera *Otello*, he protested vehemently. "The lung was injured; Tony. You need to be more recovered before you sing again, otherwise you risk damaging your voice permanently."

Tony smiled the famous little boy grin and said, "But I feel fine." Like all good actors he could be a convincing liar, and, as usual, he got what he wanted—Dr Giordano's reluctant "okay."

Jen, though distressed about Tony deciding to sing, knew better than to try to stop him. Nagging would only add to his stress.

At the first *Otello* rehearsal, Tony, his arm still in a sling, had considerable difficulty with his breathing. During the first break in the rehearsal, Mia Mitsouros abruptly lost her temper.. She felt now that she had to stop Tony from this foolhardy performance any way she could.

"Tony, it's ridiculous to gamble like this. Everybody will understand if you cancel. Are you really so arrogant you think nobody else can sing 'your' *Otello*?"

"You think I am so foolish I would risk my career for one opera?"

"Yes, actually, I do, Tony. Frankly I think you're doing this 'Show Must Go On' number for the great publicity you're getting."

"I thought you knew me better than that — how can you not understand? If I can make the voice work, I will sing. Would you not be the same?"

"I ... I don't think so, Tony." Mia bit her bottom lip uncertainly. "Because – oh, you know perfectly well how much effort it takes to project our voices in this huge theatre. If only *Otello* was a shorter role ... I'm so scared for you."

"Save your breath, Mia. I am going to sing this *Otello*."

Hesitantly Mia hugged Tony. She knew she was beaten.

....

As the Metropolitan Opera opening night performance of *Otello* progressed, the uneasy Tony gradually felt vindicated in his decision to sing. His voice was doing exactly what he asked of it. But during the third act the stage lights dimmed unexpectedly. Striding across the stage, Tony was concerned about what a power failure would do to the performance. But in the midst of his next phrase, the set abruptly lurched and revolved around him. As he put out his hand against a pillar to steady himself, he realized with dismay that the problem was not with the electricity.

He stopped singing and took a long shuddering breath. Conductor James Levine looked up at him with alarm. Tony groped for his medallion of Saint Cecilia, the patron saint of singers. The prompter in her concealed box urgently gave him the next line. The set still spun around him as Tony began to pray frantically, "Help me, Santa Cecilia, just help me get through this night." He took one more long breath and shakily resumed singing, to Levine's visible relief.

The ovation for that act was noisy with bravos. Tony bowed, grim faced. He felt frighteningly vulnerable, and almost overcome by *Otello's* love, jealousy, pain.

Mia waited in the wings for him. As they hurried down the short corridor to their dressing rooms, she slipped her arm through his.

"Tony darling you're shaking so hard I can feel it. I had no idea you were this nervous about tonight!"

"It is not the nerves; only I am thinking maybe I should not be singing so soon."

"Oh Tony I did try to stop you!" Mia said, holding him tightly against her side. "Still, darling, the hardest part for you is over."

"But I feel not so good, you know?"

They arrived at Tony's dressing room where Jen waited at the open door. Jen, his talisman. Only she could give him the kind of support he needed during a difficult performance. But tonight instead of walking into her embrace he dashed past her into the bathroom and was very sick.

He came out of the bathroom and, stumbling to the *chaise-*

longue under the open window, eased himself down and closed his eyes. Rivulets of perspiration ran down his grey face and glued his dark curls to his forehead. He groped once more for his medallion of Saint Cecilia and, finding her, moved his lips in a silent prayer.

Jen crouched beside him and put her suddenly icy hand against his cheek. She could feel her heart pounding. She tried to control the tremor in her voice as she said, "Tony, you can't go back on, not like this. Let your 'cover' finish. Everybody will understand."

Tony opened his eyes. "No, Jen. I am only tired. It is natural, my first performance since the shooting."

Jen watched him sit up slowly. He motioned to his dresser to help him with the costume change, but Jen raised her hand in a gesture which told the worried-looking dresser to stay where he was.

Tony was unused to Jen interfering. "Jen, you know I will not quit now."

Brushing her aside, he stood up and, shedding his act three costume, put on the long tunic and simple cloak of the despairing, murderous *Otello*. He sat down in his chair before the brightly lit mirror so the makeup man, who had just come in the door, could check and correct his makeup as the Moor. When all was ready Tony stood up, examined himself in the full-length mirror, and sat down abruptly as though his knees had given way.

"Five minutes," came from the public address system.

"I'm stopping this, Tony. I'm calling the Stage Manager," Jen said. She started quickly towards the door.

But Tony was adamant. He pulled himself from his chair and seized her arm, stopping her in mid step. She saw the spasm of pain cross his face, and knew it was not all physical. He looked betrayed.

"Jen, in five minutes I will do the hardest singing of my life. Always you are helping me when I have problems, why are you choosing now to make for me the trouble?" He shook his head in bewilderment. "I need every strength I have just to finish. *Per favore,* Jen. I need you to bring me the luck."

He slowly released her arm. They stared at one another. He said with more bravado than conviction, "I can do it, Jen."

Jen saw the doubt, the fear in his eyes. In an instant she was out the door and running down the corridor to consult the Stage Manager. He was standing in front of his monitors at the side of the cavernous stage, ready to call the final act. In a voice she tried unsuccessfully to keep steady she said, "Harry, Tony's too ill to finish. You'll have to hold the curtain while his 'cover' gets ready..."

But Tony had caught up with Jen, and angrily overruled her. "I am okay, Harry. I am tired, but of course I will finish."

Jen knew she had lost. This was one of the times when Tony became a stranger to her; when he became the great tenor Antonio Amato, who belonged not to her nor even to himself, but only to his voice, to that beautiful, terrible responsibility.

And Jen knew that all she could do for him now was to give him her love and support. She hugged him tightly so he would not see her tears, and, wiping them quickly away with one hand, she said, "You win. *In bocca al lupo,* my love."

Over Tony's shoulder as she embraced him, Jen locked

glances with the Stage Manager, and she realized Harry understood the situation perfectly but had no choice other than to let the star tenor have his way. Jen stood in the wings holding hands with Tony, waiting for his entrance as the final act began. Presently Mia, as *Desdemona*, finished her prayer and climbed into bed. Tony let go of Jen's hand, drew himself up to his full height, took a deep breath, and, as the Moor, walked majestically on stage. Behind his back the Stage Manager raised both his hands, fingers crossed, and with his mouth in a tight line nodded grimly at Jen.

Jen retreated far back into the wings, willing herself anywhere but here. Tension hurt her throat. Yet by the time *Otello* had murdered *Desdemona*, she was admonishing herself; she should have known Tony would pull it off. This was hardly the first time he had struggled to perform when he was ill; fortunately his concentration on stage was so intense that little short of unconsciousness would stop him. Jen began to weep. That burnished voice of honey and gold had such power to move her.

At last the curtain calls were nearly over. Before Tony's final bow he made an unusual gesture: he beckoned to Jen, still standing in the wings, to join him, Mia, Bruce and James Levine on stage.

Afterwards, as Mia, Jen and Tony made their way to the dressing rooms, Tony, gratified, said, "I knew I could finish. I told you I could do it, Jen."

He frowned suddenly, looking puzzled. He thrust his hand out in a vain attempt to brace himself against the wall, and collapsed.

....

Three hours later a disconsolate Tony sat on the side of his bed. Even the sensuous glow from the rose walls failed to reflect any colour onto his pale face. Since he had refused to go to the hospital to be checked over, the doctor who made night calls for Albert Giordano had come to their apartment. He pronounced Tony to be suffering from exhaustion and a racing heartbeat caused by the exertion of performing.

"This was possibly not the smartest thing you've ever done, Mr Amato," Dr Stephens told Tony, "singing so soon after you were shot. Didn't anyone tell you not to?"

Jen, upset and frustrated, retorted, "*Everyone* told him not to. You try to tell Tony what to do."

"Yes, uh—well, Mr Amato, I advise complete rest for the weekend, and see Dr Giordano on Monday."

"On Monday I sing *Otello*."

The doctor's head snapped up from closing the briefcase that passed for a doctor's little black bag.

"I don't think so, Mr Amato. In any case, consult Dr Giordano. But I'll be surprised if you're singing when we go to our subscription series Monday night. We'll be disappointed not to hear you, but .. ."

Jen interjected, "That's hardly the way to stop him singing, doctor. It's so as not to disappoint their audiences that singers perform when they're sick or ..."

Tony interrupted her. "You exaggerate. We sing because we like to sing. I have not noticed you stop the painting if you feel sick—why should I stop the singing?"

Dr Stephens handed Tony four sleeping pills and a prescription for more, to use if sleep did not come naturally.

After seeing the doctor to the door, Jen came back into the bedroom to an irate Tony.

"Since when do you decide to treat me like a child in front of strangers?" he asked.

"Since you started acting like one."

"It is childish to keep commitments?"

"Of course not. But to what should your commitment have been tonight? Did you owe your public tonight's performance because before you got shot you promised to sing? Or should you have made sure you were recovered so your blood-sucking audience could have years more of hearing you? What if you've done yourself permanent harm? Haven't you suffered enough on behalf of The Voice? And not only you—in some ways you've sacrificed your whole family on the altar of your singing."

Tony was angry and ill enough to lose perspective. "*You* have been sacrificed? Is a little late to start regretting that now. You knew what you were getting into when you married me. Now you want to tell me when to sing and when not? This is *my* life, *my* voice, *my* career, I love you, Jen, but not even you have the right to tell me when to sing."

Jen looked down at her clenched, white-knuckled fists. "It's my life too, Tony."

But Tony was unstoppable now, fury conveniently replacing fear. "What do you mean? You knew from the beginning we will be often apart, often lonely. You think you are the only one who suffers when I have to be away so much from my family?" Then, recklessly, the exhausted Tony delivered the *coup de grace*. "If you don't like life with me, Jen, you are free to leave; you are not my prisoner."

Jen was stunned. How could her loving concern have escalated into this? She frantically sought reasons to believe he did not know the force of his words. English was not, after all, his first language.

But now he said hoarsely, "I am going to be sick again, Jen, *Dio*, I am so dizzy ..."

Jen helped him into the bathroom. She felt almost overwhelmed by her bewildering profusion of emotions; love, tenderness, fear—fear that he meant what he said, that she was free to leave. Free? She knew she would never be free of Tony until her mind had ceased to function. Now she helped him back into bed.

"Oof, Jen, I hope that is soon over, I will keep us awake all night if I don't stop."

"You think I can sleep with you tonight after what's happened? Don't you know what you're doing?"

He grinned the little-boy grin. "Throwing up everywhere. Spreading around my favours. Metropolitan Opera, Fifth Avenue, I am not particular."

"Tony, this is no joke. How can you make light of it? After all we've just been through, with you nearly being killed, now you tell me to stay out of your business, and then you tell me if I don't like my life with you I can leave." Pain and fear goaded her onwards. "And now you think you can get out from under all that by being charming? I know you think nobody can resist your smile, but it's eminently resistible tonight, I can tell you."

His smile wavered slightly, but he persisted. "Come to bed, Jen. It has been not so good a night."

Jen turned away, and with exaggeratedly furious gestures—so Tony could not miss the point she was making—she threw open a drawer and took out her nightgown. She hurried into the bathroom, where she washed her face and brushed her teeth. To her surprise she knocked over the Lalique dish of rose scented potpourri. Odd. She was not usually clumsy. Then, turning, she stubbed her toe on the pedestal of the navy blue sink she had manoeuvred around for years.

She donned the pale blue silk nightgown, willing herself not to cry, not to let Tony know how much he was frightening her tonight, how much he was hurting her. Then she burst into tears. Quickly turning on the water to muffle the sounds, she forced herself to stop crying. But no sooner had she staunched the flow of tears and washed her face in cool water, than the weeping started up again. It took several attempts before she was able to control her distress.

Finally she opened the door between the bathroom and the bedroom. Tony lay in the big four poster bed, bright eyes closed, dark lashes against pale cheeks. Jen quietly took two blankets from the walk-in closet, intending to sleep on the murphy bed in the library. She went out the bedroom door and was closing it behind her when she heard Tony, his voice dark, husky. "Don't do this to me, Jen."

Jen stopped, turned, tried not to look at him—for she knew if she looked at him she would be lost—and looked at him.

"Don't do this to me. I need you. I know I said ... but you know without you I ... how could I live the life I have to live if you are not with me? Come to bed. *Per favore.* I have not wanted to worry you, but I have been so afraid."

He hesitated, swallowed, looked away, began again. "Why do you think I insist to sing even though everybody says don't? Because I say to myself, the bullet hurt the lung, what if I cannot breathe properly, what if I cannot sing a whole opera? What if my career is over, after all the years of hard work? I do not want to worry you, *cara mia*, I do not tell you why I must sing, but I have to prove to me that the voice and the strength are still there. I think I have proved the voice is okay, but what if I never can be strong enough any more? What if it never comes back, the stamina?"

Jen stood hesitantly at the foot of the bed, tightly hugging the two blankets. She chose her words with care, so he would not suspect how frightened she had been herself.

"Maybe this time you have good reason, Tony, but you're, oh, *we're* making an opera out of your problems ... Yes, I think you were foolish to sing tonight. And yes, you've likely set your recovery back by finishing the opera when you got so sick. But it's not the end of the world; it's not even the beginning of the end of your career. You're young, you're basically healthy, you're fit; it'll take a little time but you'll be fine—I know you will."

"You are sure, Jen?" Hope fought fear on his pale face.

Jen willed herself into a certainty. "Of course I'm sure."

"Then I feel better. You always make so much sense. What would I do if I did not have you? Never leave me, Jen."

He closed his eyes for a moment, then opened them and patted the bed beside him. "Come. Come to bed, *cara mia. Per favore.* I need you."

They looked at each other, their two solitudes slowly

merging back into the unity without which neither was prepared to live. Jen let the blankets she was carrying fall to the carpet and climbed into bed, putting her arms gently around him. He bent his head and buried his face between her breasts.

Simultaneously they whispered, "I love you," and then laughed. Tony said, "We sound like the duet, yes?"

"We are the duet, yes." Jen replied. "Oh Tony, as long as we're together, surely we can face anything ..."

He caressed her cheeks gently with his lips. She refreshed him so. His fears receded, driven away by the soft strength of her embrace. He held her tightly to him, his healing depending on her closeness. Their yearning bodies melded . And so they fell asleep, blissfully entwined.

Thirty-Seven

Selections from a review by Jamie MacTavish in the *Arts Section* of *the Sunday New York Times*.

"Friday night's audience at the Metropolitan Opera's *Otello* was treated to a rare spectacle, that of a tenor singing the role of *Otello* with his left arm in a sling. I refer of course to the great Italian tenor Antonio Amato. Amato's courageous action in throwing himself between Carlo Paoli and his would-be assassin at the Metropolitan Opera Gala on April 24, saved the life of his fellow tenor. Mr Paoli said afterwards that no-one could ask for a better friend than Mr Amato.

"Although it was rumoured immediately after the shooting that Mr Amato had been: a) killed b) mortally wounded c) would never be able to sing again, I can personally attest after last night that none of the above is the case. Mr Amato was seriously injured, having received two bullets, one in his chest, and one shattering the bone in his upper left arm. But when it was suggested to him that he should not sing this run of *Otello*, the recuperating Mr Amato is reported to have said that if the audience didn't mind looking at him with his arm in a sling, he certainly didn't mind singing with it.

"It must be said that Mr Amato's usual athleticism was hampered by his immobilized left arm. But Mia Mitsouros, performing *Desdemona* with brilliant versatility, used her considerable acting skills, aided by the rest of the cast, to create illusions of activity around the restricted Mr Amato ...

"... And what did it matter that Mr Amato was physically a somewhat static *Otello*? He continues to dazzle us with achievement after achievement. Has he ever sounded better than he did Friday evening? And has ever a singer been gratified by louder, longer curtain calls? For his courage, for his voice, for his acting, we in Friday's audience simply would not let him go. Finally a visibly exhausted but happy Mr Amato made a charming gesture. He came out for one last curtain call, with not only the splendid Mia Mitsouros, but also with his obviously cherished wife, the watercolour artist Jenetta Amato.

"And we, the audience, left, content."

The End

Jean Dell is a first generation Canadian of English and French descent. A sometime free-lance journalist, she now writes suspense novels set in the theatrical and musical worlds. She also writes and illustrates children's books.

Attending university in mid-life when her two daughters were growing up, she obtained degrees in English and French literature, and journalism.

She has played the violin and viola in several Western Canadian symphony orchestras. One of her musical passions is opera, to which she was introduced in France by her Parisian mother.

Jean Dell has travelled, mostly in North America and Europe, and has lived (too briefly) in France. She now lives in Vancouver, Canada.

ISBN 141202236-3